THE SPARE ROOM

Andrea Bartz is a Brooklyn-based journalist and the *New York Times* bestselling author of *We Were Never Here*, *The Herd* and *The Lost Night*. Her work has appeared in *The Wall Street Journal*, *Marie Claire*, *Vogue*, *Cosmopolitan*, *Women's Health*, *Martha Stewart Living*, *Elle* and many other outlets, and she's held editorial positions at *Glamour*, *Psychology Today* and *Self*, among other publications.

ALSO BY ANDREA BARTZ

We Were Never Here
The Herd
The Lost Night

THE SPARE ROOM

ANDREA BARTZ

MICHAEL JOSEPH

PENGUIN MICHAEL JOSEPH

UK | USA | Canada | Ireland | Australia
India | New Zealand | South Africa

Penguin Michael Joseph is part of the Penguin Random House group of companies
whose addresses can be found at global.penguinrandomhouse.com

First published in the United States of America by Ballantine Books,
an imprint of Random House 2023
First published in Great Britain by Penguin Michael Joseph 2023
001

Book design by Elizabeth A. D. Eno

Printed and bound in Great Britain by Clays Ltd, Elcograf S.p.A.

The authorized representative in the EEA is Penguin Random House Ireland,
Morrison Chambers, 32 Nassau Street, Dublin D02 YH68

A CIP catalogue record for this book is available from the British Library

HARDBACK ISBN: 978–0–241–66127–7
TRADE PAPERBACK ISBN: 978–0–241–66128–4

www.greenpenguin.co.uk

MIX
Paper | Supporting
responsible forestry
FSC® C018179
www.fsc.org

Penguin Random House is committed to a
sustainable future for our business, our readers
and our planet. This book is made from Forest
Stewardship Council® certified paper.

For everyone who rethought everything

Author's note: The cat is always <u>fine</u>.

PROLOGUE

The streets are silent at Tanglewood Estates. Swaying branches and the occasional squirrel are the only breaks in the slow-moving shadows, undulating shapes that stretch like caramel in the late-afternoon sun. For months now, the sole sound has been the trilling of oblivious birds and the footfalls of walkers, plodding after their dogs or just trying to break up the monotony, their eyes hungry for novelty after so many months indoors.

What the walkers can't do, of course, is peek into their neighbors' homes. Discretion is next to godliness at Tanglewood Estates, and tall gates surround each residence, blocking out prying eyes, keeping whole worlds tucked within. In one mansion, a teenage girl takes her twenty-fourth attempt at a selfie, while upstairs, her mother snaps open a jar of CBD gummies. Next door, a father of two rubs his face before turning on the camera for his fourth Zoom meeting of the day. As night creeps over the community, let's pan around the corner to the Gothic Revival, where two kids are working hard on the choreography of a TikTok dance, rattling the floor with the same song over and over and over.

Then there's 327 Tanglewood Drive, a stately manse with tall windows that look out on the lawn and the cemetery next door. Most of the house is still, a darkened dollhouse on a quiet night, beds spread with trendy duvets, fixtures gleaming in the kitchen and myriad baths.

A figure stands at the kitchen sink, shoulders hunched. Look closely—the silhouette quivers like a leaf on the marbled ivy that clings to the gate out front. Every once in a while, a large shudder takes over their shoulders.

But the most obvious motion is in the hands, moving steadily, writhing and twisting like dough on a hook.

Scrubbing and scrubbing and scrubbing at the blood stiffening in the cracks of their palms.

CHAPTER ONE

've chosen Amtrak's quiet car, so I stifle the urge to sob, to scream, to whimper in exhaustion or screech in fear of the strangers around me.

It's wild how quickly I got used to staying home. Now riding a largely vacant train feels complicated and draining, like navigating a foreign country. Virgo meows on the seat next to me, and I unzip the carrier to scratch her ears. Mike didn't want me to take her—he even reached for her carrier as I headed for the door.

Reach for me. *Fight for* me. I'm *the one you should keep from leaving.*

My breath hitches, and a sob plucks at my throat. I look down at the sandwich I bought before boarding, but my stomach has that hollow, wrung-out feeling from crying so much the past three days. I'm not sure I'll ever feel hungry again.

While I sat in the cavernous belly of Thirtieth Street Station, the vibe was fearful, hushed, crackling with distrust. Masked travelers eyed one another warily. It seems like a lifetime ago that we moved freely and breezily breathed in the air, sucking it into our bodies like milk-drunk babies. I'd felt relieved to board the train, but then a man sat behind me and now he's eating a salad, infusing the car with his hot breath.

Did I think this through? It's been sixteen hours since I shelled out $59 for a one-way ticket from Philadelphia to Washington, D.C. It might not sound like much, but my personal bank account isn't bulging. Mike's company funded our move; his new salary and signing bonus have been carrying us through my unemployment. The sandwich was another stupid $12.

But of course, my mental math is just a distraction, an anxiety more comfortable than the true problem that looms.

I gaze out the window, where pretty houses and church steeples poke out of the distance. Sabrina has a meeting at my arrival time, so her husband, Nathan, will pick me up from Union Station. I feel a squeeze of fear every time I remember this fact. I'm nervous enough to see Sabrina, and now I'll have to start this bonkers open-ended visit by finding a stranger in a train station.

My phone buzzes in the seat pocket. *Mike.* Hope crackles—has he changed his mind?

"Hello?" I keep my voice low. I shouldn't have picked the quiet car; a woman a few rows up turns to glare.

"Kelly. Hey." He swallows, and all the molecules in my body hold still. "Uh—I can't find the laundry detergent."

My insides drop. "What?"

"I'm trying to wash the sheets and—"

"Under the kitchen sink. With all the other cleaning products." Everything about the image fills me with sadness: Mike helpless in the hallway, peering at the washing machine; the fact that he's already cleaning our bedsheets, ridding them of my scent. I hear the clunk of a door springing open.

"Found it. Sorry to bother you." Static fizzes and moisture coats my eyes.

What happened to us? I want to scream. *We're supposed to be planning a life together.*

"The train okay?" he asks.

I whisk away my tears. "Yup. Text me if there's anything else, okay? I shouldn't be on the phone."

"Oh, right. Sorry."

"It's okay." I hesitate. "I'm sorry too."

"Look, let's not—" He cuts himself off, clears his throat. I know I screwed up. I thought we could move past it, but now I'm less sure than ever. "Text me when you get there. Bye, Kelly." He hangs up before I can reply, and I feel a plunge of despair.

This is not how I pictured year 34. It was supposed to be the best one yet, the year when life finally began: I had a fresh start in Philadelphia with my sweet, successful fiancé. A wedding planned, the real-life incarnation of a Pinterest board I'd been secretly updating since long before I met Mike, the invitations sent, the venue—a rustic barn near my parents' house in Illinois—locked down.

Others have it worse. I'm not sequestered in a field hospital, a ventilator controlling my lungs. My body wasn't shunted into the back of a refrigerated truck.

But this? It sucks. It really, really sucks.

I blame myself—Lord knows I've beaten myself up enough—but the caterer bears some responsibility too. Our other vendors were so understanding: *We get it, no one's holding gatherings.* But the farm-to-table eatery we'd hired wouldn't stop blowing up my phone, demanding we secure a new date or lose our deposit. My future father-in-law was underwriting the whole affair, and Mike refused to call him about it. I attributed it to Mike's overwhelm—or even his laziness, in my less-kind moments.

We fought about it. We fought about lots of things. And then, three days ago, he cracked my life in two, snapped it like a wishbone.

I catch myself worrying a nail over the gash in my palm. A gash of shame, a scabby reminder of the ugliness that poured out of me last week.

I snatch my phone back up, then reread the casual text that stopped me in my tracks yesterday. I still can't believe it's real, not something I hallucinated: "You should come stay with us."

Heart pounding, I'd given the "ha-ha" reaction. But Sabrina doubled down: "I'm serious! We have a spare room. And Lord knows, we could use the company."

That's when my hands started shaking. I was alone in our bedroom in Philadelphia. It faced the street, with bars over the windows ostensibly to keep the riffraff out, but they made it feel like a jail cell too.

"That's so nice of you!" I replied. "But I wouldn't want to intrude."

She began typing back right away. "It wouldn't be an intrusion at all—honestly, Nathan is such an extrovert, he is DYING for someone to talk to who isn't me. (And as an introvert, I am dying for him to have someone to talk to who isn't me, lol.) No pressure but it's a serious offer! Maybe for a week or two? Could be good for both of you."

Both of us. Something my mom drilled into me, a lesson gleaned from forty-plus years of married bliss: You and your partner are a team. You make decisions together. When I floated the idea, he jumped right on it.

But I wanted him to fight for me. To beg me to stay.

Crying in a mask is disgusting. Even the *thud-thud-thud* of the train over the tracks can't cloak my shuddery breath. The fabric pulls as tight as a gag with every gasp, and tears and snot soak the inside. More people turn and glare. I hear my mother's voice: *Get it together, Kelly. Get a grip.*

I send Sabrina an update: "Passing Baltimore!" I should be texting her and Nathan both, but I'm still intimidated by him.

It's hard to believe that three weeks ago, I didn't even have Sabrina's number. We'd followed each other on Instagram for years, but for whatever reason, her photos rarely showed up on my feed. And then—bored with the pandemic that just wouldn't quit, blissfully unaware that a grenade was about to blow up my life, I found myself scrolling through that roll of happy people. And the algorithm threw in a wild card: an update from Sabrina Lamont.

She's perfect. I knew her as Sabrina Balzer in high school, a tangential friend in the same nerd-adjacent clique, though we never hung out one-on-one. I remembered her as mousy and quiet; she hadn't crossed my mind in decades. *But jeez*, I thought, *look at her now.*

Thick brown waves spilled like rapids over her shoulders. She had a Frank Lloyd Wright face, sharp cheekbones and a square jaw, with sculpted brows and leprechaun-green eyes. It was a selfie from an outdoor lounge chair, and behind her stretched a sparkling pool the color of sapphires.

That night, I let the world darken as I tapped my way around her online presence, feeling that grubby rush of indiscipline, the same waterfall of want that has you finishing the pint of ice cream or wrenching off a scab, exposing the ink-red underneath. I found old blog posts by her and news articles about her and read them hungrily. I unearthed images of her at a gala and clicked through all eighteen red-carpet photos.

We all have Instagram friends we're obsessed with, right? I couldn't get enough of her glory: her mansion an hour outside D.C.; hikes through the Blue Ridge Mountains; #ThrowbackThursdays to glitzy events with her husband, Nathan, who was tall and broad and more cute than handsome with his thick red-blond beard and aquiline nose. A power couple. And sure, he had some high-ranking government job she referenced in captions, but she was no trophy wife; she's a goddamn *New York Times bestselling author*, which, Christ. What? *How.*

I ordered her award-winning romance series on the spot. It charted the heated affair between Arianna Rune, an intrepid business journalist, and Perry Creighton, her mysterious and powerful (and conveniently sexy) informant. Hours later, I finished the first book—*The Insider*—and, cheeks pink, tore into the second. I practically launched myself onto Mike that night.

He rolled away and pleaded exhaustion.

The minute I finished the latest installment, I messaged Sabrina to tell her how much I loved her books. And she wrote back and was lovely and asked how I was doing and about the "adorable fiancé" in my engagement photos and oh, we started messaging throughout the day, chatty threads that stood in beautiful contrast to WhatsApps with my friends back home in Chicago, who could only commiserate about being trapped inside with sticky children.

Sabrina recounted her attempts to make sourdough from a starter named Otis ("So cliché, right?"); I updated her on the weird things I saw on my walks around Philadelphia (bike parades, sidewalk foam parties). We cracked each other up. She admitted she, too, was having trouble keeping up with her friends with kids, whose problems felt so different from hers (no, *ours*): their constant hubbub and not a second alone with their thoughts versus our loneliness, empty schedules, and stretchy quiet moments, ones when our inner monologues started to shout.

So I let her distract me. Maybe it meant I devoted less attention to Mike's moodiness. Thinking about it now, my stomach puckers. It's not like me to be selfish.

When Mike refused to reschedule our wedding a few days ago, I told Sabrina within the hour: *OMG, Mike just told me he wants to "pump the brakes."* It popped out of me like a sneeze because she wasn't real in my mind, not exactly. I hadn't seen her in more than fifteen years.

She's the only person I've told, in fact. And Mike isn't about to tell anyone; he's displeased that I even let Sabrina into our private drama. My best friend, Amy, my mom, all the people who love Mike almost as much as I do—they don't know we're on the rocks. That for the last three nights we slept coldly on opposite ends of the bed. That the shared future we envisioned might be gone, snuffed out like a candle.

I take it as a hopeful sign that Mike wants to keep quiet about our issues. People could interpret it wrong, after all—they might think we're breaking up, which hasn't happened. *Won't* happen.

Maybe some space would be a good thing, he said yesterday. *I need to get my head on straight.*

The train's whistle shrieks outside the windows. Virgo shifts in her carrier, peering at me through the mesh.

I glance down at my phone again. My lock screen is a picture of Mike and me at Amy's wedding, him in a tux with his ramen-noodle curls combed back, me in a gown with hair spilling over my shoulders, my head fitting perfectly in the bow of his neck. I love him so much it hurts sometimes, a sandpapery squeeze on my heart. I didn't realize it until now, when I might lose it all.

Some space. A bit of distance to save our relationship. To salvage the thing that matters most.

I can do it for him.

For him, I'd do anything.

CHAPTER TWO

We pull into D.C. a little before noon, the mid-June sun high and unforgiving. I nearly drop Virgo as I hustle out, heart pounding—from yanking my suitcase down, from urgent misgivings, who can tell? I burst into the waiting area, then text the number Sabrina sent.

"Kelly?"

I whirl around and get my first look at him: He's lanky and tall, six-three or more, with copper-brown hair and trendy glasses. He's smartly dressed in a blazer, khakis, and leather tennis shoes, and in my gut intimidation crinkles anew.

He sticks out his hand, and I stare at it dumbly until he changes tack and offers his elbow.

"I haven't mastered greetings in this era," I say, setting Virgo down so I can bump my elbow against his. I nearly miss and it's terrible, like miscalculating a high-five, but then he laughs and opens his arms.

"Should we hug? I think we should hug."

I take a half step back. "Is that allowed?"

He shrugs. "We're going to isolate with you. Welcome to the pod."

It's bizarre, embracing a stranger for the first time in months. Cozy.

He picks up Virgo, but I tell him I need a sec. When I return from the restroom a few minutes later, he's unzipped the carrier and is petting my cat merrily. I watch them. He *does* look like his photos, but he doesn't move like I expected—he doesn't match the 3-D image in my brain. I thought he'd be smooth and suave, but instead there's a jerkiness there, jovial and quick.

"I'm excited to have a cat in the house." He straightens up.

"Did you grow up with them?"

"Yep—two cats and a dog." He pulls up the handle on my suitcase and starts moving. "They bring a welcome sense of mischief."

"It's true, I think Virgo is plotting world domination."

"Rina's never lived with a cat before." It's strange, hearing his nickname for her. Intimate. He chuckles. "She thinks she's not a cat person, but that's just 'cause she's so much like a cat herself."

I laugh, too, but I'm not sure what to make of it. I could ask what he means, but it feels like an overstep, soliciting a character study on his wife.

We glide up another escalator. "Did you grow up around here?" I ask. "With all the pets?"

"Charlottesville. Nice place, but I couldn't wait to move to D.C." He sets off past a line of buses that belch exhaust. "Joke's on me. Never thought I'd wind up in the suburbs."

"Your place looks gorgeous." I blush. "I mean, from what I saw on Sabrina's Instagram."

An easy laugh. "Well, in fifty-five minutes you can see for yourself."

I googled their address last night and found the cached realtor's listing. The price floored me, and the description crowed of "a GRAND Georgian Revival mansion in the Blue Ridge Mountains' most exclusive gated community atop a knoll overlooking century-old trees and lush pastureland," which was, at least, a feat of copywriting. The previous owner had Boomer taste: French country wallpaper and ruffly bed skirts.

Nathan approaches a shiny SUV, and we shuffle my things and ourselves inside. The interior is impossibly chic—seats as creamy-smooth as whipped egg whites, glossy wood on the dash. Nathan crams his mask into the console, then pauses like an astronaut testing out the atmosphere.

"Should I take mine off?" I feel like a toddler, unable to think for myself.

"Go for it." He backs out of the spot. "We'll take the risk. Otherwise, you'll spend your entire trip in quarantine." He flips on the turn signal, *tick-tock*. "We haven't been in contact with anyone else in weeks."

I wait for him to punctuate the thought with a question—*Sound good? Is that cool?*—but it doesn't come, and eventually I pluck off my mask. And here we are, two strangers-turned-pod-members, sharing the air.

"So when did you move to Deerbrook?" I tug the seatbelt too hard and it catches, resists.

"Three years ago. We were in Mount Pleasant before that." He drives casually, a few fingers on the wheel. "That's a neighborhood in the District." We pop out into the middle of D.C., hefty LEGO buildings bumped up against old churches and ornate government headquarters. I know Chicago, I know urban oases, but this feels different, like a movie set for midcentury bureaucracy.

"Do you miss it?"

"Living here? Nah." He shrugs. "We wanted more space. And it's not far."

The streets are almost empty, with lime-green scooters abandoned on sidewalks as if a spaceship sucked up all their riders. "You're fully work-from-home these days?" I ask.

"Sure am."

I'm not sure if I'll sound prying, but I keep going: "You work for the Department of Defense, right?"

"Yup. Lots of paper-pushing, it's boring." He switches lanes and we ride in silence for a few minutes and, oh, I miss Mike's comforting presence so hard I could scream. My phone tings—an alert from Zillow that a Philly home I'd saved is no longer on the market. It's an airy Colonial in Media with a picket fence hedging the backyard; how on-the-nose. When I hit Delete it's like I'm inking out the dream too.

We enter a tunnel, lights pulsing above and around us. Back out in the sun, Nathan points out landmarks as we pass: the Potomac, the Washington Monument, the Lincoln Memorial sticking up from the horizon. My heart beats faster the farther we get from D.C. From the Amtrak, my lifeline back home.

Is it still home, though? I'm not sure anywhere is home right now.

"Where'd you grow up?" he says abruptly, like he's just thought to return the question.

I frown. "Libertyville. That's how I know Sabrina."

"Oh, really! She didn't tell me that." He grins and I grin, but I feel a twinge. Am I really that . . . anonymous, to him?

"And then I lived in Chicago until February. When we moved to Philadelphia."

"How come?"

"My fiancé got offered his dream job," I recite, then blanch. It's the phrasing I've used for months—but what do I even call Mike now? And wait, why am I keeping up the charade that he switched jobs *voluntarily*, when in reality his Chicago employer let him go?

"Chicago's a great town," Nathan says. "Except for that winter."

I nod, blinking hard to reabsorb tears. Mike and I had it *so* good in Chicago. We had hobbies (*hobbies!*) and friends (*friends!*) and a sprawling prewar apartment with crown molding where the walls met the crimped-tin ceilings.

And then, right before Christmas, his firm let him go—one of those cruel rounds of cuts as VPs skimmed their year-end budgets. At his behest, I kept mum about the layoff and helped him apply for jobs all over the country—and by the end of January, he got the offer from a consulting firm in Philadelphia. I was thrilled for him—I took him out for the nicest cocktails (*cocktails!*) at a fancy lounge (*a lounge!*) and cheerfully bid Chicago adieu. Hell, I even quit my cushy marketing job at a natural-beauty brand when higher-ups bristled at the idea of me working remotely, and yes, the irony of that resignation—mere months before the pandemic—reverberates still.

I did it because I was half of a *we*. *We* were moving to Philly. *We* picked out a first-floor apartment on Chestnut. *We* set out in a moving truck—on Valentine's Day, no less—and tolerated Virgo's warbling meows for close to thirteen hours. *We* had our whole lives ahead of us: a new address, a white wedding, and, eventually, the chubby, giggly baby I'd been waiting for since I cradled dolls as a little girl.

And then. Shame rockets through my chest as I think about it again. My big, ugly misstep last week. A momentary loss of sanity, of control. A black hole of desire, sinister and limitless, springing up in my chest and taking over my body and wiping out the good. If I could take it back, I would.

The freeway bucks and swerves, broad bends through a mostly bar-ren landscape. In the distance, tawny trees and boxy office buildings scroll by. A Talking Heads song comes on the radio and, after a second's hesitation, I reach for the knob and turn it up.

Nathan's face lights up as he sing-talks the first line of "Once in a Lifetime," the bit about a shotgun shack. "Sing if you know it!"

I laugh and join in and it's true, I *do* find myself in a new part of the world.

He gestures around—he *does* find himself behind the steering wheel of a large automobile. We're both bopping our heads now, and I relax, because Nathan is an extrovert, like me, Sabrina told me so. And though I don't know where we're going, and I won't know my way around the house, and I don't know where Virgo will curl up or where I'll go when I need to scream or cry or just not be *on*, I will soon. Mike wants space; I'll give it until he comes to his senses.

I "woo!" as the song fades and a commercial bubbles on. The ener-gy's different now—we're cruising down a country lane like old friends in a road-trip movie.

"So, Nathan." I futz with the belt where it's rubbing my neck. "You're cool with the fact that I don't know how long I'll stay? It should only be a week or two."

"Of course—you've got to leave yourself an escape pod. Maybe you'll hate it."

We're bantering. I like it. "Hey, maybe *you'll* hate having *me*. We all need a get-out-of-jail-free card."

"Nope! You enter our house, you're bound forever."

I smile. "Is there a curse over the grounds?"

"Definitely. Evil spirits, witches with candy—we've got it all."

I nod. "The tower with the window juuuust wide enough for a princess to let down her hair."

He laughs as the car crests a roller-coaster hill. A winery blankets the expanse to my right, long rows of vines snaking over the landscape.

And then the gates appear, rough rock on either side of a tall wrought-iron fence. The sun ducks behind a cloud and a new song blares on, an instrumental intro, perfectly timed.

The words are threaded into the iron, curlicued and vainglorious and fringed with ivy: TANGLEWOOD ESTATES. A blackbird soars overhead and my chest compresses.

Mike. What I wouldn't give to reach for his hand right now, feel that reassuring squeeze.

Nathan taps a remote pinned to the visor and the gates glide toward us, leisurely, like a powerful man who knows the world has no choice but to wait for him.

"Welcome home," he says. And we drive inside.

CHAPTER THREE

The gates slither closed behind us. I think of the bars over our bedroom windows in Philadelphia. A few weeks ago, I awoke to the sound of someone knocking on the metal and—disoriented, half-asleep—clutched Mike in a panic. But it was just a couple teenagers hanging out in the narrow street, absentmindedly pinging the black iron.

"There's a door code in case you need to go out," Nathan says. "Not that there's much to do out there." We're rolling past what I assume are other homes: Some are set so far back that the driveways disappear into the forest. The roofs of others peek out from behind stone gates or landscaped moats of bushes and trees.

The oxygen feels different now that we're sealed inside the neighborhood. Like when the plane door closes—no going back.

I gesture behind us. "Is that the only entrance?"

"For cars, yeah. If you're walking, there's another gate that goes into the cemetery next door."

I hate spooky things, live in fear of being forced to watch a horror movie. "There's a cemetery next door?"

"Yup—Brinsmere." He clocks the fear splashed all over my face. "Don't worry, it's not scary at all. It's from the early 1800s. Designed by an architect who normally did parks, so it's actually quite pretty. Here we are." He turns in to the woods and another gate emerges. There are numbers on the stone to the left, 327, and tall iron bars curve to a peak. When Nathan taps another remote they spread open from the center, beckoning us in.

"You guys really love gates around here," I observe.

"The security was a selling point, yeah." He smiles, but his face has closed off.

I make my voice light: "Is it 'cause you do important, top-secret government work?"

He shrugs. "To be honest, Rina probably needs more protection than me. She has some nutty fans."

When I was obsessively googling Sabrina, an article had popped up about this—she'd written a long, weary Instagram caption about how frightening it was to have fans invading her privacy in D.C. She's a successful female entrepreneur who writes about sex . . . so of course some fans think they're entitled to her attention. "Has she had any scary run-ins? A stalker or something?"

The house appears, and though I've already seen it in photos, my heart booms. It's imposing in person, its colors and angles more extreme. It's perfectly symmetrical, redbrick with windows framed in black shutters. There's a slate roof with chimneys jutting out on either end, and thick steps lead to the front doors—two grand wooden slabs girdled by windows. A white portico shades the entryway, with columns flanking the doors.

It's like something from a movie, far too extraordinary to be a backdrop to the banal, to sweeping up crumbs or watching bad TV in sweatpants.

"It's beautiful," I murmur, and he thanks me.

It's only later that I realize my question about Sabrina's rabid fan base went unanswered.

Forgotten, or maybe pointedly ignored.

"Kelly Doyle!"

Sabrina, unlike her husband, carries herself exactly like I thought she would. She's gorgeous, sparkling, with bright eyes and tanned, dewy skin, effortless in a cotton dress and bare feet. She bursts from a side door and doesn't notice when Nathan reaches for her, bounding right past him and wrapping me in a hug.

Sabrina in the flesh. The woman I've been social-media stalking, then chatting with, then deifying for weeks, is in my arms. It's like waking from a dream that starred a celebrity . . . only to discover it's real.

"How was the drive?" She saunters over to Nathan and they kiss—a real kiss, long enough to make me drop my eyes.

"It was fine," he says, after she pulls away. "Not much traffic."

She squeezes the back of his neck, then turns to me. "Are you two good friends after the ride here?"

"Oh, *best* friends," Nathan says. "Prepare to be jealous."

Sabrina beams at me. "Nathan's best friends with everyone. He's like a golden retriever."

"And you're more like Virgo here." Nathan slides the carrier from the backseat.

Banter—Sabrina and I used to banter over text, and with Nathan, it worked like a charm on the drive. I take a steadying breath and grin. "What, you're saying that only someone *undiscerning* would want to be my new best friend?"

"Oh good, now there's *two* of you to give me shit."

My joke landed—I'm so relieved, my knees turn sloshy.

Sabrina dashes ahead to open the side door. They tumble inside and I pause on the driveway. The air smells sweet and I pull it deep into my lungs. After three months on lockdown, I've done it—I made it out.

I just wish Mike had made it out with me.

"Let me give you a tour." Sabrina ushers me inside.

Even the mudroom is elegant. Pendant lamps light the narrow space, and white cupboards cover the walls to my left and right.

Virgo meows. "I can't wait to see the house," I say, "but I should get Virgo situated first, if that's okay?"

"Of course! Follow me." I trail her into a broad kitchen, and then the whole house opens up around us. "Just quickly: This is where we normally eat"—we breeze through a breakfast nook with a round table and upholstered chairs—"and here's the dining room, i.e., our homage to dinner parties, RIP." I picture it: D.C.'s intellectual and creative elite seated around the fat farmhouse table.

She flounces into the next room, toward the front door, and Nathan and I follow. "This is the music room."

A grand piano dominates the space and a half dozen guitars dangle on the wall, like a shadow box of huge, pierced butterflies.

"Do you play?" I ask her.

"No, everything in here is mine," Nathan replies.

We hook into a foyer bathed in scattered sunlight. This house is huge—you could fit our Philly apartment in one corner of one floor. The reminder of Mike stings, but not as intensely. This mansion is calming me, like the walls of my heart are expanding with the space.

We trundle up the stairs, which swoop into a catwalk over the foyer. The hallway's hung with abstract art, vast canvases beneath copper sconces.

At the end of the hall she pushes open a door, and here it is, the spare room. Floaty curtains frame the windows, with views of the cemetery on one side and the front gate on the other. A chunk of mounted wood serves as a headboard for the white-quilted bed, and a mustard-yellow armchair shrugs in the corner.

"It's beautiful." I lean on the doorframe, gawping.

"Thanks—we love this room. It gets such nice light." Sabrina gestures to a walk-in closet. "I put the pet stuff in here. Hey, we'll give you some time to freshen up—come downstairs whenever you're ready."

She slides her arm around Nathan's waist and they saunter out. Mike and I were like that at first, fingertips hungry for the other's skin. And then it faded, subtly, like a day easing into night. They stride down the hallway, tall and healthy as Norse gods. I watch them through the doorway for too long, feeling my heart—fizzy with excitement just a minute ago—sink. So much whiplash today, my emotions like a kid on a swing.

Weeks ago, Mom sent me an article about how single people—those living alone—are the invisible victims of the pandemic, touch-starved and lonely. There was an interesting bit about sensors that exist only in our shoulders and back, nerve endings attuned to gentle, loving touch. The reporter noted that one reason stroking a dog or cat feels so good is that our mirror neurons imagine how the animal feels: "When you pet your furry friend, it's as if they're petting you."

That was Mom's reason for sending it: "Another reason to <3 Virgo! So glad you two have your fur baby . . . and each other." A sentiment she repeated often: *Life is better when it's shared. I'm so lucky to have your father. Together, we can get through anything.* Hell, their wedding song was "Just the Two of Us."

But three days ago, I *became* one of those sole survivors, a world of one trapped in a household for two. Seventy-two hours of torturous limbo, of dribbly tears and deep anxiety flooding my chest. My mother would be horrified if she knew about my current situation with Mike; she already thinks we're taking too long to marry in the first place. I unzip Virgo's carrier, reaching to scratch her furry rump, but she zips past me and springs onto the bed.

I cross to the boxes of Virgo's supplies—the ones I ordered yesterday as I rushed to prepare for my visit. I find scissors in the desk and yawn them apart to slit the boxes' tape, but I grab the blade wrong and slice my fingers, smearing crimson along the cardboard.

"Dammit." I sit on the bed and examine the cut. Long and shallow, blood beading in a line. A fresh wound to match the gash on my palm, a half-healed, jagged cleft above the pad of my thumb. My stomach tightens as I remember first spotting it last week. I'd been so out of control, so outside myself, I didn't even notice it tie-dyeing my sleeve red.

I hold my hand above my head (*pick me!*) until the bleeding stops, then flop back. I close my eyes and the scene from last night plays.

You have to forgive me, Mike, please. You know how much I love you.

It's—it's not about that.

So what is it about? Just tell me and I'll change it, I swear. I'll do whatever it takes.

It's not like that.

But . . . but I'm your Kell-Bell.

Even pet names are depressing in the right context. I cried for a few minutes then, wishing he'd use the nickname again, call me his. Instead he enveloped me in his arms, sniffling. I cried and cried, waiting for him to ask me, tell me, beg me to stay.

I wipe the tears from my cheeks. Maybe absence will make the heart grow fonder. Maybe he'll sit in that kennel of an apartment and realize how much he misses me, how much we love each other.

I sit up and let hope roll around in me like wine dregs in a glass.

CHAPTER FOUR

They forgot to tell me where the bathroom is, and I prod at doors until I find it. The towels are white and hotel-soft. Of course they are; everything here is perfect.

Except me. I stare into the mirror: My mask rubbed the foundation off my nose. My blond bob is overgrown and I'm in desperate need of a root touch-up.

Tired. Disheveled. *Is this why Mike won't marry you?*

I dab powder on my nose, slick on fresh deodorant. I wet my fingertips and run them through my hair. Sometimes I feel like I'm not allowed to look in the mirror if I'm not presentable.

I'm wearing opal earrings Mike got me, studs from an outdoor market we stumbled on in Kauai. The vendor, an aging hippie, asked if we were siblings, which we found both horrifying and hilarious. Though our coloring is similar, Mike and I are physical opposites: him tall and stocky, me tiny with pin-straight bob. I loved fantasizing about how our DNA would mash up: Maybe our daughter would get my ski-jump nose and Mike's long lashes. Perhaps our son would inherit my culinary prowess and Mike's green thumb. And I'd smile into the dark, pulsing with love for imaginary offspring, aching to meet them.

That was one of many incredible things about those first few months with Mike. He wasn't dodgy or withholding like other men I'd fallen for; he wasn't intimidated by the intensity of my love. This was it—this was how it felt to know how the story would end. When I daydreamed about the walk down the aisle or beach vacations with sand-speckled kiddos, I no longer had a shadowy stand-in for a partner. Boy, was I relieved.

With a sprig of tenderness, I picture him yanking warm linens from the dryer, pondering how to fold a fitted sheet. So he needs space. I'll show him I'm not clingy or needy or inflexible. I'll prove I'm not the woman he came upon last week, hands red as blood.

I'm his Kell-Bell. Surely he'll miss me soon.

I'm about to head downstairs, where I can hear their voices like a cheery radio. But at the top of the steps, curiosity tugs at me. This is where Sabrina—the woman I've been watching from afar, reading about, admiring—lives. Mysterious Nathan too. I can't help it—I pad to the nearest door and peek inside.

Nathan's office, I think: minimalist with a vast desk on splayed legs and an Eames chair. There's a banker's lamp on the desktop and floating shelves on the wall. A gleaming stone pyramid that looks like an oversized paperweight sits on the end.

Across the hallway, I push open the door to what must be Sabrina's office. It's funkier, with artwork and hanging plants forming a gallery wall over an eggplant sofa. Her desk is a collage of books and notepads and Polaroids, but the most striking feature is the wall between the windows: Hundreds of Post-it notes, color-coded and covered in her intricate cursive, stick to the wall. I read in an article that she handwrites her first drafts in notebooks, an endeavor I can't fathom.

The sticky notes flutter like feathers. I'll need to keep Virgo out of here—she'd tear them all down, have a field day.

The image makes me think of that horrible day last week, and I step back into the hallway, stomach twisting. I should go downstairs; I should stop snooping and be social. They're taking me in like an orphan and I owe them my graciousness.

But: The bedroom. Their most private space. What if this is my one chance to see it unsupervised?

The floorboards groan as I tiptoe down the hallway and poke my head inside. Light pours in from all the windows, spotlighting a king-sized bed with a tufted headboard. A huge mirror hangs on the wall next to it. I've never had one so close to the bed. Maybe it's so they can watch themselves.

I'm in her room. How is this happening right now? If you'd told me three weeks ago, when I first slipped down the digital rabbit hole of all things Sabrina, that I'd soon be standing here . . .

I peer into their en-suite bathroom. The tub is bone-white and round, like half a giant egg. Behind it is a deep, glass-enclosed shower with a bench and two showerheads.

And I jump to the sex they must be having in this shower built for two. Maybe it's because I've read her books, lingering over the most titillating scenes, or maybe it's because Mike and I haven't had sex in months, but as I gaze into the bathroom, I *see* it: Nathan and Sabrina taking advantage of the shower's marble bench, kissing hard, steam rippling like smoke, water pelting their bare skin—

"Kelly?"

The scene dissolves, *poof,* and heat rushes to my cheeks.

Sabrina's in the door, a confused smile smeared across her face. I shake my head.

"Sorry. I—I was looking for Virgo, I wasn't sure if she's allowed in here, so . . ."

"She's on your bed." She jerks a thumb behind her, blinks. "Curled up right in the center."

"I'm sorry." I'm deflated, a sagging bag of trash. My face burns so hot you could sizzle an egg on it.

It's over. I've already gone and messed it up. Why couldn't I just be normal?

But then she shrugs. "It's a good tub, right? But wait till you see the hot tub. You'll forget this one even exists. C'mon, let's get you a drink." She waves a friendly palm my way, and relief buoys up in my chest. I head for the door—I'm mortified, can't be in here a second longer—but she blocks me and I nearly bump into her.

She's taller than me and too close to my face. She's relentless with the eye contact, smiling as she arches an eyebrow. Her gaze sinks lower and stops near my clavicle. She tilts her head and starts to raise her arm, fingers outstretched, the moment slows as her hand comes closer, closer to the base of my throat. I don't breathe, I can't move. What is she doing?

Her fingers stop a millimeter from my shirt, sweep along my collar. Slowly, slowly, her arm retracts, an orange hair pinned beneath her thumb and pointer.

She blows it away like a dandelion seed, her pretty lips pursed. I'm still frozen. That was . . . strangely intimate. I'm not sure I can even remember the last time Mike was that close to me, paid that much attention to me.

Another punch of sadness. *Mike*. It's like there's a livecam trained on our apartment and every time I think of him, I tune in. I can almost see him now, microwaving leftover gnocchi.

"Cat hair." Sabrina smiles. "Okay, three drinks coming right up."

She heads for the stairs, and my head buzzes as I follow. I watch her hips swing as she swishes through the foyer. She doesn't quite move how I expected from social media either.

In the kitchen, Sabrina plucks a bottle of champagne from the fridge. "It's not every day we get a visitor."

"Everything okay with your room?" Nathan leans against the kitchen island; I envy his ease.

"It's perfect." *My* room. Sunlight and soft surfaces, a space to call my own. This morning, I was trapped in that shadowy apartment, peeking out from behind bars. But now . . . "Thank you so much, seriously. This is just what I needed."

"We're glad to have you." Sabrina eases the cork from the bottle, *pop*. "Is the kitty okay?"

"She's already acting like she owns the place." I immediately regret the turn of phrase—*I* was the one snooping around. I accept a fizzy glass. "Thanks. Um, no rush but I should get her bowls for water and food."

"Of course. Listen, I want you to treat this place like your home. I'll go nuts if every time you need something you're like, 'Sabrina, may I please use this dish?'" She crosses to the cabinet—they're all mint green and smooth, goddamn adorable—and flings it open like a game-show host. "Plates and dishes are here. Glasses and mugs are here . . ." The kitchen tour begins, appliances popping out from what I thought were cabinet fronts, *surprise!* There are double ovens stacked on the wall and a six-burner range that gives me something like an erection.

"Do you cook?" I ask, my voice breathy.

"Sadly, no." Nathan shrugs. "We've tried a bunch of those meal-kit services and we still suck."

"Well, I love cooking." I tap the edge of the stove. It's shiny and tempting, like a blank canvas. "So I can help with that. It's the least I can do. I mean, you're *housing* me, for goodness' sake."

Sabrina sets her fingers on my arm and dips her chin. "I mean it: Do not think of yourself as, like, indebted to us. There's not a power differential. However long you're here—a week or two or more—this is your home." She peers at me a second longer, then shoots a grin Nathan's way. "Honestly, we need you at least as much as you need us."

We all laugh, but she doesn't move her hand. Finally I inch away, then pull a bowl from the cabinet. "I'll put Virgo's food in the mud-room. And then you can finish showing me around, yeah?"

Sabrina smiles again. Her eyes are enormous, as doelike as a porcelain doll's.

"Of course." Her brows flash. "I know Philly never felt right for you. But here, you're home."

CHAPTER FIVE

The house is so pretty it makes my chest ache.

I keep feeling it, this wave of shaggy sorrow for how beautiful it is. I could never make a home look like this. And envy is part of it, but it's bigger than that. A feeling I get on vacation sometimes, looking out over a new landscape, tears pricking my eyes: *This is perfect, and I can't soak it in enough.*

"Everything's gorgeous," I say. Sabrina and I are in the light-filled entryway. I thought we'd start the tour, but she's still gazing up at the broad chandelier, concentric copper hoops. I clear my throat. "Did you hire an interior designer?"

"No, I did it myself." She snaps her head down to look at me. "It's fun for me, looking at something and wondering how far I can push it. Here." Sabrina nods at a keypad next to the front door. "I'll show you how to use the house-alarm thing. Nathan is super anal-retentive about security." She rolls her eyes. "You'll need the code: ten-forty-three. Oh, don't do that."

I freeze, my hands cupped around my phone. "I was writing it down."

"You can't. Everything's hackable." She shrugs apologetically. "You have to memorize it. Ten-forty-three."

"Got it. Sorry."

"It's just Nathan, with his job at the DOD—they've drilled into him that he needs to be on guard against everything. Shall we?" She leads me into the living room, prim with a stiff-backed sofa and cobalt accent chairs. "We hardly ever use this room," she says, heading into the space beyond it. "But *this* is my favorite one in the house."

It's a library—the kind Belle sweeps across in bibliophilic rapture, with shelves stretched to the ceiling and a rolling ladder slanting over the spines.

"Sabrina, it's *stunning*!"

"Thanks!" She touches the mantel of the room's fireplace. "This is why we bought the place. We had to gut the rest of the house, but once I saw this library, it had to be mine."

"It's incredible." There are cozy seats, a sleek credenza, a basket of blankets. I want to curl up with tea and a paperback. I want to don slippers and suck on a pipe.

"I'm so analog—I love the feel of books," she says. "Their smoothness and smell and everything. That's why I refuse to get an e-reader." She gives the nearest shelf a loving pat. "I was born in the wrong decade—I write by hand and take Polaroids of things I want to remember and hang on to every card and letter I get."

There must be hundreds of books lining the walls here. It's strange, I feel like I already know this room somehow—

"This was in *Market Penetration*," I blurt out. The latest book in her Heart of Desire series, a scene still seared onto my brain: Arianna bent over Perry's desk, his colleagues sipping bourbon in the parlor outside, and Perry kissing the back of her neck, his hands slipping beneath her dress . . .

"Good eye." She chuckles. "I swapped the credenza for a desk, but otherwise, this is it! Sometimes making stuff up from scratch gets exhausting."

"I'm sure." I turn away so she can't see the pink dusting my cheeks. "I don't mean to fangirl, but I have to tell you again how much I loved your books."

"Thank you! Truly, you're too sweet."

I'm sure she means it, but I feel let down: It's *exactly* how she responds to social-media comments. I don't know what I expected, but . . . bigger, truer words than her standard line, verbatim.

She flaps her hand. "I'm grateful my books brought us together. That you had the balls to reach out."

"I am too." That's more like it. "I'm an addict, honestly. I'm dying to read the next one."

"Oh, good. I'm working on it right now."

I smile even wider. "Well, if you ever need an early reader to tell you what they—"

"Sorry, I never share what I'm working on. With anyone." Her voice is stonelike—not annoyed, exactly, but not warm or apologetic either.

My chest fills with icy shame. *Why did I say that?* "Oh, of course. Sorry."

"No worries." Her eyes land behind me and climb skyward. "But speaking of—I noticed the door to my office was open."

"Sabrina, I'm sorry again, I—"

"It's fine, you didn't know. The thing is—I'm very private about my work. Especially at this stage. And Nathan really doesn't like anyone going into his office. Hell, *I'm* not even allowed in there."

"Absolutely. It won't happen again." I nod earnestly. "And anyway, Virgo loves chewing on Post-its, so we should probably keep your door shut."

"Good to know. It'll be interesting living with a cat." She gazes into the hallway, as if she can see Virgo there, and the movement strikes me as feline—the intensity, staring at nothing the way Virgo does when she seems to be watching a ghost. "Anyway, let's continue."

Sabrina glides through the halls and opens a door off the mudroom. My heart thumps as I follow—*is she annoyed, have I overstepped, is it already time to pack my bags?* The basement houses faded Persian rugs and a sectional sofa. There's a bar in the corner and a cool, musty wine cellar where shelves of dusty bottles form a compact maze.

"Last thing on the tour!" She's back to her bubbly self, and the tourniquet-like squeeze on my heart eases. A glass door opens into a screen porch with Acapulco chairs and a cushioned wicker sofa. "The mosquitoes are vicious here. This makes it bearable—until it gets too hot to be anywhere other than the pool, that is."

Other than the pool. It hits me, another punch of *how the hell is this happening?* It's like I'm being punked, led through an immersive space carefully engineered to read "Perfect Life." This is a dream; soon I'll wake up, sweaty and lonely and a hundred miles away.

If only Mike were here with me. If only any of this were mine.

And then she slides the screen door away, and it's cerulean and glorious: that amoeba-shaped pool. Sabrina must've been sitting in one of these deck chairs when she took the selfie that caught my eye and tipped over the first domino. Was that just three weeks ago?

"Do you swim?" She squints at me. It feels like a test.

"Absolutely! I was on the swim team, remember?"

"That's right."

I can picture high school Sabrina in group photos, but I remember her only in shuffled movements: tall and hunched, her bad posture making her height more noticeable. She sported unremarkable clothes and a low ponytail, plus a shyness so intense it seemed to upstage her.

I have one clear memory of her, one that crackles with meaning like a word blipping out of a garbled call. Ninth-grade English with Mrs. Dreier; we were studying Shakespeare and had to write our own sonnets, iambic pentameter and all. The teacher read her favorites aloud and Sabrina's was one of them, a deft, lilting poem about observing the perfection of other girls. I still remember a line comparing their ponytails to "*feath*-ered *plumes* that *rip*-ple *in* the *sun*." I stared at her, shocked that such pretty words had sprung from that quiet form, as she grew redder and redder.

I never told her how much the poem impressed me. Maybe that's why I reached out all these years later. Correcting yesterday's wrongs.

I notice a round lump on the patio's corner. "Is that the hot tub?"

She shades her eyes with her hand. "It is! Use it whenever you want." Above it, string lights cling to a limey tree. My pupils are red hearts. It's beautiful and perfect and the only thing missing is my partner.

Hang on to this one, my mom said of Mike almost five years ago, grinning at the pictures I'd pulled up on my phone. *You two could really take care of each other.* She loved him before she'd even met him.

And I loved him almost as quickly.

"Have you eaten?" Sabrina starts heading back inside.

In the kitchen, she tosses things onto the counter and I assemble a cheese board. Sabrina seems impressed with the final product—snazzy on a marble slab I found under the sink—and I shiver with pride when she takes a picture for her Instagram. She makes plates for herself and Nathan and apologizes for needing to get back to work.

"But I'm sure you want a little time to yourself too," she says, because she doesn't understand my loneliness, how even my skeleton aches for affection. "Make yourself at home."

And I'm alone once more. In this grand kitchen, so gorgeous it belongs at the end of a home-renovation show. The wave of separation is even stronger this time, like homesickness for a life I'll never have. The Talking Heads song trumpets on in my head. It's true: This isn't my beautiful house, that wasn't my large automobile. She isn't my beautiful wife.

I'm still on the outside. Same as it ever was.

CHAPTER SIX

I text Mom to let her know I arrived, then check my email: updates from Zillow, from bridal magazines, reminders of the plans that are slipping away, like something tossed overboard. I don't know what to do with myself. In some strange, bone-deep way, it feels like the pandemic has robbed me of my identity—who am I without my friends, my hobbies, the fiancé I looked forward to someday calling "my better half"?

I picture the stunned look on Mike's face when he found me last week. *I don't know who you are,* he stammered, hands curling into fists. His eyes hardened from shock into betrayal. *This is a side of you I've never seen.*

My stomach pretzels. Why couldn't I be *good*? Sweet, loyal Mike deserves better than a loose cannon like me.

After all, I didn't know I was capable of what I did either.

Enough. I stuff the thoughts down, pushing hard like I can squeeze them through a sewer grate. Mike assured me it's not about that; he can't articulate what the problem is, and maybe that means it's surmountable with a little time apart. I wonder what he's up to right now.

With a flap of sadness, I picture him calling for Virgo and remembering she's gone.

I tap his name on my phone—no answer. Anxiety hops and swirls like chickadees. Is this what I've signed on for? Tootling around an even more unfamiliar home? Alone in this dining room, I get the eerie feeling that none of this is real—that I might not exist. If a Kelly falls in the forest and no one's around to hear it . . . ?

Go for a walk, Kelly. I change into tennis shoes and, after a moment of furious debate, text Sabrina that I'm heading out. As soon as I step into the soupy air, the unease mellows—there's greenery everywhere, wildflowers hedging the drive and crinkly-barked pines stretching several stories high. I try calling Amy. I open Google Maps and zoom into Brinsmere Cemetery—Nathan insisted it's not creepy, and I'd like to get my first visit over with, know what I'm living next to. I'll walk the perimeter until I find an opening.

At the end of the driveway, I have to key the code in twice to get it right. This whole development must've been cleared from the woods, and as I walk I admire the trees that remain—fat knots distorting their trunks, squirrels scurrying over their roots. The cemetery appears in pieces through a fence of metal poles. Yet another jail cell—am I inside or out?

My phone rings and I smile at the screen.

"How's Virginia?" Mike's voice is reedy and weak. It cheers me, in a twisted way; him mourning my departure is a good sign.

"Okay so far. I'm trying to find the entrance to a graveyard now."

"Why? You hate cemeteries."

A tender nip to my heart—he really knows me. "You're right. But this one's more like a park, apparently."

"A park full of dead people?"

"Well, they're buried. There's not, like, a *Sixth Sense* thing going on."

A flick of laughter. My heart twinges harder; I can still make him laugh.

"How is it with your friends?" he presses.

"Fine. They're being good hosts."

"Are you sure you're good there? You don't really know these people, right?"

My chest lifts—he already wants me to come back!

But then he pricks the bubble: "I mean, maybe you could go stay with Amy instead?"

I slump. "She didn't invite me. And Amy has a kid—she doesn't need to be looking after me too."

"I guess."

I sigh and peek through the bars again. Geese waddle over the grass, as non-aerodynamic as feathered kettlebells. "How are you doing?" I ask.

"I'm okay. I successfully finished the laundry."

"That's good." I hate this, walking on eggshells whenever we talk. We're so lucky to have found each other—can't he see?

"I miss you," I say. My heart pounds. I can't believe I'm afraid of how Mike, my love, will respond.

"It's really weird not having you here," he finally replies.

My shoulders wilt. He needs to come to his senses, realize we're perfect together.

"I should go." I struggle to keep my voice from trembling.

"Okay. Bye, Kelly."

Yet again, he didn't fight for me to stay.

The entrance in the gate is almost invisible, identical to the fencing around it but for the latch at the top. Inside, I make my way toward a hill prickly with crumbling monuments, some hundreds of years old.

When I crest the hill, I see a roundish valley with headstones set up in concentric circles. A carved angel looms in the center, the markers around it like patrons at an outdoor concert.

I look over my shoulder at the tippy-top of Tanglewood Estates— from this elevation, I can see straight into my room and Nathan's office. I'll need to draw the curtains, lest I put on a peep show for the ghosts.

In the basin's center, the angel is mottled gray-green, genderless and imposing with thick wings and a laurel wreath atop its chunky curls. One arm hugs a stone book with ATWOOD carved into the cover.

There's a symbol inscribed in the statue's base: a triangle centered in a vertical rectangle so its corners touch the rectangle's top and sides. It looks a bit like a child's drawing of a home.

"You scared me!"

I jump and whirl around. A woman stands gobsmacked a few yards away. She's middle-aged and shaped like an avocado, with tough, leathery skin and beady eyes. Under each arm, half-moons of sweat darken her linen blouse.

"Sorry!" I pull my mask up. "I thought I was alone out here."

"You look like you've seen a ghost." Her Southern accent deepens and she breaks into a smile.

"Well, we *are* in a cemetery!" I joke. "I'm Kelly. I'm visiting from Philly." I jerk a thumb at Tanglewood behind me.

"Diane. Where are you staying?"

Undeniable small-town-gossip vibes. Hey, I like gossip. "With some friends. The Lamonts?"

She rears back. "They're having guests? *Now?*"

I grow a bit defensive: "I needed people to isolate with. We're a . . . pod."

She frowns. "How well do you know them?"

"How well do *you?*"

She tilts her head. "I know the husband's a fed and the wife writes porno."

I laugh to keep it light, but my belly curdles. "Sabrina writes romance novels. She's a *New York Times* bestseller."

Diane narrows her eyes. "Well, nice meeting you."

I'm not particularly sorry to end the conversation. "See you around."

Clouds have rolled in, a bruisy shade of indigo, and the breeze jostles into action. But now that I'm in the center of this grassy bowl, I'm not sure which way I came from. I pull out my phone to check the map, but the blue dot jumps around, then settles on a spot outside the graveyard. I give up and start walking, leaning against the grass's soft pitch. The wind rustles again, restless, and I feel my heart thrumming in my chest. Finally I spot the rooftops of Tanglewood Estates and nearly sprint to the gate below.

Drops splatter onto my arm, my collarbone, the crown of my head. I'm at the fence but I can't find the damn exit. I rush one way, then the other, squinting at the top of the fenceposts as the wind cups the rain and lobs it back at me.

I find the latch, finally, and hurl myself through, breaking into a run as the sky cracks open above me.

CHAPTER SEVEN

"I hate that it's storming." Sabrina sets a bowl of salad on the table in the breakfast nook. "I wanted us to watch the sunset from the pool for your first night."

"That's saying something, because normally Rina loves a good storm." Nathan's plunking down silverware.

"Summer storms are cozy! Good for writing." She fluffs the greens with broad wooden spoons. "I like to pretend I'm in a Brontë novel."

I'm lingering with a glass of water. It feels momentous, picking out My Seat in the breakfast nook.

"Hopefully not *Jane Eyre*," I crack, then consider. "Wait, aren't *all* their novels creepy?"

"Sit, sit," Nathan says. They drop into chairs directly across from each other, so I pull one back in-between. Thirty minutes earlier, they let me throw together some pasta, and now they indicate I should serve myself first. Sabrina uncorks a bottle of wine Nathan dragged up from the cellar.

Once we've filled our plates, Sabrina holds her goblet aloft: "To Kelly gracing us with her presence!"

"To you two for having me in your beautiful abode!" Our glasses clang.

"I love this house," Sabrina says. "It's like our own little world."

I match her grin and feel that little-kid glee buoying up once more, a bit of hope among the misery. Here, I can breathe. I can find myself again and return to Philly a better partner—the Kell-Bell Mike fell in love with.

"Speaking of the Brontës," Nathan says between bites, "Rina told you this place is haunted, right?"

"No . . ." I plaster on a smile but feel a twinge in my chest.

"The house is almost two hundred years old. Sometimes we hear footsteps at night." He waggles his eyebrows.

"Nathan, enough." Sabrina sips her wine. "Any noise is the house settling. This home has nothing but good vibes. It's so safe and comfy— you'll see."

Nathan's super anal-retentive about security. Earlier, Sabrina blamed it on his job, but . . . "Is that part of why you moved out here? To be somewhere safe?"

"Partly," Sabrina admits. "Deerbrook's crime rate is basically zero."

But the period at the end of her sentence feels charged. "Did something happen in D.C.?"

"Actually, yes." She clasps her hair behind her neck. "I got doxxed."

"Oh no."

"Yeah. It was scary." She looks down at her plate. "I said some things about incels and men's rights activists on Instagram. A few had been harassing me, and one day I'd had enough. But they struck back. Found my home address and personal email and phone number and blew them all up with threats. We had to get the police involved. It was . . . a lot."

I glance at Nathan—his jaw has tightened and his fingers have curled into a fist.

"I'm so sorry," I say. "That's awful. I saw that *Us Weekly* piece about your Instagram post, but it didn't mention . . ." I stall out. *Jeez, Kelly, don't tell her you read articles about her.*

"The cops told us to keep it quiet—it's like having a stalker, acknowledging them only makes it worse." Her shoulders jump. "We were already thinking about moving, but that put us over the edge."

I nod. "How'd you decide on Deerbrook?"

Nathan glances at Sabrina, as if checking who should answer. "It was on our radar because a friend had family in the area. And we liked all the green space."

"Nathan always felt cramped in D.C. And to be fair, you could touch both sides of our townhouse if you stood in the middle." She demonstrates, arms in airplane position.

"D.C.'s not meant for someone my size." Nathan gestures near the top of his head. "On the Metro I was like . . ."

"An American Girl doll stuffed into a Barbie Dreamhouse," Sabrina supplies.

"Thank you." Nathan guffaws. I glance at Sabrina, expecting an I-made-him-laugh beam like mine from the car ride here, but she only smirks. They must be accustomed to the sudden hooks of each other's minds.

Not like Mike. Before the pandemic locked us inside and brought out the worst in us, we could still delight each other with a goofy joke. Back in February, we passed the time on the thirteen-hour drive from Chicago with a game: pointing at things along the road and spinning out silly hypotheticals. *We should buy that abandoned skating rink. We should move into that RV park. We should get jobs at the water park on that billboard.* Imagined futures tied together by *we.*

I jab my fork into a tortellini, piercing it like an eye. "Are most of your friends in D.C.?"

Sabrina nods. "Now I regret not befriending any of our neighbors. I'm jealous of my friends in the District with their *pods.* Everyone in Tanglewood is old or stuffy or busy with their kids, you know? We're the weirdest people here. The only ones with zero interest in joining Colonial Country Club."

"Luckily, we're pretty good at the us-versus-the-world thing." Nathan holds her gaze.

My chest sinks. How long has it been since Mike looked at me like that?

"Speaking of neighbors," I sputter, puncturing the moment, "I met one at Brinsmere—Diane. What's her deal?"

Nathan furrows his brow. "Doesn't ring a bell."

Sabrina looks like she wants to say something, but then she sips her wine.

"She seemed surprised you have a guest," I press. "And she knows what both of you do for work."

"A busybody," Sabrina observes.

"And *that* is why we have the privacy gate." Nathan pushes his plate away. "It's nice to feel protected. Cut off from everything. You'll see."

"I hope you like it here," Sabrina adds, a bit shyly. "I still feel like you're a mirage—yesterday I asked you to come. And today you came!"

I flash back to the conversation with Mike.

I'm thinking about going away for a bit.

What? Where?

My huge gamble, all in—surely he'd choose me over being alone. *To stay with my friend Sabrina. Outside D.C.*

The one you've been texting with.

Right. I stared at him, my hopes as high as a tightrope walker teetering in midair.

And then the words I dreaded most, ones I couldn't unhear and he couldn't take back, words that slid through me like a fillet knife, sharp and quick: *Maybe you should.*

I glance up, registering that the Lamonts are waiting for me to reply. They're even cooler in person than I'd hoped. Perhaps it'll rub off on me.

"I *know* I'm going to love it here." I smile hard. "I'm so glad I came."

The wine does its work, slackening the space around us. After dinner Nathan zooms to the basement and emerges with another bottle, and we glide into the library.

I briefly panic about where to sit. Nathan drops onto an armchair and Sabrina plops on a cushion near his feet, transforming it into a throne. I take the loveseat and this feels nice, a cozy distance between us, and, God, it is marvelous to be around people. A bellow of wind and rain makes the lamps wink, and Sabrina lights candles that fill the space with towering shadows and their woodsy perfume.

Warm, witty Nathan makes the air spark with his quick jokes and easy banter. I stick my foot out and play-kick his shin when he teases me good-naturedly, and he fumbles to fight back, an impromptu game of footsie. Sabrina, with her lopsided smirk and husky voice, keeps the conversation moving, pushing us onward when a topic grows dry or nudging us back on track when Nathan and I fall too deep into a joshing digression. The wine is saline and crisp and the chemistry undeniable. We open a third bottle. We let one candle flicker until its wick dwindles and drowns.

I let the thought swirl, a betrayal to Mike: *I could get used to this.*

The house *is* noisy at night, groaning like an old man settling into a La-Z-Boy.

I miss Mike. I miss the bulk of him next to me in bed, the way he murmurs in his sleep. I miss the plans I'd knitted for both of us, starting with him signing back on to a wedding.

I don't know how to put this, he said. *I . . . I don't want to re-up the vendors.*

And my brain did a desperate scramble: *You want different vendors? No. Not that.*

What, then? And I'd braced myself, sure it was because of what I'd done, how I'd messed everything up.

I think I need to pump the brakes. I'm not sure about . . . getting married.

"Not sure" isn't "definitely don't want." I can still fix this. Right?

I stare at the ceiling and let the future play out like a filmstrip, home movies in reverse: Mike and me hosting a wedding, buying a house, exploring Philadelphia, building a life. Preparing ourselves to make tiny humans that are half him and half me, beings with their own mysterious quirks and opinions and penchants and personalities who'd one day blow our minds with the way they saw the world.

Alone in this foreign bed, I mourn those kids as if they're real. I'm almost thirty-five. So many friends are struggling with fertility issues. What if those figmentary fetuses are the closest I'll get to motherhood? This is *not* what I was counting on—for me, for my ovaries, for humanity at large.

A new sound, soft and scraping. I push the covers down and turn on the lamp.

Something's wrong.

Another scratch, and it snaps into place: The bedroom door is shut, even though I'm sure I left it cracked so that Virgo could come and go. I hurry over and pull it open, and she sidles past me, giving my shin a head-bump.

Who closed the door? I peer into the hall and think I see the shadows move, but it could be the wind strumming spindly branches outside. It's dark here, a downy dark so different from the orange-tinged night of Chicago or Philadelphia.

I creep down the hallway. Night spills in from the bathroom window, and through it I can just make out a yard tentacling into the woods beyond. I flip on the light and gaze at my reflection.

I'm not crazy, I shrieked at Mike, hearing the words like they were coming from someone else. *You won't even* look *at me. It's like I don't exist.*

My nightgown's twisted off-center; my hair's tangled and wild. I flick off the light and watch myself disappear.

CHAPTER EIGHT

'm braced against a desk and someone's behind me, fingers sliding along my waist. I reach back to stroke Mike's bushy hair but wait, it's glossy and long. I glance over my shoulder and she shoots me a secret, knowing smile as she slips her hand beneath my dress. I gasp as the feeling builds like steam in a teapot, like water in a geyser, like—

My alarm blares and I jolt awake. I breathe hard for a moment—that felt *so real*. I'm as turned-on as a teenager, swollen and sensitive.

Not to mention flustered, sheepish, confused. A sex dream about *Sabrina*? It's clear where my subconscious pulled from: Sabrina's book, that frenzied, secret hookup in Perry's study. But I've never so much as kissed a girl.

A headache bangs at my temples, the consequence of all that wine. Virgo, cat-loafing at the foot of the bed, winks coolly.

Someone's in the kitchen, clattering around. It'll be strange, seeing my new housemates first thing in the morning, in that blinky, pre-coffee stage. I'll have to be friendly and *on*, and they will, too, in their own home.

"Good morning." Nathan dumps sugar into his coffee with a flourish. It's exactly how Mike takes it, and my insides tumble down.

"Morning." My headache intensifies. Did I embarrass myself last night? I didn't black out, but my jokes were dumber and I laughed too hard at them. My cheeks warm as I remember my toes tussling with Nathan's. Is it already time to book my train back?

"How'd you sleep?" he asks.

"Really well, thanks!" It's an automatic fib. "Is there more coffee?"

"Just made a pot."

I cross to the coffeemaker, flail around for a mug, and then stick my head in the fridge, seeking milk. We're stuck in the excruciating loop of him helping and me bleating *thank you!* like a wind-up doll.

Mug in hand, I drag my laptop into the dining room. I send my résumé into the void, *whoosh*. My unease is an illness, attacking my cells from the inside. Last night I felt at home; why am I swinging back into Awkwardville like a dang rocking horse?

My phone rings on the table and my heart lifts.

"Hi, sweetie!" Amy cries. My eyes fill at the sound of her voice— God, I miss her. We became friends in the break room during my first week at Juna, the natural-beauty company I called home for a decade, and we quickly became inseparable. We went clubbing in our twenties; we lived together as we celebrated our joint thirtieth birthdays. She moved in with her now-husband the same week I moved in with Mike, and that's where our paths diverged: She threw together a dynamite wedding in five months flat, while Mike and I fumbled through the last four-plus years, all the way until . . .

"Amy! It's good to hear your voice."

"Wait, what's wrong?"

I clear my throat. "Do I sound weird? I'm not sick, cross my heart."

"Thank God. I'm calling to thank you for that super thoughtful box you sent. I told Greg I'm using one of the bath bombs tonight and no one's allowed to talk to me."

"You're welcome! You deserve some TLC."

"You're the best, seriously." A car honks in the background. "I'm at the playground with Liam. I thought we'd be the only people here."

"I miss that kiddo."

"He misses his Auntie Kelly! How are things? How's Mike?"

I pin an arm to my stomach. "I'm actually in Virginia for a few days."

"What? Why?"

"I'm staying with friends." I swallow. "We're quarantining, don't worry."

"Where's Mike?"

I wince, picturing him alone in that shadowy townhouse. I flash back to our first night in Philadelphia: sharing Greek takeout at the kitchen counter, giggling as we dragged pita through a tub of tzatziki. "He's at home. We . . ." My voice betrays me, cracking like land in an earthquake.

She lets out a sympathetic noise. "What's going on?"

My desire to not tell her is like a force. Mike doesn't want anyone knowing our business, and I don't want to burden my friends with something that'll (presumably, hopefully) blow right over. Amy *loves* Mike and me as a couple—along with her husband, we're a perfect foursome.

And unlike me, she's a stellar partner. She didn't breach her husband's trust and mess everything up like I did to Mike.

"Kelly. It's *me*. You don't have to be Miss Perfect Relationship with me." She grows quieter, like she's holding the phone away from her mouth. "*Liam, give that back, that's not yours!* So wait, why are you in Virginia? With who?"

The decision locks into place: I'll tell her *after* Mike and I work things out. When I can breathe again. "I'm staying with a friend from high school."

"Do I know this person?"

"No . . . we kinda rekindled our friendship out of pandemic boredom. They have all this space and a pool and everything." Inspiration strikes: "Mike will probably join me here soon."

"Oh, nice! A pool—sounds awesome. *Liam, come back, please.* I'm sorry, can I call you later?"

We hang up and I stare out the window, my guts knotting. It's not Amy's judgment I fear so much as her disappointment, how bummed she'd be if we broke up. And telling her the truth would make things feel too real, too irreversible.

I text Mike a photo of Virgo. He doesn't reply. I stare at the screen, dazed and teary.

Sabrina wanders through the music room just then and rears back when she spots me. "I'm sorry! Do you want me to leave?"

The sight of her flashes me back to that illicit dream, and I blush.

"Of course you shouldn't leave." A ripple of sobby laughter. "It's *your* home."

She crosses to me. "What's wrong?"

"My friend was asking about Mike, and I hate lying to her, but . . ."

"Shh. I know everything's hard right now." She crouches to wrap me in a hug. She holds my face against her soft bust and she smells nice and it's a confusing moment for my entire body.

"You'll figure things out," she murmurs into my hair.

And it's strange: When she says it . . . I believe her.

CHAPTER NINE

That evening, Sabrina and I carry brimming wineglasses through the basement and set them on the edge of the pool, which sparkles with the night sky. Sabrina dives in without hesitation.

"Is it cold?"

"Only for a second." She sidestrokes away.

I ease myself in. The water's like cold knives and when I dip my shoulders, then my head, the frigid rush sweeps through my blood. We gather in the deep end, legs pumping like eggbeaters. Fireflies strobe in the lawn and, once again, I marvel that this is my . . . well, *their* life, and mine for the time being.

"Remember having to tread water for twenty minutes in gym class?" Sabrina's breath is hitched from exertion.

I find myself observing how her hair fans out over her clavicle and look away. "To get an A, you had to keep your hands out of the water the whole time too."

"I forgot that part." She leans back so her feet buoy to the surface. "I'm sure I didn't even attempt it."

Were we in the same gym class? I can't picture her shuffling out of the locker room in a one-piece. "I bet I did." I kick my way toward my wine.

"Swim team, right?" The underwater lights shift from purple to pink, illuminating the slick skin above her bikini top.

For a second time, I catch the thought and shove it away. It has to be the dream—it's coloring my whole day. "Yep. I swam competitively in grade school too."

"Cute. Did you love it?"

"I didn't have a choice—when I was nine, my mom dropped me off at swim practice one day."

"Wow."

I shrug. "You know how it is: *We're the parents, you're the kid*. It was probably good that I was getting regular exercise." I snicker; Sabrina still looks wounded.

Finally she smiles. "I remember your mom. She was always volunteering for stuff."

"That's true." I can't picture either of her parents. "She wanted to be in on the action. Know what was going on."

She dips her head back. "Does she know about you and Mike?"

My pulse ticks up. "No. Honestly, you two are the only ones who do."

She doesn't reply. Her eyes are glowing orbs, reflecting the pool lights.

"It still doesn't feel real." I let out a sobby laugh. "We've never even come close to breaking up before."

Crickets chirr; overhead, something whiffles past . . . hopefully not a bat. Suddenly I need her to understand it—why I have to undo this, make him trust me again.

"We met right after my thirtieth birthday," I say, my voice thick. "I was capping off a decade of the worst dating luck. My college boyfriend cheated on me with my best friend. The guys I dated in my twenties kept ghosting, and then, right before I met Mike, I went all in on Trey, this hot producer who was in and out of Chicago for work—turned out he had a wife and two kids at home."

"What a dick." She sets her hand over mine on the pool's edge and I stare at it, heart like a nail gun.

"And then . . . it was like the clouds parted, you know? Mike bought me a drink at a bar, and then we got together every night for the next six days. That week felt like *years*." I chuckle sadly. "When he loved me back—I felt so *lucky*, like I'd woken up in a Nancy Meyers movie. Like, I saw his laugh in slow motion and our marathon dates at warp speed."

She's such a good listener, her attention present and complete.

I glance away. "We—I know you'll get this, because I see it between you and Nathan. Mike felt like home in this way I hadn't felt since I was a kid." I pause, my throat tightening. "You know what I mean?"

"I do. Except that I didn't have that feeling as a kid—Nathan was the first soft place to land." She rests her elbow on the pool's ledge. "When we got together, I was like: *Oh, this is how it feels to be a family.*"

"I'm sorry—I didn't know that. About your parents."

She shrugs. "We don't talk anymore. Semi-absent dad, narcissistic mom."

"They're still in Libertyville?"

She nods. She looks like a mermaid, lit by soft rainbow lights.

"I guess that's why I don't want children," she says. "I have no model for good parenting."

"You'd be a great mom. You're so nurturing." She smiles sadly and I flinch. "Sorry, I don't know why I said that. I guess I never even questioned it for myself—I always figured I'd have kids. Two, so nobody had to be an only child like me." I feel it again, a prickly pressure in my chest: *Why did I mess everything up with Mike? Why did I self-destruct?* "Anyway, I'm glad you and Nathan found each other. What you have . . . it's beautiful." Jealousy bulges in my belly, but admiration, too, warmth.

"Thank you. And I'm sorry about Mike. It's such a cliché, but I'm sure things will work out as they should."

She touches my shoulder again and my heart is puffing up, swelling like those time-lapse videos of tender flower buds.

"Oh, Kelly." She pulls me into a hug and it doesn't quite work in the deep end. She wraps her wet arms around my shoulders and our legs tangle and we're sinking down, down, laughing and sputtering as we shriek and slip and accidentally grab each other, her hands on my neck, my arm, my ribs. My head dunks under and there's that sudden slick quiet, and the water's cool and kind and Sabrina's calf grazes my waist as she kicks back to the surface and I'm tingling, still, everywhere she touched me.

I allow myself a moment suspended in the crystal water before I come up for air.

CHAPTER TEN

I feel the mattress shift—that gentle, far-off pressure of the cat landing on the foot of the bed. But when I look around, Virgo's next to me, eyes aimed like lasers into the darkness.

I scramble for the light—if Virgo's here, what the hell's at the end of the bed?! The room turns white and I blink hard: nothing. But Virgo doesn't take those almond eyes off whatever she's staring at. The hairs on my neck won't stand down, and finally I throw off the covers and head for the bathroom.

Anemic starlight seeps in from the window, and as I wash my hands I peer outside, past the inky pool and swath of lawn, into the woods beyond.

My heart jerks—what was that? I could swear something moved, dark and vaguely humanoid, lurching sideways among the trunks. The trees sway like drunk old men and I stare so hard my eyeballs tire.

Nothing.

I struggled to fall asleep tonight, my brain sifting through shifting images of Sabrina in the pool, of Mike fumbling under the sink for dusty cleaning products, of the night—exactly a week ago—when I ruptured the relationship that meant everything to me. It's a horrible feeling, knowing what you've done is irreversible. That you've fractured life into the grand tectonic plates of Before and After.

I turn on the bathroom light, squinting into the brightness. Benadryl—I need Benadryl or melatonin or sleeping pills, something to calm me in this new place, with its shivery environs and creaking interiors. I fling open the medicine cabinet and rummage through its shallow shelves: a creased box of Band-Aids, a bottle of Tylenol, a shower cap folded inside a white square. The feeling kicks in like a match to a burner—I want to look and look and look, I need to *know*. If I could just see what's in here, understand what's tucked inside this home . . .

Suddenly I've time-traveled to a week ago, to the floor of our home office in Philly. The room was in shambles thanks to me: folders and loose papers ripped and scattered, Mike's heavy desk tipped on its side like a derailed train, his monitor cracked from edge to edge, desk lamp crimped into a funny angle like a broken limb. I'd pulled out the desk drawers and flung them on the floor one by one. I'd ripped a mirror off the wall and the framed print next to it, checking for something, anything, behind them, and the shards on the floor, half-clear, half-reflective, formed a jagged confetti that I barely registered as I lifted the rug to check underneath. A metal edge tore into my thumb, but I didn't notice it until later, when the blood had stained my sleeve and grown tacky in a channel down my palm.

I was there and not there, more energy than matter, a black hole in the center of a swirling, chaotic galaxy, unhinged, out of control, a silent airhorn blaring like it does before a binge or an orgasm, *do it do it do it*.

Then Mike's hand clutched my shoulder. I froze, heart like a bass drum, and went cold when my eyes met his: betrayal blazing, anger so big his arms shook. His grip tightened, and the pressure clarified my thoughts.

I'm not crazy, I screamed. *You won't even* look *at me. It's like I don't exist.*

I don't know who you are anymore, Mike said, jaw clenched. *This is a side of you I've never seen.*

His words were a pin to a balloon, and I disintegrated into sobs. But it was too late. The beginning of the end.

But also the end of the beginning, the apex of a creeping unease that had begun long before I found myself crouched in the eye of a hurricane. Months earlier, I could tell that Mike and I were drifting apart. It started shortly after we moved to Philadelphia and intensified during the lockdown and I couldn't talk to anyone about it but I knew, *knew* something was wrong. Mike brushed off my concerns: *It's a global pandemic, of course something's wrong.* But I couldn't shake the feeling there was more he wasn't telling me.

And there was a woman. A coworker. Aubrey, a lipsticked analyst with hair as black as an oil spill and one of those soft, giggly voices that makes men lean close. I met her during our first week in Philly at the one happy hour Mike's company sponsored before the pandemic shut down gatherings. It was obvious Mike and Aubrey had already hit it off, and extra obvious to me that she was gaga over him. When I tried to joke about it later that night, Mike was annoyed, defensive. His sternness was a pebble in the windshield of my trust in him, a chink that forked and spread.

And then, when the shutdown descended like a velvety stage curtain, he grew secretive—I swear he did. He snapped the office door closed for what seemed like too many meetings. He smiled down at his phone when we were meant to be miserable together. I was alone—jobless, friendless, identity-free—and when the weather warmed and they resumed their office happy hours but informally, in a park, partners were "no longer invited," he insisted, to keep the group size small. And he always volunteered to make grocery-store runs and he'd rush out into the day and leave me alone in the prison-bar apartment and what was I *supposed* to think, dammit, how was I supposed to feel?

Proof, I needed proof. While he shuffled away for yet another visit to our local "essential businesses." It started simply enough: I rifled through drawers, skimmed his emails. But then I couldn't stop; my suspicions couldn't be for nothing, because what would that mean about *me? Do it do it do it*, the screechy gremlin inside my head screamed. So I did.

There was nothing; I was wrong.

But the damage was done.

I can't believe you don't trust me, he said, voice quaking, eyes red and flinty. *How can I trust you now?*

And then, a few days later, he refused to re-up our wedding vendors. He didn't *call off* the wedding, we didn't officially *break up.* But now he's there and I'm here and I'd give anything, *anything,* to take it back.

There's nothing in the medicine cabinet to help me sleep. I swing the mirror closed and return to the bedroom. Virgo lies like a sphinx in front of the closet, gazing into the dark.

CHAPTER ELEVEN

wake early to a text from Mike—a photo of the sun rising over the art museum, he must have gone for a run—and smile. Maybe the distance is working! I head downstairs to cook breakfast for everyone. I'll show initiative, demonstrate my value. I rinse and dry and chop, and the movements soothe me. It's sensual, cooking for someone. Conjuring something to touch their lips, their teeth, their tongue.

"What's this?" Nathan materializes in the doorway, delighted. I feel a blare of warmth at the sight of him. He's got this quirky confidence that makes him handsome—magnetic, somehow.

I turn away, face hot. Like the thought is a betrayal to Mike. "I'm making breakfast. Hope you like eggs."

"Huge fan." He helps himself to coffee, then peers over my shoulder, oddly close. I reach for the egg carton but knock over my glass and spatter orange juice all over the counter.

"Dammit." I crouch and rummage below the sink while sticky juice drips onto the cabinet door.

"What are you looking for?" Nathan leans over me, presses a paper towel onto the countertop puddle.

"Cleaning spray." And when his footsteps disappear into the mud-room: "Oh, is that where you keep the supplies?"

"Indeed." He returns and proffers the bottle. "Can I help?"

"Nah, I've got this." I straighten up. "You can entertain me."

"With pleasure!" He crosses to the kitchen island and plops onto a stool. "Now what? Want to see my ribbon-dance routine?"

I laugh and toss the wad of soggy paper towels in the trash. When I glance back he's still watching me, his attention intense and unapologetic. Interactions feel so . . . different in this house. Deliberate, loaded. Maybe it's the contrast with the frosted air of our Philly apartment. Or maybe it's the library, Sabrina's latest book come to life. Last night's swim feels charged in my memory too—how our wet skin kept connecting.

But . . . but I'm sure she's just a touchy-feely person. Glancing at Nathan, I feel an abrupt instinct to prove I respect their marriage. "I've been meaning to ask: How did you and Sabrina meet?"

"UVA." He folds his forearms on the counter. "We didn't start dating until a few years after graduation, but we were friends."

"Wow, so you've known her almost as long as I have."

"Guess so! Her sorority and my fraternity did events together."

I can't help myself: "I didn't peg you as a frat boy."

"Oh, c'mon, I'm a gun-toting good ol' boy." He chuckles. "Of course I belonged to a stupid frat. Corn-fed Rina—now, *she's* the surprise sorority girl."

My heart quickens. I crack an egg over the pan and try to sound casual: "'Gun-toting'?"

"Of course. I gotta be ready to defend my family." He smiles as he says it, but I can tell he means it. His weirdness around security—it keeps coming up.

"Why, because of your job?"

Once again, he clams up at the mention. It's scary but also . . . kind of hot, how he does something important, mysterious, marbled with danger.

Finally, he shrugs. "Because I feel safer with a gun in my nightstand."

"Your *nightstand*? Loaded?" This I do not like. Security codes, gates, fine, but a weapon feels like another level.

"Wouldn't do me any good empty, would it?"

I turn around to stare at him.

"Relax, Kelly." He chortles and saunters over to me. "You're in our circle. That means you're safe no matter what."

He's close, too close, and my body betrays me, responding with a rush of heat. I shake my head. "Okay. Sorry. I know it's your house. But I . . . I really don't like guns." I focus on flicking my wrist so the egg flips.

"Whoa! I've always wanted to do that. May I?" Behind me, Nathan reaches for the saucepan's handle. I feel his torso against my back, closer than any man since Mike. After a second's hesitation, I place my hand over his, and my stomach erupts with butterflies.

"Show me?" His voice wafts across my neck.

My whole trunk's fluttering. "You just . . ." We jerk the pan together and the egg tips again, sizzling. Nathan cheers and lets go, then claps a hand onto my shoulder.

He keeps it there. We both stare down at the egg, spotlit by the hood light. Okay, so he and Sabrina are *both* handsy.

"You really know your way around a kitchen," Nathan observes as I twist away to grab a plate.

My cheeks burn. "It's just an egg."

He checks his phone. "My first meeting is about to start. I'll come back down for breakfast after, okay?" He holds my gaze for a beat before smirking and sauntering off.

I can still feel his handprint on my shoulder, menthol-tingly. I stare into the saucepan, where butter's turning into swirly smoke.

The next day, I'm finishing a cover letter in my room when Sabrina knocks on the doorframe. I smile involuntarily—being around her is so *fun,* the embodiment of the zappy chemistry that infused our texts before I showed up here. She's been tucked in her office all day, so I'm delighted to see her midafternoon.

"Am I interrupting?"

"Of course not!" I lean forward in the mustard chair. "What's up?"

She sits on the edge of the bed. "I wanted to ask you something. I've been writing up a storm, and I'm not actually sure if I can use any of it—it's so different from my other books."

"Uh-huh?"

She twirls a bit of hair. "I know I told you I never let anyone read my work at this stage. But . . . I don't know, I was thinking . . ."

Thump, thump, thump—my heart's like a happy dog's tail thudding against the floor.

"Would you be willing to read it? And tell me what you think?"

Eeeh! "I would love to! It would be my honor." I look away and try to wrestle down my grin.

"Perfect. You have to be honest, though."

"Cross my heart." I press a hand to my buzzing chest. Is this really happening? Just a few days ago, her work was for her eyes only; now she's pulling back the curtain, beckoning me inside her head. This feels like confirmation—I knew *I* was feeling the best vibes, but now I know it's mutual.

"I'm just so happy I'm here," I blurt out. *Oh God, was that out loud?*

But then she smiles. "I am too." She stands. "Okay, I'll print it out soon."

The rest of the day, I'm like a kid on Christmas Eve: giddy and impatient as we carry dinner into the basement and eat in front of the latest HBO hit; giggly and hyper while we choose a peppy vinho verde from the wine cellar and debate the merits of prestige television. *Go upstairs, Sabrina,* I beg silently. *Turn on the printer.*

I'm getting ready for bed when she appears in the doorway again. She looks almost shy as she holds out a stack of paper, clipped at the top. "It's only the first few chapters. I'll give you more soon."

When she's gone, I vault into bed, propping pillows behind my back and snuggling beneath the covers. I suppress a smile as I snatch up the manuscript. *Elite Deviance.* She's always been good with the double entendres.

It picks up right where *Market Penetration* left off: Arianna and Perry are engaged and cohabiting in a luxurious apartment in the Financial District. There's a wonderfully sexy opening scene—their anniversary, Perry in a three-piece suit, slooowly buttoning the back of her eveningwear—and then the action kicks off: Arianna receives an encrypted list of angel investors mere hours before—*dramatic chord!*—a bomb erupts at a conference, killing half the names on the roster. Ooh, I like this new thriller direction.

But that's not what makes goosebumps sweep from wrist to wrist.

One of Sabrina's many talents is introducing new characters, and I can almost hear the swell of soulful strings as Taylor Finnegan strolls into a scene. In slow-mo, she steps out of a cab and gazes at the skyscraper in front of her, fair hair billowing in the Manhattan breeze, eyes ice-blue and—

Wait. My heart bangs against my sternum, louder and louder, like someone at the door determined to be let in.

I reread the description. Taylor's short and slight, with a glossy bob grazing her shoulders. Freckles sprinkle her upturned nose, and her most striking feature is her eyes, irises the colors of sapphires. She's an advertising exec from the Midwest. And—if my intuitions are correct—she's being ushered in as a new love interest.

Something flowers in my chest, a secret, surprised glee.

This woman—she sounds like, well, *me*.

CHAPTER TWELVE

I read it all in one gulp: seventy-five pages of a charged, slow burn as the mysterious Taylor befriends the couple, eager to help clear their names, and the attraction between them grows and grows like a loudening bass line, an invisible triangle crackling between them. One night in bed, moaning with ratcheting intensity, Arianna secretly pictures Taylor whenever she closes her eyes. The sample ends on a cliffhanger, the moment when, cheeks flushed, breath hitched, I think, *Oh my God, the threesome is finally happening.*

I sleep restlessly, hot and bothered and wondering, perhaps idiotically, if I really might have inspired this Taylor character. What would that even mean?

And why should it matter when my true love is several hundred miles away, sleeping alone in the bed we bought together? My stomach tightens. I should focus on restoring Mike's trust in me, not letting my imagination run wild with girlish self-aggrandizement.

The next morning, I'm so distracted on my walk that I almost miss the stranger directly in my path. She's wearing a mask—that's what I notice first, the light-blue shield over her nose and mouth, which she snaps into place upon spotting me, like someone sending up a flag. Above it, her eyes are friendly, and I break into a grin before pulling my own mask up. A fellow rule-follower! There are too few of them in this neighborhood.

"Hi!" I stop six feet away. "Are you lost?"

"I'm trying to find the cemetery." She has cropped hair and wide-set eyes. "I've been trying to find the gate for, like, fifteen minutes."

"I can help with that. You're a block short." I start moving and wave her along. I'm prematurely excited—how great would it be to have a walking partner? "Are you new here?"

"I am! I just moved in with some family friends."

"Oh, I'm a refugee too." I cringe. "Sorry, not to make jokes at the expense of *actual* refugees. Where are you coming from?"

She laughs. "D.C. And don't worry—actually, I think you're the first person in Tanglewood to check your privilege ever."

"Wait, are you calling Colonial Country Club"—I gasp—"*colonialist?* Never!"

Her eyes twinkle. "I could hug you! . . . if I didn't believe in science!"

We reach the gate and I beam. "I'm Kelly, and this is the gate."

"Nice to meet you, Kelly and gate. I'm Megan. I was gonna cut through the cemetery and walk to a juice bar out on Route 309—wanna come?"

We fall into step and eventually lower our masks. She asks where I'm staying and gasps when I describe it: "That's my favorite house in the neighborhood! Is the inside amazing too?" She's a few years younger than me, a fellow Leo, and like myself, she's between jobs ("Wait, are we the same person?" I joke). She's excited that I used to work at Juna ("That hashtag-play-all-day campaign was *you?* It was brilliant!"), and it's the most pleasant rush—the easy patter of getting to know someone new, someone curious and socially fluent. She also has a cat—Louise, an excellent pet name—and she reacts with appropriate glee when I pull up photos of Virgo. By the time we pass under Brinsmere's peaked front gate, we feel like old friends.

"What made you decide to leave D.C.?" I ask as we traverse the cracked sidewalk down US-309. It's car-clogged and shade-free, too hot in the sun.

She gazes across the street. "A breakup, honestly."

"Oh my God, me too!" I blanch. "Er, relationship trouble, anyway."

"Seriously?" Her brows reach toward her hairline. "What happened?"

I give her the CliffsNotes version without hesitation—she's a stranger, after all—and her sympathy's like a warm compress.

"I'm sure you'll patch things up," she tells me. "Everyone's losing their minds in the pandemic."

"Thanks. I know what you mean." *I need to get my head on straight,* he said. I'll let him and he will, simple as that. All of this—the mansion, the Lamonts, the curious thrill of Sabrina's new book—is secondary. "Is that . . . what happened with you?"

Megan squeezes her eyes closed. "Not quite. My ex stole all my money and tried to get me fired."

"*No.*" We reach the juice bar and I stop.

But she nods, heaves a tired sigh. "It's been . . . a lot."

I press a hand to my chest. "How did he try to get you fired?"

She looks at me sharply, and my stomach sinks—I've gone too far, asking probing, painful questions of someone I've just met. "I'm sorry, that was rude of me."

She peers at me a second longer, weighing, then glances away. "No, it's fine. My ex was tossing around wild accusations. Luckily my company had my back. But . . . yeah, the money thing is what brought me out here. I couldn't keep up with rent." She shakes her head again. "It's like, I have to laugh or else I'll cry, you know?"

"Totally. Man, I'm so sorry." I thought I had it bad with Mike, but that was nothing. What we have is salvageable—worth fighting for.

In our case, the only one spitting out wild accusations . . . was me.

I glance through the café's glass doors. "Juice is on me, all right?"

Once we've snatched up our order and agreed to "do this again soon," she raises her brimming cup: "To better times ahead."

When I thud my drink, green as a beetle, against hers, camaraderie wells in my chest. Coming to Virginia was the right call. I went from total isolation to two hosts and a soon-to-be friend in the blink of an Amtrak ride. Megan and I chat animatedly as we head back into the neighborhood and part ways a few blocks from the house, and as I approach the driveway I wonder how long I should wait to text her to make plans, I don't want to seem—

I freeze, one foot in midair. Coldness shoots through my arms as I take it in, the horrifying sight.

A bird lies still, its feathers a lattice of brown and tan. It's tiny and round, a soft umber baseball. There's a wound on its neck, oozing blood.

It's bang in the middle of the driveway, a few inches from the gate. And facing out, facing *me*. I stagger back and look up and down the road and into the trees along the gate.

"Who's there?" I listen hard until layers of sound answer me: nearby birdsong, insects buzzing, the roar of a distant lawnmower.

No reply. Like whoever else is frozen, listening too.

I gather my courage and sidestep to the keypad—but then I pause, three numbers in, realizing that the gate's slow arc will intersect with this creature, hurting or even dragging it across the pavement. Tears spring into my eyes. Finally I call Sabrina, who rushes outside and pauses on the other side of the iron bars.

"Poor thing." She drops onto her haunches.

Is it breathing? Are its beadlike eyes staring back? "Is it dead?" I ask.

Sabrina lifts a nearby rock. I gasp and move to stop her, but then she reaches through the gate and uses it to nudge the bird. It rocks lifelessly.

"Who would do this?" I squat, too, and that's when I catch it—fear in her eyes. But when she turns to me, a smile spills over her face like soap in a carwash.

"It's nothing to worry about," she says. "Probably a hawk. Or a cat—don't they leave things at people's doors? Maybe a stray can tell we have a cat inside now."

I stare at the bird's tiny face, its open eyes like black caviar. Maybe she's right. I'm being paranoid again—imagining threats where there are none. Even as a quiet, anxious kid, I had trouble weighing what I should actually be afraid of.

We stand. "Let's go in," she says. "I'll have Nathan bury it in the woods."

I'm not sure I can do it—hear the gate swinging outward, know it's hauling that feathered form across the cement.

"Trust me, okay?" She grips the bars. "Come inside and we'll take care of it."

Finally I nod. When I've crossed the threshold and stepped onto their driveway, she pulls me to her.

"Make sure he buries it somewhere nice," I say.

"I will." She strokes my hair and it's strange; it's not how my friends hug me. "You are so damn sweet."

CHAPTER THIRTEEN

Taylor moves into the spare room.

Arianna and Perry's spare room, that is, a chic guest suite in their downtown Manhattan apartment with views of the Statue of Liberty. Still, the parallels are unmistakable. There's *a wingback chair the color of goldenrods*. A *live-edge wooden headboard* hand-sanded by Perry, because he makes furniture—the hottest hobby. From my deck chair by the pool, I glance back at the house and remember Sabrina's words in the library: *Sometimes making stuff up from scratch gets exhausting.*

The second excerpt is even better than the first. Things are getting serious between the three of them, and the way Sabrina describes their shared sexual escapades . . . damn. I chew my lip as I drop into another R-rated scene, heat flocking to my groin.

But then I hear something—a steady crackling in the trees. It sounds like footfalls and I look up sharply, squinting into the tapestry of green and brown. One more snap and wait, was that movement? I sit sideways and the eerie feeling intensifies, whining like microphone feedback, someone's there, waiting, watching—

"What is it?" Sabrina calls, and I jump a mile. I twist around and see her near the screen porch, a Polaroid camera dangling from her hand.

"I thought I saw something."

"Maybe a deer." She makes her way over, then points at the papers on my lap. "You're reading it!"

"I'm almost done." I grin. "Sabrina, this is your best writing yet. I *love* the dynamic with Taylor."

She doesn't reply, just smiles and sits next to me.

After a second, I notice the rectangle in her other hand. "What's that?"

She opens her palm and I reach for it, my fingers trailing across hers. It's a Polaroid of *me*, one that makes my heart thrum—I'm stretched on the deck chair, holding up her pages. Cheeks pink, knees kinked, a small smile on my lips.

"You looked pretty." She holds my gaze, her raised eyebrow like a question mark. It's too much, the photo, the compliment, the lascivious scenes with Taylor Finnegan, the strange stirring in my chest and tummy, and I look away, eager to change the subject.

"I—I forgot to tell you: I met a new neighbor yesterday," I say. "Megan."

"When?"

"On my walk. Before I got distracted by that dead bird." I glance at her. "Maybe we could have her over in the backyard or something?"

She tilts her head. "I'm not sure how I feel about having guests right now."

". . . Except me, right?" I ask, all needy.

"Oh, you're not a guest. I'm talking about strangers. You—you're home." My heart squirms but in a good way, battered by the intensity of her eyes.

My phone rings, jolting me back. Mike's name appears, and it's disorienting, like I'm in one universe and he crept in from another. The unmoored feeling you get when the movie ends and the cinema flicks the lights on.

"Take it." She stands. "I have more writing to do."

I watch her walk back to the house, phone vibrating against my thigh. And I pick up.

"Kelly, hey." His voice makes my heart speed.

"How are you?" I ask.

"Okay."

The silence hisses. Shame on me for thinking I'd stay long enough to forge a friendship with Megan . . . and, God, for fantasizing about myself in Taylor's role. This book, this mansion, none of this is *real*— Mike is home base, my rock. I picture myself reaching for his firm shoulders and pressing my cheek against him, breathing in his familiar scent.

"How are you liking Virginia?"

"Still getting used to it." I'm struck by an instinct to tone down how luxurious it is. "It's . . . isolated. Rural. I keep thinking I see movement out of the corner of my eye." As if on cue, something clacks in the trees.

"There could be bears. Coyotes. Maybe wolves."

Tell me you miss me, beg me to return. "You know me with my overactive imagination. No city noise to drown it out."

"Makes sense."

Tears shoot into my eyes. How, *how* is this so strained? "Mike, I miss you."

"I mean, I miss you too. But you're the one who left."

Ouch. I sit up. "What? You told me to leave."

"You . . . you told me you were leaving." His voice pinches. "I don't know how you're rewriting this in your head, but you're the one in Virginia. I didn't go anywhere."

Acid surges up my windpipe—*no*. "You said you wanted space. To, quote, 'get your head on straight.'" I swallow. "I'm sorry. I thought this is what you wanted. Should I come back?"

My heart thrashes. If he were here, I'd clutch his callused hand in mine and we'd remind each other to breathe. I miss him. I want to thread my fingers through his, wrap his freckled arm around me.

I try again: "Or do you want to come down here? There's plenty of space." I don't know if I have any right to invite him, but I don't care. Though I hate being the target of his prickly temper . . . there it is, a ribbon of relief too: *He doesn't like that I'm gone.*

"Babe?" I prompt. Sweat trickles down my chest. *Say the word and I'll be yours again.*

"No, you're right, I did say it was a good idea." He grunts. "I mean, I hope you didn't just go along with it because I said that. But yeah. It could be good for us."

Us. He used it, the royal "we." We're still a unit, two points connected to form a single line. This is the most agreeable he's been since he pushed off the engagement, and my heart clutches at it like the crane of a claw machine. "You know I'm here for you." I chuckle. "Even if I'm . . . *here.*"

"I know. Hey, I should get back to work."

"Love you, Mike."

A second passes. "Talk soon." The phone beeps and he's gone.

"What the hell?" I whisper aloud. Was that conversation productive or further severance? Should I even be here?

I turn toward the mansion; the back windows reflect the robin's-egg sky. I make a decision. Nathan and Sabrina aren't impartial; they only know what I've told them about Mike, so they've only heard about him at his worst. I'll call someone with institutional knowledge of my relationship. Someone who was next to me at the bar when it all began.

"Kelly! I'm so sorry I didn't call you back. I'm a hot mess right now."

I push my own needs aside. "Amy, are you okay? Is there anything I can do?"

"It's nothing acute. Just the general chaos of trying to keep everyone in the house, like, clean and fed and healthy. How are you?"

"Not okay, actually. I have to tell you something, and I'm so sorry I didn't do it sooner."

I bring her up to speed on Mike and my difficulties. I'm crying by the time I get to today's mystifying exchange with him.

"I have no idea what he wants or if I should stay here or go to him or *what,*" I finish, the words galloping out before another sob can take over.

Another sympathetic groan. "I'm so sorry, Kel. I wish I could give you a big hug."

I sniffle. "Thank you."

"Are you feeling supported? Are Serena and what's-his-face giving you lots of hugs?"

"It's Sabrina." Her question makes images flash: how Sabrina and

Nathan both seem to like touching me, hugs and taps and arm-grabs that don't feel anything like friendly consolation. The thought is like a stomp on a piano and I shake my head, refocus on Mike. "They're being fantastic. But they don't *know* Mike. They don't know us as a couple like you do."

"Mmm." I picture her nodding. "Well, how can I help? Do you want me to listen or give advice or . . . ?"

"Advice!" I wipe my eyes. "Please. Based on everything you know . . . how do I get him back?"

It hangs there, melodramatic, high-schoolish.

Finally: "You might not want to hear this, but I think you should take a step back."

I twist onto my side. "Like, let him come to me?"

"That's not what I mean. Have you zoomed out and asked if this is definitely what you want?"

Coldness dumps through me like sleet. "What are you talking about? He's my guy."

"Okay! I'm just asking. I'm a big fan of Mike. But . . . to play devil's advocate, there *are* things you've said you don't like about him. Like how he doesn't know what to do with himself when he's upset, or how he hates the beach and you're a total water baby. Or, or how he's a picky eater so you don't get to try out weird recipes anymore."

Hot tears snake down my cheeks. "Jeez, Amy, did you have that list all ready to go?"

"No! I'm sorry. Shit." She sucks in a breath. "I had to ask. Mike's a good guy, but that doesn't mean . . . how do I put this? It doesn't mean you don't also get to decide if the relationship is right for *you*."

She's said it—she said it and she can't take it back and now it's sinking into my worldview like a drop of blood in a pail of fresh milk, it mixes its way in and even if the liquid still looks bone-white, I know it's there. My stomach churns. It's like a hex, one I can't unhear: *Maybe you're not right together.*

"Of course he's right for me." I wrench my voice out of its screechi-est range. "I've known it for almost five years. We've *both* known."

But I flash to myself on the floor of his office, the room in shambles, blood trickling down my wrist. Is that really the behavior of someone who . . . ?

"Got it," she says. "I'm sorry. Obviously you know yourself and the relationship better than I ever could. I just . . . I love you a lot." Her voice breaks. "I want you to be happy. In whatever form that takes."

Then help me get Mike back, I think, but it's too pathetic to say aloud a second time. This was a mistake—now Amy pities me, Amy from her own pandemic zone of a rumpled toddler and loose toys and stockpiled Purell, the *universe* contained inside her hip Lincoln Square apartment.

Of course she can't understand what it's like to be almost thirty-five, unmarried, and childless in the midst of a global pandemic. She has no idea how it feels to witness the love of my life drifting away, like I'm a tourist on the curb watching her bus pull into traffic. *Wait for me!*

"Thank you," I say instead. "Thanks for listening." I do mean it, even as I want to strangle her through the phone.

"Call me anytime," she says, "anything you need." And we hang up.

Were Mike and I happy? I flash back to the crushing sameness of the last few months. The lockdown spotlit our differences—how he always played podcasts, uncomfortable with the downy silence I craved; how he thought TV was a waste of time, whereas I love trashy shows.

None of it bothered me when we had friends to see, jobs to commute to—when we fell into each other's arms after a long day's work, relieved to be home. Now there's *only* home, nowhere else to go.

Well, *a* home. Now I truly don't know where to hang my hat.

I shake my head as if to clear the thoughts. Sure, Mike and I don't agree on everything—but what couple does? We work in all the ways that matter.

I let myself in through the basement, feeling it again with every step—this sense of not-mine, how I have no claim to the comfy den or bar in the corner, the wine cellar spangled with bottles they brought inside before me. I pause on the bottom stair; Nathan's and Sabrina's voices are slinkying down the stairwell, tense, angry tones I haven't heard before.

"How the hell do you expect me to do that?" Nathan snarls.

"Fine, whatever," Sabrina hisses. "Thanks *so* much for having my back."

"Well, if you don't tell me anything—"

"I said it's *fine*."

"It's . . . not . . . *fine*." There's the tinkling crash of glass shattering, and my limbs go cold. Did gentle, cheery Nathan just break a dish?

I shift my weight and the step groans, and one of them lets out a quick "Shh." I mouth a profanity and start stomping up the stairs.

Poking my head into the mudroom, I surmise that they're in the kitchen—*ugh,* I'll have to pass them. Nathan's sweeping the shards into a dustpan, and they're both relaxed and chipper as I pass. My ears heat, but Sabrina chirps, "Ready for the next few chapters?"

As I shoot into the foyer and fling myself up into my room, I replay their spat in my mind. The broken dish must've been an accident. I wonder what the argument was about—bills, work, pandemic comfort levels. Hopefully nothing to do with me.

I plop onto the bed, cringing. *Nathan and Sabrina argue?* I feel guilty for witnessing it . . . and weirdly disappointed that their relationship isn't perfect. But then I see it from another angle: Hey, every couple has issues. Long before we slipped into this limbo, Mike and I had the occasional screaming match (one even culminated in a trip to urgent care when Mike kicked the sofa and broke his toe). Conflict is a given; rough patches are normal.

Call me anytime, Amy said—*anything you need.*

And she meant it. To her, it's true.

But I know what I need—I need Mike. And now I know she can't help me with that.

I'm on my own out here.

CHAPTER FOURTEEN

An hour later, Sabrina bursts into my room, agog. The humidity has waned and puffy clouds are moseying along the sky and they've had a great idea: We can spend the afternoon hiking. They made up! I'm so relieved. And this is just what I need—clean air, a fresh perspective. A chance to exorcise that nonsense Amy spouted about my relationship.

I volunteer to pack a picnic lunch and we're buoyant in the kitchen, filling Tupperware and rustling up paper plates and bamboo forks. The hair I pulled back flops forward as I'm chopping beets.

"Here." Sabrina tucks a lock behind my ear, and for a microsecond, her fingers linger on my jaw. It's tender, the sweep across my cheek, and I stare at my blood-red hands as I thank her. I flash to the last scene I read, Taylor reaching for Arianna's face, slowly guiding it to hers. My cheeks warm and I steal a glance at Nathan, who's still hunting in the cabinets for a water bottle.

"You have the prettiest hair," Sabrina says. "It never gets frizzy."

I think of Taylor, her shiny locks "the color of cornsilk."

"My stylist would beg to differ. I'm in desperate need of a cut and color."

"You really don't like compliments, huh?" Nathan whirls around, clutching a canteen.

"I don't want to sound arrogant."

"You're not, though," Sabrina counters. "*I'm* telling you you're beautiful. And you're disagreeing."

My heart thumps. Beautiful—me? "Sorry, I'm not trying to reject your—"

"Ugh, don't apologize!" She waves her hand good-naturedly. "I think you're hot. You can't convince me otherwise."

I turn away before she can see the uncontrollable grin on my face.

"Well, thank you," I manage.

"That's more like it!" Nathan cheers.

I take a deep breath. "Sabrina . . . you know you're intimidatingly beautiful, right?" My voice sounds funny, like someone else is saying it. Nathan's watching us, laid-back as ever.

"Thank you. I *love* a compliment, especially when it's about my appearance. A chink in my feminist armor, I guess." She levels a wicked smile my way. This is definitely not the girl I remember from high school, timid and on-edge.

She seals a Ziploc bag. "Okay, question for both of you: What's the compliment you like receiving the most? A therapist asked me this once."

We're quiet for a moment.

"That's a deceptively hard question." I scoop the beets into a bowl. It'll take so much scrubbing to get the crimson off my palms. "What's funny is that neither one of my parents ever paid me a compliment—it was like, 'Oh, you got a four-point-oh, sounds about right.'"

"My mom too," Sabrina replies. "I think she's jealous that I got out of Libertyville when she still lives in the beat-up house she grew up in."

Envy—I'd never felt it from my parents. Just concern. I was a sensitive kid, and anxious, always worrying about things I couldn't control. Trait neuroticism, according to the child psychologist two towns over. But I got good at taking emotional temperatures, at reading rooms.

I learned which strong emotions were better left unexpressed. Which thoughts freaked people out, so they shouldn't be shared.

"I'm sorry, Sabrina," I say.

She nods at Nathan. "Meanwhile, his family's so adoring, it makes me sick."

"It's true!" He raises both hands. "They're my biggest fans. Like, kept all my preschool finger paintings."

"That's how Mike's mom was too," I say unthinkingly. A rush of memory: The sound of Mike's angry sobs spilling down the hallway the day after his mother's funeral. I sprinted into the bedroom and found him clutching his knuckles, leaning against a wall that bore a fresh, blood-streaked dent. He pointed to his phone, its screen newly cracked, and I lifted it from the floor to read a text from his father, criticizing Mike for crying during the service.

His mother was the sweet one, doting and kind; an aneurysm, sudden as a lightning bolt, took her life right after Mike and I moved in together. I felt his devastation like it was my own, a marshy grief that wouldn't let go. I clutched his hand as the moments between thoughts of her started to lengthen like taffy and his guilt did, too, his fear of forgetting her. We went for long, quiet walks and watched documentaries about the afterlife and slowly climbed out of that crater together.

"Yours *never* paid you a compliment?" Nathan repeats, pulling me back.

I snort. "The only time my dad said he was proud of me was after he first met Mike."

"Ew," Sabrina blurts out. After a shocked second, we all laugh. "Not ew to Mike. I'm sure he's great. But ew to thinking that partnering with someone is a huge accomplishment."

Nathan nods. "It's luck, right? Rina and I were lucky to meet each other."

"And you were lucky the timing was right." I work my hands over crimped hunks of kale, massaging in the dressing. "You were in the right headspace to commit."

"You still haven't answered my question." Sabrina slides my dirty cutting board into the sink. The knife glistens red. "What's the compliment that makes your day?"

I consider. " 'You're kind,' I guess? Or 'you're loving.' Maybe 'generous.' "

"'*You make me feel good,*' basically. Huh." She nods thoughtfully. "Well, Kelly, you do make me feel good. And not just 'cause you're hot."

"Seconded," Nathan adds. "The feeling-good part but also, you're a very beautiful woman."

I laugh again, wishing they'd never stop. It's not flirting if the married couple's right in front of me; these are genuine compliments, ones I want to pack on ice and save. "Thanks. Nathan, what's yours?"

"My favorite compliment?" He hits Sabrina with a small, private smile. "That I make the people I love feel safe."

Sabrina makes a gagging noise but wraps an arm around his waist. He kisses the top of her head and I feel a punch of jealousy. I like their house, I like Tanglewood, I'm weirdly happy here. But their love's a reminder of what I'm fighting for with Mike.

"Rina," he says. "Your turn."

She pulls away from him. "That I'm bold. Ballsy. Willing to go there."

"Well, as a reader and fan . . ." I clasp my hands. "I can definitely say that's true."

She touches my chin as she passes, a gentle hold so our smiles can meet. "Thank you," she says. "Now let's get out of here."

We pile into the SUV and head for the mountains, which soon elbow the horizon: layer upon layer of green-tinged triangles sloping toward the sky. Our ears pop as we near them, and though I thought I didn't like country music, it's jolly and fitting as Nathan cranks the volume.

We sing along to the chorus of "Wagon Wheel." Sabrina turns around and grins. "'A southbound train'! This song is about you."

"But do I rock you, Mama?" I joke, then blanch.

"You rock us," Nathan affirms. "Rina, help me look for the turnoff."

The tires crunch over gravel as we pull into the parking lot, a level point in this sea of crinkled land. The sky feels closer here, like someone lowered it with a pulley, the unbroken blue so rich and bright I could almost brush my fingers against it.

In the woods, shards of sunlight pelt us like hail, trees and shrubs bow at our feet, and sculptural mushrooms blip out of logs. Every once in a while the trail swerves and we find ourselves along a ridge, where we pause to gaze at the moss-green mountains shrugging in the distance.

My heart expands with all the empty space. *Beautiful*. Me. Not just beautiful—*hot* too. It's a conversation I'll replay forever.

Mike stabs into my thoughts, like a picket sign thrust above a crowd. I shouldn't be so happy here with my new pod; it isn't fair. Maybe I should go home to him. Buy another Amtrak ticket, beeline for my love. If distance isn't working, closeness must be the answer, right?

Sabrina asks me to take their photo. Behind them, a huge bird carves arcs in the sky. I envy it—two muscular wings and it's never stuck in place, never held back by southbound trains or barred windows, by the strangeness that's unfurled between Mike and me.

Nathan tickles Sabrina's waist and I get the perfect shot, laughter on both of their lips.

I should be focused on Mike, on winning him back.

So why does the idea of leaving this place, these people, to rush back to Philadelphia feel . . . unfathomable?

CHAPTER FIFTEEN

"I'm not going in there." Sabrina's eyes flash.

I'm still peering into the dark, trying to make out any forms inside, but Nathan turns sharply toward Sabrina.

"Of course you are. What, we hiked all this way to *not* go in the cave?"

At the trailhead, I'd vaguely clocked the name—Gebhardt's Cavern—but I didn't put the pieces together even as we zagged into a sudden ravine, gray stone looming on either side. Now here's the open mouth: a rough half-circle four feet high, with chunky rocks sloping out of sight at the base. Hairs prickle along my neck and arms. The only way in is down.

"Exactly," she counters. "Because I'm here for daylight. And fresh mountain air. Neither of which is present inside . . . that." She waves her hand.

"Oh, c'mon. We'll just see what the first chamber looks like." He turns to me, grins. "Kelly's going in with me. Right?"

I glance back and forth between them; I hate being the deciding vote. But Nathan's plea is stronger, so I nod. "As long as there aren't any bats. I am not a fan of bats."

"You and all of humanity this year," Nathan notes. "Rina, I'll go first. I won't let anything happen to you."

"I'm not going."

"But you can—"

"*I said no.*" Her voice bounces against the rock, fading somewhere over the gorge. Birds go silent, and the air frosts over. I stare at the ground, squirming in the bristle of this sudden spat—the second time today I've heard them take this tone with each other.

Finally Nathan whirls around and clambers into the cave. It's steep, a scramble, and when his heel slips, he slides a few inches.

"Careful!" I call uselessly.

Sabrina turns to me and I flinch.

"Kelly, get down here!" Nathan's voice floats up from the maw. "It's awesome."

Sabrina raises her eyebrows. I look at the cave. Back at her. Taylor flickers in my mind, her fearlessness and nerve. I drop my backpack and scrabble into the mouth.

The tunnel slants into a broad cavern. It's damp and cool down here, and Nathan holds out a hand as I step onto the floor.

"Amazing, isn't it?" He doesn't let go, and our palms hang between us like a hammock. My stomach jumps.

But then I hold my phone up, and it *is* amazing, like stumbling onto another planet. Slick stalactites dangle from the ceiling like stone icicles, some pinkie-thin, others as thick as tree trunks. A steady *drip-drip-drip* marks time, and I follow the halo of Nathan's flashlight to a black semicircle on the far wall: another opening, calling to us like a portal.

"Let's go in deeper." Nathan's already listing toward it. "One more chamber. Okay?"

I glance behind us, where filtered sunlight spills down the craggy ledge.

He squeezes my hand. "I'll keep you safe. Promise."

He lets go and starts picking his way over the rocky ground. I follow, pulse hammering, alert and frightened but exhilarated too. We reach the passage and Nathan slips inside, disappearing into the dark.

I swallow hard, then hopscotch over a series of fat rocks toward the pinprick of light I take to be Nathan's phone. When I get close and sweep my light upward, I gasp: Nathan's facing me, eyes wide, staring at something behind me. I whirl around and my foot catches on a rock—*whoa*—I start to fall but Nathan catches me, both hands on my back and then sliding around my waist, holding firm until I find my footing. He stays like that, my back tight against his torso, and my body responds, leaning into him.

"I didn't mean to scare you," he murmurs, his mouth close to my neck.

But you did, I think—*though you're goofy and good-natured, you're also high-powered and mysterious and you promise to keep me safe as if you know something I don't*—

"You gotta see this. Hold up your light."

I do as I'm told and then let out a gasp that echoes around the cavity: There's another opening in the rock wall, several feet tall and vaguely vaginal, and inside it a ruffle of ribbed crystal glitters back at us. It's blue-white and sparkly, more beautiful than the ice storms that turn Chicago into a fairyland.

"It's incredible," I whisper, turning my chin toward him, and he drops his hands and steps back, as if he's just realized he's hanging on to me. I straighten my shirt. "Er, should we head back to Sabrina?"

"Sure." He grins at the twinkling stone. "She would've loved this."

There's a chittering sound that seems to crescendo once I notice it. Slowly, I swing my flashlight up, then yelp: At least a dozen bats dangle from the ceiling. I beeline for the exit and Nathan follows, beaming his phone ahead to light my path.

A few days later, we stay up past our bedtimes, lounging around the music room and sipping what Nathan calls "house scotch," which is amber and buttery and always glittering in a decanter on the bar cart. These are some of the longest, sunniest days of the year, and that's how they feel, luxuriously slow, golden and stretchy like the cheese in a gooey panini. I especially love our evenings as a trio—cocktails in the library or a movie in the basement or, the other night, a board game in the dining room, with Virgo batting at the game pieces.

I needed this: people to pass in the kitchen and tell when something funny happens during the day. They recount Virgo's shenanigans and I learn the names of supporting players in their lives: Sabrina's sharklike publicist, Nathan's tyrannical boss. We unhook the velvet rope and let one another into our lives. I fear, in a frail, faraway way, that this might be *too* much time together, that they'll get sick of me, but right now I'm an addict, high on their presence.

On the couch, Nathan's strumming an acoustic guitar, and Sabrina's back is against the armrest, her toes on his thigh. Whatever friction I detected the other day has dissipated like smoke. They're perfect together. If only Mike were here, his arm slung across my back.

I send him a text: "If you're still up, give me a call." He doesn't answer right away, so I add: "Just want to say good night." Still nothing. My lungs tighten. But then I notice the tambourine Nathan's holding out for me. I grab it, smiling, and push my phone into the rug.

They're working so hard to make me feel welcome. It's intimate, inserting myself into their lockdown routine. *We're pretty good at the us-versus-the-world thing,* Nathan said that first night, like these walls contain their entire universe, and now I'm part of it, and Sabrina jingles the ice in her glass and Nathan flubs a chord and I marvel at how . . . how *everything* this feels, like the rest of the Earth doesn't exist.

Related: I might be drunk.

Nathan plays whatever Beatles songs pop into his head and we sing along, clapping after every number. Finally I bid them good night and climb upstairs, swaying a bit. In my room, Virgo is curled on the rug and I step on her tail, and she yowls and bolts away.

"I'm sorry, monkey!" Now I'm wide-awake. I turn on the lamp and drop to my knees, checking for her under the bed, peering into the corner. I crawl over to the dresser and press my cheek to the floor, and Virgo's smooshed against the wall, her eyes huge.

"It's okay." I should let her be, but my brain, gooey from the whiskey, won't relax until I know she's forgiven me. I stretch my hand beneath the bureau and tap something—crinkly, plastic, flat. I press my fingers down and slide it out.

It's a small stack of Polaroids, furred with dust. My pulse quickens as I take in the first: It's a young woman in a scalloped, see-through

piece of lingerie—black lace and mesh over her small breasts, red lipstick smudged along her mouth, kohl lining her bright-blue eyes,
straight ice-blond hair hanging over her face. She's sprawled on a chair,
gazing up at the camera, her tongue teasing the corner of her lip, and it
reminds me of those American Apparel ads from decades ago, overex-
posed and unblinkingly sexy.

My heart bangs against my sternum. I know that chair. Upholstery
the color of an egg yolk, the back a swooping curve. I turn to it, the un-
assuming reading chair in the corner.

But more importantly . . . *I know that face.* Something cracks in
me—how stupid was I, thinking Taylor was based on me? She's here
and more beautiful than I even imagined. Eyebrows thick, smile symmetrical and knowing. She's like the glow-up version of me.

Hands shaking, I drop the Polaroid on the bed and take in the second
one. My stomach somersaults: It's a waist-up photo of this woman in
the same black bodysuit, this time with the halter top untied and slipping down her chest. A man—*holy shit, that's Nathan*—stands behind
her shoulder, arms wrapped around her, his face angled down as he
kisses her neck. She's thrown her arm back and tangled her fingers in
Nathan's red-brown hair as she gazes at the camera, exposing her pale
throat.

That's Nathan. Nathan standing just the way he stood in that cave
yesterday. Nathan not wearing a shirt. Nathan with his face buried in
the crook of this mystery woman's neck, one hand on her breast. It's like
the R-rated version of one of Sabrina's book covers, two hot people
emanating lust.

I flip to the final photo and nearly drop it. The anonymous woman is
the star again, with the lacy top pulled back up. But there's something
wrapped tight around her neck—it's black, perhaps a bandanna or tie—
and Sabrina's clutching the ends in a fist. Sabrina's turned away, showing the camera her profile, sideswept hair, and bare back. She looks
determined, her spine stiff as she pulls the noose taut. The blond woman's mouth is open as if she's mid-word, her eyes trained beyond the
camera.

I slide the Polaroids into a pile and flip through them again. BDSM—

Sabrina put a bit of it in books two and three, and certainly whatever's in these photos looks consensual. I sit on the bed, drunk and in awe. The new book is semiautobiographical, then. A Taylor really did stay in this bedroom. Someone who posed for these photos, liked them, kept them. Lost them when they slipped beneath the dresser.

I'm . . . intrigued. Confused. Embarrassed that I ever thought Sabrina's work-in-progress might be a thinly veiled proposition. Turned on too. This went on right here in my room: clothes drifting away from bodies, fingers finding skin.

I lie back on the bed, head spinning. My gaze falls on Sabrina's manuscript, still stacked on my nightstand.

I switch on the lamp, settle beneath the covers. I find the passage that's replaying in my mind, the first time they're all three together. I read it two times, three, then close my eyes, picturing it.

I see it again and again, every moment, every move. And in my mind, Taylor's face keeps flickering back and forth between this mystery woman's . . . and mine.

CHAPTER SIXTEEN

My foot bobs as I wait at the table. I'm excited to see Megan, but my attention's been hijacked by the woman in the Polaroids—Taylor, as I keep thinking of her. It's been two days since I found the photos, and all I can think about is figuring out who she is. I clicked through every Instagram Sabrina ever posted, searching for clues, any hint of someone who fits the description. I scrolled through the comments, too, and the 1,200 people she follows. I closed the door and scoured my room but found nothing but a few forgotten gum wrappers. I padded into the library and plucked the Heart of Desire books from the shelves one by one, poring over their acknowledgments sections, copying down names to google afterward.

Nothing.

I've pulled the photos out several times to prove I didn't hallucinate them. She's a phantom. And the less I find about her, the more desperate I am for info.

"Kelly!" Megan is smiling broadly behind her mask—I was so lost in thought, I didn't even see her enter the bistro's back porch. I stand to hug her, but then we catch ourselves and exchange awkward fist bumps.

"It's good to see you!" I scrape my seat toward the white wicker table. The backyard of the Deerbrook Noshery is as adorable as the Yelp reviews promised: ivy shrouding the surrounding fence, vases of wildflowers bull's-eyeing the tables. "I'm so happy we're doing this."

"Me too! It almost feels like the Before Times." She pulls off her mask. She looks a bit like a Bratz doll: round eyes, sharp chin. "I'm glad you texted me."

A waifish server with a long black braid hands us menus. I feel skittish, off my game, but Megan is merry as she scans the menu.

"So, tell me everything!" she chirps. "How's the semi-ex? How's the job search going? Oh, and what's Virgo been up to?"

I relax as I tell her about the jobs I've applied for. I show her a photo of Virgo sitting proudly in an unused fireplace. As I slip my phone back into my purse, I wince, realizing I haven't contacted Mike in two full days. "As for the semi-ex, well . . . no developments there." I spread the blue-plaid napkin on my lap. "What about you? Any updates?"

"Not really, no." She twists a straw wrapper around her finger. "A lawyer friend is trying to help me get my money back, but there's so much to document—it's a mess."

"You can't, like, call the police and say he stole it?"

"Well, no, 'cause it looks like I initiated the bank transfer myself." She scrubs her hand over her face. "Like I said: complicated. And frankly, kind of mortifying."

"That's awful—I'm sorry." Poor Megan dated a *grifter*? Once again, I thank my lucky stars that I met Mike: one of the good ones. Sensing she'd like a subject change, I snap my menu closed. "Anyway. How are you liking Tanglewood?" I laugh. "I say that like I've been here forever, when it's actually been, like, less than two weeks."

"Is that all?"

"Yep! And I don't have any immediate plans to leave." I take a sip of water and a lemon seed hits my tongue. "Is your visit . . . open-ended?"

She nods. "For the time being. My aunt—that's what I call her, even though we're family friends—was so nice to take me in, but I hate feeling like a burden."

"I know what you mean!" I set an elbow on the table. "The friends I'm staying with won't even let me pay for anything."

"What are they like? Your hosts?"

I flash back to the washed-out Polaroids that've hung, scrim-like, over my brain the last couple of days. I see them every time I pass Sabrina or Nathan in the hallway—Sabrina's fist around the play noose, Nathan's lips pressed to that woman's throat. I'd kill to meet her, to know what it's like to be the one let into Sabrina and Nathan's marriage.

Honestly, it's ridiculous how much time I've spent thinking about her. She's an invisible force floating around the mansion—a ghost with unfinished business.

I jump, registering Megan's expectant stare. Wow, she's trying to engage in normal conversation and I'm acting like a space cadet. "Sabrina and Nathan?" I finally say. "They're great. They . . ." And then my mind shorts out. *They took a lover. They held an NSFW photo shoot with her. They kissed her neck and touched her chest and wound fabric around her throat . . .*

The waitress appears, thank God, and Megan orders first, grinning warmly as she hands back the menu. When we're alone again I shake my head. "Sorry, I don't know why I'm so scatterbrained today. But I want to hear what's new with you!"

Like a slalom skier, she carves the conversation into easy realms: hikes and wineries in the area, television the whole country's binging, books everyone's talking about. She's charming and I'm off my game— I thought our lunch would distract me, but the mystery woman still buzzes in my mind.

We part ways in the parking lot, her heading to the grocery store, me steering Nathan's SUV back into Tanglewood. I feel guilty for being so preoccupied—maybe I'll text her an apology. As I turn in to the subdivision, though, my mind doesn't linger on her. It pauses on Mike, whom I hardly talked about at lunch. During that impromptu juice-bar excursion, I told Megan all about our relationship, but today Mike has barely crossed my mind. Like my attention is a limited commodity, and all of it's draining into . . .

Her. The woman in my room, wild and free. Mike wouldn't even know what to do with a firecracker like her. Yes, a deep, logical part of me aches to get back together with him, to slip back into the cozy assuredness of our relationship . . . but I can't help wondering what life must be like for the real-life "Taylor." She gives heteronormativity the middle finger. She bleaches her hair and poses for sexy photos with confidence I could never summon.

As I wait for the gate to the Lamonts' driveway to open, my inner voice grows to a shout. *She* wouldn't have quit her job for a man without a second thought. *She* wouldn't have moved halfway across the country, no questions asked. *She* wouldn't be in my sad, half-dumped, jobless, pathetic shoes . . .

I jump, realizing the gate's been open so long it's starting to close again. I lean on the gas, thrusting the car past the gate seconds before the metal scrapes the SUV's sides.

Enough silly daydreaming, a part of me admonishes, the practical, prudish, pragmatic side. *Stay focused on Mike and the future you've worked hard for.*

But then I hear Amy's words again, forbidden fruit, the spores she puffed into my brain so they could take root and sprout like invasive weeds: *Mike might not be right for you.*

I kill the engine and sit in the driveway, stomach squeezing. Guilt ripples through me for even pinning down the bad thought, but it blossoms like a wildflower and there it is, ready or not: *What if what I thought I wanted and what I actually want . . . aren't the same thing?*

CHAPTER SEVENTEEN

While Nathan drives to Rosslyn, Virginia, for some top-secret meeting in a secure facility, Sabrina and I go for a walk; it's a perfect summer day, the sun high and the sky crackly blue. We stroll down the driveway, past the gate that plugs the end. We turn onto a cul-de-sac, where trees fold us into a jungly tunnel.

One-on-one time with Sabrina always feels special—colors are brighter and the minutes hurtle by. Today, there's a new current running through my chest, because I've made a decision: I'm going to ask her about the Polaroids.

I've exhausted all other avenues for identifying this woman, and it's not my fault that I found them in my room, cobwebbed against the wall. I've weighed the pros and cons. Yes, Sabrina might feel defensive or embarrassed or even violated. But she also might open up about them. And that possibility, however tiny, floods me with hope.

Out of nowhere, she clutches my hand. I freeze, insides compressed. She leans toward me and I see it in slow-motion, *What is happening?*

"A bald eagle," she whispers. My pulse restarts, throbbing through me. "In the tree."

She lets go and I can still feel her fingerprints. What is *with* the

Lamonts and their casual hand-holding? I spot the bird's white head, bright as a shock of paint, and pull out my phone to take a few shots. When it lifts off, I open my camera roll to see if I caught anything.

But—that's not right. There's a run of pictures I didn't take, Virgo outlined in the bay window. My pulse is a metronome as I flip through them.

"Hey, do you know who took these?" I hold out my phone. "They were taken yesterday." The uncanny sense that the mansion has eyes . . . what if it's not just my paranoia? What if we aren't alone?

"I did!" Sabrina steps away, grinning.

"What?"

"Virgo was perfectly silhouetted in the window, and your phone was sitting out."

The cold that jolted through me mellows, but another part of me is still waving its arms: *That's weird!* "You used my phone?"

"I didn't go *into* your phone, obviously. I turned on the camera from the home screen."

I don't know what face I'm making, but after a second she deflates. "Sorry. I won't do it again."

I shake my head, horrified that I've hurt her. "No worries." I heave some cheer back into my voice: "Virgo is a supermodel, right? She does her little thing on the catwalk."

Maybe I'll post the photo to prove I dig it. For now, I send it to Mike. Once again, he doesn't reply. I picture him mooning around the Philadelphia apartment right this moment, scummy plates on the counter, dust dampening on the bathroom tile, and feel a flare of frustration. Why won't he answer me?

Diane turns onto the road ahead of us, this time with a seventy-something blond woman. They stop short, unfriendliness wafting off them, and Sabrina does the same.

"Hi, Diane! Nice to see you again." I turn to the blond woman. "I'm Kelly. I met Diane the other week."

"Lydia," the stranger replies. She has feathery wrinkles around her mouth and eyes.

I jump as fingers clutch my wrist. "Have a good day!" Sabrina tightens her grip as she starts walking again, and I hurry to keep up. Their heads swivel as we pass.

"Ugh, Diane," Sabrina hisses once we're out of earshot. "I forgot to fill you in after you met her. I didn't want to get into it in front of Nathan."

"Oh, yeah?"

She rolls her eyes. "She's read all my books."

I stop short. "What?"

"Yup. Sends me these long, judgy emails afterward enumerating her issues with the plot and reminding me I'm a terrible person for putting smut out into the world."

I shake my head. "That's wild. And . . . kind of ironic. She thinks they're bad for humanity yet she can't stop reading them?"

"I know! I haven't told Nathan because I don't need him thinking she's another unhinged fan. She's harmless, but—*such* bad vibes."

We pause at an intersection and a car rolls past. The driver, a bald, bespectacled fellow, waves. It's strange, not being able to see people in the homes we pass, not over the tops of gates and strategically placed trees.

"This might sound weird," I say, "but is there any way Diane could be a little more unhinged than you think? Could she be watching us?"

" 'Watching us'?"

"Or, like, coming into the backyard? I thought I saw . . ."

Sabrina's looking at me like I've lost my mind. "You *saw* her? In our backyard?"

"Sorry, no. It's more a feeling than anything. But I'm sure it's . . ." I trail off. Why can't I keep my freaky, alarmist thoughts to myself? "Forget I said anything."

She pulls at her necklace. "I told you people in this neighborhood don't like us. Which, whatever, I don't need everyone to like me. I'll take their passive-aggressive bullshit over obnoxious fans any day."

"Like the doxxers?" I blurt out.

She nods. "I didn't tell you the worst part. Obviously it was stressful and scary, but Nathan could *not* handle it. He was out of his mind with anger and impotence and, like, righteous indignation. At a certain point,

I was like, 'Now I'm devoting as much energy to calming you as I am to dealing with this.'"

I think back to the time Mike surprised me with a trip to Costa Rica—how he turned purple, nearly apoplectic when we arrived at the ATV rental spot after sloshing through tense mountain roads, and the owner apologetically said they had no usable four-wheelers left. Mike raised his voice and fists in tandem and the poor guy's eyes widened, like Mike was about to grab him by the shoulders. Mike didn't touch him, of course. But he, too, doesn't take well to not getting his way.

"I get that," I say. "I love men, but they can be such babies."

"That's not all." She steps over a dandelion sprouting from a crack. "This one doxxer showed up at our place and wouldn't leave. Just standing on the sidewalk and staring menacingly. Like, dude, get a life. Anyway, the cops said they couldn't do anything since he wasn't technically on our property. But when he was still there in the middle of the night, Nathan lost it. He walked out there and punched the guy in the face."

"What?"

"I know! Thank God he didn't bring his gun down with him." She shakes her head. "So the guy's bleeding from his nose, and get this, *he* calls the cops on *Nathan*. He wanted to press charges. Luckily we'd been documenting his, like, vigil outside our place and the DOD's lawyers threw some scary language at him and made the whole thing go away."

"Jeez." I flash back to the morning I heard them arguing in the kitchen—the sudden clang of porcelain shattering on the floor. "That's bananas."

"Right? I was so mad at him. Nathan, I mean, for acting like a five-year-old. And then the *DOD* gets involved? He was mortified." She turns to me. "By the way, don't mention it to him. He hates me telling anyone."

It's odd, being let into their shared secret. I nod vigorously.

"Thanks." We walk on. She ruffles a branch where fat blossoms hang like Christmas ornaments. It's a moment from a fashion magazine, the way the sun hits her cheekbones and ripples her hair. She catches me staring and I look away, blushing.

"Hey, I'm glad you haven't left yet." She whacks my hand gently with the back of her fingers. "Wish you'd forget about Philly and move down here already."

I don't know it's happening until it's done: I flutter my fingers back and then they catch, they slide together, our fingers interlocked like a picket fence.

She holds my gaze, smiling serenely, and that whole side of my body lights up, purple and warm.

I take a deep breath. "Hey, can I ask you something?"

She nods. The better I know her, the more intense her beauty is, all cranked-up like a light on a dimmer switch.

"I . . . I stumbled on these Polaroids in my room, there's . . . this woman in them, she's . . ."

Sabrina's face contorts with every word, morphing like a cartoon: eyes widening, lips drawing into a worried line, jaw tightening with horror. She pulls her hand out from mine and clutches my forearms.

"Did you show them to anyone?"

I shake my head, feeling childish and small.

"Or tell anyone about them? Where are they?"

"They're in my room. I didn't do anything with them. I know they're . . . not mine to see."

She slackens and releases my wrists. "Okay, phew. Sorry, it's . . . she really would not want those getting out. Nathan, too, with his job." She starts walking again, staring straight ahead. "I'll grab them from you when we get back. Thanks for letting me know."

She flashes a tight-lipped smile and my cheeks blaze with shame. Dammit—I definitely can't ask for more details now.

At home, she charges directly upstairs and waits while I fish the photos from the dresser. I get a crisp "thanks!" and watch her disappear into her office, then hear the grinding sound of a wooden desk drawer opening and closing.

I sink onto my bed, heart thumping. Why did I have to mention it? Did I just ruin everything?

Sabrina's words keep replaying in my mind. The first concrete thing I've heard about this woman, a detail I weave into my understanding of her.

She really would not want those getting out.

CHAPTER EIGHTEEN

spin possibilities like silk. Is this woman a public figure? High-ranking like Nathan? An avowed virgin, a married woman, Nathan's subordinate? I wonder where she is now, and if she's figured out the Polaroids aren't with her. She has Boss Bitch vibes, so I'd like to think she's having a sexier pandemic than most—shacking up with multiple lovers, maybe, or partying at a villa in Ibiza.

Sabrina's phone rings and I hear her trot downstairs, answer it, and bang around the laundry room for a moment before opening and closing the basement door. I slip into my bathroom, which overlooks the backyard, and watch her pop out onto the pool deck and sit on a chair. She rubs her neck as she speaks and I wonder what's stressing her, and if it has anything to do with me, but more importantly, an idea is taking shape, prickling at the inside of my pelvis—

This is my chance.

I've got to get answers while I can.

I shoot down the hallway, slip inside her office, and cross to her desk, the room's wooden nucleus. Who knows what else she's stashed here? *I'm so analog,* she said during the whirlwind house tour. *I hang on to every card and letter I get.*

I cross to the desk and take in the mosaic of stuff scattered on top: advance copies of romance books by other authors, Post-its and paper scraps with notes scribbled on top, even a wrinkly napkin with an intriguing stream of consciousness on the front: *Fall from balcony—man she was w/ claims she wrapped her legs around him, mistake—witnesses? Neighbor??*

My heart thumps like I've buckled myself into a roller coaster. I throw open the drawer on the right and rummage through pens, paper clips, rubber bands that ping and roll beneath my touch.

I kneel and yank the left-hand drawer, but the brass knob bites my fingers—locked. Where's the key? I sweep my palm along the drawer's bottom. A rough edge slides into my skin, the sliver a tiny fang, and I pull my hand out and stand.

I plunge my fingers between the pillows and cushions of her purple couch. I fling my face onto the ground and search the dusty floor below the furniture. I dash across the hallway and confirm through the bathroom window that Sabrina's still out back.

My breath feels as quick and light as a hamster. *Think, Kelly.* If she locked up the photos and headed downstairs, the key is either in her office, on her person, or somewhere in . . .

I rocket downstairs and spin into the mudroom. I heard her pause here—I heard banging, like she was using a cabinet or drawer. I open the lower cabinets and rifle through rows of cleaning products. I drag a stool in from the kitchen to reach the hanging cupboards: woolen dryer balls piled in a bowl; a basket of winter gloves; a sticky bottle of fabric softener.

No key.

I yank a flashlight keychain off a hook near the door and aim it behind the washer: dust bunnies, ducts sticky with cobwebs. I can't get a good look behind the dryer so I hold my breath and slide my hand into the gap.

My fingers brush something—is that mesh? I yank it out, then blink at the ball of dirty black. A cold, floaty feeling washes through me as I unfold it. I recognize this bodysuit. Pretty lace scalloped down a plunging neckline. The bottom a latticework G-string.

It's the mystery woman's getup from those Polaroids.

The conclusion is a whisper in my ear, unstoppable: *And now it's mine.*

I shove it into my pocket and race upstairs, locking the bedroom door behind me. Determination fills my chest.

In a rush, I unzip my fly and step out of my pants. I rip my top up, feeling the release as my head pops past the collar, and wriggle out of my bra. I stand there, naked, arms shaking, heart pounding, a surge of disbelief rippling through me: *Are you really going to do it?*

And then I pounce on the bodysuit. I flick it open and shake the ties of the halter and pierce the leg holes with my feet, first the left, then the right. Then I'm sliding it up my body, tying the halter around my neck, tight as a noose, tight as the black fabric Sabrina looped around Taylor's throat.

I fling open my closet door and focus on the full-length mirror on the back. My breath catches in my throat. It fits perfectly. My small frame, my cute butt, the overgrown blond hair lanking on my shoulders . . . I admire it from different angles, smoothing my hands over my hips, my torso.

I close my eyes. I picture the Polaroid again, Nathan's hands instead of mine, his beard tickling my shoulder, his lips on my neck. I flash to us in the cave: Nathan's strong arms around me, his bristly chin so close to my ear. I blink my eyes open and stare again, surprised, hungry, more into my reflection than I could even explain.

Mentally I flip to the photo with Sabrina and pluck a black T-shirt from a nearby hanger. I roll it up and, pulse banging, cheeks pink, wind it around my neck, once, twice, gathering the ends in one hand and holding them out just so. Like the fist is Sabrina's. Like she has to make me hers.

I stare and stare and then let the fabric go, watching it float down my body and pool on the floor. One photo left. From the hallway, Virgo scratches at the closed door, meows, but I ignore her as I step closer and closer to the corner of the room.

Ears burning, heart roaring, hips on fire, I lower myself onto the yellow chair.

I lean back, knees bent to the side, and imagine the flash of the Polaroid camera, the heat of its flare. My lips part, breath hitched, and form that knowing smirk. The tip of my tongue finds my upper teeth. Teasing. Powerful. Everything.

My pulse thunders and sweat pricks at my chest. Sunlight spills in from the windows and lust fills me up like steam and my hand finally, finally slides across my thigh.

My shoulders buckle; my torso twists. But I don't stop until my breath erupts in my own silent scream.

CHAPTER NINETEEN

Fireworks—they're still on, Sabrina tells me in the kitchen, her eyes sparkly with childlike glee. She hasn't mentioned the Polaroids and I haven't said a word about the bodysuit tucked in my closet, but I've felt different since that day. Bolder, more at ease. Like I tapped into whatever fearless energy Taylor brought into the house and can channel it like a medium.

"So the Fourth of July isn't canceled?" I dry my hands on the towel dangling from the oven door. This morning, right when I wasn't thinking about him, Mike finally reappeared to ask if I had Independence Day plans. I'm putting off answering his text. I can feel Chicago Kelly lurking in the corners of my mind and demanding answers—the moony part of me that was once so stoked to marry him. But I'm not ready to bring it into the light just yet.

"Not the pyrotechnics." She unrolls the top of a bag of chips. "And they're the best part. Do you want to invite your new friend to watch with us?"

"Megan? Maybe." I feel a flash of surprise—when I suggested inviting her over earlier, Sabrina was so put off by it. But this is different, I suppose; an invitation to a public event, not their house.

And then the surprise boomerangs back: I don't particularly *want* to invite her. I don't want to share the Lamonts.

"We've got a secret spot to watch them from." She smiles as she crunches. "The highest point in the area."

It clicks. "The cemetery?"

"Bingo." She swallows. "We get a private show."

"Are we allowed inside that late?" There are signs: The graveyard closes at dusk. I feel an old knee-jerk spurt of fear at the idea of being in there after dark. But then . . . staying here has changed my relationship with fear. Cross-wired it with novelty, with excitement. With seeing things as if for the first time.

"We use the side entrance. It's worth it." She pushes past me, touching my shoulder as she passes. My skin heats. "You'll see."

We head out as the sun is setting, turning the clouds' undersides violet and fuchsia. Fireflies blink and swirl, and the cicadas' hum makes the trees seem charged—watchful and sentient. A few mansions are lit from the front, but most are shrouded in darkness, with melted-butter light seeping from windows that peek over towering gates.

We reach Brinsmere, and Nathan swings the gate open. Darkness is descending quickly, like someone yanked the rope on a stage curtain. Graves that were so pretty by day now look Halloweeny, macabre. I trip on a root and flail. Nathan makes a "whoa!" sound and catches me, one hand on my arm and another on my waist, and I look into his face and time freezes. *Nathan's hand on the bodysuit, pressed to Taylor's ribs.*

"Thanks." I pull away, grateful he can't see me blush.

Sabrina clicks on her flashlight and heads up the hill. The sky's hazy denim now, and old tombstones stick up like gnarly teeth. She reaches the top and stops in an open patch. To the left is the bowl of the gravestone "amphitheater," the angel just visible in the center. It looks alive—alert. Sabrina spreads a blanket on the grass. On someone's grave, maybe. We crack open IPAs and the whole thing feels illicit, thrilling, like we're teenagers in a closed-off part of town.

"What time do they start?" I take a loud, frothy sip.

"The fireworks?" Nathan rests his elbows on the blanket. "Whenever it's dark enough. This town is so podunk, it's hilarious."

"Well, except that it's super ritzy," Sabrina cuts in.

"Was that classist of me?" he says. "Fine. It's the boonies, but with piles of gold."

"That would be *The Goonies*," I break in, and happiness twinkles through me when they both laugh. I sigh. "Who knew I'd like the suburbs?"

Sabrina giggles. "Right? Even though it's a ghost town."

"Literally!" Nathan sweeps his arm across the tombs.

"Deerbrook felt much less isolated when we could drive into D.C. for dinner or a show," Sabrina says.

"You must miss it," I observe.

She pinches her can so the metal tings. "You know what I was just thinking about? We all miss our friends and routines and lives, sure." A gust of wind makes the treetops whisper. "But I didn't realize how much of my job came down to being face-to-face. Like, my publicist drives me bananas over email, but a few times a year I'd meet her for drinks in Manhattan and remember how much I love her." She sits up. "Nothing's casual anymore. Nothing's off-the-record. I miss hearing gossip at romance conventions. I miss meeting readers at festivals. We're all in a vacuum now, fumbling around in the dark."

"Totally." I lean forward. "Like, I'm great at in-person interviews but so awkward on calls with recruiters. Zoom is no substitute for real life."

"That's true for my job too," Nathan adds. "So much used to be decided on the golf course."

Sabrina's voice flattens: "Handshakes for major arms deals."

Nathan shifts to face her, and something passes between them, shutting me out. I feel a flapping desperation to be back inside—back on their side of the fence.

"That's exactly it!" I lie on my back. "There's no relationship-building." *Except with you.* I think it so hard I half-wonder if I said it aloud. *You are my only relationship.*

Nathan flops onto his side, propped up on one elbow, and smiles at me from above. His mouth is so close to my bare shoulder that *oh my God is he going to kiss it, my shoulder, and if he does what will I—*

A distant pop makes me jump, and we snap to attention.

"It's starting!" Sabrina's face is awash in the first firecracker's red glow.

The explosions are spectacular, big and bright and booming, spheres of fire and showers of wild sparks. Glowing spiderwebs drip light like tears. Incandescent tadpoles scream as they whirl, and novelty firecrackers make lopsided hearts and smiley faces.

But my favorites are the traditional ones, massive neon chrysanthemums, canvassing the sky with color and light and a great *pow* of thunder. The fireworks display goes on and on and I don't want it to end, even when we reach the finale, even when it fills me with rapture, all the sound and smell and sight, the way it painted the sky.

When it's over I drop back, almost panting. For a few seconds we're silent, listening to the final reverberations. Then Sabrina sighs happily.

"I needed that," she says, as if it were a mug of coffee or a good massage. Or a . . .

"I forgot how much I love fireworks," I say quickly. "Once, I was flying out to visit my parents on the Fourth and I got to see a bunch of them from above. They looked like little fireballs hanging all over the place."

"'Balls hanging all over the place'!" Nathan helps Sabrina fold the picnic blanket. "Weird, that's also the title of my sex tape."

"Sex jokes are Nathan's love language," Sabrina stage-whispers as we head for the gate. "Anyway, balls are the least-interesting thing in porn. They look so small and scared."

I let out a surprised laugh.

"Rina's more of a boob person." Nathan takes my elbow again as I navigate around a headstone. "It's one of many things we agree on."

"That's good," I say awkwardly, and then the silence swells. I feel them listening, their ears like black holes. They're testing me—seeing if I'll lean in or slink away.

Blame my Midwestern repression, but I've never been the kind of person who could have these conversations. Friends would bring it up cheerily—Amy loved recommending female directors she'd discovered—but I always felt shy.

I gulp in the cemetery air. "I like lesbian porn, personally." I say it loud, my confidence feigned.

"Us too." Sabrina reaches the gate and fumbles with the rusted latch. "There are some cam couples we really like. I didn't think I'd like amateur stuff, but it's actually hot. Because you can tell the attraction is real—they aren't acting, like in porn."

"If you can call that 'acting,'" Nathan adds. He makes his voice breathy: "'Doctor, let me show you where I need treatment.'"

Are we still earnestly discussing porn, or did Nathan seal it off with a joke? I want to be as sexually free as them, as liberated and cool. I cast around for a way to keep the conversation going—

"Do we have any food at home? I'm starving," Sabrina says, and the chance to be let into their hip and sexy world scampers off like a rabbit in the night.

Inside, Nathan pulls snacks from the cupboards and corrals us into the screened-in porch. The screech of crickets and katydids rattles the screen and boils the air. Sabrina sprawls on the wicker loveseat, Scheherazade about to spin a tale, then pulls something tiny from her purse.

Is that a vibrator? I flash to the second book in her Heart of Desire series, the lovemaking session where Perry unveils an array of shiny toys and he and Arianna sample them one by one, an erotic buffet. But then Sabrina closes her lips around it and the tip glows blue: a vape pen. She sucks slowly, luxuriously, letting it swirl in her lungs before exhaling a pearly cloud.

"It's super smooth," she tells me.

I glance at Nathan. "Don't you work for the government?"

"Conveniently, the lockdown's put a damper on drug testing." He shrugs. "Still, I won't partake."

Sabrina tumbles onto her hands and knees and crawls toward me. She stops, her legs an inch from mine, and holds the vape pen up to my mouth like a cigarette. My eyes meet hers—*flash*—and then I lean forward and take a deep drag, her fingers just touching my lips. I turn my head and blow out a long, lazy stream.

"Damn, that is smooth."

She sits back and takes another hit. "Strong too."

Nathan's brought a Bluetooth speaker with him and he puts on something bluesy. The song sounds like America, and that's fitting, because it's the Fourth of July.

Wait—that was a high observation. Oh no. My thoughts already have that roly-poly quality, where every thought that makes it to the surface has three thoughts charging after it from different angles, analyzing it, giggling at it, arguing with it.

Wait, why "roly-poly"? See, there I go again!

"Y'know, I'm still clinging to the fireworks' effect on me." My voice is fuller, thicker, like it's shooting out of my throat differently.

"Their effect on you?" Nathan pops a pretzel into his mouth.

"Yeah. The way they made me feel." There's a silence, is it a long silence? I think they're waiting for me to say more and I feel a cold lurch of embarrassment, because, whoops, I forgot what I was trying to say, or what I was thinking, even.

There's a tingly feeling spilling down my spine, liquid gold, and it reaches my tailbone and pools so that my entire pelvis is warm and sparkly. I look down and realize the sparkles, though invisible, are covering me exactly like the lace bodysuit, clinging to my hips and torso and around my neck. Sabrina's still kneeling before me and my God, she's maybe the most beautiful woman I've ever seen. She smiles and the sparkles bounce and twirl.

And then—something happens. Something forbidden and wild, not me at all. Like the pot and attraction have charged up my insides, they're wearing me like a Kelly costume.

No, a Taylor costume. I'm Taylor now, transformation complete.

I lean forward, palms flat on the floor. Sabrina's face is so close and she looks up at me, full on, so bright I could cry.

Before I can think, I close the gap between us.

And I kiss her, hard, on the mouth.

CHAPTER TWENTY

As our lips touch, a million thoughts run through my mind at once, all in a microsecond, a computer's hyperthreading, a multitude of sparks charging out of a center point, a big bright-red firework that lights the whole night sky.

Oh my God. I'm kissing Sabrina.

I'm kissing a woman.

My friend.

My friend since high school.

Her husband is right there.

I'm screwing everything up, they're going to kick me out.

Her lips are so fucking soft.

I'm ruining everything.

Mike.

I'm cheating on—

She kisses me back and the thoughts drop away, like someone hit the Mute button. She grabs the back of my head and I could kiss this mouth forever, I could breathe in her breath, I gasp as our tongues meet and now the sparkles are everywhere, fully charged particles, like those fireworks we saw, the ones that danced and spun.

I pull away with a surprised laugh. Now the thoughts come back, an electric circuit: When our lips touch the current flows and those thoughts go away but now they're back, back, back, baby.

Embarrassment and guilt spray through me like a fountain. *Mike. My hosts. A* woman. "Whoa, sorry." I lean back, mash my hand against my brow. "I don't know what came over me."

When I dare to open my eyes, Sabrina hasn't moved away, and she's looking at Nathan, some silent conversation passing between them. Finally she turns back and it's the sun, her full-on attention so blazing hot it could incinerate me.

"It's okay, Kelly." She tucks my hair behind my ear, then runs her fingertips down my jaw. They leave a trail like a comet, like those weeping-willow fireworks. When she's touching me, the voice is quiet. When her skin is against my skin, that's all there is. "No pressure, obviously. I can go back to the sofa. But . . . it is okay. With both of us. If you want."

My whole body is thrumming. I look at Nathan, who nods. I turn back to Sabrina. Her huge green eyes. Her lifted brows. The expression that's inviting me into something—a running leap from a cliff, no going back.

I can't answer because I'm beyond words, I'm a humming closed circuit, charged and alive. I lean forward and kiss her, hungrily, so ferociously I want to eat her whole, and then her hands are under my shirt, unhooking my bra, undressing me with unbelievable speed and skill.

Now Nathan is on the floor, too, and I grab his chin and kiss him hard and run my fingers through his coarse, lamplight-colored hair, and it's like I'm wearing the bodysuit even though it's up in my room, the Polaroids have sprung to life and I'm living them, it's all here and there are textures everywhere, hard and soft, and I want to sample them all, that erotic buffet.

After a few minutes Nathan suggests we go to their room, and so we dash upstairs, Sabrina holding my hand as if I might not remember the way. As we turn down the hallway, Mike flashes in my mind—Mike, *my* Mike, and a shard of gloom starts to impale my heart.

But then Nathan throws open the bedroom door and all thoughts of Mike scatter, like napkins on a windy day. Moonlight spills across their bed and we launch ourselves on top, laughing, undoing all the hard work of buttons and buckles and zippers so that we can feel skin, all that skin, Nathan's hairy and rough, Sabrina's smooth and warm. I see it all, the flesh I've been picturing since that first day, since I saw their tiled shower and pictured them like this, body parts that are somehow awe-inspiring yet exactly what I expected.

Sweet, goofy Nathan turns bossy and serious, switching positions, running the show. Sabrina is relaxed and unselfconscious, smiling as she kisses me. I catch a glimpse of us in the mirror, the one that hangs near the bed. It *is* hot to be able to see. I think again of the Polaroids, of the scenes I read and reread in Sabrina's new book, the moments I imagined in this very three-dimensional space, and now I'm in it, part of it, it's finally real.

When it's over, we crash down on the bed and I can feel them on either side of me, smiling as aftershocks rock through me. Finally I crack open my eyes, run a hand across my forehead.

"That was incredible," I tell them, looking from one to the other.

I feel warm and safe and still sparkly, glittery champagne. I'm on their bed but floating, too, alert and dreaming. I close my eyes and Nathan rolls over to kiss my shoulder and I smile into the darkness, trying to hold on to what's just happened. But my pot-soaked brain starts doing that channel-flipping thing where the thoughts move too fast and in unexpected directions, zooming like a school of fish.

Soon I'll fall asleep, and the weight of Nathan and Sabrina around me might already be asleep like warm safe bedding.

But first a thought blips through the chaos, almost nonsensical yet full of clarity and light:

I'm never going back.

CHAPTER TWENTY-ONE

I wake and blink in confusion—where am I? Pain bangs at the inside of my skull, and that's what reminds me: It's the headache I always get after smoking pot. More sensations shake me awake: That sound is Nathan snoring. The weight on my waist is Sabrina's forearm. My arm is asleep, painful tingles, because it's smashed beneath me, a cuddle foul.

I open my eyes and gasp. *Oh my God oh my God oh my God.* Did that actually happen? What was I thinking?

Cautiously, I peel back the sheet and slide my legs over the top. I shimmy down the center of the bed and hold my breath as one foot hits the floor, then the other.

My eyes and cheeks feel red and hot. I can't believe I convinced myself I could—what, metamorphose into the woman in the Polaroids? I'm an idiot. What have I done? I can't stay here—it'll be too uncomfortable for everyone. I need to book the first Amtrak out of D.C. . . . but I have no idea where to go next.

I slink around, slipping my clothes on as I encounter them. I finally spy my underwear dangling from the open drawer of Nathan's nightstand. I creep closer, shame roasting my face; they're ugly, blue-and-green-striped cotton, and lolling inside out. I snatch them up and spot a flash of metal that makes my heart thump before I even know why.

I lean closer, examining. Of course—it's the gun he mentioned, black and shiny. I've never been this close to a loaded gun before.

Nathan rolls over and I rear back, then dart into the hallway. How am I supposed to face these people when I just witnessed them in their most intimate moments? When I stared into Nathan's face as he . . . while I . . .

I scuttle into my room and close the door. From the center of the bed, Virgo gazes at me knowingly. Like she can tell what I've done.

Cheater. The thing I was terrified Mike would do to me, I've done to him. Guilt whiffles through me like a tarp. I flop on the bed and watch the light from the windows bleed from gray to white. Birds pipe up—morning. How the hell can I be in this house now, sober and lucid?

I step into the shower as tears stream.

Mike.

Through it all, since the week we met when I decided *Yes, this is my person, thank God I can say goodbye to all that nonsense,* I didn't even let myself consider that we wouldn't end up together. Picturing my life without him in it felt dangerous, like chanting "Bloody Mary" into a mirror. Even when I convinced myself he was having an affair with Aubrey (*who's unfaithful now?*), I cared because he was mine.

But now . . . now I'm confused. I think of Nathan and Sabrina and feel a surge in my chest, my hips, my whole body. They're bright and shiny in my mind's eye, so intelligent and giving and *hot*.

From almost day one, I loved Mike, a warm, safe, spongy love that felt like relief, a slackening in my shoulders. We had cozy, comfy sex in a handful of go-to positions at a frequency that tapered off over the years, but that's the long haul; that's normal.

I can't believe I had a threesome.

Mike floated the idea, two years into our relationship, when I asked what he wanted for his birthday: There were apps, he said, where we could find a third, and wouldn't that be fun, a one-time ménage à trois? And I'd *freaked out* at the suggestion. Burst into tears on the spot, sulked around the apartment for weeks. Because I took it to mean I wasn't enough—he wanted to sleep with someone else, a loophole in our monogamy. God, I was hurt.

But . . . now I'm not so sure. Because applying that same logic, that same math to what just happened would mean *I* was the Lamonts' escape clause, a meaningless one-off . . . and that's not how it felt at all. As I towel off, my body swings between two extremes: an ugly, gray guilt when I think of Mike, but when I flash to last night—writhing on their sheets, feeling so good it was like my brain was scrunching, crumpling into a red-hot kernel of pleasure—well, it's clear which side is Technicolor.

But oh, how can I face them? Humiliation loops through me as I pull on clothes, as I brush my teeth, as I steel myself and creep downstairs. *Please don't let anyone be there.* But there's clanking in the kitchen, and I freeze. I'm not sure whether I want it to be Sabrina or Nathan, which encounter I dread more.

I take a deep breath and waltz into the kitchen as part of my body looks on in horror, *turn around run away go back.* They're *both* in the kitchen, dammit, and they grin at me.

"Good morning!" Nathan sounds . . . normal. He's rumpled in sweatpants and a UVA T-shirt, but I picture him the night before, torso slick with sweat, and embarrassment rockets through me. The toast pops up, *bing,* and I think wildly that it's mocking me.

"Morning!" I match his cheer, then lunge for the coffee right as he turns toward the fridge and we end up in a weird, jerky dance.

"How'd you sleep?" Sabrina unfolds the arts section of a newspaper. The kitchen island is scattered with pieces of the *Blue Ridge Times,* and I stare at her, wide-eyed.

"Sometimes Rina does karate in her sleep," Nathan adds. "Took me a long time to get used to."

Okay, we're acknowledging it. "Yeah, I . . . woke up and thought you two might want more space." I'm lingering, carton of creamer clutched in front of my chest, when he plants a hand on the fridge and leans over me. My knees wobble, my God, *want.* Is Sabrina seeing this?

"We both want to make sure you're feeling okay about everything."

His blue eyes bore into mine. "It's . . . whatever you want it to be. We can talk about it, not talk about it, pretend it never happened . . . you decide."

I smile in spite of myself, then feel that crow of guilt sitting on my shoulder. "I . . . look. It was the best night I've had in a long time. I've never done anything like that before."

"Coulda fooled me," Sabrina calls. I glance over and there it is again, a rush of warmth in my groin.

No, Kelly. Get it together.

"It's just that . . . well, I'm still with . . ." Before I can even utter Mike's name, a lump clogs my throat.

"I'm sorry about Mike." Sabrina stands, hands clasped. "We knew you were trying to make it work, and that wasn't . . . we shouldn't have . . ."

"No, don't apologize. It's all on me." I turn away, crying.

Nathan clicks his tongue and wraps me in a hug, all big arms and bristly beard. "We won't mention it again, then."

But the thought of pretending it never happened fills me with a frantic, flapping sorrow. Oh, what a mess I've made—alienating everyone who shows me affection.

But then a distant part of me, one that crystallized last night, works its way to the surface. The untamed part of me. Taylor.

My voice is a whisper, but somehow I do it, I form the words: "I— I don't think that's what I want either."

Nathan's head turns toward Sabrina. I hear her get up and cross to us.

"What do you mean?" she asks cautiously.

I step out of Nathan's arms and look into their faces. I can feel my ethical brain, the practical, grown-up part, screaming for attention: *What are you doing? Think about your engagement, your identity . . . your future.*

But I can't, not yet. Because—unlike when I let the gleeful demon run loose and destroy Mike's office, or even when it explored Sabrina's office and the mudroom and rummaged deep in their medicine cabinet— this time, what it pulled off doesn't feel entirely . . . wrong. Yes, I shouldn't have done that to Mike. But being with them felt natural in a way I can't explain.

"I don't know," I admit. "I don't know what I'm saying." Finally I chuckle. "When I woke up, my first thought was that I needed to catch the next Amtrak out of here."

Sabrina looks wounded, but Nathan raises his eyebrows. "You're gonna make me drive back to Union Station?" After a charged moment, we crack up. The tension drops, like smoke sinking to the floor.

"Stay! You should stay with us." It's the second time she's said it in a few short weeks, but this time it's so different. "I mean it—as long as you want."

"Really?" My heartbeat's nearly a drumroll.

"Yeah, don't leave." Nathan leans against the counter. "We could even do that again sometime. If you want."

Again? I'm like a cartoon character who just sprinted off a cliff, legs still beating in midair. "You're serious?"

"Totally. We had fun, you know?" Sabrina beams. "We're not swingers or anything. But . . . Nathan and I finally talked about it, and it turns out we both secretly wanted that to happen."

They wanted that to happen. *They wanted that to happen!* I'm smiling so big it hurts, and I swallow, tapping into that fearless Taylor energy. "I'd been thinking about it too. A lot. But I wasn't about to act on it." I turn my palms to the sky. "I'm so vanilla! I've been a boring straight chick for as long as I can remember."

Sabrina nods. "And obviously we didn't want you to feel pressured or uncomfortable or anything."

"Especially since—I mean, the reason you're here . . ." Nathan peters out, and the air stiffens again.

Mike. Of course it's not that simple. Of course I'm conveniently omitting him from my calculations.

But . . . hasn't he been omitting me from his too? He's screening my calls, barely responding to my texts. Even before that, he refused to re-up our wedding vendors. Unilaterally, no discussion, just an announcement: *Change of plans!* Didn't he basically quit on me?

I gaze at Sabrina. I like her so much it's a force, a wave of heat. My feelings toward her are carnal and wild, set deep in my brain, my hips. And Nathan—those mischievous eyes, that goofy grin. The way bantering with him makes me feel sharp and funny and like I'm enough.

I finally, finally ease the cork off the thoughts I've been holding back: Maybe Mike and I weren't as happy as I insisted we were. Amy wasn't wrong; I never did like his loud podcasts or aversion to ethnic food or the side-eye he shot me when I binge-watched TV. Not to mention how badly he dealt with negative emotions—witness how he hid his joblessness and our relationship foibles, for one thing. Or how, whenever he grew angry, he squeezed his fists and stomped his feet like a toddler. *Why do I keep telling myself I need to be with him?* Sabrina and Nathan are everything he's not—accepting and unconditional and so goddamn emotionally intelligent.

I grab Sabrina's hand to my left, Nathan's to my right. "I'll stay." We wind our fingers together and they exchange a smile over my head. "Have you ever opened up your marriage before?" I ask carefully, thinking of the Polaroids. This is it—time for answers.

"We did, yes. We had a partner for a while." The way Sabrina jumps in makes me suspect she didn't mention my discovery to Nathan. "Also a woman." A *partner*—I wonder how it progressed to that, a bona fide relationship.

"You don't seem that surprised," Nathan observes.

"Well, I'm almost halfway through Sabrina's latest manuscript. And there's this Taylor character . . ."

Sabrina giggles. "That obvious?"

I say it without thinking: "Honestly, when you first described her . . . I secretly hoped she was based on me."

"You're so different." Nathan's words prompt an awkward beat, but Sabrina shakes her head.

"You're both wonderful. And the relationship was great. For all of us."

They don't care that I haven't done this before. In fact, I'm lucky to have them to guide me into this brave new world. "How long ago were you with her?" I ask.

They exchange another glance. "Oh, ages ago," Nathan says.

"It ended amicably," Sabrina adds. "When we . . . when it ended, she lived in D.C. and we were here."

"Got it." So Taylor's a city girl, getting through the pandemic in her own badass way. "Are you still in touch with her?" I'm not sure what answer to hope for: If they are, I'll have to deal with my own jealousy. If they aren't, it suggests we're going down a road that—should it go awry—could shunt them out of my life forever.

They exchange a glance that makes my heart thump. This was an easy question, a binary.

"It's actually really awful." Sabrina's eyes skitter to the floor.

No. I have no idea what's about to come out of her mouth, but I know it's big and bad and it has the potential to turn this entire offer on its head. That means it's the last thing I want to hear. *Stop there.*

She sighs. "Right now . . . she's missing."

CHAPTER TWENTY-TWO

rock backward. "*Missing?*"

They both nod gravely. "From the District," she says. "We heard it on the news. They still haven't found her."

"That's terrible." My fingers fan against my breastbone. It's incomprehensible, something from a true-crime special. "What do they think happened to her?"

Nathan rubs his beard, his eyes pained. "It's been long enough without any sign of her that . . . they figure it's something bad. But we have no idea. Obviously, we're hanging on to hope."

"Jeez. I'm so sorry." This isn't right at all. She's supposed to be, like, on a yacht near Santorini with a cadre of partners. Or living in a sex-positive group home off the grid or, hell, alone in a boho loft somewhere, independent and free. Not *missing*.

Because I feel like I know her. Through my peephole view, I understand her, her unabashed sexuality and unapologetic sense of self. This mystery woman, she's iconic, invincible. Though she doesn't know it, she let me in on a little secret about the Lamonts. Showed me what's possible, how *not* to be a perfect Midwestern wife-to-be.

She's . . . well, she's me.

I realize my mouth is hanging open and I gulp. "What happened?"

"Like Rina said, we have no idea."

"Honestly, it's been horrible for both of us," Sabrina adds. "I'd rather not talk about it."

I feel chastised, befuddled. *You're being silly,* I tell myself. *You don't know this woman. Her disappearance has nothing to do with you.*

Sabrina smiles shyly. "Here's the thing: Having you here—it's the first time we've smiled in forever."

"It's true." Nathan's chuckle is round and sobby. "You came along, and God, I wasn't sure I'd ever laugh like that again."

Warmth floods my chest. I let the mystery woman go, because she's not the one Nathan and Sabrina want to be with. That's me; I won. It's cheesy but I force it out: "You two make me so happy."

Sabrina grins. "Wait, I know what this moment needs."

She thumps downstairs, then returns with a bottle of bubbly. We joke as she pours it into glasses—a splash of orange juice on top, "we're not *lushes,*" she says with a laugh—and we drift into the library and it's just like the day I arrived, *clink,* but even better, friendlier. No more wondering when this'll come to an end. I truly belong.

Nathan scoops up a tambourine that floated in from the music room and shakes it whenever we all crack up. I feel its happy chimes inside me, like we've leveled up to a higher vibration. I have the sense I'm in a lucid dream, a dimension where the outside world can't touch us.

"Oh, one thing," Nathan says. "We should keep"—he gestures around—"all this to ourselves."

I was expecting this, on account of their silence around the mystery woman, but still, my neck and scalp go cold. I force a smile: "You don't want people knowing you've taken a *lovah?*"

"Because of his job," Sabrina jumps in, her face twisting with sympathy. "High-profile, high-up. I know it's hard. We hate being so secretive too. But . . . it's not the kind of thing we want getting out."

"Got it." It won't even be that hard. Secrets are easy to keep when the world is on lockdown. I'll have to be a bit evasive with Amy and maybe my new neighbor Megan, but my occasional Zoom happy hours with friends don't skate anywhere near my sex life.

And other than that, the only person I ever talk to is . . .

"Mike," I blurt out.

They both turn to me as tears prick my eyes.

"You can't tell him."

"*Nathan.*" Sabrina swats him with the back of her hand. She turns to me. "We're not trying to steal you away from anyone. But would you really want to tell him anyway?"

"It's not that." The thought reaches my lungs, my clavicle, slithers up my throat and finally pops out of my mouth, words I've never said aloud before: "It's over."

Tears flow and Nathan pulls me against his chest. I cry into his shirt, just like I've done to Mike so many times. The sobs are ugly but ribboned with relief—that steady gush of releasing something you've pushed down.

Mike. I loved him, love him still, but the *in*-love part faded long before the pandemic. And then we were two plastic pieces in the Game of Life, pink and blue, hurtling toward a family because we never thought to check for an off-ramp. *Pump the brakes*—that was how Mike put it all those weeks ago. We both knew it, deep down. We were waking from a trance and realizing we didn't have to move forward just because we said we would.

I pull away, sniffling. "I need to talk to him. To really end things."

Nathan nods. "Of course. You need closure."

"And if we're going to try this, we should do it the right way," Sabrina adds. "I know we all got, you know, caught up in the moment yesterday, but . . ."

"Totally. I'm—I'm not cool with cheating." I rub my brow. "We'll have to—oh God. We'll have to tell all our wedding guests. The vendors. This is gonna suck."

Sabrina strokes my arm. "It will. But we'll be right here waiting for you."

My heart squeezes like a fist. "You think I should do it now?"

"Rip the Band-Aid off, no?" Nathan says.

"It's up to you," Sabrina says, "but the sooner it's done, the sooner you can move on."

"What are you going to say?" Nathan tries to sound casual, but I can tell he's concerned. Which is irritating.

I glance around the library. It's like the walls are wobbling, the colors shifting—my perspective reorienting itself to make room for this insight. After that awful college boyfriend and string of disappointing dudes, I took it for granted that Mike was the One. Decision made, done, on to the next level of the game. It felt risky to even *consider* a future without him. Doubts—I left zero space for them.

"I'll tell him I've had some time to think, and we need to officially break up. Don't worry, I won't say anything about last night. It's not . . ." I trail off. It's not what? Relevant? The reason I'm officially ending things? It's all that and more, but it almost doesn't matter, because for once, I feel a thrilling blast of certitude—not from the anxious voice chanting *make-it-work-make-it-work-make-it-work* but from a deeper knowing, a confrontation with the part of me that's known for a while. So what if it took a wild night with these two for me to face it?

"I'll go for a walk," I say, giving my eyes one last wipe. "I'll call him now."

"We'll be here," says Sabrina. The woman whose soft skin I can touch again soon.

I snap my shoulders forward, straight as a fence, and stand.

CHAPTER TWENTY-THREE

I stare at Mike's name for a long time. I'm on a bench in Brinsmere, across from a headless stone cherub and a perfectly round pond. A turtle suns itself on the edge and when I finally touch my screen, the critter tips into the water, *bloop*.

My heart's like a machine gun as the FaceTime rings and rings.

"Kelly. Hey." He looks concerned and sleepy and I tear up on the spot.

"Hi, Mike. We need to talk." My voice crackles and overhead a crow caws.

His eyes drop. It's like he already knows.

"I—I want us to be honest with each other," I say.

"What is it, Kelly?"

I can barely get the words out: "I don't think we should be together."

His lips quiver and his face reddens, but he just stares into the camera, waiting for me to go on.

"You're great. And I don't regret a second I spent with you." I try to swallow the rock in my throat. "But we've been growing apart for a while, you know? And I . . ." A shudder runs through me. "I didn't want to see it. But now I'm facing the truth. I love you, Mike. But . . . I can't marry you."

He looks away, tears trailing down his cheeks.

"Mike, say something."

"Shit." His jaw trembles. "I did not see that coming."

"It's what you wanted, isn't it?" Some defensive part of me needs him to agree. To take responsibility for kicking off this series of events.

"Of course it's not . . . shit, Kelly." He runs a hand across his forehead. "I thought you wanted to make this work."

Confusion blares in me. "But you didn't want to get married."

"I wanted to *postpone* the wedding. Figure some things out. God, don't you think if I wanted to . . ."

Hot tears surge down my face. He shakes his head, eyes flashing, and I reflexively hold the phone farther out. *Am* I throwing everything away? In Philly I begged him to come around, to acknowledge we were a perfect fit. But now . . .

"All this time to think," I say, "it made me realize you were right. You did the *brave* thing, pumping the brakes. I'm—am I all alone out here?" I watch his nostrils flare, his face redden. "Breathe, Mike. Let's take a breath." As I loudly suck in air, my chest brims with alarm. I don't know what I'll do if he has a meltdown or begs me to change my mind. All the cells in my body stand still, waiting.

Finally he sighs. "Maybe you're right." He gives his head a slow shake. "Maybe we're better as friends."

My heart lunges. "I *really* want us to be friends. Please tell me we can do that." He's taking this better than I expected, and I relax. He truly will be okay.

He presses his lips together. "What's your plan?"

It takes me a moment to figure out what he's asking. "I'm gonna stay here. For now, anyway. I think we both need space."

He squeezes his eyes closed, then nods. "You're right."

"We probably shouldn't talk for a little while." I wish I could hold him tight—while I get to return to Sabrina and Nathan, he's all alone in Philly. "Will you be okay? Can you call Leigh or someone?" He's not close with his sister, but I can't picture his bro-y friends offering a shoulder to cry on.

"I'll be fine. Don't worry about me. Are *you* okay?" His blue eyes pierce the screen and abruptly, my head gets floaty—*Is this really happening? Are we truly breaking up?* I have the peculiar feeling that I stepped out of my own life and into a separate story.

"I'll be okay," I say. "But God, this is *weird*."

"Sure is," he shoots back, and we both laugh. Then, like it's just occurred to him: "Wait, what about the wedding?"

I frown. "We'll cancel it. I can email our guests."

"How's *that* going to look?" Something flares in his eyes.

I press my lips together. "Like the truth?"

"What, you want to put it on blast that we . . . that you . . . ?"

"I can put it however you want," I say, irritated. Mike hates airing dirty laundry, and a called-off wedding is as filthy as it gets. His father, the preppy, stiff-upper-lipped Ohioan who was bankrolling our nuptials, will be especially displeased. But this is the situation, and he'll have to deal with it. "People deserve to know."

"Why? It's nobody's business but ours."

"They think we're having a wedding, Mike! They're going to notice if it never materializes."

"We don't have a date," he points out. "We could cancel the vendors and deal with everything first."

Now he's trying to postpone the inevitable. But . . . I think of Taylor, how in-charge she seems. I want to get it over with so that I can truly cut ties.

"It'll be easier once people know," I insist. "And maybe you can call the vendors? Get the deposits back?"

He lets out a heavy sigh and we segue into logistics. We always worked well as a team, smooth and efficient, and my heart aches knowing this is our last shared project—a joint effort to undo the culmination of five years together.

That's a long time to invest in someone. I know about Napoleon, the chihuahua he adopted in college. He knows about my childhood vacations on Mackinac Island. We have inside jokes and catchphrases that make sense to us alone.

Had. They'll all be buried in the time capsule of past tense now.

When it's time to hang up, neither of us is ready. The sun ducks behind a cloud and coats the cemetery in a steely gray. I should get back to Nathan and Sabrina.

"Take care of yourself, okay?" I say.

"You too."

I hesitate. "Love you, Mike."

"Love you too." And when we hang up, the bawls that convulse my lungs are the only sound in the cemetery.

Finally I stand. My head feels congested; my stomach is hollow, and my balance is off.

Mike. I picture him still frozen in his office, reeling from the news. It's funny how revelations can be both shocking and inevitable.

I pass the angel statue again, pausing to run my fingertip through the symbol on its base, the triangle enclosed in a rectangle. I gaze up at the book in the crook of its arm: ATWOOD. I press my palm to the angel's sandaled foot and the cool stone steadies me.

As I exit the cemetery, something light and quick flutters in my chest. I did it! I did the brave and sexy thing. The Tayloresque thing. I've cut Mike loose and now I get to come home to my new life.

But when I reach the foot of their driveway, my blood frosts over.

Something furry and dead is heaped below the gate, legs sticking out at grotesque angles. My insides fold in two—is that Virgo?!

I step closer and oh thank God, it's not Virgo but a raccoon splayed on its back. Its belly is pulpy, pied fur and guts. Its head lolls back and barbed teeth snarl from its open mouth.

Roadkill. But how did it get here? Or was it killed by a bird of prey? It's *exactly* where I found the dead bird that Nathan buried in the woods.

Heart pounding, I take a few steps back. And only then do I look up at the gate. I let out a clipped "Oh!"

Because there's a note on the gate: capital letters on plain white paper, taped to the iron bars.

LEAVE.

CHAPTER TWENTY-FOUR

swing my head this way and that, watching for someone watching me, whoever's behind this. Seeing no one, I rush inside.

Nathan's playing an old Ben Folds song on the piano, and when I heave open the front door, he stops. The minor chord bounces around the foyer, unresolved.

"How'd it go?" Sabrina darts in from the dining room. "Are you okay?"

I rush them out the front door, babbling. When they spot the gruesome scene, Sabrina's jaw drops, but Nathan just looks grim.

"This is a threat, right?" I cry. "Why would someone threaten us? We have to call the cops."

They trade meaningful looks.

"*What?*" I'm nearly in tears.

Nathan eases my shoulder around, so our backs are to the grisly sight. "There's a surveillance camera on our gate." He points. "Let's watch the footage first."

He herds us into his office and I look around with fresh eyes; it's weird that there's a room I'm not allowed in. Like I'm a child barred from the formal dining room with all its expensive china.

Nathan's been so dodgy about what he does for work. It'd probably sail over my head—acronyms and military minutiae—but it's wild how little I know about even the broad strokes.

While he enters password after password into his computer, my eyes sail to the floating shelves on the wall. There are books on them, a framed picture of Nathan with Hillary Clinton. There's that green stone pyramid, perhaps eight inches high, and *wait*, I recognize the symbol on it: a triangle trapped inside a rectangle, the figure on the grave marker.

"How was the call?" Sabrina asks, stroking my arm. I still feel dizzy and overstimulated, my stomach cramped.

"We . . . I . . ." I break down crying again, even though I thought I was dry. "Sorry, I'm fine. It went as well as it could. But it's . . . hard. I haven't wrapped my head around it yet."

"Of course it's hard." She rubs my shoulder. "Even when it's amicable, you need to grieve the ending."

"Like you and your ex, right?" I ask. She used the same adjective for their breakup: *amicable*. She glances back at Nathan.

"Found it!" Nathan waves at his screen, and we flank his shoulders. He plays the black-and-white footage. Shortly after I strode outside this morning, two figures appeared.

"Michelle's kids," Sabrina observes.

Two boys—small, maybe middle-school-aged—fake bravado as they carry a bundle to the door. One drops the dead raccoon onto the pavement and the other struggles with a loop of packing tape before smoothing the sign against the gate. They nod, giggling and grossed-out, and take off.

"Who are they?" I prompt.

"Neighbors." Sabrina sighs. "Harmless kids picking up their parents' vendetta against us."

"A *vendetta*?"

Nathan weaves his fingers behind his head. "We told you people don't like us here. They think we're uppity city folks who don't want to fraternize with them."

"Which is true." Sabrina shakes her head. "Lydia, that woman we saw with Diane—she's their grandmother. I'm sure they've heard her say some nasty things about us."

"Well, we should tell her. Or their mom—Michelle?" I point to the screen. "This is unacceptable."

The Lamonts exchange another glance.

"They're stupid kids," Sabrina says softly. "And it's a pandemic—I don't want to be ringing people's doorbells. Unless it escalates, let's leave it, all right?"

"I'll bury the raccoon," Nathan says. "I'm sure they found it by the road—they're not going around torturing animals."

I make Nathan rewind to the day I found the bird. Sure enough, a few minutes after I left for my walk, these big-eared boys crept over with a bird on a piece of cardboard.

"Kids can be so cruel." Sabrina reaches for me. "Kelly, you're okay?"

"That's a lot to process." Nathan grimaces.

What awful luck: a breakup and a threat all at once. I picture the sign again: *Leave*. Well, I'm doing the opposite.

"I'm okay," I tell her. After a moment's hesitation, she kisses me, a long, slow kiss with her fingers whorling the nape of my neck. I kiss her back, then let her pull me into another hug.

Sending the mass email is hard; I make Sabrina read it over and hit Send for me as I recoil from my laptop, cringing. In it, I'm honest: *We realized, lovingly and mutually, that staying together is not the best choice for either of us.* A second later, my chest goes cold: I was supposed to share it with Mike first. Well, too late now.

Almost instantly, the replies start rolling in, earnest announcements that folks are *there* for me, or *here*, or wherever people float to provide moral support when we're all on lockdown. Ten minutes later, Amy calls.

"Kelly! What happened? Are you okay?!"

"Thanks for calling." I'm not sure I have the energy to talk to her. "It's what I said in the email. We both took a little time to ourselves, and . . ."

"Wow. I know he was being weird about the wedding, but . . ." She makes a *huh* sound. "I can't believe you didn't tell me."

I cringe. "It only happened this morning. I'm sorry—you've been so supportive. But I needed to get it over with."

She softens. "I'm worried about you."

Maybe she thinks I'm lying about the breakup being mutual; after all, last month I begged her to help me win him back. Well, fine. If people are busy pitying me, no one will suspect I was the one who . . .

But oh, my brain is quick to spin excuses. Yes, I technically cheated, but *Mike* stalled the wedding. He encouraged me to leave. And when I fell for someone (some-*two*) new, it was as natural as stepping off a bus.

"Thanks, Amy. And I'm sorry I didn't tell you first." I ask how she's faring in Chicago. I admit I don't feel like talking about the breakup, and we hang up, friendship intact.

The dining-room window looks out on a grove of pear trees. I watch their branches sway in the breeze. I feel empty again, strangely removed from my life upheaval. It's done. Wedding retracted, guests alerted. Sexy new possibilities waiting in the wings.

I move like someone possessed: confident and determined, stepping softly. I find Sabrina on the sofa in the library and drop to my knees next to her. I kiss her yet again—it still feels new and I focus on the softness of her lips, the truffle taste of her mouth. I feel sexy and wanted and entirely new.

I glance over my shoulder. "Nathan! Get down here!"

And after a second, he does.

CHAPTER TWENTY-FIVE

Ahh, the high of crushing on someone new. I'd forgotten how good it feels, the lightning every time our eyes meet, the warm smoke that rushes through me at a gentle kiss or nuzzle or palm on my shoulders. The hot-pink lust roaring at the drop of a hat, like a hose cranked on and then, abruptly, unkinked.

I'm surprised by how quickly I grow comfortable with it all. I kiss Sabrina's temple when she's perched on a kitchen stool. I climb out of the pool and wrap my wet arms around Nathan's waist when I catch him watching me swim laps. Perhaps it's because I was imagining it for so long—Sabrina and Nathan but also Arianna and Perry, with me as Taylor, proxies for this perfection. It's like we're magnets, sensing one another's pull: hands to torsos, lips to heads, shoulders jockeying for puzzle-like fits when we cuddle.

And the sex! Who knew I liked sex this much?! With Mike, I thought my libido was low-to-average; sex was predictable and pleasant, a perfunctory affair.

Here, I'm insatiable.

We have sex at least once a day for the first week—more threesomes, not nearly as confusing or logistically difficult as I'd have thought, just three people enjoying themselves, letting someone take the lead while the odd man out finds a way to contribute. Or watch, which is excellent too—watching and being watched, arousal rising en masse like the room temperature. I stare into that strategically placed mirror on their wall and nearly grin. *Look at you.*

Then, one night, Sabrina knocks on my door while I'm reading in bed. Nathan has been working in his office all evening, so I figured we were taking the night off.

"Did you bring me another section of your book?" I fling aside the paperback I filched from her library.

"Not exactly. I'm still figuring out the middle." Her glossy kimono yawns open when she sits on the bed. She squeezes my foot where it lumps beneath the comforter, and I giggle.

"What's up?" I say softly.

She leans forward in lieu of answering, and our lips touch, and she tangles her fingers in my hair and pulls me closer and it's still sweet and soft and new, yet so familiar, so right.

I pull away. "What about Nathan?"

She sits back, confused. "What about him?"

"Is it really okay for it to just be us?"

She laughs kindly. "Of course it's fine. It wouldn't be practical to, like, exclusively have threesomes."

She kisses me again and she's right, fair point, but apprehension still swims in my head: Did everyone know this rule but me? Is this how things went with their ex? Does it mean . . . have they continued to have sex without me?

"Relax," she whispers, stroking my neck.

But I'm nervous. Sprawled on my bed, making out like teenagers on the soft duvet, I feel the doubts creep in: *Can I really do this?* It's so different from a threesome, where I can let Nathan take charge. How did this work with their ex? Will I be bumbling and incompetent in comparison?

Looking back on it now, I realize I've had crushes on women as well as men—all the way back to high school, really—but I always added an adjective: *friend* crush, *work* crush, *talent* crush. Spacers that neutered the attraction before I could examine it through my own heteronormative lens. There was one Juna colleague I loved being around in a way I couldn't really explain, but I chalked it up to her (and her wife) being exceptionally hip. Now that I think about it, the clues were all there—but I dismissed them, cozy in my assumed straightness.

Virgo hops on the bed, sauntering over my calves with her usual nonchalance, and we both laugh.

"You're so tense." Sabrina drags her fingertips down my arms.

I roll off of her. Through the window, the moon winks down at me. "Sorry. It's just . . . you're the first woman I've had sex with, period." Again, I picture her with their former lover, the gorgeous blonde who sucked them out of their monogamy.

Her eyebrows lift. "Well, then I'm lucky you're so good in bed."

I chuckle. "I really want to be good. For you."

"The thing is . . ." She looks away, thinking. "It's not about technique, right? It's about paying attention and being generous and, like, noticing what the other person likes." She settles a hand on my hip. "And in that sense, you're excellent. You care, and what else could anyone want in a lover?"

I worry, still, that Nathan will feel jealous or left out—sulky from neglect. But maybe that's projection, my own insecurities left over from a monogamous past. And my anxiety slips away as I focus, as I drop into my senses, until nothing matters but what's happening in that soft-lit spare room.

A few nights later, I find myself alone with Nathan. He kisses me on the screen porch and pulls me onto his lap, and when he stands, lifting us both, I laugh against his lips.

"Should we get Sabrina?" I ask.

"Naw. I want you all to myself."

I let go of his shoulders and slip my feet back onto the ground. "She won't . . . I mean, are you going to tell her? Did she tell you that . . . the other night . . ."

He looks amused. "I mean, we're not giving each other blow-by-blows. But I assume you two have your own thing going on." He kisses my ear.

"You're right. Sorry I'm being weird." I sweep my hand through his hair. "I don't know why I'm asking about ground rules. I just . . . don't want to do anything wrong."

"Relax." His whisper sends sparks down my spine. "There's no playbook. We're feeling it out."

"So to speak," I add, a classic Nathan joke, and he responds by tickling me and tossing me onto the wicker sofa.

When it's only us, he pushes me, dilating my comfort zone. He tugs my hair and bites my neck and I grin through each gasp, trying to mirror his urgency. I think of the Polaroids, of their ex like a pawn in their arms, and feel a rush of heat.

Then, abruptly, he moves his fingers. Now he's touching me more deeply and it's like a key change, major to minor, the feeling sharp and taut and high-pitched.

"Hey." My voice is mostly air.

He moves faster. I reach for his hand.

"Should I stop?" he asks. The sensation is neon and frenzied and I like it but I don't, did I even know I had a G-spot?

"Don't stop," I pant. Nathan doubles down and it's like a river rushing toward a waterfall faster and faster and I'm not sure I like it but—

I explode, knees and hips bucking, gasping for air. He watches, pleased. It takes a moment for my brain to clear, like it's a shaken-up snow globe.

"That was . . ." I murmur into his neck. *Weird. Intense. A little scary.*

"That was gorgeous," he supplies. Definitively. He kisses my neck and stands. I lie still and stare at the ceiling, still shuddering.

After a few more times, I come to appreciate it: how in bed, Nathan is animalistic and in charge. He leans in to growl compliments that make me gasp and clutch him close: *You looked so hot in that sundress* or *God, I love watching you in the pool* or, once, *I have never wanted someone as bad as I want you.* Logically I assume he directs this kind of dirty talk Sabrina's way, too, and Taylor's back in the day. But, oh, it works.

I do wonder about the ex. They never mention her—too painful, I guess. I google for a missing woman who fits the vague description, but it turns out, nationwide, thousands of people disappear every *day*. In a bizarre way, this soothes me. It's mere coincidence their lives intersected with one of these missing-persons reports.

I owe this woman a debt of gratitude: She paved the way for the Lamonts to invite me into their marriage. I don't want to be a paranoid new girlfriend, digging in the past, comparing and contrasting herself with her lovers' last partner.

That was the old Kelly. And I don't miss her at all.

CHAPTER TWENTY-SIX

’m at the dining table when it hits: an email from Mike, [no subject].

My gut pretzels while cold washes through my lungs. I race to open it, both wanting and not wanting to know what it says.

Hi Kelly,

I'm not sure how to start this . . . I feel like a well-heeled gentle-man writing a letter like it's the 1800s. Did you see the NYT article about how letter-writing is up during the pandemic be-cause we all have too much time on our hands? I guess we're living in a Jane Austen novel . . . these days I look forward to my brisk afternoon walk.

I can't stop thinking about you. I'll come right out and say it . . . I miss you. Looking back on all we had and all we've been through, I see I made a mistake. I'm a much better man with you by my side. Who's going to remind me when to use lie and lay? Who's going to hug me tight and tell me everything is

going to be okay when shit gets dark? Who's going to follow
me down the wrong trail on a hike in Costa Rica and still have
me laughing? There's no one else I'd rather be lost with than
you.

It's not too late . . . we can still do this. Forget the wedding, we
can go to the courthouse whenever you want . . . or have the
wedding of your dreams when everyone can get together . . .
I'll do whatever you want because I still want to have adven-
tures with you. You're my Kell-Bell and I'll always love you.

Love,
Mike

I'm bawling by the time I get to the end. It's all there, everything I
wanted: self-reflection, an admission that he screwed up, even a promise to make the wedding happen, now or later. My stomach twists. *We
could still do this.* Call the farmhouse venue in Grayslake, email our
guests, re-up our vendors. Make it like the recent past never happened.

But—but I don't want to wipe out the last few weeks. My heart
buckles, heavy and stiff. Poor Mike, alone in that shadowy apartment.
Doubting himself, replaying all our memories. Hurting. I should be
there for him. I push back from the table, then rocket up the stairs.

At the top, I pause—I was going to run into my room, but the light's
on in Sabrina's office. I hesitate a second longer, like a squirrel in the
road, then rush down the hall.

My knock pops the door open and I lock eyes with her. She's
crouched over her desk, wide-eyed, like I've caught her red-handed.
She shoves what looks like a stack of notecards into the desk's lowest
drawer, then swivels her wrist to lock it. The hairs on my scalp prickle—
I know that locked drawer well. What's she stuffing inside?

"Oh no." She clocks the tear tracks on my cheeks. "What is it? Come
here."

I step into her arms. She strokes my hair, then shuffles us onto the
purple couch.

"It's Mike." I reach for my phone. "Here."

She reads it with her lips drawn, her eyes sliding back and forth like a ventriloquist dummy's.

Finally she leans back. "Ah, yes. The 'so, listen' email."

"What?"

"I've gotten it after breakups too. And—I could be wrong, I don't know Mike—but in my experience, it's more about aversion to bad feelings than genuinely reconsidering." She hands the phone back to me. "Breaking up is awful, and a lot of people—maybe men in particular—have a knee-jerk reaction: *The way to make the bad feelings go away is to undo whatever's causing it.* Instead of sitting with the hurt. You know?"

"You think that's it?" I don't mean to sound defensive, but . . . ouch. She doesn't even *know* Mike. Who is she to decide if he's genuine or not?

"I do. But grief is normal, right?" She smiles kindly. "You were together for *years*. The relationship mattered."

"It did." I let out a hiccupy sigh, then look up. "I really thought Mike and I were on the same page. That it was mutual."

"This email doesn't mean it wasn't mutual. Or that it wasn't the right call. He's just floundering." Her arm slings across my back. "And actually, this is . . . never mind."

"What?"

She swallows. "No, it's not my place to say."

"*What?*"

Her shoulders slump. "His email . . . I don't know, if I were you, I'd be kinda annoyed. For one thing, he didn't apologize. And for another, everything he says he misses . . . it's like, ways you took care of him."

"What are you talking about? He apologized." I swipe at my phone, befuddled, then wilt. "Okay, he said he made a mistake."

Her eyes flash. "A mistake is buying the wrong kind of nut milk. What he did . . ." She shakes her head and there's a beauty to her anger, indignation glinting like light on a shield. "I'm just saying—you have every right to be hurt by what he did."

But then I look away, because she doesn't know how I destroyed his office—how *I* set everything in motion. "*He's* the one hurting," I say. "I didn't ask for this. I wasn't trying to, like, punish him for 'pumping the brakes.'" My fingers claw into air quotes.

She rubs my shoulder. "I know. You're not like that. I'm sure it's hard to see him in pain." She sighs. "But, I dunno. It seems a little . . . manipulative. Like he's calling all the shots. Oh, *now* you want Kelly back, now that you don't know whether to use *lie* or *lay*."

Mike, who couldn't find the laundry detergent. Mike, who was never great at handling his own hurt. My heart rate zooms as the realization buoys up, pushing over the horizon like the sun at dawn. She's . . . she's *right*. And with that lens in place, everything he's said . . . everything he's *done* . . .

"I mean, hell, he let me move across the country for him and then called off the wedding." I blink at her. "Unilaterally, without talking to me. Knowing full well that I didn't know anyone in Philly." I continue the diatribe silently: *And when I messed up, he didn't even stand by me.* And now he's changed his mind, so he expects me to, what . . . drop everything and skip back to Philadelphia for him?

Her head bobs. "Totally. Not to mention: Not letting you tell people about your pain so that you could get some support. I mean, if you hadn't blurted it out to me . . ."

"You're right. You're so right. God, even sending this email after we agreed not to talk . . . it's not fair." My heart whacks against my ribs. "And now I'm pissed. Should I call him? Or not respond?"

She considers for a second. "Let's get Nathan's opinion. He's our resident straight man."

It strikes me as she rises and knocks on his office door—my secret lovers are giving me advice for dealing with an ex. Unprecedented times, indeed.

They shuffle in together, and Sabrina prompts: "Kelly, show him."

He reads the email, scratching his beard, then sighs. "Goddammit, Mike. Poor dude is *struggling*."

The fury thaws a bit. I do care about Mike—I can't help it, I've cared about him for so long it's encoded in my DNA now—and I hate when people in my orbit are suffering. "I know. And I'm annoyed with him, but I also don't like the thought of him alone and spinning out."

"Of course. Because you're a sweetheart." He plonks down next to me. I squeeze his arm gratefully—it was kind of him to react with empathy, labeling Mike *struggling* and not *an asshole*. Any guy who can successfully juggle being with two women must be high in emotional intelligence.

"What should I do?"

He squeezes my knee. "If I were him, I'd want a reply even if it's not what I hoped to hear. He's gotta be glued to his phone right now."

"Good point," Sabrina murmurs.

My stomach folds this way and that, twisting like a fortune cookie. "So how should I respond?"

"With clear boundaries," she says. "Get your laptop. We'll send it together."

Hi Mike,

Thanks for being honest with me about your feelings. I care about you so much, but I don't see our breakup as a mistake. I know it's hard right now, and it's hard for me too, but I really think the best thing is for us to not talk to each other for a while. I hope you're getting a lot of support. You'll get through this.

Kelly

My anger has fully melted into a puddle of sadness by the time I hit Send. I thank Sabrina as fresh tears begin to fall, and she pulls me to her.

"It's just . . . it's hard, seeing him like this." I wipe my nose. "And— and what you pointed out, how controlling he was. It's really upsetting to think about too."

"Of course." She squeezes my hand. "I don't know if this'll help, but I, for one, am furious at him. I want to cut off his balls and slap him in the face with them." She mimes it, flailing her fist near my head, until I laugh.

"Thanks. That does help."

"Good. Because I mean it."

"She's right!" Nathan calls. "Anyone who messes with our partner messes with us."

There's a beat—*partner*, he said *partner*, and does he simply mean *sexual partner* or . . . ?

"One of my favorite things about you is your complete lack of a poker face." Sabrina kisses my temple. "You're giving deer-in-the-headlights. Is it because Nathan called you our partner?"

I nod stupidly. "I didn't want to assume, but . . ."

"Who are we kidding?" Nathan throws open his arms. "It's pretty obvious what we're doing, right?"

"A . . . a throuple?" I cringe—though the characters use the term in *Elite Deviance*, it sounds silly when I say it.

"Yes!" Sabrina clutches my hand. "An adult relationship. All equal partners."

"Featuring the two most beautiful women I've ever seen," Nathan adds.

They grin and I grin and we all three burst out laughing.

CHAPTER TWENTY-SEVEN

"You seem . . . fine."

It sounds like an accusation. I turn my face up to the stippled sunlight.

"I told you, Amy. It's rough, but . . . it's kind of a relief. Some part of me saw this coming."

"*Really?*" She catches herself. "Sorry. I'm just . . . surprised. Last month, all you wanted was to get Mike back. And now it's been, like, two seconds since you guys called off your wedding, and you sound happier than ever. Happier than *me*."

Is that what this is about? "Amy, talk to me! Are you going bananas at home? You don't need to hide it because you think I'm fragile right now." The wind shakes a maple bough overhead, sending winged seeds pirouetting.

"Shoot," she replies. "I didn't mean to make it all about me . . ."

Stalemate: She can't grouse about being trapped with her family to a fresh-off-a-breakup friend. I can't divulge the *real* reason for the pep in my step. We've been circling each other for twenty minutes as I wandered the neighborhood. Now all I want is to hang up and rush home.

Calls with Amy feel flatlined, a mottled gray-brown—nothing interesting or vulnerable or weird, just two old friends skimming the surface. And the beigeness of our calls throws into stark contrast how colorful this morning felt with Sabrina and Nathan—the fluorescent jolt of watching Sabrina dive into the pool and then surface, smoothing her wet hair; the silly yellow lunch break when Nathan monkeyed around on his ukulele.

I'm not stupid—I see the many potholes ahead, feel a clench in my chest whenever I think about Down the Road. And it's uncomfortable, lying (even by omission) to Amy. But Nathan still wants us to keep our relationship under wraps, and I get it; taking this relationship public would lead to some serious fallout. I picture my parents, gobsmacked and horrified; my Chicago friends, smiling and blinking before lighting up a text thread, one I'm not part of: *WTF???* Even my most progressive friends would be thrown by this.

And who could blame them?

I was the envy of all as Mike's doting partner. He was the total package, and I was a catch—*American Gothic,* explicable and well matched. The future I'd painted for us visible in the background: house, minivan, chubby babies. My stomach cramps. I'm not ready to confront those feelings yet, what being in this new relationship means for my stated desire to be a mom. Society's expectations or my dreams? Can you really disentangle them enough to say for sure?

I step off the curb, hooking left past an empty playground. Amy and I say our goodbyes, *loveyoumissyou* by rote, and I sever my connection to that drab, far-off Elsewhere.

Nathan's in the kitchen gazing at an iPad, oversized headphones pinning down his hair. He slams the screen facedown on the counter as soon as he notices me, then pulls down his headphones.

I try to be nonchalant as I cross to the fridge. "Have you seen Sabrina today? I might cook these frozen scallops tonight."

He laugh-snorts. "She's having trouble with her book, so she did the thing where she smokes pot to relax but ends up more anxious. I had to bring her cereal and close her in a room." He waves his hand. "Anyway, we both love scallops."

I feel an internal beep of jealousy: I can't possibly access their shorthand and institutional knowledge. Though they both strive to make me feel special, we're not in an equitable relationship, not really. They share a deed, a life—a last name.

I pull the scallops from the freezer and notice the mess I left last night: cabinet doors open, last night's plates scabby in the sink. My ribs tighten—how did I miss this? Sabrina likes the house impeccably clean, and I've been trying to keep it that way. Which is not my natural state; Mike and I would let things get bad and then blast nineties pop and have a cleaning party. Once, we wound up in a dance-off, whooping at each other's moves.

Aww. That was a good moment. For a second, I miss him. And *it*, the ease of a "normal," sanctioned relationship that made everybody comfortable.

Not to mention: one I didn't step into *years* after the other players.

On autopilot, I reach under the kitchen sink for cleaning spray, then catch myself and fetch it from the mudroom. When will this house truly feel like home?

"Thanks for doing that," Nathan calls as I spritz the counters. He and Sabrina have consistent reactions whenever I do a chore: Nathan thanks me and Sabrina insists I don't need to do it, *No, really, please don't feel like you must*. Socialization, I guess: Girls learn to never make someone feel put-out; boys learn others are there to serve them.

"No problem." I clunk open the dishwasher. "Maybe you can get me a French maid outfit."

"Ooh. The sexy live-in help." He doesn't mean anything by it, but the discomfort intensifies.

Utensils clang as I rinse them in the sink. "Y'know, normally when someone moves in with a couple, there's a power differential, right? Like, a maid or governess or whatever."

He grimaces. "I didn't mean—"

"No, I know. It's just . . ." Can I really do it? Be this . . . vulnerable? "I'm worried I won't ever be on your level. You're a legal unit and I'm an add-on. I'm wondering how . . . with the last woman . . ." His face contorts with discomfort and my need to assuage it surfaces: "Sorry, I don't know what I'm going on about. But hey, feel free to think of me as your sexy governess. That's my favorite Gothic cliché. But it might raise some eyebrows since you, you know. Don't have children."

His elbow thuds onto the island. "Rina and I actually tried to get pregnant. Years ago. It took a while to get there—I wanted kids, she was less sure. But then we started trying, and . . . well, it didn't go well."

Whoa. Right after I moved in, while Sabrina and I swam around the darkened pool, she told me she never wanted children. Now I'm pulled in two directions: an urge to back away from this story, so intimate and not his alone to tell, but also desperate for him to keep going.

"What happened?" I finally ask.

His eyes squeeze shut. "Two miscarriages. One right after the other."

My gut drops like an elevator in a shaft. "I'm so sorry."

He's telling me stuff about Sabrina, things she herself hasn't brought up. This isn't fair to her . . . but I'm also desperate to hear more.

"I wanted to keep trying, but Rina was done. She wouldn't discuss it. Not even adoption."

I could give you a baby. The thought comes to me fully formed, knit together as if my brain were a womb. It's ridiculous—outrageously inappropriate.

But then another part of me sits up, indignant. *If we're truly in an equal relationship*, it points out, *I should be part of that decision too*.

"I'm sorry," I say again. Carefully: "I've always wanted a family. I definitely didn't think I'd be turning thirty-five without that piece in place."

He nods, then slips from the stool, as if he just realized he crossed a boundary. I feel a wave of sympathy for Sabrina—that she went through that, her own body growing and then rejecting a bundle of potential deep inside, not once but twice.

But also that she wasn't the one who told me. Now I know this without her consent.

"Well, we can talk about that later," he says, patting my knee as he passes. "I'll get to work on that French maid outfit."

He starts to turn around, and hope blossoms—will he continue the conversation? But then he snaps up his iPad and saunters away.

I lean against the counter, feeling the dishwasher's hum. Was that unsupportive of me, gossiping about Sabrina with her husband?

I have no idea how to navigate this. But I already feel like I've screwed up.

CHAPTER TWENTY-EIGHT

Megan's smile is so genuine, so expectant, that I might scream.

She taps a nail against her Millennial-pink mug and tilts her head, waiting. She's asked me something.

I have no idea what.

"Say that again?" She *very nicely* invited me out for a coffee, and I *very rudely* blew her off for a couple weeks, and now we're on a patio and it's too warm to be drinking hot coffee and when I'm away from them all I can think about is Nathan and Sabrina, an addiction, *sabrina-nathan-sabrina-nathan.*

"I asked how your family's doing! In Illinois."

"Good memory!" I blink. "They're good. They were already home-bodies, so they're doing fine." I shake my head. "Sorry, I'm being spacy again."

"Is it the breakup?" She makes a sympathetic face. "I couldn't concentrate on anything for *months* after mine. And not just because it actively blew up my life."

"It could be the breakup, yeah." I take a breath; I can do this—I can open up to Megan. "It's so strange. Saying goodbye to everything I thought I wanted. I could see the future so clearly: white wedding, two-point-five kids. And now I'm . . . rejiggering my life plans."

"I get that. My ex and I were crazy in love for a while. I never thought it would end the way it did." She shakes her head. "I'm almost glad it crashed and burned so spectacularly—there's no room for wanting to get back together or wondering if it was the right decision."

"Same. I mean, different circumstances." We both laugh, and this is better; we're connecting. "But I know it was the right thing."

"So, Kelly." She leans forward conspiratorially. "What do you want now? What's next?"

That's easy: Nathan and Sabrina. I want them near me, next to me, on top of me.

"Not sure yet." My heart pounds. I take a sip and coffee burns my tongue.

"Fair." She leans back. "Well, you seem to be holding it together. I can't believe you're only a few weeks out from the official breakup. What's your secret?"

My stomach twists. "I guess it's the support I'm getting from my hosts." I sound like a robot.

A warm smile. "What are they like?"

Gorgeous. Smart. Unbelievably good in bed. My chest sinks—this is exactly what I was afraid of. She's confiding in me and I'm lying through my teeth. Because all I *want* to talk about is how damn happy I am; how I'm falling, hard and fast.

"They're both awesome. As far as lockdown setups go, I hit the jackpot." And then it pops out of me, something we could casually promise in pre-pandemic life: "You'd love them—maybe we can all hang out sometime."

Her eyes brighten. "I'd love to come over! I'm dying to see the inside of that beautiful house."

Shoot. I gulp. "Thing is, they're not super comfortable with me having guests."

"Ah." She's unbothered. "Well, maybe we can hang out there when they're not around."

"Maybe? They kinda never leave." This conversation is giving me seventh-grade vibes and I'm not sure how to fix it: *Mom says you can't come over after school.* "Sorry, I don't mean to be rude. But I'm so glad we're getting together again." I smile and she smiles and it's like I've lost all my social skills—I can't think of a single thing to say.

Megan changes the subject, but I can feel it, how I'm the worst coffee date of all time, carefully weighing my words before talking about this, my Summer of Secret Love, the "roommates" I fear I'll out. She keeps the energy up, joking and chattering, but I'm sure she can tell I'm being evasive—I *am* hiding something, the thing that's most important to me.

She's ready to walk back into Tanglewood together, but I say I need to use the restroom on the way out. She doesn't mind waiting, but I insist as the awkwardness crests and finally hurt flickers in her eyes and *ugh,* I suck. She heads out and I let ten minutes pass, watching the clock as heaviness seeps through my limbs. *Bummer.* Turns out my fears were founded: For now, anyway, I'm not super capable of making new friends.

But as I walk back to the house, the grip in my chest eases. Even before the pandemic, Nathan and Sabrina were content without the company of their snooty neighbors. Maybe I was wrong about needing other friends in Deerbrook. Hey, we're *all* running in tinier circles than ever, hunkering down with our pods. It's like the pandemic has cinched in the drawstrings of our lives, and somehow I won the lottery: I get to isolate with my two favorite people.

I turn in to Tanglewood, push the code into the keypad. The gates slide open, welcoming me home.

I haven't put on makeup in a while and it feels foreign, tacky against my lashes and lips. Surprisingly, the break seems to have done my face good: My skin is clearer, my under-eye bags shrunken, freckles sprouting like dandelions on my nose and cheeks.

This relationship looks good on me.

"Daaamn," Nathan says when I find him strumming a guitar in the music room.

"Agreed." Sabrina struts in, resplendent in a flowy caftan. "Ready to go?"

I've joined them for grocery runs, but we've never gone to D.C., all three of us. As we drive past the gate, I feel a flare of anxiety: *Is this okay? Are we safe?*

I almost laugh. I used to travel the world, head to music festivals and hot-yoga classes, the air thronged with breath and sweat. Now I'm scared to leave a gated community.

A date! We're going on a real, live date. It feels a bit like taking the relationship public—though there'll be no PDA, Nathan reminds me—and I'm as giddy as a teenager on her way to prom.

In D.C., Nathan turns in to what looks like an abandoned lot—but no, it's a brewery, the taproom a weird paddock with red booths and pub tables propped crookedly in the dirt. The place has a cyberpunk feel: a fat sandbox with cracked plastic buckets, robot murals along the aluminum fence. Nathan approaches the "bar" (a long table with a lineup of kegs) and orders from a mustachioed man.

"I got the gose, the IPA, and the stout," he says a few minutes later, setting them on the table. "I figured we can share."

"My favorites!" Sabrina reaches for the darkest one.

"They didn't have a pilsner?" I ask. ". . . Not that these don't sound good."

Nathan is flabbergasted. "Do you want me to—"

"No, it's fine!" I grab a cup. "These are great. Thanks for getting 'em!"

"You're so easy," Sabrina says. "I love how you'll just go along with whatever."

I squint at her. I'd like to be laid-back and cool, *a pleasure to have in class*, but something about her phrasing feels weird. How did Mike put it? *I hope you didn't just go along with it because I said that.* Moving here, he meant. Aka the best decision ever.

A couple arches their backs over our table to let a family pass, and we pull away instinctively.

"It's weird being in public," Nathan observes.

Sabrina nods. "I wonder if we're on the verge of everything opening back up."

I catch the zigzagging fruit fly of discomfort I'm feeling, *aha:* Things opening up denotes an end to the pandemic . . . and what does that mean for our arrangement?

"Can I ask you something?" I say.

"Of course." Sabrina smiles, those perfect teeth lined up like soldiers.

My heart thuds. "Have you thought about what will happen when the pandemic ends?"

Nathan raises his eyebrows. "In general?"

"No—with us."

They glance at each other. I feel it like an electric shock, Milgram's punishment, the way they can communicate with their eyes.

Sabrina turns to me. "Of course it's crossed our minds. But since we have no idea when that'll happen, well . . . why not take it a week at a time?"

"I guess." I stare at my cup. "But it's gonna look weird if I stay here post-lockdown, right? Like, what adult woman randomly lives with a married couple?"

"The pandemic's changing all the rules." Sabrina waves her hand. "Everyone is looking at themselves like: My life doesn't have to be what I thought it was. So I wouldn't worry about that. We'll all come out of this quote-unquote 'weird.'"

"And anyway, no one can touch us here." Nathan swigs his beer. "I'll make sure of that."

I squeeze the cup in my hands. "So . . . is that the plan? We'll keep living together and pretend it's platonic?" My pulse picks up as I force it out: "Honestly, it's hard for me. Keeping it a secret? And I get it and I'm happy to do it, but . . ." I think of my stilted calls with Amy and the awkwardness of my coffee date with Megan. "I mean, how did you do it with your past partner?"

Their eyes meet again, *zap*. "She was fine with it." Nathan shrugs. "She agreed it was nobody's business but ours."

I picture her in the Polaroids, eyes piercing and fierce, slim shoulders squared. Of course she was chiller than me. Of course she didn't need external validation.

To my horror, tears fill my eyes. "I like you both a lot. I like *this*. And I wish we could shout it from the rooftops." An exhaust pipe pops in the parking lot and I jump. "Sorry, I didn't mean to get so . . . intense." *Needy. Clingy. Unable to trust.*

Sabrina touches my shoulder. "Maybe it'll change once Nathan gets another job. But for now, who cares about telling other people? We know what we've got is good."

I dab my leaky eyes and shake my head. "Whew! I'm fine. *We're* fine. No more double IPAs for me. Hey, let's get a selfie, yeah?"

They crowd around me, beaming as I take a few shots, then Nathan plants a kiss on my temple.

"Don't post that one," he barks. I sober up on the spot, like a finger snapping.

He clears his throat. "I mean, it's just for us."

"I wasn't going to post it—I'm not stupid."

Sabrina looks engrossed in her purple nails. I wrestle down the prickling irritation: He's simply being cautious. What kind of person snarls at their partner like that? "I'll delete it," I add, thumbing the garbage-can icon.

Sabrina stands and sets off for the bathroom and Nathan checks his work email. After a moment, I pull out my own phone.

And I gasp.

My beloved Kell-Bell,

I know we agreed not to talk for a bit, so I hope this is okay. It's hard for me not to talk to you when I'm used to hearing your voice throughout the day . . . I took it for granted. Last night on our call, Leigh told me the best gift I can give you is my honesty, so here goes: I made a horrible mistake, and I'm an idiot . . . you are my person and I'm just putting myself out there praying you'll want to give it one more shot.

Feel free to delete or ignore as you see fit. I don't deserve you, but I'll always love you.

Love,
Mike

CHAPTER TWENTY-NINE

My stomach quirks. "Nathan, look." I shove my phone under his nose and he squints to read it.

"Woof." He leans back. "Are you going to reply?"

"Should I?"

"Well, do you think he'll keep contacting you?"

"Maybe? Ugh, I don't know. I've never broken up with him before." My heart bangs. *You can be fierce, too, Kelly. You can set the terms.* "I kinda want to call him. Is that a terrible idea?"

He crosses his arms. "You know him best."

"Yeah, I want to get it out of the way." I slide ungracefully out of the booth, hands shaking, and head for an empty corner choked with weeds. My jaw locks up as I tap on Mike's name.

"Kelly?"

"Hi."

There's silence and, for a wild second, I think he's hung up. And then—a juddery groan, the sound of throat-clearing. He's been crying.

"Mike, it's okay."

"It's—it's not, though." I hear several Darth Vader breaths. "I keep thinking about what you said—how this was my idea. But, Kelly, I just needed a minute. You destroyed my office because you got this idea in your head, and then you expected me to be . . . fine. I didn't want to frolic around, replanning our wedding, while I was working on forgiving you."

I might throw up. "You told me this wasn't about your office." My voice shakes, accusatory. "You said that—"

"No, I *did* forgive you—I love you. And the problem wasn't you or us—it was the lockdown. All this time to *think*, it's not healthy. Of course you felt like I was pushing you away. But it was just me losing it and wanting to, to change things, to blow shit up."

Deep breath in, deep breath out. *It's not about the office,* I tell myself again. Two people letting go of the *fine* to make room for the *great*.

I sit on a low bench made from cinder blocks. "I hear that, but . . . isn't that kinda what you're doing now? Trying to change things instead of hitting Pause and, like, being honest with yourself?" When he doesn't answer, I force the words out: "Because I had some time to think too. And . . . I'm sorry, Mike, but I came to the opposite conclusion."

A loud, slow exhale. "That's it? After five years, that's it?"

I look up at the gloomy clouds. "I'm sorry. I know this sucks."

We're both quiet. A pigeon toddles toward me. I'm glad we're having this conversation over the phone. I don't miss the shaking arms and tomato-red face that accompany not getting his way.

"I just . . . I dunno, I don't think it's over," Mike says.

My irritation intensifies: He keeps doing this, not listening to me, not acknowledging that I'm part of this decision too. And now he's interrupting me on my *one* day out. And so the thought I've been pussy-footing around pops out of me: "I started seeing someone."

"What?"

Shit. The stupid impulsive gremlin's at it again; I promised Nathan and Sabrina I wouldn't say anything, and though I'm not naming names, that wasn't smart. But I have no choice but to lean into it now. "It's new, obviously, and I'm not telling people about it—Amy doesn't even know—but I really am moving on. And I want you to free yourself to do the same." And here I start to cry, picturing it. "I want you to meet your soulmate and be so goddamn happy everyone hates you a little bit."

He's crying too and now I wish we were together, I wish I could hold his callused hand.

Finally he swallows. "How did you even meet someone? Wait, you didn't start seeing them *before* we . . . ?"

My body grows cold. The line fizzes between us.

I know what he's asking: Did I cheat? Did I sleep with someone else before we'd officially called it quits?

"Kelly?"

What blares into my mind right then is Lara—an old friend from Chicago who never met her father. Her mother was vague about it: *He didn't want to be a dad, so he left.* It wasn't until Lara was in her twenties that her mom told her the truth: She learned she was pregnant *after* they'd broken up and decided not to tell him. He never wanted kids, so why bother? Essentially, she told her daughter the truth but switched the order of the pivotal events: the pregnancy and his departure.

And though I was horrified when Lara shared this, now I get it. I understand why her mother made that snip in her timeline. A reordering, like that CRISPR gene editing, lift and drop, an innocuous fib to justify her actions and make herself seem—

"Sorry," Mike says. "I don't know why I said that. I know you wouldn't do that."

So I let him draw his own conclusions. I keep things vague, like Lara's mom did. "I'm really sorry, Mike. I'm not trying to be hurtful. I . . . I want us both to heal." I listen to his muffled sobs. "Breathe, Mike. Take a deep breath with me."

His sigh makes the line sizzle. "I want you to be happy," he finally whispers.

An unbuckling sensation in my chest. This is what I wanted, of course, but hearing him let go for real is big and hard and bittersweet. Short, spastic breaths rock through me as I cry.

"Thanks, Mike," I manage. "You're talking to your sister? You're not going through this alone?"

"Yeah, Leigh's driving out this weekend."

"Good."

An ambulance shrieks past; I watch Sabrina and Nathan at our table, finishing our beers. I long to head back to them, but another part of me wants to stretch this out, our wistful farewell.

He sighs. "I guess this is goodbye, then."

"It is. Goodbye, Mike." I feel like I'm play-acting at being an adult, mature and evolved. And I remind myself of everything I had to convince Mike of: *Tough* isn't *bad*. *Uncomfortable* doesn't mean *wrong*. Like bodybuilders, we break ourselves down in order to grow.

"You're pretty fucking fantastic, Kelly."

And I laugh through the tears, feeling the invisible lead capelet floating off my shoulders. "You are too, Mike. You are too."

CHAPTER THIRTY

I'm in deep.

I skim around the house, pausing in sunbeams, basking in the UV rays and in the long days of us, "US" rays, Nathan and Sabrina, the suns that make me glow and grow.

It's symbiotic. The best kind of relationship, mutual and positive. Making all three of us happier, stronger, bigger, a triangle that keeps expanding. No more fretting about Mike or setting up a false juxtaposition, Mike versus the Lamonts, a bad-faith whataboutism. I loved him and I told myself we could be happy together, but it never felt anything like this.

It doesn't hurt that the sex is like nothing I've experienced before. They're both so good at taking charge in the bedroom . . . which makes perfect sense. Nathan is this brilliant paper-pusher with an enigmatic, high-powered job, and Sabrina is this effortlessly bossy badass who runs her household the way she runs her writing career: competently, without hesitation, getting everything exactly right. I read the next section of Sabrina's manuscript, in which the three team up in and out of the bedroom, and Arianna's inner monologue summarizes my feelings: *If everyone knew how good they could feel,* she thinks, *the world would be a different place.*

Well put, Arianna. Everything is . . . good. Suspiciously so.

And in the absence of bad things, my mind gets to work.

It zooms down to the level of a nanometer and zeroes in on a hair.

It's long and flaxen, draped precariously over the bathroom sink. I lift it, frowning. I hold it against my own part, confirming it's too long by six inches at least. And I feel it, the little demon deep in my brain, gleefully coming back to life.

It's hers. The woman they loved first.

The mystery woman.

No, the missing *woman.*

It's ludicrous, *not again*, and, while my heart thrashes and my fingers throb, I remind myself that if they're not thinking about her, I shouldn't either. It's just my annoying, high-strung brain.

I don't know when I first detected the gremlin, but I remember the moment I realized not everyone had such a devil on their shoulder, spewing fear. As a toddler, I heard about divorce and worried my parents would split. I learned about orphans and foundlings and abandoned, feral children and fretted that their fate would become mine.

No one wanted to hear about the gremlin, I learned. It made them uncomfortable. I stuffed the thoughts down and focused on seeming together, on excelling at school and pleasing teachers and coaches and it all seemed to be working until—

The college boyfriend, his cheeks pink: "We ended up making out, I think we should see other people."

And then Trey, a decade later: the Facebook message from his wife, "Just thought you should know." I'd collapsed to the floor in the kitchen, where Amy found me sobbing.

You know how serious food allergies get more intense with every exposure? It was like that, each betrayal turbocharging the distrust.

But I'm stronger now, emboldened by Sabrina's and Nathan's affection. So I talk back, pulling breaths into my belly: *It's just a hair. It means nothing. I trust them and like them and things are so good.*

Please don't do this again.

My heart wins out, my trust and tenderness toward these two people. I blow the hair off the sink.

When the unease resurfaces, I make up an errand to get me out of the house. The puff of cold air at CVS's sliding doors makes goosebumps spring up. Someone takes my temperature and dribbles slimy sanitizer onto my palm.

Supermarkets, corner stores, pharmacies—they're smack in the center of the Uncanny Valley, the Venn diagram of Before and During. At first glance, they look normal—anemic lights, wide aisles—but everything is . . . *off*. Lines on the floor separate those waiting at the registers; shoppers wear masks and wing suspicious glances at one another. Dead-eyed employees and plastic shields guard the toilet paper and Clorox wipes.

I'm about to check out when I feel it again: eyes on me, a sensation like the whine of a dentist's drill. I turn and see someone dart around the endcap, and I straighten up and march into the next aisle.

She pretends not to notice me, entranced by a rainbow of greeting cards.

"Hi, Diane."

Her eyebrows jump. "Oh! Good to see you, ah . . ."

"Kelly," I supply. Again.

"That's right. Stocking up on the essentials." She snatches up a card and studies it, then crams it back onto the rack. *Birthday, from couple.*

Irritation roars up like tinnitus: *enough*. "Listen, Diane, I don't mean to be rude," I begin—

"Then don't be."

I scoff-laugh. "I'm sorry?"

"Look, I don't know what you're doing in Tanglewood with *those* two." Her voice curls in disdain. "But I don't associate with them, and by extension, you."

A cold prickle slinks up my neck. This is far beyond snooty-neighbor or erotica-averse disdain—she acts like she has a *reason* to hate them. Details line up in my mind like the pins of a lock: The Lamonts moved to Deerbrook three years ago . . . maybe their ex visited them here before she went missing. And maybe Diane, queen of the busybodies, knows there's a link between her and them.

"What is your problem with the Lamonts?"

She crosses her arms. "I don't trust them."

"When we met, you made it sound like you didn't even know them."

"Exactly. I don't." She turns. "Now, if you'll excuse me . . ."

"Wait!" My heart pounds. "What can you tell me about—" I stop short. I almost said *their ex*. Guilt washes through me—I nearly spilled their secret. And if I can't trust myself . . . who *can* I trust?

She takes another step. "I *was* a fan of Sabrina." She's too close—way closer than six feet. "But that was before they moved here. They're liars, and if you haven't figured that out by now—well, you're either a sucker or you're just like them."

My ribs contract. "You have no idea what you're talking about." She *must* be referring to their ex. Did she see a woman coming in and out and get annoyed when they shut down her prying questions?

"Don't say I didn't warn you." She whirls around again, and something about the motion, awkward and shuffling, tickles my sense of déjà vu.

"Have you been creeping around their property?"

She freezes with her back to me. Finally her head swivels, too fast, like she's possessed. "What did you say?"

"Looking in. I saw someone out there. More than once." At least, I think I did.

"Are you calling me a pervert?"

A mother and daughter farther down the aisle glance our way. Doubt prickles my chest like pop rocks. This isn't like me, causing a scene.

"Sorry—that's not what I meant. I think I'm losing my social graces." I offer a bashful smile.

She narrows her eyes. "I'm not one to speak ill of other people." *Like hell you're not.* "But Sabrina and Nathan—they're nothing but trouble." She points a pudgy finger at my face. "And if you're not careful, you'll get wrapped up in it too."

I speed home, pulse whooshing in my ears, and scare the crap out of Virgo when I burst into the mudroom. She takes off, limbs akimbo.

Sabrina's on the pool deck, filling a notebook with her loopy cursive.

"I just had the weirdest run-in with Diane," I announce, dropping onto the chair next to hers.

She raises her sunglasses. "Not her again." She listens, an amused smile on her lips. When I've finished, she leans back, facing the sky. "Ohh, Diane. Every neighborhood has one."

"Why would she call you liars?"

She winces. "After our ex disappeared, the cops came around a couple times. Just following up with all her acquaintances." She clicks the pen in her hand. "Then right afterward, get this, Diane rang the doorbell and asked what that was all about. When we politely told her it was none of her business, she accused us of hiding something." She rolls her eyes. "She's the ultimate busybody."

Ahh, so it *was* about the ex. "You think that's what she meant? 'Trouble'?"

She settles her hands behind her head. "As you know, she also thinks I brought, like, *smuttiness* into the neighborhood. Lowering property values with my sex-positivity."

"But she's read your books."

She giggles. "That's the best part, right?"

Sabrina suggests I change into a suit, and I let it go, tying the strings of my bikini and then plucking a sun hat from the mudroom. I dive into the deep end, then watch as Sabrina steps out of her coverup and sweeps her hair into a ponytail. God, I love looking at her. I think I love *them*, though I couldn't say so, not when it's only been a few weeks. But it rockets out of me, a liking so intense it could power the Eastern Seaboard.

Nathan seals himself in his office that night, so Sabrina visits me in my room, nuzzling my neck and kissing my temple, my collarbone, my belly. When she's done, I try to return the favor, but after seeming close for an uncomfortably long time, she touches my cheek.

"What's wrong?" I ask, feeling like a failure.

"It's not you, I promise," she says. "I'm just . . . in my head tonight."

"You're sure?" I know I shouldn't take it personally. I've been in her shoes plenty of times.

"Completely. Come here, please." I climb up next to her, and in the softness of her cuddle, the smell of her shampoo and warmth of her arms, I relax. *This is good.*

CHAPTER THIRTY-ONE

One evening I follow Nathan and Sabrina into their room and ask, coyly, if we'd all fit inside their tub. We haven't hooked up in their bathroom yet, even though sex was all I could see when I first laid eyes on that egglike bath and broad granite shower. They exchange a quick glance, weighing.

"I'm not sure it's big enough for three," Sabrina admits.

"You two can use it," Nathan says, all magnanimous. "I'll bring up some champagne. I have a bit more work to do before bed."

Bubbles form a blanket of foam as the tub fills. Sabrina steps in first, then rests her head against the ceramic ledge. I settle on the opposite end. My foot nestles against her waist and she massages the arch. *Mmmm.* I read somewhere that baths evoke early, pleasurable stages in the womb.

I think it again, defiant: *So what if Nathan and Sabrina are my everything?* Megan texted me again today, inviting me along on a run, but I demurred. I feel bad—I'm sure she's lonely—but she doesn't need the kind of friend who ducks questions and lies by omission anyway.

Nathan appears, smiling, with two glasses of fizzy champagne. He shuts the door behind him and Sabrina takes a deep sip.

She's quiet tonight. It's as if ennui is wafting off of her, a deep, unsettling hum.

"Is something wrong?" I rest my arms on the tub's edge.

A long sigh. Finally: "It's not anything you've done, if that's what you're worried about."

Well, I wasn't until you said that. "With Nathan, then? Not that it's any of my business." I think back to the things I shouldn't know—how Sabrina saw Nathan bloody a doxxer, how Nathan wanted kids but Sabrina's womb wouldn't allow it. That tense argument I overheard from the basement stairs. I wonder what else they keep from me, what they say in the darkness.

She sets her glass on the floor. "I'm worried he prefers you." She chokes out a single, mirthless laugh. "Okay? I'm not proud of it. I don't think of myself as a jealous person. But . . ."

I stare, shock coursing through me. She's . . . hell, she's *Sabrina Lamont*. Objectively spectacular, the best of the best.

"No way. You know how devoted he is." As the words tumble out, I worry they're all wrong. "I'm—I'm sure it's just a novelty thing."

She shrugs. "It's not your fault. But I know what I see. We've been married for quite some time."

"I know that," I say, too quickly. I want to comfort her, but is she asserting her dominance, reminding me she's the OG?

I splash my hand into the water and sit up. "I'm sorry you feel that way. I want this to work." I lean forward, hitting my stride as a caring, supportive partner. "This is real. I love being in a relationship with you two. What do you need?"

She plays with a handful of bubbles. "I shouldn't have brought it up. It's my own insecurity, I suppose. After . . ."

She's quiet long enough that I can't help myself: "After your last partner?" Did they ever take baths in here together? Feel the slickness of wet skin?

Sabrina's cheeks redden. "It was . . . different. With you, we're all three in balance. Which is *good*. But the last time . . . Nathan doesn't know that, well . . . ." Her eyes widen, opening a portal to this secret.

My pulse canters. "What is it?"

"She floated the idea of being together," she says. "Her and me.

Leaving Nathan. And I couldn't, of course—that was totally counter to what we were trying to do, you know? And we never talked about it again, but . . . how do I put this? I'm gonna sound like an egomaniac, but." She sinks lower. "It was easy to feel secure when I was the belle of the ball. And now I see you and Nathan together. You're so, I don't know, *effortless*." She wipes away a tear.

"Oh my God," I murmur. "And Nathan has no idea?"

Her eyes widen. "Not at all—and please, please don't tell him. It would really hurt him."

"Of course."

She tips her head back. "So if I struggle with jealousy sometimes, that's why. Or if I worry you and Nathan are going to kick me out, well . . ." She laughs again, harder. "I'll shut up now."

My heart crumples. *She* feels like the outsider? The thought fills me with gooey tenderness. "Aw, Sabrina. We're not going anywhere."

She lets out a snotty laugh. "Well, not *now*. There's a global pandemic."

We both chuckle, letting the tension break. I still can't believe it—she's worried Nathan prefers *me*? My ego's bubbling like the fizzy froth on our bath.

I drain my champagne flute. "Do you think we all three should talk about it?"

"No, no." She shakes her head. "I shouldn't have mentioned it. Please don't say anything to Nathan, okay?"

I want to—I want to sit him down and tell him we need to make sure she feels included. But if I were her, I'd make the same request. "I won't say a word."

"Thank you." Relief washes through her. "And thanks for listening." She sits up and crawls forward to kiss me.

"Of course. I'm glad you told me."

She sits back with a splash. "I *like* that Nathan is so into you. It's part of why this works." Her eyebrows flash. "It's fun for me to watch you drive him wild."

"Oh yeah?"

"Mm-hmm." She stands, foam clinging to her skin. "Should we get out? I'm getting hot."

I pull the plug as she wraps herself in a towel, and then I grin. "Why don't we go in the hot tub? Since we're already wet."

Sabrina knocks on Nathan's office door as we pass, and we leave footprints on the stairs and through the screen porch. Outside, the crickets and katydids chitter so loudly, I could swear the air is vibrating. Nathan yanks off the Jacuzzi's lid and I step inside first. Nathan sits next to and above me on the tub's edge.

It's a breezy night, and a full moon casts silvery shadows. We chat as the water fizzes and swirls, bubbles eddying like clouds in those far-off pictures of the Earth. I observe Sabrina and Nathan together, our conversation echoing in my mind, but I don't see it—any evidence of the favoritism she observed.

After a while, Sabrina slides onto the bench next to me and we're kissing, hands moving slowly, Nathan's fingers finding the nape of my neck. When I lean back Sabrina nudges Nathan's knees apart. He stands on the bench and disrobes, and when he sits back down on the ledge, his hand returns to the back of my head, beckoning me closer.

My eyes flash to Sabrina—isn't this what she was talking about? *She* lays the groundwork, but he wants *me* on my knees. But when we lock eyes, she nods and gives me an encouraging smile. So I turn and she slides her hand around my waist as I kneel on the bench, and I lower my head, water bubbling at my chin.

Nathan's breath goes juddery. Sabrina's hands slip around me in the water, teasing, touching, and steam and pleasure flush my cheeks. Nathan's fingers tighten and pull my head closer, and I love doing this, I'm good at it, he slides his hips forward and—

The sound hits me first: the crash of a breaker hitting the beach, water and bubbles swirling and churning. A rush of unexpected heat.

It's all so abrupt it takes me a second to realize what's going on. But by then, it's too late.

Nathan's holding my mouth and nose beneath the surface.

And I can't breathe.

I try to lift my head, but his fingers tighten around the back of my head. I feel them pressed into my scalp, ten taut nooses.

I yank backward, desperate, but there's nowhere to go with Sabrina behind me, firm against my shoulder blades. As I shove my back against her, her arms lock around my waist.

Bubbles shriek in my ears, and hot Jacuzzi water, sharp as acid, shoots into my nostrils. Adrenaline barrels through my limbs as my lungs start to burn, and I try to cough, to scream, but no matter what I do my body just keeps inhaling more water. My brain cues the alarm, flashing blue and red and a high-pitched siren, *I need air I need air I need air*. All I feel is water burning through my skull and catching in my throat, foamy as a washing machine. My eyes spring open but I can only see the wild rush of bubbles and, beyond them, my own bare feet, toes curling in fear as chlorine burns my corneas.

Nathan forces himself deeper, he's crossed the threshold and I can feel him quivering in that animal way and behind me Sabrina squeezes me harder, pushing her weight against my back, pinning me in place, her pawn.

And suddenly, it's all very, very clear, a neon bolt of lucidity streaking through my water-logged skull.

He's not going to stop. He won't let me breathe.

I'm going to pass out.

And then I'm going to drown.

CHAPTER THIRTY-TWO

Nathan cries out and his fingers spring open and I twist away, staggering to the other end of the hot tub. My cough grows deeper and deeper until it's that foghorn sound, a monster's call.

"Do you want me to get you some water?" Sabrina finally asks.

I'm coughing so hard I'm crying, sweat and snot and hot tub water all pouring out of me. Nathan reaches for me but I recoil from his touch. A wringing sensation roots deep in my stomach, then rises and rises until I lean over the side of the tub and retch up a small, clear stream.

"Oh my God." Sabrina sets a tentative hand on my back.

I whirl around to glare at them. "What the *fuck*?"

A bewildered look flickers between them, which infuriates me more.

"Are you kidding me? Neither of you had any idea I was *drowning*?"

Sabrina holds her hand out. "Kelly, relax."

"*Don't tell me to relax.*" Another coughing squall rocks through me, harsh and low. "You pushed my head under. And you"—I snap my head toward Sabrina—"were squeezing me so tight I couldn't step back."

Nathan gives his head a horsey shake. "I didn't push your head under."

"Are you okay?" Sabrina cuts in, shooting him a warning look. "Kelly, look at me. Are you hurt?"

"I'm—I could have died." I hate that I'm still crying. I shake my head and stand up straight, because I want them to see my anger, dammit, not that I'm sad or scared.

"But you didn't!" Nathan hurls back.

"I couldn't breathe!"

"*Enough.*" Sabrina splashes between us, throwing her hands out like Moses parting the Red Sea. "Everybody calm down. Kelly, I know you're freaked out, and I think we should get you inside and dressed. And Nathan—"

"No!" My fists plow into the water. "You do not get to act like this is some dumb recess scuffle where we're both at fault."

"Not at all." Her voice is lower, soothing, that Cate Blanchett purr. She touches my shoulder and, just the tiniest bit, I relax. "That must've been awful. It should not have happened and I'm so sorry you felt like I was trapping you." She peers at me, her eye contact relentless, and finally I nod at the water.

"As for you." She swings around to face Nathan. He looks wilted and sheepish and helpless, like a flaccid dick. "You owe Kelly an apology."

His breath is quick, his mouth a downturned curve.

"I didn't mean to," he finally says.

I cross my arms as Sabrina groans.

"Okay, fine." He lifts both palms in surrender. "I'm sorry. I am. I had absolutely no idea."

"That's the problem," I snap.

"That can't happen again." Sabrina stands taller, facing him. "Nathan, look at me. You have to be careful. You can't get carried away." His face falls as she leans closer, almost hissing. "That. Can't. Happen. Again."

They're both frozen, two statues, and her words roll around my head. Her modulation—its syncopated rhythm follows me as I climb out of the tub with all the dignity I can muster. It echoes as I yank my towel from the lounge chair and stomp inside, water pattering, and as I pause in front of the wine cellar, glaring at the beehive of dusty bottles while I secure the towel around my waist.

I didn't hear it. I felt it. The meaning of her last word.

You have to be careful. You can't get carried away. That can't happen . . . again.

I lie in bed and wrestle down the thought. I'm being stupid—obsessing over Sabrina's inflection, reading way too far into Nathan's idiotic but accidental head-dunk. Aren't men's heads empty when they . . . ? I read that somewhere, ancient religions using sex to find meaning. To find God.

Me, I'm finding shapes in the clouds that were never really here. Sabrina didn't mean *again*-again. There wasn't some earlier incident they don't speak of. Nathan hasn't gotten carried away before with her or . . . or with any past partner . . .

I resolve to ask Nathan in the morning, but in the kitchen he's quiet, still sulky from last night. *Well, screw you too.* Sabrina, luckily, seems cheerful, swanning around the downstairs in one of her pretty kimonos. I wait until we're alone in the breakfast nook to bring it up.

"Can I ask you a question?"

"Of course." She looks up from her phone.

"Last night—I know it was an accident, obviously."

Her eyes darken. "Of course. Are you feeling better about it? It was such an in-the-moment thing."

"I know. I was wondering . . ." I wrap both hands around my coffee mug. "Has anything like that ever happened before?"

She stares at me for a second, eyebrows knitted, then breaks into a calm smile. "Of course not. And it won't happen again."

"Okay." I feel foolish—what did I expect her to say? "Well, hopefully we can all move past this."

"Definitely. Was Nathan still pouting this morning?" When I nod, she rolls her eyes and touches my hand. "It's over. I promise. There's nothing but good vibes here."

I meet her eyes and nod vigorously. Of course she's right.

I can't move my arm.

The realization jerks me awake, confused panic morphing into pins and needles as I roll off my shoulder. Nathan and Sabrina are asleep beside me, their chests moving gently. Beyond the open windows, the sun is rising, and peachy light blankets them both. I feel a bud of tenderness at the sight. In the dawn glow, when Nathan looks cute and boyish and Sabrina looks elegant and wild, I can adore them unabashedly. I can forgive them for the hot-tub incident. I can keep the deep suspicions, the voice murmuring *This will never work*, at bay.

I stare at the ceiling for a moment. I don't miss Mike, but . . . sometimes I miss that certitude, the life mapped out ahead of me. Watching friends struggle with kids or even infants, I feel my own desire for motherhood cooling. Parenting in a pandemic seems miserable, and who knows how long this dark period will last?

I sigh and swing my feet over the side of the bed, then jump at movement in front of me. But it's my own reflection in their huge, rectangular mirror. I'm perfectly centered in it, and with the coral light kissing my neck and cheek, I look . . . different. Sexier, edgier. I drop my shoulders and angle my chin up and—

There it is: I look like *her*.

Taylor, the missing mystery woman who sat right on this bed, who probably did things I haven't tried. I wonder where she stood when she asked Sabrina to leave Nathan for her. I wonder if he ever suspected anything.

I stand and move closer to the mirror, watching the shadows slip across my clavicle, my face. I pause and run my hand over my neck, my bust. I lean in close, so close, looking for fingerprints on the smooth surface. Wondering if Taylor stood right here and admired herself like me.

I spot one, a half-moon near the frame, and raise my own hand to press next to it. But when my fingers jab the mirror, I pause.

Something's off.

I pull my arm back and the sensation stops, but I know there was something, some impossibility my subconscious picked out and is waiting for the rest of me to see. I push my hand back along the frame, pressing my fingertips flat.

And then it clicks.

No way. I rock back, heart pounding. Then I raise a trembling finger and send it closer to the mirror again. It grows larger in the reflection as if Taylor were on the other side, ready to share a spark like Adam and God on the Sistine Chapel.

Tap—the tip of my finger hits the mirror and flattens against the glass. My shoulders tighten and my jaw locks up. *No.*

But it's true. No matter how I crane my neck around the finger, I can't see the telltale gap between my flesh and its reflection, the sign that the mirror is one-way, reflecting from its back. Instead our fingers kiss, real and fake.

Which means the mirror coating is on the *outside.* Which typically means the mirror is two-way glass, reflective on one side, clear from the other.

Which means someone can look through it from the far side.

I grasp the frame and try to swing it toward me. It doesn't move.

This wall seals off their walk-in closet, and I dart to its door, which is closed, as always. I tighten my fingers around the knob, pulse like a jackhammer, blood on fire, and turn. Surprise: It swivels under my hand. I fling open the door and grope the wall for a light. I slap it on, *bing,* the space floods with light—

"What the fuck?" I breathe.

It's a mirror on the outside, but in here, it's a window.

And centered in it, balancing on three spidery legs, trained on the bed like Virgo when she's spotted her prey, is a camcorder.

CHAPTER THIRTY-THREE

I slump against the doorframe, weak with shock. I flash back to everything that's happened in this bed. What if any of it got out, making its way to my parents, my friends, employers former and future? Lord, the handful of times I've been tied up and blindfolded here—was that for the camera's sake, did they arrange themselves so the lens would get an unobstructed view? I saw those Polaroids, the light BDSM vibes. Have they been . . . what, making cam videos without my knowledge?

My entrails thrash and my throat begins to burn. I feel that deep pull, like a hand reaching all the way through me and scooping back up—nausea swims higher and higher and I sprint to the bathroom just in time to—

Vomit hits the sink, painful and sharp, coming out of me at a hundred miles an hour. Under the nightlight's glow, the liquid bubbles against the porcelain.

I look up at myself—eyes and nose red and streaming—and fling my finger against this mirror, too. It hits the glass with a plunk and I can see the white moon of my finger pad reflected in the thick glass.

Obviously, Kelly, this isn't a two-way mirror. There's a medicine cabinet behind it.

I cup a shaking hand under the tap and rinse my mouth. *Okay*. I review my options. I could tiptoe out of the bedroom, stuff my things into my suitcase, and try to find a local cab company. I could pretend I never laid eyes on the camera and refuse to have sex in here again.

Both things are unrealistic. But I really, really don't want to do what I know I *should* do.

I suck up a few more mouthfuls of water, then pat my sweaty face dry. Morning—I'll wait until everyone's up. But when I open the bathroom door, Nathan is sliding on his glasses.

"You okay?" he asks, loud enough to rouse Sabrina next to him.

"What is it?" she says, and when I open my mouth to answer, I start to cry instead. They both sit up with alarm, and then Sabrina notices I've left the closet light on. She nudges Nathan and nods toward it.

"Oh shit," he mutters.

Quick as a cat, Sabrina is out of bed and standing next to me. "You saw the camera, right?" And when I nod, she slips an arm around me. "We would *never* film you without your consent. Never. We have this for ourselves and have never, ever used it for you."

"We were thinking about asking you," Nathan adds, lumbering over. "Feeling you out on it. It's fun, watching it back later."

"Like how people do boudoir shoots. We plan it out and I wear pretty lingerie and everything."

Taylor's lacy, scalloped bodysuit plunges into my mind.

"It's just . . . a thing we do," Nathan says. "This weird-ass two-way mirror was here when we moved in—let's not think about *that* too long—and we got a camera for it that doesn't have Wi-Fi connectivity, so nobody could hack it. But we haven't used it in a while."

"Never with you. *Never*." Sabrina shakes her head. They've formed a wall between me and the closet.

I want to believe them. It's weird, it's super weird, and why wouldn't they tell me when kinky shit is already wafting between us, but . . . God, maybe it's true. *They're* weird. Sexy and eccentric and totally strange.

I hate that it's part of their appeal. That I'm never quite sure what I'm getting myself into, and it kind of turns me on.

I cross my arms. "Show me."

Nathan frowns. "What?"

"Show me what's on the camera. Then I'll know if you're telling the truth."

A stretched-out second as they both stare at me. Then Nathan shrugs and turns to it. He clicks the camcorder off the tripod and carries it over. The battery is dead, which is a good sign. He digs in the closet and then jams a charger inside, and the flip-out screen lights up, all cheery.

Nathan looks up. "Do you want me to hook it up to a TV, or—"

"Jesus, Nathan." Sabrina face-palms. Nathan still looks confused and I take pity: "No, this is fine."

He hits Rewind and, leaning close to the tiny monitor, I watch the Lamonts have sex in reverse. I blush as I figure out what I'm seeing: Sabrina taking control, a toy levitating into her hand. Then she's pulling on a lacy bra, wiggling into a jacket—a backward striptease. Then onto the end of an earlier video: The two of them are cuddling on the bed, and then they float up into—

"Are there dates?" I demand. I'm aroused in spite of myself. Nathan presses a button to zoom out to a grid of videos, a still-frame signifying each one. He points: the latest is the only one filmed after I moved here.

My shoulders droop. "I'm sorry I doubted you." Guilt is tumbling through me, leadening my insides. It's Mike all over again—my paranoia running unchecked. "You must feel so . . . violated. I should've trusted you. I don't know why I'm like this."

Sabrina rubs my back, making a shushing noise. Nathan clicks another button on the camera, *beep!*, and it zooms out again to a wider grid of more videos.

I watch as he swings the monitor closed. "Can we go back to bed?" he asks, all cheery.

"Wait." Something's bothering me about what I just saw. I feel it, a flutter of alarm.

"What is it?" He reaches for the power button.

Don't do it, Kelly. Let it be. You thought you saw something and you're about to humiliate yourself again.

"The last row. The previews." My stomach hardens. I lift my index finger again, the one that's been so busy today, testing mirrors, singling out the closet.

I know what I saw. Not two naked bodies—three. "You made videos of your last relationship?"

They exchange another look.

"We told you about her," Sabrina says, her eyes warning.

"Let me see it." I can feel it dawning on me, that detail that isn't right, like a light in the distance that's stretching, growing, taking the shape of headlights—the front of an oncoming truck.

You trust these people. You like them both. Don't screw this up—they'll only give you so many chances.

"We can't let you watch it." Sabrina knocks Nathan's arm away. "That's not fair to her."

"Just let me see." Bile scalds the back of my throat.

You're being crazy. You're being demanding. You're pushing them away, Kelly, just shut up and be glad they're willing to forgive you.

Nathan squeezes his brow. "Kelly . . ."

But now the air-raid siren is going off inside me, *find it find it find it,* and the only way to calm it is to know. "Show me," I say again, heart banging. "Show me now."

Because I know what I saw in the last row of videos, the freeze-frames in tiny squares.

The moment slows as, deliberately, painfully, Nathan yawns the screen open and pivots it toward me.

And then, in a rush, I snatch it from him. Hands shaking, I use the arrow buttons to jump down through the grid and zoom in.

I hit Play, blushing when I confirm what I'm viewing, then scramble to pause it. I can't see the third person's face clearly, but I get the idea: She's petite with a curtain of blond hair. She's sandwiched between Nathan and Sabrina.

And the video was taken on May 20.

"This is your ex?" I demand, looking up at them. Sabrina's lips are a thin line. Nathan's shoulders hunch as he nods.

I jump to the next video. May 16. May 5. April 29.

My brain does a quick, squiggling scramble for another explanation, but I know there isn't one.

Less than a month before I moved in, their ex wasn't missing at all.

She was naked on their bed.

CHAPTER THIRTY-FOUR

My fingers fly open and the camera thunks to the carpet.

"Kelly—" Sabrina starts to say, but I take a step away from her, heart thrumming like a hummingbird's.

"*You lied.*" I'm pointing again, this time at her reddening face. "I asked you when that ended. And you said it was a long time ago."

"Look, we were . . ." she begins, and when she hesitates my heart grabs at theories: This isn't their ex at all, but a random hookup? Or . . . or they broke up a long time ago and this was a random sex-with-an-ex situation? But jeez, when did she even have *time* to go missing? Did they—

"We should have been clearer with you," Nathan cuts in.

Coldness slops through me. "What?" I want to pause time, rewind to before I touched that godforsaken mirror.

Sabrina wets her lip. "We actually did . . . we stopped seeing her in May. These were our last times together."

May 20, the final video said. *May 20.* And now I'm mentally rewinding, hurtling through my personal history with Sabrina and Nathan, reeling as I factor in this new detail: I finished Sabrina's books and contacted her around Memorial Day; *days* after their breakup, she and I were chatting nonstop. She was cheerful and open even as her heart scabbed over—not to mention, sometime between then and now, said ex *vanished*. And Sabrina kept right on texting me like nothing was amiss in her life.

"This is absurd," I nearly shout. "You didn't—when we were talking every day, I had no idea you . . ."

I flash back to that first afternoon here—how we raised our flutes of foamy champagne and Sabrina shot Nathan a private grin: *Honestly, we need you at least as much as you need us.* Is she a psychopath? Are they *both* psychopaths? Just how terrible am I at reading people? Suddenly I crave Mike, my sweet, loyal Mike, how he never lied to me, not even when he knew that the truth—that he wasn't able to move forward with the wedding—would hurt me.

"Why didn't you tell me?" I clutch my hands in front of my chest. My heart's pounding so hard I picture it rippling the air between us.

Sabrina touches my arm. They are always touching my arm and *no,* I yank away.

"This is exactly why." She looks wounded. "At first, of course we didn't talk about it—we didn't tell anyone about our relationship—"

"Same as with you!" Nathan butts in.

"Right. So there was no reason to bring it up. But then, when we got together with you . . ." She glances at her husband. Our partner. "We were afraid you'd think it was a rebound thing. Which it's *not.*"

"It's true," Nathan adds, in that defensive tone men use when they're worried they won't be believed. "This was *not* the plan when you moved in."

I can feel my chest defrosting, starting to open back up. "But . . . but you lied to me." Tears gush down my cheeks. "I trusted you."

Sabrina takes a step toward me. "I know. We're so sorry, Kelly. We . . . it was a bad call."

Nathan is discomfort personified, shoulders hunched, hair askew. He doesn't move and I have the thought that if I poked him, he'd pop like a balloon.

Finally he groans. "I'm sorry, Kelly. I'm really sorry." He runs his fingers through his hair. "We didn't want you to think this is a thing we do. Luring people in or whatever."

"I wouldn't have thought that." My voice bristles. Is it even true—would I have run the other way? "I wish you'd been honest with me." I want to believe them—I want it so badly that my ribs ache. "I—I don't get it. How did things end? When did she disappear? Isn't there, like, an active investigation if it happened so recently?"

"There is. But we had nothing—*nothing* to do with that." Sabrina shakes her head earnestly. "It's like I said—she was in the District, and we have no idea what happened or where she is."

I stare at them, searching their faces. Their eyes are round and wide, begging to be believed. "That's it? There's nothing else you aren't telling me?"

"Hand to God." Sabrina raises her palm, and after a second, Nathan notices and throws his palm up too. There's something cartoonish about it, endearing.

Finally I nod, and they both slacken. Sabrina swipes at her tears and my stomach crumples. Here's my partner, someone I deeply like—maybe even love. I know what to do; I can be who they need me to be. I cross to Sabrina and wrap her in my arms.

Nathan walks over to us. "I'm glad you know the truth now." He cups one hand on the back of Sabrina's head and another on mine. "You have to understand—you saved us. We were so upset when we found out she'd gone missing." His voice wobbles and my stomach tightens—that was a few short weeks before I arrived. How could they move past it so quickly? Were they *not*, in fact, over her?

But he answers my unasked questions: "Then you came along." It's potent and bright, like a squeeze of fresh lemon. "You make us happy, Kelly." He kisses me, a long, slow kiss with his fingers on the nape of my neck. Then he leans in toward my ear, his voice a whisper. "So happy and so . . . well, see for yourself." He lifts my hand off the small of Sabrina's back and drags it along the inseam of his sweatpants. *There.* I feel her watching me as I grin and kiss him again, reaching for his waistband.

He backs onto the bed and as I climb onto his lap, I have the thought—the thought that women are not supposed to have, the catty thought, competitive, buying into that poisonous, patriarchal messaging that there's not enough for everybody, that other women aren't your friends. It blares in my mind right as Nathan finishes:

I'll be so good, they'll never think of her again.

CHAPTER THIRTY-FIVE

"I promise it's not you." I stroke Sabrina's arm. I couldn't orgasm despite her best efforts, and now my room feels twitchy, unfinished. I forgot to close the curtains and we're reflected in the window, pretzeled in a restless cuddle.

"Are you sure?" She herself had no trouble. I failed to notice the lopsided nature of hetero sex before I got tied up in all this—if the man gets off, we can deem the sex *over,* period.

I suck in a breath. "I think I'm still processing everything about your ex."

It's been two days since our showdown in their bedroom. She and Nathan are acting like it never happened. I guess for them, it's settled. My shoulders tense. Will this go poorly, my surprise inquisition?

"Oh yeah?" she says. Flatly, I think. Or am I just expecting her to resist?

"I want to know more about her." I struggle to force out the words. "Now that I know it wasn't that long ago, I'm kinda spinning."

"Kelly, there's a reason we don't talk about her." Her voice comes out strangled. "There's a lot of pain there. It's still raw. I mean, imagine if Mike went missing right now—how hard that would be."

I stare at the ceiling, unable to breathe. I feel like I'm being carved out, eviscerated. Because I heard the unspoken sentiment between every sentence:

You do not get to set the conversation.

We loved her more than you'll ever know.

I set the rules.

It's not your house—you just live here.

"It's not fair, you know." I pull myself up to sit. I hate that I sound like a toddler, but I'm quaking with frustration. "We're in this supposedly 'equal' partnership, but it's not equal at all. Why are *you* always making all the rules?" It shoots out of me, deadly as a bullet: "I bet *she* didn't like that either."

The fury in Sabrina's eyes is like a blast of white light. "You didn't know her." The whole room's silent, like the particles in the air have stopped vibrating. Her anger is a molten force. "To you, she's an abstract concept. But to us, she's *real*. And thinking about her is like a knife in my gut. So we are not going to talk about it." She straightens up, a little calmer. "That's . . . that's a boundary I'm setting."

My gut kinks with guilt. She's right—she doesn't owe me details, she needn't thrust my curiosity up above her own pain. I'm the selfish one, demanding answers, looking to soothe the dark part of myself that suspects there's more they're keeping from me.

I remember something Amy once said. I'd fallen into a bad habit of sharing my relationship anxiety with Mike, blathering on about how I worried he might leave me, that he might not love me enough. "You know, intimacy isn't telling your partner everything," she said. "Total honesty is actually pretty toxic to a relationship. What matters is *trust*—believing that, day after day, you can keep showing up for your partner."

I didn't do that with Mike. I have to do better this time.

"I'm sorry, Sabrina. That—that wasn't cool, trying to force you to talk about it."

"Thank you." She wipes a pretty tear. "And thanks for understanding. It's really, really hard." Her eyebrows lift, suddenly emphatic. "You won't try to talk to Nathan, will you? Please tell me you won't. It . . . I'm afraid it won't go well."

Her eyes hold mine, intense and unblinking. *Was* I planning to run off to Nathan? It seems childish: *Mom said no so I'll try Dad next.*

"'Won't go well'? Like, he'd be even more upset than you?" I shake my head. "Not that there's anything wrong with how you're reacting. *I'm* the insensitive one." *I'm afraid it won't go well.* It sounds ominous, a plea and a warning. Of what?

"I don't want you talking to Nathan about it." I jump at the sudden grip of her hand. "Please. Can you do that for me?"

"Of course." My heart's like a bird's, the beats piled on top of each other.

She releases my hand and leans back. Relief floods her face—relief at the idea that I won't provoke her husband. I flash to Sabrina standing like a warrior in the hot tub, each word a blow to a sandbag: *That. Can't. Happen. Again.*

I think I love Nathan. But how well do I know him, really?

I fall asleep wishing I could go elsewhere for information—I'll feel better as soon as I know more. There must be some sign of her here—more of her belongings, maybe, or evidence of their relationship—and my fingers itch to poke around the house. Perhaps her full name is on a document somewhere, the element missing from my internet searches. But I never get the place to myself; there is, after all, nowhere to *go*.

But the next morning, the Lamonts are in the kitchen when I come downstairs.

"We thought we could go to a winery tonight!" Sabrina announces.

Column of light, heavenly chorus! "Ooh, the one you were telling me about?" I make a big show of considering. "That sounds lovely, but I actually have a Zoom with some Juna friends this evening."

"Oh yeah?" Sabrina tilts her head.

"Yup. But you two should go!"

Her eyes narrow. "Is tomorrow better?"

I shake my head, keeping my voice level. "Honestly, it'll be nice to have some podcast-and-chill time." I wave my hand. "And you need . . . Lamont time!" I almost said *couple time.*

"Works for me!" Nathan murmurs, carrying his mug to the sink.

Sabrina's still watching me, concerned. I give her my calmest smile. *Please, trust that it's nothing*, I silently scream. *Trust me so that I can get back to trusting you and Nathan.*

Finally she shrugs. "If you're sure."

"Totally. I'll hold down the fort."

Hours later, as the sky is darkening, I watch the gate close behind their Lexus. My heart's already thumping like I've joined the line outside a haunted house. I let time pass in case they turn around. When I'm sure they're gone, I spring into action.

I start in the basement, searching under the couch cushions and beneath the bar. I stick my head into the wine cellar, where dusty bottles stare back at me. Now I've got that prickly, tingly need to keep going, to *know*. To get answers while I can.

Nathan's office—the room I'm not allowed in, of course there's something there. My pulse revs as I step inside; it has the eerie, aggressively quiet air of a space you're not supposed to be in.

My eyes roam the room: floating shelves with the green stone pyramid on top, etched with that strange symbol; the broad monitor on his huge desk, all of it imposing and defiant, a white man's lair. His windows look out over the cemetery, and as I watch, a flock of geese lift off and form a ragged V. Leaving so soon?

I drop to my knees, checking under Nathan's desk and loveseat. I peek beneath the cushions and behind the pillows and I yank at the top drawer, *where is it it's somewhere there must be something here—*

And then I freeze.

I flash to the horrified look on Mike's face when he caught me in Philadelphia, the office around me torn to shreds. *What are you doing, Kelly?*

Doubt yawns open inside me and guilt rushes in. They trust me and I adore them and I need to stop before I mess things up for all of us.

And suddenly it's clear, like a stereo blaring on: *What a bad, homewrecking partner I'm being.* Stirring up drama, digging into the past. I push the door closed and turn on my heel, prepared to give up on the endeavor.

But now I'm face-to-face with Sabrina's office, another closed door. When Sabrina snatched up the Polaroids—mere days before we finally slept together—she crammed them into a locked desk drawer. And, distracted by Taylor's lacy bodysuit, I never found the key.

The hairs on my arms and neck rise in a wave. I pop open the door; twilight coats the room. When I approach the desk, my eyes zero in on the lower-left drawer. I grab the handle—still locked.

Where the hell is that key?

It's got to be in the room—no reason she'd carry it around the house. I peel back the cowhide rug. I grope through the stacks on her desktop, checking below the mouse pad and keyboard. Finally I drag her little stepstool under the window and, balancing on my tiptoes, pull the hanging plants down one by one.

It's in the last one I try, glinting on top of the potting soil, shaded by the Pothos plant's marbled leaves, which fall in tendrils like Rapunzel's hair. I nearly lose my balance coming down from the stool, and then I'm on my knees again, jamming it into the drawer.

It fits, and then—synth chord!—it turns. My ribs contract. My hands feel like they're buzzing, fully charged. I close my fingers around the small knob, steel myself, and pull. It slides toward me with that grating feel of wood-on-wood.

It's a messy pile of paper goods—envelopes and cards and God knows what else. The three Polaroids are on top and I take them in, hungrily, like they're a drug I've been detoxing from.

Finally I set them on the floor and open the first few cards—all from Nathan, birthdays and anniversaries commemorated with his chicken scratch. I sift through playbills, ticket stubs, curls of photo-booth printouts, a coffee-stained prix-fixe menu. It's like skiing backward through time, watching Sabrina catch shows and dine out and engage with the world.

My fingers close around the drawer's deepest item: a kraft-paper envelope held closed with a red string. My heart speeds again, but I try not to get excited: It's probably more random debris, a scrapbook minus the binding. I can feel my guilt looming in the distance, too, like it's a landmark up ahead on the road: I'm not ready to face it yet, how every paper I thumb past is a betrayal of Sabrina's trust.

I unwind the string, then slide my fingers under the flap. I close my hand around—*yes*—another waxy stack of Polaroids. They make a plasticky crinkle as I yank them out, and a chill shoots up my spine as I take in the first: a selfie, with Sabrina's long arm expanding into the bottom corner. Smooshed against her face is the woman. They're outside—is that the Lamonts' backyard?—and as I flip through the small stack, I find another off-center selfie where they're kissing, then one of Taylor kissing Nathan's cheek. It's the G-rated version of the photos I found in my room, more adorable than sexy.

Nathan looks ebullient in every photo, and the intimacy between all three is obvious; there's an ease you can't fake. My stomach cramps with jealousy. No way did *this* woman creep around their mansion while they were away or dig through their locked drawers, dark questions knocking at the door of her consciousness . . .

But then I get to the last photo. My back freezes over and my throat and chest compress.

No.

I hold it closer, not wanting to believe what I'm seeing.

There's the mystery woman again, shot from the knees up, this time in a plain black bra and underwear. Her arms hang by her sides, her expression vacant.

But the worst part is the bruises.

One is above her hip bone, the size of a deck of cards.

One is rough against her neck, a purplish 8.

And the worst one is over her right eye, darkness streaking over the cheekbone and lid.

I drop the whole pile, not ready to confront the inevitable conclusion. But there it is.

Someone hurt this woman, choking and beating her.

And then she disappeared.

CHAPTER THIRTY-SIX

For a long time, I sit stock-still. Finally I slide the photos back into their envelope and wind the red floss around the fasteners, tightening it like a noose. My fingers slither below the drawer's other contents—it all feels sickeningly cutesy now, cloying shit cloaking evidence of assault. I almost lose my balance as I slip the key back into the planter, standing on my tiptoes while my heart beats double-time.

What . . . what the hell do I do now?

I stand and hustle out of the office, then drop onto the yellow armchair in my bedroom, the one where *she* once sat. I can't ask Sabrina or Nathan about the photo—not when I came across it digging through their personal effects. Do I have an obligation to report this to someone? I don't even know the woman's name—let alone what the Polaroid proves. Who did this? If it was Nathan (or, hell, Sabrina herself), why would they keep the photo? Why wouldn't they destroy the evidence?

What do I do now?

The hissing gremlin reminds me there are other rooms I haven't checked yet. I stand and dart down the hall, teeth chattering like I'm out in the cold. The camera in the bedroom closet—there are videos of her on it, and though I don't have her consent to watch them, maybe there's a clue there, something other than taped sex. It's a weak lead but the only one I can think of.

I hurry to the closet door, fling it open, and—

The camera's gone.

I stare at where it should be, the brick of air atop the tripod.

Wait. Okay.

This makes sense. I freaked out at the sight of it, so they put it away. That was the right move, the respectful thing to do.

But who beat that poor woman?

We are not going to talk about it, Sabrina said. *That's a boundary I'm setting.*

That awful evening in the hot tub—I flash back to Nathan's defiant sneer, to Sabrina's sobering admonishment: *That can't happen again.*

What are the people I love capable of?

"Kelly?"

I jolt—I didn't hear them come in, and now they're calling my name and jogging up the stairs, *shit shit shit.* I fling myself into the closet, pulling the door nearly closed, but *goddammit, Kelly, they're obviously going to yank it open to change their clothes.* I'm frozen, trapped, and I watch through the two-way mirror as they spill into the bedroom.

Sabrina beelines for the bathroom, but Nathan's still coming for me, and I watch in horror as he saunters closer, closer—

But then he turns at the bed and walks up its side, inches away from me. I rear back as if he can see me.

He crouches and disappears from view, and the gun in the nightstand blinks into my mind. Then I gasp as he pops back up with a crumpled sweatshirt in hand. He yanks it over his head and turns to stare at me.

At the mirror. He can't see me. He doesn't know I'm here. Still, I press my hand over my mouth and back away as he stares, tilting his head thoughtfully.

He leans even closer and I hold my breath. He reaches up and digs out an eye booger. Then he turns and ambles out of the room.

I wait to hear him galumph back downstairs, *oh, please stay in the bathroom, Sabrina,* and then I dart out and into my bedroom.

I turn off the lights and change into pajamas; I text them both, "Sorry, I totally passed out, see you tomorrow!"

They don't reply, and my fingers find my call log before I even know what I'm doing. I tap on Favorites and names stare back at me, with tiny, round avatars to their left.

Mike.

Years ago, I added a silly photo to his contact info: He's holding a puffin in Iceland, so happy, he's nearly in tears. He never liked this picture, his face dopey with joy, but now it makes my heart bulge.

With Mike, there were no secret windows or hidden cameras. No woman from his past creeping closer and closer to the present. Things were quiet, predictable. What's so bad about knowing where the story's going next?

Plink, I tap his name and now the image is larger, filling the screen, and my phone says *calling . . . ,* dot-dot-dot like it knows it's a bad idea. Panic unfurls in my chest. What am I doing—what will I say if he picks up? After everything, after I told him not to contact me, after I scolded him for getting back in touch? I hit the big red button, *abort.*

My heart thumps; my cheeks glow red, and something spiky rolls around my chest. A full-body cringe, and then I turn on airplane mode and fling my phone onto the floor.

In bed, Virgo curls against my leg as my brain treads the deep groove of a scratched record, over and over and over again, repeating the facts like they're a rosary, an incantation, a curse:

Their ex is missing.

Somebody beat her.

They nearly drowned me in their hot tub.

I stare up at the ceiling, which transforms into a projector screen that glows even when I close my eyes: a blowup of that Polaroid, the bruises like fat plums on their ex's face, hip, and throat.

The next morning, sunlight muscles through the windows and everything looks less bleak. There's a text from Mike—*Did you call me?*—and I chide myself for the temporary insanity. Mike's no longer my fiancé; I can't scurry back inside the gopher hole of my past whenever things get tough. And anyway, I'm not his Kell-Bell anymore, agreeable and weak—forgiving him wholesale after he shoved me off a cliff in Philly, then muzzled me from discussing it with anyone.

I message him back: *Butt dial, sorry!*

As I brush my teeth, I make a decision: I'll talk to Nathan behind Sabrina's back. He doesn't know she forbade me from discussing this woman, and I can't pretend everything's normal until I have answers.

Gag orders: no longer my thing.

I get my chance when he wanders out to the pool and dips a skimmer into the water, scooping up twigs and leaves and fat dead flies. The August sun presses into my skin as I make my way over to him.

"Can I help?" I call, keeping my voice friendly.

"Nah, this shouldn't take long."

Which means I need to act fast. "Can I ask you something?" I shade my eyes with my hand. Hopefully he can't see my quick, shallow breaths or the way my fingers tremble.

"What's up?" He leans way out to ladle a brown-black seed pod.

"It's . . . it's about your ex." I perch on the edge of a deck chair. "What's her name?"

He focuses on the water's surface, expressionless. "Beth."

Beth. "Right. I'm sorry to bring it up, but I keep coming back to the fact that she went missing. After you broke up." I swallow the sharpness inching up my throat. "I'm just . . . I'm so sorry you had to deal with that. Have there been, like, detectives talking to you? Do they have any leads?"

He sets the skimmer upright and leans against it. "It *has* been awful. We talked to investigators, yeah—they interviewed all her friends."

I expect him to go on, but he's quiet. "Where do you think she is?" I finally prompt. It sounds so stupid aloud.

"I think she was killed." His shoulders droop and coldness soars through me, *holy shit.* But then he rushes on: "I mean, she's been missing for months now. That's what normally happens in these cases, right?" He lets go of the pool skimmer and it clatters on the tile. He sits next to me. "Beth had this ex who kept harassing her in D.C. even after they broke up. A cop and an unbelievably good liar." He gives a hard, macho sniff. "It was so fucked-up. One time Beth called nine-one-one, and her ex's subordinate showed up at her door. You know how cops protect their own."

"That's awful," I murmur.

He stares at his feet. "We tried to help her get a restraining order, but they said she needed evidence of a crime. Hell, Beth's own family wouldn't listen—everyone said it must've been a misunderstanding. It felt like Rina and I were the only people on the planet who knew what was going on."

I wrap my fingers around his forearm and give a reassuring squeeze. It's an infuriating, terrible story . . . but it's also what I needed to know.

An abusive ex, still harassing and stalking her. Evidence of a crime.

And there it is, the explanation for the Polaroid in Sabrina's locked drawer.

All my paranoia, those inky suspicions that Nathan and Sabrina aren't as good as I want to believe—it was my overactive brain again. There's an explanation for everything: They implied their breakup with Beth was far in the past so I wouldn't feel like a rebound. After all, if they were being shady, wouldn't they have hidden her from me altogether? Sure, they finessed the truth a little, but only for my sake. They were still more honest than they'd had to be, right?

And why should the way Nathan dunked my head underwater for a moment have any bearing on that? Sabrina's comment held no words between the lines: *That can't happen again.* It was an accident, one she didn't want to repeat.

So I choose to let it go. Hey, this is the new-and-improved Kelly, modern and evolved. She coolly navigates a three-party relationship without getting bogged down in labels or the murk of the past. Who among us doesn't have some baggage?

"We told the detectives all this. Obviously." He shakes his head, his eyes steely. "I wish there was more we could do. I told her I'd protect her, I . . ."

He drops his head into his hands and his shoulders rumble, racked with grief. I rub his back and feel that heavy ache in my throat and arms.

"I'm so sorry, Nathan." I press my cheek against his shoulder. "Shhh, it's okay."

When he finally sits back, he looks dazed and sheepish. He's only the second man I've ever seen cry like that. He trusts me enough to be vulnerable—and I trust him too.

"Beth had a hard life," he adds. "She grew up poor and her parents sent her away when she was a kid. Just abandoned her and pretended she didn't exist. And then all the awful stuff with her ex . . ." He clears his throat. "We wanted to . . . to be a solid thing in her life. Something she could count on."

Poor family. Sent away. I file them away, two items for my shadow box of details about her. I take Nathan's hand. "You always make me feel safe."

This does it—this makes a smile play across his lips. He kisses my hand, and for a split second, all is right with the world.

CHAPTER THIRTY-SEVEN

I'm thirty-five today and my God, look how far I've come.

I'm adored by not one but two incredible humans. Not to mention, of course, Amy, my parents, friends back home, et al.—humans who blow up my phone first thing in the morning, showering me with birthday messages, making me feel loved. I push down the complicated twinge that comes from remembering how little I've talked to my old friends, and how I'm hiding the source of my joy from them, lying by omission. Whatever. I've heard a lot of things about quarantine birthdays, but mine's off to a stellar start.

Mike leaves me a cheery voice message ("Hope it's okay to break our no-talking rule for this . . ."), and the rumble of Philadelphia's streets scores it like background music. For the first time in forever, I smile at the sound of his voice—I'm so glad he's coming around, and his message fills me with cushiony relief.

He's good; things are good. Me, I'm freaking *great*.

The security system is beeping so fast, we can't keep up. A delivery driver appears at the entrance to Tanglewood with a colorful cloud of peonies and gardenias from my folks. We dash to the gate to collect treat after treat: cookies from Amy, chocolates from my college friends, wine from the Juna crew. I give myself a break from the fruitless job search and spend the afternoon by the pool, fielding birthday wishes on my phone.

One text pops out like a wrong note: "I'm bringing over cupcakes—I'd love to see you and say happy birthday, but I'll leave them at the gate if you're busy!" My heart crumples; I forgot I told Megan my birthday in that first zippy conversation as we sucked down green juices and joked about our astrological signs. I've been dodging her invitations ever since our awkward coffee date.

I compose my reply in the Notes app so she won't see my typing, and flinch as I hit Send: "That's so kind of you—thank you! We're running around all day so I can't hang out, so sorry. Hope you're doing great and thanks again!!"

The cringe doesn't last long, as other birthday messages pour in, and Amy sends a video of little Liam wishing "Auntie Kewy" a "happy buthday," and the sun is shining and I have it all.

I take a selfie in front of the pool—ooh, like the one that sucked me into Sabrina's life back in May, a whole season ago. I noodle over the caption for a while, feeling my heart overflowing, needing to capture that happy gush without hinting at our relationship. I can't be the only one who's grateful the pandemic roused me from the trance of busyness.

> #cornycontentwarning! This past year has been a real challenge, and the last few months have been the most difficult of my life. But I'm also so grateful to year 34 for pushing me to take a leap of faith and make choices that are authentic to me—who I am and who I want to be. Even in the middle of the pandemic, I'm realizing that the life I never expected is better than I dared to hope. I'm so grateful to those I get to love . . . and I'm happier than ever. Cheers to 35—and to bravery and change!

I'll take it down if Sabrina or Nathan objects, but I don't think anyone will read into it. Besides, they can't be mad at me today. It is, after all, my birthday.

Sabrina made a reservation at a swanky seafood restaurant in Alexandria, and I slick on a cat-eye and run a curling iron through my hair. I hear Nathan in his office, next to my bathroom, and his face lights up when I flounce through the door.

"Kelly!" He's backlit by the open windows, so that columns of slanted light skewer the room. "You look fantastic." He stands from the desk and draws me to him.

"The pyramid." I point to the green paperweight as I pass. "What does the symbol mean?"

"It was a housewarming gift." He barely glances at it. "For moving next door to Brinsmere."

"Really? That's it?" Teenagery disappointment soaks my voice. He nods.

"You clean up nice!" Sabrina calls, materializing from the hallway.

"What time is the reservation?" Nathan slides his hands around my waist.

Sabrina giggles. "Seven-thirty."

"Plenty of time, then." He nuzzles my neck, then lifts me suddenly, and I squeal and wrap my legs around him.

"Here? In your office?" I ask, grinning against his kisses. I'm so rarely in here at all—let alone for sex.

"Well, it *is* your birthday." He chuckles and drops me onto the stiff sofa.

The doorbell rings again, the chime of someone at the far gate, the one that leads into Tanglewood. I start to sit up, but Nathan wrestles me back down.

"Leave it," he says. "We'll get your presents later."

"Aren't you Miss Popular?" Sabrina adds. She grabs Nathan's shoulder to jokingly push him out of the way.

She kisses me too, and runs a hand along my side. When it's over and I'm flushed and breathless and floating in the stratosphere, I murmur, "Let's do that forever."

At the restaurant, the hostess steers us to a table overlooking the river. Each dish is more delicious than the last, and we try one another's food, stabbing forks onto plates, lifting one another's cocktails, laughing, swallowing, sharing. God, I like these people.

Sabrina pushes away her plate. "So, we wanted to run something by you." The air has darkened, the river dimming into an inky black. We're lit by the candle on our table now, an upward glow.

Nathan's suppressing a smile, light flickering in his eyes.

I gasp. "Is it a naughty idea?" The frankness with which they discuss sex fascinates me. It reminds me of parents divvying up household chores: *I've got to work late so y'all can hook up without me. Who's picking Betty up from soccer?*

Sabrina laughs. "It is, actually. You once told me your favorite scene from Heart of Desire is the one in Perry's office. When he's late for a meeting and his coworkers are waiting outside, right?"

"You're making me blush." I tuck some hair behind my ear.

Nathan smirks. "Well, as you know, the office was based on our library." He clasps his hands. "We want to re-create it. All three of us, somehow."

"Obviously it won't be exactly the same, but . . . I don't know, are you into it? Now that I'm hearing it aloud, I sound like a megalomaniac: 'Let's role-play a scene from my book.'"

"No, I love it." I shoot them a giddy grin. "I've always wanted to be Arianna Rune."

A humming excitement pervades the car on the way home. We're ditzy with anticipation, and I feel something like pride: This is because of me, my birthday, my presence. My sexual liberation and trust in these two magnificent humans. All my life, I believed I only had the capacity to love one person at a time—that my care, compassion, and affection were limited resources. But with Nathan and Sabrina, I see how love begets love. Being with both of them feels as natural as breathing. I'm more *me* than I've ever been. Mike who?

At home we bum around the bar cart while Nathan makes us Manhattans. When we're all on our second cocktail, Nathan and Sabrina disappear upstairs to change into business attire—they're really going for it, straddling the line between goofy and game. I wander into the library and run my fingers along a row of spines.

A burst of inspiration: I find Sabrina's books and pull out *Market Penetration*. I revisit the scene, heat building inside me as I read. There's a roaring fire in Perry Creighton's office—a detail I can replicate on this cool mid-August night. Logs hulk in a basket next to a stack of newspapers, and I unfold a *Blue Ridge Times* and strip off the front page, then twist it into a cylinder. I do the same with the next two sheets, peeling away pages like an onion's layers.

My eyes dart across the headlines before I crumple each piece. A real estate section, something about the local high school's first virtual graduation.

I almost throw it away—I crunch up the sides and have already begun the wringing motion when I freeze, my whole body a question mark, *What did that say?* Dread plumes deep in my belly.

Moving slowly, slowly, I reverse my movements: twisting my wrists the opposite way, unwinding the paper I'd been squeezing into a log. I clutch the top and bottom and, heart pounding in my ears, horror filling my shoulders and throat, pull it back into a rectangle.

It's the photo that grabs me, the smiling headshot in a plane of urine-yellow paper. Ribbons of text about zoning laws and tax relief programs surround the picture like a matte.

I know that face, the straight teeth and big eyes and smooth, unlined face.

The headline's blunt: SEARCH EFFORTS INTENSIFY FOR MISSING DEER-BROOK WOMAN.

The first line is unmistakable: *Police are seeking answers in the disappearance of 31-year-old Elizabeth Kessler.*

Elizabeth. "Beth." The woman in the Polaroids.

And a few paragraphs in, another sentence makes my blood turn to slush: *Kessler was driving a 2018 Acura MDX that was last identified on a security camera on an unmanned gate at the intersection of Rosemont Boulevard and US-309.*

My heart thunders against my chest. I know that spot. I've passed by it dozens of times.

It's the entrance to Tanglewood Estates.

CHAPTER THIRTY-EIGHT

No. No. No.

I keep rereading the line, willing my eyes to be wrong, craving that cool rush of relief when you realize everything is fine. But it's right there, in black and white.

Red all over.

A woman they loved was last seen a stone's throw from their front door.

My instinct is to drop the paper on the kindling and watch it go up in flames. As if by deleting the evidence, I could delete the knowledge from my brain too. Slip back into that cozy second when I was building a fire for some raucous birthday sex, waiting for my partners to change into costume and find me relaxed and resplendent on the credenza.

The newspaper hovers in the air, shaking like a leaf, and oh it's because my hands are trembling, and my jaw, too, my teeth chattering in the sudden cold of this horrible discovery. I sit on the loveseat and draw in a few breaths. Then I force my eyes to focus one more time:

Police are seeking answers in the disappearance of 31-year-old Elizabeth Kessler. Nearly 200 people joined a candlelight vigil

Sunday to mark the one-week anniversary of the last time she was seen.

Kessler was last spotted on May 24 driving out of the District of Columbia and heading west, District police said. Kessler was driving a 2018 Acura MDX that was last identified on a security camera on an unmanned gate at the intersection of Rosemont Boulevard and US-309. The vehicle has not been located, officials said. Police did not provide a description of what she was last seen wearing.

A Deerbrook native, Kessler most recently served as an associate fellow at the Center for Modern American Security in Washington, D.C. At the vigil, held at Westridge community garden, friends and family expressed dismay at her disappearance.

"We are beside ourselves with grief and worry," said Nancy Atwood, the woman's mother, reading from a prepared statement. "Elizabeth is a talented and driven young woman, and we're praying for her safe return. We implore everyone in our community to help get her home safely."

Anyone with information on Kessler's whereabouts is asked to contact Northwest Detectives Division or call 911.

My brain scrabbles for an explanation, like a squirrel in the bottom of an emptied pool, clawing for a way up up up and out of this hell.

The woman they lied about, the person who filled the slot I currently occupy, was last seen *here*. And they kept this detail from me. Let me think she vanished from her home in D.C. That had to be intentional, a crime of omission.

I let the newspaper drop to the floor, but gray smudges mark my fingers still.

What else are they keeping from me? Christ, do I know these people at all? I flash to the Polaroid in Sabrina's drawer, bruises bulging on this woman's eye, throat, and side. I think again of the look that zapped between them in the hot tub: *You have to be careful, Nathan. You can't get carried away . . .*

I'm breathing so fast my hands and feet tingle and my head swims. *An unmanned gate. Her last known location.* On my very first day here, when we rolled past the same palisade, Nathan made it clear: The swinging iron gate with its curlicue lettering is the only way in or out of the neighborhood. My brain circles around it another time. If she entered and was never seen again . . .

I glance down at the paper once more. The angel on my other shoulder pipes up: They're not idiots—if they wanted to withhold info from me, they might not, say, *leave a newspaper article outlining the case against them folded in their library.* I cling to the thought as I force my breath to slow. In, then out.

But then our conversation from last week echoes in my head, our teary triangle in front of the closet where a camera sat as watchful as a sphinx: *There's nothing else you aren't telling me?* And Nathan and Sabrina raised their palms, scout's honor: *Hand to God.*

There's a creak behind me, then footsteps, and I stand and whirl around—I can't see them yet, but Nathan and Sabrina are descending the stairs. Fear stabs at my lungs and I look around wildly, as if searching for somewhere to hide. My eyes settle on objects: I could dive behind the chaise longue; I could grab the iron poker from the hearth, hold it like a bat.

They freeze in the foyer, near the foot of the stairs. Nathan's in a crisp navy suit, looking giddy, the way all men get when they dress up. Sabrina, now in a blazer and pencil skirt, looks concerned.

"What is it?" she asks.

"We don't have to do this if you've changed your mind," Nathan adds, smiling magnanimously. "Or we can save it for another time."

I shake my head and swallow hard, trying to find my voice. "It's not that."

"What's going on?" Sabrina takes a step toward me and I flinch. She notices and her face darkens.

Instincts tussle in my chest. *You love these people—I'm sure there's an innocent explanation.*

You don't even know *these people. What if you're in danger, and asking them about their dark secret will only make it worse?*

"What's going on?" Sabrina comes closer and touches my wrist. A part of me longs to pretend I never saw this—to kiss her hard.

No. This matters. As their partner, I have every right to ask about their past and understand why they lied.

I open my mouth and it's one of those moments when you hear your own words as if someone else were uttering them. "I found an article about your ex. Elizabeth. About her disappearance."

Sabrina squeezes her eyes shut. "Okay, wow. I thought it was something about the rimming."

A surprised laugh puffs out of me. I regain my composure. "It . . . it rattled me," I admit. "I know you don't like talking about her, but seeing it in print—it made it real." Something's keeping me from pouncing, from telling them I know she was here.

"I'm sorry, Kelly." Sabrina blinks her giraffe eyes at me. "That must've been so jarring."

"Talk about a mood-killer," Nathan adds, flumping onto the arm of the loveseat.

Sabrina sighs. "Do you want to talk about it? I can't believe this happened on your birthday, of all days." She glares at the newspapers next to the fireplace, as if they're at fault. "What did it say? Just that she'd gone missing?"

My heart speeds and my head feels floaty. *She doesn't know I know.* The detail they've withheld—the part linking them so directly to her disappearance. They have no idea which article I picked up.

"Right, just that she was missing," I say. "It was so weird reading about her, her career and background and stuff." My pulse bangs. "You said you talked to detectives? Did they tell you what they knew? The, the where or when or how?"

I look back and forth between them, fighting to look natural. Nathan's still hunched on the loveseat, his face as blank as stone. Sabrina clutches her hands in front of her stomach.

Tell me the truth, I beg. *Please, tell me.*

"They didn't tell us anything," Sabrina says. "We were interviewed like any other friends."

"So you lied to them. About your relationship."

Sabrina's head cocks. "Kelly . . ."

"It was always for me." Nathan clears his throat. "I'm the one who wanted it to be a secret. From day one."

"So they still don't know anything? She just . . . disappeared from D.C. one day? They know she was in the District?" *Correct me*, I beg silently. *I'm not even being subtle. Tell me the truth.*

Sabrina looks me square in the eye, and I feel it, a falling, crashing sensation, like breaking through the ice and dropping down, down, down toward a lake's silty floor.

"That's right," she says, her voice level. "We have no idea what happened to her."

CHAPTER THIRTY-NINE

They lied to me and they're lying still.

What bulges next is a desire to back away, to put some distance between us. My brain whirs, rushing to come up with a plan.

"I'm sorry," I say, willing my jaw to unlock. "But, um, I think the mood is kinda ruined for the night. I actually—you know, it's been so long since I've stayed anywhere else or had a little alone time—what if I stayed at a hotel tonight? You know, a staycation."

They look mystified. "A staycation?" Nathan repeats.

I nod. This is unbelievably stupid; no way they're buying it, but I need to get out. "I'll—I'll grab my things and maybe I can borrow one of your cars?"

"But you'll be alone on your birthday." Sabrina looks wounded.

I smile, force my shoulders down and back. *Get it together, Kelly.* "It's what I want. And then you two can enjoy some time together too." I awkwardly wave my hand at them.

"Are you sure?" Nathan is giving in, his voice taking on a what-the-hell tone.

"Yes! Let me get my stuff." Calmly, Zenlike, I ascend the stairs, resisting the urge to take them two at a time.

Shit. Shit. Shit. I grab my laptop and a handful of clothes, then stuff everything into a tote. I can't leave without Virgo, and my heart gushes with relief when I find her curled in the closet. She wriggles as I scoop her up with one arm, and I fight to hang on to her and—

"Everything okay?"

I whirl around and Sabrina's in the doorway, arms wrapped around her waist.

"Nathan booked you a room at the Ritz-Carlton in Tysons Corner." She leans against the frame. "We can give you a lift?"

My insides twist. Is it bad if they know where I'm staying? Is it worse that I'm having that thought, and that I don't want them to drive me because some freaked-out part of me wonders if they know where Elizabeth—or, *oh God oh God,* her body—is now, and they'll drive me straight past the exit for Tysons Whatever and deep into some dark, empty forest and—

"I'm sorry you saw that about Elizabeth. This is not what we wanted for your birthday. You know I don't like talking about her, but." Her eyes gleam with tears. "I'm sorry, Kelly. We should've been upfront with you and now I'm so worried we messed everything up."

I stay frozen by the bed, hands tingling, knees threatening to give out. Virgo starts struggling again.

"Don't worry about it." I force the words out. "I'll be back soon. And—and thanks for booking me a room, that's so nice. I'll drive my-self, if you don't mind."

"Of course." The air between us is cold and bristly. "Whatever you want." She turns and walks into her office, then shuts the door.

Rolling around my head is one giant, voiceless scream. It peals and echoes as I rush downstairs and streak up the hallway. In the mudroom, I drop Virgo into her carrier, scoop up my purse, and yank Nathan's keys from the hook.

I reach the SUV and fling Virgo and me inside. At the gate, the car's window takes forever to sink into the door. I'm so anxious that it feels like a small miracle when the code still works, but the gate, too, takes its time spreading open.

My fingers drum on the steering wheel. Cones of canola-colored light funnel out of the headlamps. Bugs wink in and out. I'm jealous of them and their tiny wings, how they're never held back by iron gates. Or by the chaos in their panicked minds.

Of course, they also can't stop setting off on suicide missions toward beautiful, blinding lights.

As I arc onto Tanglewood Drive, I can't shake the feeling I'm forgetting something. Hell, I'm forgetting *everything,* leaving nearly all my earthly possessions in the closet, but there's something else I should've taken care of before bolting, some obvious detail I'm overlooking . . .

At the gate that'll dump me on US-309, I glance up at the camera—the last one to see Elizabeth alive. I wonder where it feeds into—the gate's unmanned, and Nathan said he can only access footage from the camera on their driveway. Why did anyone think to check this one in the first place? Who thought to ask Tanglewood to turn it over?

Once I'm out of the community, I pull over. What's my plan? Am I forging ahead with the night they arranged for me, a "staycation" in the suburbs? I'm not sure what other options I have. I can't drive Nathan's car to Illinois and show up at Amy's door, all *never mind the Grand Theft Auto.* I squint at oncoming headlights. This is ridiculous. What am I doing?

Finally I pull up directions to the Ritz-Carlton. After a while, Tysons Corner pops up in the distance, a clump of skyscrapers twinkling in the night. A sign welcomes me to "America's next great city." A tagline set in the future. Tomorrow unspooling like you hoped—nobody can promise that.

I park in a garage and a well-dressed man with droopy eyes hands me a key. I follow a porter to a suite and perch on the massive bed. A white comforter hangs over it like meringue. I nearly hit the ceiling when someone knocks on the door, but it's just a hotel employee with a litter box and scratching post for Virgo. Five-star accommodations, indeed.

I have more missed calls and texts from Sabrina than I can count, each one baffled but kind: "We're here for you." I put my phone on Do Not Disturb mode. The missives dissolve some of the barbed panic.

But then I think of the article again and fear pinches my chest.

For the first time in a long time, I'm somewhere new, and alone. There's a lock on the door and a security desk downstairs. So I relax enough to let the murky thoughts hatch anew: Did Nathan and Sabrina have something to do with that woman's disappearance? Did they hurt her and then cover it up, get away with it? What caused them to break up—how badly did the relationship end?

Overwhelm hits me like a wave, and I lie back on the bed. Virgo moseys over and curls against my thigh. She's not a lap cat, never has been, but she smiles reassuringly in that blinky feline way and even extends her front paws to touch my fingertips. I twiddle my fingers as tears pour into my ears.

Get it together, Kelly. Use your head. I took Nathan's car. I'm at a five-star hotel in a random city in Virginia. What do I do now? Call the cops?

And say what—I found sexy photos of a missing person in a house you probably know she's been in . . . and I have a random and unverifiable suspicion that Nathan gets carried away during sex sometimes?

The police already know everything in the article. Nathan and Sabrina said they've spoken to law enforcement.

But . . . the Polaroid showcasing those ugly purple bruises. Shouldn't Sabrina have given it to the cops, introduced it as evidence?

Ugh, if only I could *talk* to someone. I sit up and wipe my eyes. Virgo starts licking her chest, violently thrusting her head back.

My urge, oddly, is to call Sabrina about this. I think of Mike a few weeks after his mother passed, red-eyed at the kitchen table, taking pulls from a bottle of Jameson. *I just want to tell her,* he said. His gaze was glassy as he slammed his fist on the wood. *All I want is to call her and tell her: My mom died.*

I didn't get it then. Now I feel the twisting frustration: *Can you believe it, Sabrina?*

But there's another instinct tugging at my consciousness, one at least as intense. The same want-want-want that had me tearing through Nathan's and Sabrina's offices last week.

I need to know more. And for the first time, I have enough info to learn everything.

I open my laptop, wait a moment for the Wi-Fi to connect. I open a fresh search.

Elizabeth Kessler. Washington, D.C. Missing.

There it is, the same article I saw. My insides curdle as I read it a second time. My eyes snag again on the description of Tanglewood's gate, crosshairs on a corner I know well. A quote from her mother, the woman Nathan said abandoned her.

But then I notice something wildly obvious, three words that change everything.

A Deerbrook native.

Elizabeth was from Deerbrook originally. A new explanation slots into place and I cling to it like a raft in a storm: Maybe Elizabeth and the Lamonts *had* broken up, and she was heading to Tanglewood to see a family member.

The idea is like a wallop of leaden relief and suddenly I'm exhausted, sleepier than I've ever felt in my life. This roller coaster of a night has worn me out and I barely have time to slip off my shoes before I pass out, fully dressed, the lamps still aglow around me.

I jerk. Where am I? Virgo's at the end of the bed and she squints at the door, then leaps down and saunters under the bed. The scene fills in around me: crisp gray sofa, glass coffee table, bay windows overlooking the black sky and city lights.

"Kelly?"

I freeze. My ears perk up like Virgo's. *No way*. No way did I just hear Sabrina's voice.

"You in there?" That's Nathan. My pulse explodes. I scramble to stand, then creep to the door and peer through the peephole.

Their eyes and noses bulge in the fish-eye lens.

My body starts to shake, first my hands, then my jaw, then my arms and legs all jagged with adrenaline.

There, the bull's-eye of the mistake I left behind, the oversight that's been plaguing me since I tore down their driveway hours ago. The article from so many months ago—I smoothed it out and dropped it on the living-room floor. I left it in plain sight for them to spot and lift and read. A cursory skim would reveal that I hadn't told them the truth—the article wasn't just about her disappearance; it mentioned the location too.

They know I know they lied. They know I know she was there. Like any good newspaper article, the one I left behind reported the who, what, where, how . . .

I gasp as it hits me. *When.* How did I miss it? The article said she was last seen May 24—*four days* after the three of them recorded their final sex tape.

"Kelly?" Sabrina calls again. My heart thunders in my chest.

Who knows what they want with me?

CHAPTER FORTY

My eyes dart to my purse on the floor. I rush over and snatch it up, noticing all the missed calls from both of them.

"Kelly?" Nathan bellows through the door. "We know you're in there."

"Jesus, you sound like a Bruce Willis character." Sabrina clears her throat. "Sweetie, we're sorry to show up like this, but we wanted to make sure you're okay." I don't answer and I can feel them both listening. "We messed up so badly and I'm sorry, but you have to let us explain. We . . . we can stay out here and talk if you want."

"In the *hallway?*" Nathan murmurs, so softly he must think I can't hear, and a tiny part of my heart softens. This is *Nathan*—the goofiest gent I know. Nathan, who makes silly jokes blaming everything on my cat: *Dammit, Virgo, didn't I tell you to empty the dishwasher?* Nathan, who once, as the credits rolled on a grim, Oscar-nominated war movie, whispered, "Do you think there's a blooper reel?"

Sabrina ignores him. "Thirty seconds, Kelly. So we can be honest with you. Then, if you still want out, I swear to God, we won't bother you again."

She says it like I have a choice, but I don't. I'm trapped. Slowly, I return to the door.

"What are you doing here?" I call into the wood.

"We just wanna talk," Sabrina says. "We tried calling but your phone is off or something. We were worried. The guy at the front desk told us which room you're in."

I hesitate, heart galumphing in my chest. "I've got my phone, you know. I could . . ." I trail off. I could, what—call for backup? If they *try* *anything*? Are they aware I'm considering the possibility that they're cold-blooded murderers, somehow responsible for Elizabeth's death?

"You can call the police if you want—they already know everything." Sabrina sounds so sad, and confusion puckers my gut. "We want you to know the truth."

Boy, do I want them to convince me. I want it so, so badly. "Tell me why you lied to me. And what happened the night she disappeared." My teeth are chattering so violently, I can barely speak. "I know you were with her."

"I swear to God, we weren't," Sabrina replies. "We didn't see her that night—she never showed up. Or even contacted us. And the phone records back that up."

"Can you open the door?" Nathan blurts out.

My pulse is a roar, like waves percussing the sand. Finally I slide the chain into place and crack the door, letting the metal catch. "I want to know everything."

Sabrina nods. "First of all, I swear, we had nothing to do with her disappearance. We know absolutely nothing. We talked to the detectives so many times, and I wish we had something useful for them."

"We have them on speed dial. Look." Nathan swipes at his phone, then holds up the screen: Detective Peskowitz.

"We can call them if you want," Sabrina says again. "I don't know if they'd pick up this late, but if that's what you need to feel safe, we'll do it right now."

I glance at the clock next to my bed—it's just past midnight. My chest is already beginning to thaw. "She didn't say *anything* to you? Before she disappeared?"

They both shake their heads hard enough to whip their hair. I flash to Sabrina in the bathtub, her face damp and coral pink: *She floated the idea of being together. Her and me. Leaving Nathan.* I promised I wouldn't disclose this to Nathan, but now all bets are off.

"You're lying." I peer at Sabrina. "You told me she was looking for an exit ramp even before she—"

"Her abusive ex was still harassing her," Sabrina says quickly. She does *not* want Nathan to know about Elizabeth's proposition. "The woman she dated right before we all got into a relationship. But that was nothing new."

"The woman?" I repeat, confused.

"We tried to get the detectives to look into her, but there wasn't anything linking her to the disappearance," Nathan adds. "But who knows if her cop buddies were protecting her."

Whoa—when Nathan brought this up next to the pool, didn't he say her ex was a policeman? No . . . he said *cop* and I jumped to conclusions. I frown, annoyed with myself.

"We've gone over it and over it—there were zero warning signs," he says. "We saw Beth the week before and she was totally normal."

Another puzzle piece snaps into place: the breakup they never mention. The tiny date on their final sex tape and the look in their eyes when they talk about her, syrupy sad.

They call her their ex, yes. But it's only because they couldn't date her anymore.

"You didn't break up at all," I say. "You were still dating when she disappeared."

They both nod.

We didn't want you to think this is a thing we do, Nathan said as the camcorder lay still between us. *Luring people in or whatever.*

My voice shakes: "Why did you invite me to stay with you?"

Sabrina's shoulders stoop—another glimpse of her awkward high-school self. "To distract us, I guess. We were sick with worry, and there was nothing to do, so much time to fill, and—and I thought it would be good for you, too, a location change . . ."

I lean against the wall, head swimming. It was their own version of

sending the "So, listen" email. Trying to revert to how things were before the hurt. Refusing to face the pain head-on. "I want to know everything about your relationship with Elizabeth," I say. "From the
beginning."

"Okay, that's fair. Elizabeth was friends with both of us. *Is.*" Sabrina
looks into Nathan's face as she speaks. "Nathan met her through work,
and then we were seated together at a gala and we all hit it off."

"When was this?"

"Maybe three years ago?" Nathan creases his forehead, remembering. "She lived in D.C."

Sabrina looks down at her hands. "After we moved, she loved spending the weekend with us in Deerbrook. As friends, until late last year,
when the relationship . . . changed."

"She's the reason Tanglewood was on our radar," Nathan says. I realize this tracks with what he said at our very first dinner as a storm
throbbed against the windows—that a friend had told them about the
subdivision. "She has family there. An aunt and cousin and their kids."
His face crumples. "They're the ones who left that raccoon outside."

"And you saw her aunt with Diane. Lydia?" Sabrina shakes her head.
"They all hate us."

"Why?" I ask. "You told me the dead animals were about people
thinking you're snobby."

Sabrina touches her neck. "Isn't it obvious? They think we had
something to do with Elizabeth's disappearance. Or that we know something we're not telling them."

"Why would they think that?" But then the answer locks into place:
"Because she disappeared on her way into the neighborhood. And they
think she was coming to see you."

"Exactly." Sabrina pulls at a snarl in her hair. "But we have *no idea*
why she drove to Deerbrook. She didn't tell us she was coming."

"Couldn't she have been on her way to see her relatives?" I point
out.

Nathan opens his rough palms. "Maybe, but she *never* went to see
them. She avoided them like the plague when she visited."

"Why?"

"She didn't talk about it," Sabrina admits.

"How convenient." I frown. "C'mon. You're telling me she hated her relatives but wanted you to move close to them?"

"She didn't tell us to look there." Nathan looks bewildered. "She just—we only *knew* about it because she'd mentioned having family there. Hell, she was campaigning for us to look at Bethesda."

"Or to not leave D.C. at all," Sabrina adds.

I shake my head. "What about her mom? She's quoted in the article—you said her parents abandoned her."

They exchange a baffled glance. "They weren't in touch. But I'm sure her parents still want her found." Sabrina blinks. "The cops expect you to make those kinds of statements when your kid goes missing, right?"

"All we know is that she got in the car in D.C. and never made it out," Nathan says. "That's it. We gave the detectives everything we could think of."

They keep repeating this line, but it can't be true. Not when they're so aggressively tight-lipped about our relationship. "You didn't tell them you were sleeping together, though, did you?"

They shake their heads.

"But everything else, everything relevant—I swear to you." Sabrina swipes at a tear. "We're so sorry."

"It was stupid of us to not be up-front about it," Nathan says. "We were trying to avoid . . . this. Ruining things."

Through the slim crack I look them both in the eye, one after the other. I can feel it, how desperate they are for my forgiveness, and my stomach folds like a soggy paper plate.

From the start, they lied about the timeline: *We dated, and then she went missing.* Truth is, she went missing when they were still very much together.

But . . . I can understand the tiny snip, the copy-paste to make it all sound more palatable. Like my friend Lara's mom whispering a lie about her daughter's father. *I got pregnant, and then he took off.*

Or me, sitting on that low cinder-block fence with Mike on the other end of the line. *We broke up, and then I fell for someone new.*

"When I picked up the article you'd seen, oh my God." Sabrina smooths her hand over her hair. "I know how it looks. We really wanted the chance to explain. We . . . we love you so much, Kelly."

Love. There it is, the word I've been craving. Cool water in the desert, a balm for a burn. I feel it sink into me, down to the level of my DNA, infusing every cell with specialness. My heart's confused about how to respond. It was shocked a second ago, astonished, betrayed, but now I feel it reaching out of my rib cage like an open hand.

Not so fast—the paranoid part of me pulls me back, scraping its claws against my chest. All the half truths and obfuscations . . . I need to lay them out, examine them one by one. I feel nauseous and jangled and somehow both keyed-up and exhausted.

Suddenly I know what I need; I need it so badly the pull is oxygen-urgent. "Can I take a minute to process?" Their faces fall and guilt shoots through me but no, I need to *think,* dammit. "I'm sorry. I love you both—you know that." My chest flutters as I say it aloud. "Thanks for telling me the truth. But I need to sit with everything. Get my head on straight." I wince, hearing it: Mike's exact wording, back when I didn't realize we were beyond repair.

Nathan looks gutted, but Sabrina nods. "Charge anything you want to the room."

Shame clogs my throat. "Are you sure?"

"Of course." She shoots me a sad smile. "It's your birthday, after all."

"When are you coming back?" Nathan looks childish and afraid.

"Hush." Sabrina loops a brave arm around him and turns to me. "Will you tell us if you need anything? Anything at all."

I nod stupidly. We stare at each other, waiting for someone to speak, and then Sabrina's hand shoots out. Her fingers fall over my knuckles, clenched against the door, and I squeeze her hand back and Nathan closes his large fist over mine and it's dark and deep and tragic, not knowing if we can fix what's broken.

I finally pull my hand away, and they saunter out of sight.

CHAPTER FORTY-ONE

A gun fires, *bang*, and I startle awake. It's bright now, sun soaking through those filmy curtains. I don't hear it again. A truck back-firing, maybe.

I slept late, somehow—it's almost eleven. I've got an emotional hangover, that dull headache and sore stomach and mangled, scooped-out feeling. But I have a fresh perspective too: All of last night's concerns look milder in the daylight. For Sabrina and Nathan to trek out here to talk with me . . . they must really care.

Sabrina texted hours ago:

The house feels so empty without you. We feel sick about everything we've done, all our bad calls and stupid decisions when we should've just been honest. We're still holding out hope you'll give us another chance—a chance we don't de-serve. You're the most amazing woman and the best partner in the world. But we'll understand if you never want to see us again. We'll be heartbroken, because we love you so much, but we understand. If that's the case, feel free to call an Uber

(I can send more $$ if need be) and we'll collect N's car later.
Miss and love you, Kelly. Xoxo.

My heart clutches. It's so goddamn *nice*. They messed up, yes, but who hasn't? I'm certainly not perfect. "The best partner in the world"—I know it's a lie. But I drink it in, I reread the words until they blur, I pull them inside and let them warm me.

I stretch and pull on yesterday's clothes, then trek to the lobby for black coffee and a bowl of milk for Virgo. When I get back to the room, she slinks to the sofa and gazes out the window, as if waiting for somebody.

I turn on my laptop again. It's strange, come to think of it, that Elizabeth's name isn't front-page news—or that, at minimum, a true-crime community hasn't popped up around her, sifting through suspects like this real woman's disappearance is a big game of Guess Who: family members, the Lamonts, the violent cop, who (twist!) isn't a beefy dude like I assumed. Elizabeth's a beautiful, young white woman who worked a relatively high-profile job in D.C. Who kept it mostly under wraps? Hell, who kept the Lamonts' name out of the news?

You can ask them. This is what people in relationships do, they talk stuff out instead of fleeing, pressing their foot to the gas of a borrowed SUV. I find what I'm looking for in another news article: *lead detective Jennifer Peskowitz.*

There it is, confirmation of their story. No way were they faking the pain that crinkled their faces and throttled their voices. Sabrina made that clear as soon as I started asking about Elizabeth, in fact: *To you, she's an abstract concept. But to us, she's real. And thinking about her is like a knife in my gut.*

Something else leaps out from the articles: Her mother's name is Nancy Atwood. *Atwood*, the name on that grave marker I'm always passing, the towering angel with a symbol on the tombstone below. A symbol—which looks a bit like an A, come to think of it—on the stone pyramid in Nathan's office too. A housewarming gift, he called it. So Elizabeth's mother's family has some prime real estate in the graveyard connected to Tanglewood . . . which also points to her having relatives there.

I rack my brain for their names, then check social media. There's

Lydia Atwood, the sour-faced woman I saw walking with Diane. With a few clicks, I confirm that her daughter's named Michelle, and that she's the beaming grandmother of the boys who dumped roadkill on our driveway, and that they all live in Deerbrook.

I exhale and lean back. It's all aboveboard. It clicks together like a zipper, seamless and smooth.

I make a decision: I'll be a good partner. I won't add to their shame and grief. I'll tell them I understand. I'll tell them I believe them. I'll carry Virgo to Nathan's car and move back into their spare room.

I picture the love in their eyes, their arms thrust open. The thought cheers me—here's my chance to make everything right and be the prodigal son, back home. My chest eases and I stand. *Onward*.

At the entrance to Tanglewood, I pause, zeroing in once more on the camera at the gate. Elizabeth occupied this exact three-dimensional space right before she disappeared, probably at the hands of her abusive ex. I shake my head as the gate finishes sliding away.

Doubt's prickling my gut now—we're in the midst of our first big misunderstanding, navigating uncharted territory. But I again visualize the joy on their faces, how they'll slump with relief, and lean harder on the gas.

When I spot the mansion, my heart booms. For some reason I think of horror movies, of Hill House—not sane—and almost hear the musical cue, a pipe organ's frightening blare.

Just nerves. I'm not good at this—setting my paranoia aside and leading with trust. I push away the neurotic inner child and the twenty-something who worried everyone she loved would betray her. I couldn't do it with Mike; I'll do better this time.

I half expect them to gather in the windows or throw open the side door, their mouths thrilled half-moons, but the house remains silent and still. I park and, clutching Virgo, traverse the driveway. Sabrina's car is here, so they must be home. The old suspicion wriggles in my chest: *Is something wrong? Did something happen to them?*

No, they just aren't expecting you. I'm almost to the side door now. In the yard a crow, nearly Virgo's size, twists its neck and hunches its inky shoulders. It holds my gaze for a beat, then lifts off, disappearing among the treetops.

It's quiet, too quiet. I reach for the bubbled numbers on the door's keypad and then, at the last second, knock instead.

Silence. Virgo shifts in her carrier. Five seconds pass, ten. I adjust my hold on her and knock again, then ring the doorbell.

Still nothing. I take a few steps back and try to peer into the upstairs windows, but in the midday sun they're all mirrors.

I hear something. The knob jiggles and the door cracks open.

"Kelly?" Nathan frowns, then opens the door a bit wider.

I smile nervously. "Hi."

He glances behind me. "Why'd you ring the doorbell? I thought . . ." He shakes his head.

"Um, it felt presumptuous to walk in after I took off." I smile again, bigger this time. "I'm back. I thought about everything you said and I . . . I'm sorry I doubted you. I just want to go back to the way things were." I'm babbling and Virgo yowls. "Can we come in?"

He hesitates again, then swings the door open. All the buoyancy I drummed up on the drive is gone. They begged me to return. Did they not mean it?

Inside, I set Virgo's carrier on the floor, and Nathan leans against the basement door, eyes unfocused. A horrible thought: *They changed their minds.*

"Where's Sabrina?"

He stares for a moment, then shakes his head. "Sorry, I didn't—we thought you were gone for good."

My guts contract. This is not the warm welcome I was picturing.

"She's downstairs," he adds, as if he just heard my question. "I'll go get her." He turns and shuffles down, feet galumphing. I wrap my arms around myself as they discuss in hushed tones. I can't make out any words. Should I wait for them or head to my room? Why isn't Sabrina hurtling up the stairs, teary with relief?

After a beat, I start making my way to the foyer. My head is buzzing; if I screwed things up here, I truly have nowhere to go. Are they upset I didn't come home with them last night? Has Sabrina reconsidered her standing invitation now that the betrayal of my departure has set in?

"Kelly!" I turn around and she's hurrying toward me, arms outstretched. I step into the embrace, yearning for it like a baby craves milk, but her stiff shoulders don't melt even in the warm hold of the hug.

"I'm so sorry I left." If she let go, I'd beg, I'd drop to my knees and wrap my arms around her calves. "I'm sorry I didn't trust you."

"Oh, Kelly." She rests her chin on the crown of my head.

"I should've come back sooner," I add. "I shouldn't have run off in the first place. I—I'll make it up to you however I can."

"Shh. It's okay." Her voice sounds heavy and sad.

I feel a flash of shame as I say it, the pathetic thing, twitching with neediness and clinginess and all the things I swore I wouldn't bring into this relationship: "You aren't happy to see me? Should I go?"

"Of course we're happy to see you," she replies. I hear Nathan walk into the room behind me and feel her chin lift. "You made us realize some things," she continues. "Like, how much processing we still have to do. We're in the middle of some . . . intense discussions, is all."

"Aha," I say. It checks out—inviting me into their home, acting so normal and cheery mere weeks after their partner disappeared definitely smacks of denial.

But God. If they call for a break or separate or divorce or whatever, we're all done for.

"We're glad you're feeling better about everything," she says. "We love you."

I grab for it, the L-word, like a stray dog scrabbling for scraps. "Sorry I doubted you." I lean back and wipe my eyes. "I'm sorry I stirred all this up. I didn't mean to, but—"

"No." Sabrina shakes her head. "Don't apologize. It's all on us." Her eyes meet Nathan's and something passes between them. I feel it again, the zap of being left out.

But this is their grief to process. *Their* partner vanished, not mine. Of course this is stretched across their shoulders. A yoke.

You're not unwelcome, I tell myself, an internal shout. *This isn't about you.* But the stinging pain in my chest won't listen. I feel unwanted, rejected, more of an outsider than ever.

"Is there anything I can do?" I ask. Their nos come quickly, little bullets. Well, time to behave like the supportive partner I swore I'd be. "I'll give you two a little space."

"Thanks," she replies. "We'll . . . we'll be downstairs." Her gratitude is like a hot poker and the singeing sensation continues as they close the basement door behind them. They thump down the steps, head into the den, and murmur in tones too low for me to hear.

I feel heavy, sludgy. I make a sandwich I'm too sad to eat. I trudge into the library and slump on the loveseat. I watch the light from the window slide across the floor, but still, they don't climb out of the basement. I'm certain they're talking about me. How they'll get rid of me now that I'm living here, maybe; how they'll ask me to leave. My heart cramps like a calf muscle.

And then resolve snaps together in my stomach. We love each other, dammit, and I won't leave without a fight.

I stride into the kitchen. I'll make them a five-star dinner, pull out all the stops. I'll set the table and light candles and we can discuss it—us, them, everything—over a mouthwatering meal, the egalitarian throuple we vowed to be.

But first, wine.

(And maaaybe a tiny part of me recalls that the wine cellar is located in the basement, where they're hanging out without me. Coincidentally. Conveniently. Maybe.)

I noisily open the basement door—I'm not trying to eavesdrop, after all—and they fall silent, as if someone hit the Mute button. I trundle down the stairs, each step louder than the last, and when I reach the bottom I don't even glance into the den.

I sense them frozen, staring at me as I reach the door to the wine cellar. I close my hand on the knob and twist.

It won't turn.

"Kelly?" There's desperation in Sabrina's voice, breathlessness.

It's a strange sensation, this delayed resistance against my palm, and I tilt my head, confused. I try again, harder this time, and feel the knob clutch against me.

Like someone's holding it from the other side.

My pulse explodes. Fear puffs up my hair, floods my limbs.

"Wait." It's Nathan this time and they're coming for me but I ignore them, my entire body focused on the mystery in my palm. I clutch both hands around the knob and lean all my weight against it, pulling like my

life depends on it, throwing my torso back like this is tug-of-war. The door trembles, it vibrates like white-knuckled fists in an arm wrestle, and I tug-tug-tug *ha, I'm winning* and suddenly the door breaks free and swings open, me with it, and I'm soaring backward I've lost my footing I can't get my hands back fast enough to—

A face. Time stands still, quivering, as I lock on it and . . . wait.

I *know* that face.

I've never seen it in person but I've studied it in tiny photographs. On my laptop screen. In pictures I pulled out of Sabrina's drawer. In a tapestry of black dots, bunched and spread on newsprint. And once, long ago, in risqué Polaroids I found beneath my—

My head hits the cement floor: a flash of light, so sudden and dazzling it's like looking into a tractor's high beams. A crack so loud it seems to split the earth, or at least my skull. Pain follows, a swooping agony, *eeeuuuuurrrrrrrrn*, like the boomerang roar of a race car careening around a track.

Now I'm bouncing upward, lifting off the ground. My whole head hurts—a big bell, struck.

And then the world goes dark.

CHAPTER FORTY-TWO

A sea of empty bookshelves—naked wood as far as the eye can see.

"Don't try to move."

The voice is the flame that touches the end of the firecracker and makes the truth blaze: *Elizabeth*.

Thoughts shuffle in to frame it: *Elizabeth was in the goddamn wine cellar.*

Those aren't bookshelves; it's the basement's exposed ceiling. I'm on the ground. I start to turn my head but there's a white-hot point of pain on the back, and I cry out.

"I told you not to move!" Her Southern accent twangs and I realize she sounds concerned, not malicious.

I start to sit, but the pain pulls like gravity. "What's going on? How long was I out?"

"A second or two," Sabrina answers. Her head pops into view and they're all leaning over me, like that scene at the end of *The Wizard of Oz—you* were there and *you* were there and . . .

"I'm so sorry," Elizabeth says. "I didn't mean for you to fall. Are you okay?"

I sit up, more slowly this time, and take her in. Sitting back on her heels, she's even tinier than me, but rounded and soft, no harsh angles. In the wine cellar behind her, I spot a small red backpack.

"You're Elizabeth," I say. She gives me a slow, cowlike blink, then nods. I look at Sabrina, then Nathan, then back at Elizabeth. "What are you doing here?"

Sabrina lowers her hands in a calm-down gesture. "Let's sit down and discuss this like adults." She turns to me. "Are you okay? Can you stand up?" There's kindness in her voice but I'm still dizzy with confusion. They're all looking at me like *I'm* the surprise, the one who doesn't belong.

I nod, which sends a clang of pain down my neck. Nathan touches my elbow, but I yank away and head into the basement den.

Sabrina perches on the sofa and Elizabeth drops onto a cushion next to her. I narrow my eyes—that's my spot. I sit on the floor near Nathan's feet.

"Okay," Sabrina says, opening up the afternoon's proceedings like an emcee. "First and foremost, we owe Kelly an explanation."

Not an apology?

"Elizabeth showed up this morning," she continues. "We—we had no idea she was in town."

I look at them one by one. "What, she just rang the doorbell?"

"I still knew the code," she says quietly. "I was waiting until I could get them alone."

"Why?" I snap, my insecurity flaring. *So that you could steal them away from me?* She turns to Sabrina and I study her. She could be my stunt double—same petite stature, same blue eyes and smooth blond hair. I'm equal parts fascinated and horrified. Elizabeth is . . . *here.* The real-life Taylor, the woman I've been turning over and over in my mind is inches away. It's like when I first got to Tanglewood and kept goggling at the house, the pool, the Lamonts in the flesh—objects of my obsession brought to life.

"She just got into town," Sabrina says, the way a mom speaks for her child. "From Santa Fe."

"Santa Fe?" My eyes bug. "Wait, all this time that the police have been trying to find you, you were . . . in New Mexico?" I almost laugh. This is stupid. Preposterous. Am I dreaming?

"That's right." Elizabeth shrugs. "I bought a train ticket in cash and used a fake name. Once I got there, I started working on a farm. Gave myself a new backstory—a fresh start." She sniffles and turns to the Lamonts. She's so helpless. It feels practiced, somehow. Affected.

"I missed y'all so much," she says. "But I knew I had to get my head right."

She drops her chin and Nathan and Sabrina make soothing noises. My stomach feels rock hard, clenched with alarm.

I don't care. I want to stand up and scream it. I don't care how she escaped or what she's been up to or if she befriended all the animals on her magical farm and turned it into a goddamn PBS show. The woman Nathan and Sabrina were in love with is alive, and back, and sitting on the blue-gray sectional sofa in our partially exposed basement.

"Things hit a breaking point with her ex," Sabrina says, glancing at me, as if I'd opened my hands and said, *Tell me, please, why she decided to disappear!* "We told you how she was harassing Elizabeth. She kept showing up at your house and bringing her gun, right?"

Elizabeth nods, eyes glimmering with tears. "And the one time I fought back, she shoved me into a wardrobe."

"We documented it that time and helped Elizabeth file a restraining order," Sabrina adds. It's like they're piecing this story together, writing an agreed-upon history. Elizabeth's hand floats to her throat and I realize they're talking about the Polaroid in Sabrina's desk drawer.

"That's right. But it didn't do any good. She got put on administrative leave, and that made her more furious." Elizabeth curls her hands over her belly. "It's like I said—I felt trapped. Not by y'all, but like, I had this sense, this *knowledge* that the only way to break the cycle was to disappear."

"I still wish you'd told us." Nathan's whole face is scrunched. "We could've helped you." He's gazing at her tenderly, the way a baby looks upward while nursing, and my stomach convulses. *Why are you telling me this why do you think I care what the hell is she doing in this house?!*

"I know that, Nate." She holds his eyes before collapsing into more sobs. Nate and Beth and Rina—everyone's got a pet name but me. Mike surfaces in my brain, smiling as he cupped my face: *My Kell-Bell.*

Acid reflux barbs through me, razor-sharp. I force air into my lungs. *Relax, Kelly. They're just being kind to her—she's a battered woman who quite literally broke into their home with nowhere else to go.*

Sabrina presses a palm to her shoulder and Elizabeth grabs it gratefully. My guts twist in jealousy. I think back to what I learned in the bubble bath: Elizabeth wanted the two of them to run off together.

"Elizabeth was smart," Sabrina continues. "She took out a bunch of cash and stashed a go bag in her trunk."

"Oh, and the camera at the gate?" Nathan sits up, animated. "Turns out she drove up, but then changed her mind. She never actually came in!"

"The detectives didn't tell us *that*," Sabrina adds. Elizabeth still hasn't let go of her hand. No—I'm not losing them to her, not without a fight.

I pull in another long inhalation. *Don't be paranoid,* I remind myself. *You know how much they love you.*

Elizabeth nods excitedly. "See, exactly! I didn't want to give the detectives any reason to come after you two. And I couldn't ask y'all to lie for me." She looks at her feet, a doe-eyed Botticelli subject. Nathan and Sabrina are lapping it up. "Plus, I knew if I saw you, I'd lose my nerve and not be able to go through with it."

"But you *did* sic the detectives on them." I can't help myself. "By showing up on that security camera. And, I hate to say it, but you're kind of putting us all in a bad situation by being here now, right?"

Nathan and Sabrina stare at me like I've said something vulgar, and my ears and throat grow hot. The Kelly they love is compassionate, agreeable—now's not the time to push them.

I swallow the rock in my throat. "Elizabeth, I'm sorry you went through that," I say. "But why are you here? Now?" I point at the floor. I leave the second part unspoken: *What does her reappearance mean for me, for us?*

Elizabeth keeps crying and finally Sabrina touches her chin, then tenderly lifts her face. Elizabeth's answer is a whisper meant only for Sabrina, but I hear it: "I couldn't stay away."

Elizabeth's face moves closer. The heat between them feels palpable, like the shimmering waves wafting off the concrete on Chicago's hottest days.

Wait. Sabrina's not turning away.

And as I watch, floating in a bubble of horror and disbelief, Elizabeth and Sabrina kiss.

CHAPTER FORTY-THREE

"Sabrina! What are you doing?" The words shoot out of me, and the two pull apart and turn, four sand-dollar eyes. All along, I assumed we were a unit, a closed system, but as my pulse races and everybody stares at me, I realize they never promised me exclusivity. Blackness sucks at the corners of my vision. What if I got it all wrong?

"I'm sorry," Sabrina murmurs, scooting away from Elizabeth. She looks up at Nathan, guilt splashed across her face.

"Let's all take a beat." Nathan bounces his palms toward the floor. His voice sounds on, fake, the tone he must use to address a boardroom. "Emotions are running high."

"You could say that," I blubber, my voice round with hurt.

"I'm sorry," Sabrina says. "I wasn't thinking."

"I leave for twelve hours and you forget I exist?" It ekes out of me between sobs.

"Not at all!" She stretches to set her hand on my knee.

"You gotta understand—when Beth showed up, we weren't sure if you were coming back," Nathan says. Rejection forks through me like a lightning bolt.

"We're *glad* you're back," Sabrina chokes out. "Christ, we're glad both of you are okay. We just . . . shit." Her fingers push against her brow.

Elizabeth's staring at me and, through my tears, I meet her gaze defiantly. God, she's pretty. Sitting across from her, I feel like her uglier stunt double. Another sob lurches through me. *Now there's nowhere I belong.*

"When you came back, I begged them not to tell you about me," she offers. "They said you're trustworthy, but I couldn't take the risk. No one can know I'm here; Nate and Sabrina are the only people on the planet I can trust."

"Plus, if her ex's jealousy was a source of violence, well." Nathan shrugs. "You can see why Beth didn't want us to tell our new partner she's here."

"Not that you're jealous! Or violent!" Sabrina adds.

"Or your ex," I point out.

"I'm real sorry." Elizabeth lists closer to me. "I told them this, and I'll tell you too: I'm sorry for all this bullshit. I never meant to hurt anyone. And I definitely didn't mean to get you wrapped up in any of this."

I narrow my eyes at her. I've never liked reckless people. You think you're above reproach because you refuse to be conscientious, to think ahead—to consider the consequences of your actions? Because you insist on hoisting your own needs above everyone else's?

But then I shush the cruel thoughts. I'm not here to judge Elizabeth. I'm here for Nathan and Sabrina, my loves. The ones I came back for. The ones who feel like home.

So I nod. "Thanks. And again, I'm sorry for everything you went through." I glance up. "Nathan, Sabrina, I was going to surprise you with a nice meal. That's why I came downstairs—to grab a bottle of wine. Should . . . should I make us something?"

They look at one another and the air calcifies around us, turning pointy, uncomfortable. But then Nathan smiles: "I gotta say, Kelly's a hell of a cook."

Everyone chuckles, the tension broken, and we stand.

And then, Lord help me, I walk into the kitchen and begin making dinner for the woman I love, the man I love, and their missing ex.

I hear them retreat to different corners of the mansion: Nathan to his office, Sabrina to the library, Elizabeth still in the basement doing God-knows-what. My hands shake as I rinse and dry and dice. *What's she doing here? What's her endgame?* The knife waggles as I position it, and its thumps against the cutting board make me jump. Chopping through a carrot, I imagine the blade slipping, neatly severing a finger from my hand. *Thunk. Thunk. Thunk.* I can't believe I'm doing this. Making coq au vin and mashed potatoes for this woman, the one I replaced.

The chicken, steeped in wine, sizzles on a skillet. A drop of white-hot oil hits my wrist. I hear Sabrina get up and I freeze, but then she walks into the bathroom. I'm piecing together a nice meal by rote, cringing as I picture it touching Elizabeth's lips and tongue. I splash brandy into the pan, ignite it. Nathan's footsteps make the ceiling creak. The stew thickens. I could scream.

The breakfast nook is a bit tight for four, so Sabrina sets the table in the dining room, cloth napkins and wineglasses and it's so fully absurd I laugh as I carry the serving dishes out to it. It's like a magazine photo spread: *Perfect Tablescapes for a Welcome-Home Meal to Remember.*

I flinch, thinking again about the homecoming I pictured for myself. *Kelly, you're back!* But Elizabeth beat me to the punch. The prodigal son out front, stealing my thunder. I can't wait until this woman leaves us alone for a moment and I can ask Nathan and Sabrina how they're feeling about her reappearance.

Is this happening? Are we really going to make small talk and clink glasses and remark on how goat cheese adds brightness to the mashed potatoes when *Elizabeth has been hanging out in the American Southwest just so she could come back here to . . . what? Hide in the basement like a squatter?!*

We take our seats, Elizabeth kitty-corner from me. She looks like that Disney princess, Aurora—the sleeping beauty, docile and sad. We fill our plates and Nathan pours the wine. It's so tense and awkward that I could die, I could actually burst into flames.

"So how did y'all meet?" Elizabeth asks.

Nathan and Sabrina are conspicuously tongue-tied so I answer. My insides feel like they're on fire.

"We didn't mean for it to happen," Nathan blurts out. Sabrina's face contorts like a Picasso painting, but he can't help himself: "We—I'm sorry, Kelly, I don't mean to be rude. But, Beth, we weren't . . . we were still grieving. We didn't forget about you. We just . . . well, it happened."

My heart capsizes. I stare at him, careful not to blink until the tears are reabsorbed.

"I think what my husband is trying to say . . ." Sabrina says, and we all cringe, hearing it through our own lenses: Elizabeth the ex, Kelly the rebound-slash-third-wheel, and Nathan the . . . well, *Nathan*. It's the stupid Talking Heads song again, and we ask ourselves: How, *how* did we get here?

Sabrina clears her throat. "We have so much love and respect for both of you." Does Sabrina ever lose her cool? Even now, she's talking like a therapist. She looks back and forth between Elizabeth and me— Old and New; Former and Present; sometime inhabitants of that damn spare room. "We want everyone to feel comfortable and safe."

Safe. I flash back to those nights in bed with Nathan, fear and excitement rocking through me, no safe word, no telling him to stop. The incident in the hot tub; the loaded gun hunched in his nightstand. The cloud of suspicion around them both that terrified me but made me feel alive, too, always on my toes.

Versus all those nights with Mike. Cotton candy at a carnival in Lake Forest; that brief, glorious period when Virgo wanted to play fetch for hours, before one day glancing at the fabric mouse and turning back to us like, *Pshht, you expect me to get that?* How we cuddled on the couch on our last day in Chicago and listened to audiobooks on the long drive to Pennsylvania and how we could still make each other laugh, hooking into goofiness at the most random times. And sure, sometimes he had the emotional regulation of a four-year-old, and our relationship wasn't exactly passionate. But I never doubted he was one of the good ones. He'd never lead me into a lion's den like this.

"I understand," Elizabeth says. She sets her hand on top of Sabrina's and they exchange a tender look; jealousy simmers inside me again. "I'm the one who left. I didn't want y'all to wait around for me. I missed you both, but . . . I want you to be happy."

I stare into my glass, at the oxblood moon of pinot noir inside.

"You're safe, Beth." Nathan's fierce protectiveness makes me envious too. "We won't let anything happen to you."

"I know. I always feel safe with you." She looks back and forth between them, her eyes soft and teary, a lovely Southern belle. "I missed y'all so much."

She's like a baby bird in need of security. I feel it again, the love like warm sunlight beaming between them, and the envy and rejection and, and *outsiderness* make me want to sob.

"Are you going to see your aunt?" I ask loudly, popping a hunk of chicken into my mouth. Everyone looks at me, alarmed. "Lydia, is it? I know she's in the neighborhood. And your cousin and the cousin's kids, right?" I want to push her on it—tell her how everyone hates the Lamonts now, how the boys dragged dead animals here in a childish attempt to scare us away—but her face crumples and I feel awful again.

"I don't know. I haven't thought that far ahead."

"It's okay, Elizabeth," Sabrina shushes. I stare at my plate. We're all ice sculptures.

Finally I stand. "Everyone finished eating?"

It breaks the spell, thank God. I turn away swiftly, before they can see my tears.

CHAPTER FORTY-FOUR

Nathan shepherds us into the living room and cues up a Tom Petty album. Sabrina drops onto the couch and Elizabeth sits next to her again, sideways, toes against Sabrina's thigh. Sadness drops through me like a stone in a ravine. Will that ever be me again?

Nathan pours us tall glasses of scotch from the bar cart. He really doesn't know that Elizabeth asked Sabrina to run off with her? From where I sit, Elizabeth's favoritism is obvious. Is that why she's here, to drive a wedge between Nathan and Sabrina?

Their eyes and fingers linger when Nathan hands her a drink. *Oh my God—what if Elizabeth told* him *the same thing?*

I slug back my whiskey and set the glass on the rug. The three of them chat as if this weren't the strangest goddamn tableau of all time. I study Elizabeth. *What are you doing here?* I notice that, though she touches the glass to her full lips, she isn't really drinking.

I can't take it anymore. "So . . . what is the plan?"

They all turn to me, wide-eyed. An immediate wash of regret— I can't keep doing this, being so demanding and making everyone uncomfortable.

I can't if I want them to still love me.

"What do you mean?" Nathan asks.

"For Elizabeth. Are you staying, are you gonna contact your family, are we all going to, like, live together in secret for a while, or . . . ?"

There's a long, awkward silence.

Elizabeth's lips quiver and she looks away. "I'm sorry, Kelly. I don't have a plan." I think it again: *You're reckless.* "Given the pandemic, I assumed that when I got here Nate and Sabrina would be . . . alone."

"You said you got here this morning," I point out.

"No, that's when I came inside."

A jolt of alarm. "Holy shit. How long have you been here?" The blond hair, the occasional feeling of being watched. Has she been crouching in that bedroom closet, spying on us through the two-way mirror? Sneaking around the house at night, standing in the doorway of the spare room and vowing to take it back? "You've been watching me, right? From the—"

"I got here yesterday," she says. "I was traveling by night, paying taxis in cash, trying to keep a low profile. I walked in from Brinsmere." She plays with a lock of hair. "When I got to the house and saw you inside, I freaked out. I was gonna turn around and walk back out of Tanglewood, but then—it was wild, I thought I was hallucinating—I spotted Renee. My ex? At the gate. I thought she was in D.C., but she was prowling around Tanglewood, like she was waiting for me. And I could tell she couldn't get into the property, so I figured the best thing was to wait and get inside as soon as I could." She blinks. "The safest place for me was actually here."

I look at Sabrina and Nathan. "Renee was here? Trying to get inside?" Is *that* whom I've seen around the property—the press of eyeballs I couldn't ignore?

Nathan nods. "We confirmed it with the security camera."

"Why?" They all look confused and I shake my head. "Why was she trying to get in?"

Sabrina shrugs. "Same reason the Atwoods hate us: She thinks we weren't telling the truth about Elizabeth. That inside, we must have bloodstains on the floor or her shackled in the basement or something."

Her eyes widen, like she's surprised by what just popped out of her mouth.

They're lying to you. It's the voice again, hissing, insistent. Her whole story is ridiculous. I'm supposed to believe that, months after she disappeared, Elizabeth *happened* to arrive the same hour as her villainous ex?

"So I showed up earlier today," she continues. "It felt like a lucky break when you took off last night. And you still weren't here this morning. So I . . . I walked inside. I had no idea how they'd react, but . . . well, you know how amazing they are." She beams at them; my stomach cramps.

They're acting like this isn't the most outlandish tale they've ever heard. And she probably hopes I haven't noticed that she's avoiding my number-one question.

"Why come back now?" I press. "Sounds like you pulled the whole disappearance off pretty well." The air changes again, another tang of discomfort, and I grow impatient. "Can anyone tell me what's going on?"

"She's been through a lot of trauma," Sabrina says. She gazes at me and for a wild second I'm not sure whether she means Elizabeth or me.

"Anybody need a refresher?" Nathan lifts his empty rocks glass.

"I want to see the video." They all turn to me sharply.

"What?" Nathan says.

"The security footage. From yesterday." I stand. "You saw Renee on it? I want to see it too." My heart bangs inside my chest. Is this it? The moment I catch them lying to me . . . again?

"You're right. We're asking you to take a lot at face value." Sabrina gets up from the couch. "Shall we?"

I follow her upstairs, with Nathan and Elizabeth trailing behind us. "Did you *tell* someone Renee was skulking around the property?" I murmur to Sabrina. "Doesn't Elizabeth have a restraining order?"

She groans. "You want us to call her friends at the Deerbrook PD? And say what—that she came to our gate and then walked away?" At the top of the stairs, she turns to face me. "Elizabeth *does* have a restraining order. She even got Renee suspended from the force, remember? But tell me, Kelly—how do I accuse someone of being within a hundred yards of a *missing person*?"

I'm speechless, sputtering. Sabrina closes her eyes and gives her head a tired shake before continuing into Nathan's office. She's right, it was a stupid question. But since when does Sabrina talk to me that way?

Nathan plunks down in his Eames chair. As he wakes his computer, my eye snags on the stone pyramid on the wall.

"This is . . . what, your family crest?" I lift it from the shelf. It's caked in dust, and my fingers leave shiny streaks where they've wiped it clean.

Elizabeth nods. "I gave that to them when they moved in. I had it in a closet and it was sort of a joke—like, now you're on Atwood territory."

"I'm in," Nathan says. I shove the dusty green triangle back into place and we crowd around him. On the monitor, I'm driving up in his SUV earlier today, my expression rattled. He rewinds to this morning, and there's Elizabeth, her backpack slung over one shoulder, darting up to the gate and letting herself inside.

In reverse, star- and sunlight strobe. Now it's my birthday and I cross the threshold on my way *to* Tysons Corner, the SUV moving jerkily. A jogger bobs past. We get home from our seafood dinner, and then we leave for it. We take turns popping outside to collect birthday treats for me.

"There," Sabrina says. Someone with a baseball hat arrives at the gate, a small box clutched in her hands. "Renee was carrying something— we have no idea what."

My neck prickles and hairs pop along my arm. The figure pulls out a phone and glances up, and Nathan hits Pause at exactly the right time. I take in the glimpse of face: dark hair, sharp nose, angular jaw.

I'm bringing over cupcakes, the text reads. *I'd love to see you and say happy birthday, but I'll leave them at the gate if you're busy!*

So they're mistaken. "No, that's the new neighbor. The one I hung out with a few times—Megan."

The three of them exchange a piercing, panicked look.

"Her name's not Megan," Elizabeth says. "That's Renee."

CHAPTER FORTY-FIVE

My heart ticks like a bomb. "No. No way. Megan's not . . . she's straight, she . . ." But then the penny drops. My eyes widen. "Wait, *you're* the ex who stole her money! And tried to get her fired! That was *you*!"

Elizabeth's jaw drops. "Hold on, *you're* friends with my *abusive ex*?"

"She's a grifter!" I point at Elizabeth as my eyes dart to Nathan and Sabrina. "Can't you see? I bet she already asked you for money. We can't trust her!"

"You can't trust *me*? Nate, you've got to get her out of here. She's colluding with Renee!"

"Enough." Nathan stands, suddenly terrifying. "We are going to discuss this like adults."

Elizabeth glares at me, so I stare right back, lips trembling, defiant. Finally Sabrina touches my arm.

"Nathan's right," she says soothingly. "I'm sure we can get to the bottom of it." She waits for me to turn to her, then murmurs, "It's okay, Kelly. Really."

She squeezes my hand and there it is, proof that she's *my* partner, in my corner. Elizabeth sees it too; her eyes narrow, and I feel a spritz of victory.

I suck in a breath. "Megan is . . . I thought she was my friend." I feel that crumbly sensation you get when, midway through an argument, you realize you're wrong. "We bumped into each other near Brinsmere not long after I moved in. We only hung out a couple times before I ghosted her. But she told me her partner drained her savings." I cross my arms. "Sure, some of what she said was a lie. But was that part true? Did you steal from her?"

"Kelly—" Sabrina tries to warn, but Elizabeth shrugs.

"I took almost ten thousand dollars. After everything she did to me, it felt like the least she could do."

Sabrina's and Nathan's mouths drop. I turn to them, fists clenched. "Did she ask you for money? Is that why she's here?"

"Don't talk about me like I'm not here." Her eyes flash. "And how do I know you're telling the truth? For all we know, Renee *sent* you to—"

"I went to high school with Kelly," Sabrina says softly. "I can vouch for her. I can vouch for you *both*."

"Renee is the rat here," Nathan adds.

I scrape my memory: that initial run-in, how Renee seemed surprised and delighted that I lived in this mansion. She targeted me—she knew all along. "God, she kept asking about you two, but I was all hung up on not accidentally saying anything about our relationship." I scrub my hands over my face. "I thought nothing of it."

Now the memories are flickering, faster and faster:

That's my favorite house in the neighborhood! Is the inside amazing too?
I'd love to come over! I'm dying to see the inside.
Maybe we can hang out there when they're not around.

"That bitch." Elizabeth stomps her foot.

I'm teary, ashamed. "I'm sorry—I feel so stupid. She was obviously trying to use me."

"I bet she was triggered when you ghosted her." Elizabeth drums her fingers. "Was this the first time she came to the house?"

I frown. "I think so."

"So she decided to show up and see if you'd let her in." Elizabeth rubs her brow. "She risked being on camera to get back into your good graces because you were her only in. That sounds like Renee—trying to pump you for info."

"She's a master manipulator," Sabrina notes. "You bumped into her, like, your first week here, right?"

I nod. Alarm flutters through the room, gasps and nervous hand motions.

"I bet she's crashing with Lydia," Elizabeth says.

It takes me a second: "Your aunt? *She* likes Renee?"

"They all do. Michelle too." Her fingers twist together. "They love her. Thought she was the best thing that ever happened to me, and wouldn't believe a word I said even though I had the bruises to prove it."

"Wow, this is starting to make sense," Sabrina says. "They're like a real-life true-crime subreddit that's convinced we made Elizabeth disappear."

"Or that we're hiding her," Nathan points out. "It makes sense now that we know Renee didn't do anything."

"And now you *are* hiding her," I add.

"Fair point." Nathan grimaces. "For once, Renee's right."

A beat. My head thrums and swarms like a buzzy wasp's nest. For me, the facts aren't lining up: How could Elizabeth's family be Team Renee when the abuse allegations were serious enough to get Renee suspended? Renee duped *me*, sure, but I didn't have a blood relative calling her a liar and cataloging evidence of battery.

Elizabeth exhales, puffing out her cheeks. "Well, this has all been terrifying," she snips. "Unless there's anything else, I'm going to shower and go to sleep."

There's a desperate, ticking silence. Possessiveness roars up in me. "Take my room. I'll sleep with Nathan and Sabrina."

She eyes me. Her nose twitches. "Thanks, Kelly."

"You're welcome."

We stand there another moment, eyes locked like horns, and then she turns and swishes out of the room.

And finally, finally, we're alone. I clear my throat, nerves twitching.

"So . . . has anyone given any thought to what this means for the three of us?" We hear the soft sough of the shower next door.

Nathan looks at me, vacant-eyed. "We're going to need a minute, Kelly. That's not exactly the most pressing issue on hand."

His words hit me like a slap, and my insides drop as though they're being sucked through a pneumatic tube. He's right—I was rude to their abused ex right in front of them. Not a great look.

"We should clear the table," Sabrina says, glancing at the door.

An idea cracks open. "I'm going to grab some of my things," I say, before scuttling down the hall.

In my room, I flick on the light, feeling that hot rush, fingers itching. The bed's made differently—someone already changed the sheets for her. Virgo is coiled on the end, impervious to the unfolding drama. I glance around desperately, then spot what I'm looking for: that red backpack, whatever Elizabeth brought into this house. An answer, perhaps, to the question that's making everyone squirrelly: Why did she return?

I know it's an invasion of privacy, but I can't stop myself. And after all, didn't she invade *my* privacy by entering our home?

I whisk the backpack off the floor. My heart's like a bass drum, the grand one that brings up a marching band's caboose: harder and harder, faster and faster, so loud it drowns out the sounds around me.

"What are you doing?"

She's in the doorframe, a huge towel wrapped around her tiny frame.

I freeze, my hands as red as the backpack hanging from them.

Her eyes narrow. "Get your hands off my shit. *Now.*"

CHAPTER FORTY-SIX

I let go of the backpack and shoot her an apologetic smile.

"Just grabbing a few essentials. Trying to find my pajamas."

She nods warily. "Your dirty clothes were on the floor. I put them in the closet."

"*Thank* you," I reply, though what I actually mean is much more obscene.

"You're welcome." She takes a step toward me, somehow straight-backed and dignified in a towel.

She watches as I whip a few of my things from the nightstand and closet. My fingers brush against the bodysuit—*her* bodysuit—and I stiffen.

"You know you're only here because I left," she murmurs.

No. I slowly turn to her, feeling hollow and cold. "What did you say?"

She crosses her arms, still leaning in the doorway. I hear the clatter of the Lamonts cleaning up downstairs—out of earshot. "They opened up their marriage for me." She shrugs. "Something they thought they'd never do. And you're a stand-in. Hey, I get it"—she gestures around—

"everyone's lonely, it's a pandemic. But I was their first. And they've been waiting for me. Holding out hope I'd come back." A soft, blinky smile. "And, shoot, here I am."

I stand, pulse thudding. There's a ringing in my ears, sharp as a root canal. "They might buy your damsel-in-distress bullshit, but I don't. You're a snake." I narrow my eyes. "I'll figure out what you're doing here." Her eyes zip to the backpack behind me, then back up.

"What, you think you're going to get *me* kicked out?" Her chin juts.

I tilt my head. "You act like you're the one with all the power. But all I have to do is call nine-one-one." I move one step closer. "Or, you know who else's number I have?"

Her eyes widen as it dawns on her: *Renee*. "Nate and Sabrina would never forgive you," she snarls.

"Maybe so." I open my palms. They're shaking but it doesn't matter—she sees it, my upper hand. "All I'm saying is: Don't cross me."

Virgo vaults off the bed and gallops under it, breaking the spell. I finish gathering my things, arms quaking, and flash Elizabeth a big, square smile. "If you need anything, let us know," I say, like a proper hostess. "Good night."

She closes the door behind me; my heart slams against my chest. I'm a few steps into the hallway when she opens it again, and I tense, but it's just to let Virgo out.

My knees wobble as I head downstairs. *Have I ever spoken to anyone that way?* I didn't know I was capable of it.

I pause on the last step and grab the banister, breathing hard. I'm there again, on the floor of Mike's office, the bull's-eye in a room that looks like a crime scene—furniture overturned, glass shattered, things ripped apart. Blood soaking into my sleeve and oozing along the cracks inside my wrist.

I don't know who you are, Mike said through clenched teeth. *This is a side of you I've never seen.*

I twist around to look up the stairs. Adrenaline streams through me. I don't know who I am either. Did I really do that? Will she tell them what I've said?

But as I turn and hook through the foyer, indignation rises. How dare she? Telling me I'm on the verge of getting kicked out—I'm not a placeholder. I'm their partner.

And I need to figure out what she's doing here.

I pause at the kitchen's threshold. Sabrina and Nathan are wordlessly thunking cups into the dishwasher, scooping leftovers into Tupperware, erasing all the evidence of our charged dinner. I have the wild, eerie thought that once they're done, they'll have cleared me away too, deleted my hours at the house since I came back from Tysons Corner.

I clear my throat. "Elizabeth's all set up in my room."

"Good. Thanks." Sabrina stomps into the mudroom, then ferrets around in the cabinets. "Did someone move the spray cleaner?"

"Oh sorry, I probably stuck it under the sink." I rush to grab it and she plucks it from my hand wordlessly. Are they still annoyed that I dared to ask what this meant for our relationship? I perch at the island. All our spark is gone, the electricity and ease that made us *us*.

All because of Elizabeth. I feel a scrunching sensation in my chest. Our relationship's shoved off its axis, spinning wonkily and on the brink of toppling. I never should have left; I should have stuck by my loves, looked them in the eye instead of snatching up Nathan's keys and tearing out of here.

None of this would have happened if I'd stayed where I belonged.

"Do . . . do we have a plan for tomorrow?"

Nathan power-sighs. "Nobody has a plan. And nobody has some secret agenda they're keeping from you. We're all taking it an hour at a time. Okay?" He raises his eyebrows at me, exasperated, and I blink back tears.

I nod, gulping down the knot of emotions snarled in my throat. "Sorry. I'm going to bed."

"Night," Sabrina says flatly, spattering bleach onto the island. I drop my chin and hurry out.

Upstairs, I pause in front of Nathan's office. I replay the security footage in my mind, Elizabeth confidently slipping through the gate. Like she belongs—like they were expecting her.

My stomach twists. They want me to believe that Elizabeth *happened* to arrive at the exact same moment I took off. But isn't it more likely that she was in touch with one or both Lamonts? Maybe they invited her in after they presumed I'd left for good . . .

The last text I got at the Ritz-Carlton: *Feel free to call an Uber and we'll collect Nathan's car later.* Was that a subtle, passive-aggressive hint to GTFO?

Nerves crawl across my shoulders, buglike, as I continue on to their room. I shouldn't have run away, shouldn't have been rude to their wretched ex. Shouldn't have broken into Sabrina's locked drawer or hidden in the closet on the other side of this glinting mirror. They'll never love me now, and I can't blame them—I think I hate me too. I'm not a grifter, but I'm no more honest than one: I lie and dig and betray, betray, betray.

As I lie alone in Nathan and Sabrina's massive bed, though, spiky anger creeps into the swampy hurt, then overtakes it.

Fuck Elizabeth. She's the catalyst, not me, the one who screwed up our happy island. All of our tension, everything that's gone wrong traces back to her.

My last thought before I fall asleep is that I hate this woman. Not me. Elizabeth. She's the interloper, the spare.

And I need her gone.

I get a horrible night's sleep: jagged dreams of abandonment; pulses of rejection; grubby envy as I replay Elizabeth kissing Sabrina over and over, like a canker sore I can't leave alone. We all sleep restlessly, bathroom breaks and comings and goings, awakenings I barely register in the dark.

Finally, I wake for real and hear Virgo mewling in the hall. I roll off the bed, my whole body wrung-out and sore, and stagger to the door.

It's bright out here, the open landing washed in morning sun, and I blink as I piece together the scene. Virgo's sitting in front of the spare room, meowing. When she sees me, she starts to pace.

Huh, the bedroom door is open a few inches—didn't Elizabeth close it last night? She probably doesn't want Virgo piano-keying across her torso at this hour; I head down the hall to shut it.

But when I get close, Virgo darts inside. I sigh and start to go back to bed—what do I care, everyone's already choosing Elizabeth over me— but inside she starts warbling again.

I rub my eyes, confused. Virgo bolts out of the room and back inside; it's an odd time for zoomies, those normally come in the evening. She stops short in the dark tongue of shadow between the door and frame and stares at me, *mrrow*.

Hairs pop along my neck and arms. Is Elizabeth just ignoring Virgo's shenanigans? No one could sleep through that. I creep closer and call, "Sorry about my cat, she's used to sleeping with me in there."

No answer. Virgo disappears back inside, her orange tail fat and bristled. The seconds seem to spread out as I set my fingers on the door and push. "Elizabeth?"

Virgo is on the floor near the foot of the bed, bobbing her head the way she does when I bring a new toy or piece of furniture inside, like she's working up the courage to investigate.

"Virgo?"

She chirrups, tail swishing.

Then the fear hits me. All at once, like diving into a pool. My muscles tense and I rear back, abruptly certain that something is wrong. I get the eerie feeling this room isn't mine, that I've opened the wrong door and stumbled through a portal. I'm not here—I'm elsewhere.

Slowly, slowly, my eyes sweep over the butterscotch-colored floorboards. To the bottom of the bed frame, then the edge of the comforter, the fluffed horizon where it folds over the mattress.

Above it, a foot. And then my eyes hurtle forward, hungry, *shooom*, they charge up the rest of the bed and take it all in at once: pale legs, gray underwear, thin cotton tank top askew on her slight frame, nipples and knees pointing up at the sky.

The broad splotch of blood, cardinal-red and soaking half of her hair and dyeing the duvet from her shoulder to the top of her head. A deep wound over her ear, wet as a mouth.

I rush forward and reach for the other shoulder, the Good Samaritan part of me duking it out with the repulsion. *This is a human being. You have to help.*

And then I take in one more detail, one more jumble of input my brain assembles into something familiar, wrong, terrifying.

Elizabeth's eyes, wide open. Vacant. Unblinking.

And then I start to scream.

CHAPTER FORTY-SEVEN

It's the scream I've been holding back for so long, the scream that's plugged my windpipe ever since I yanked open the door to the wine cellar and stumbled into this nightmare. Ever since I realized how much the Lamonts were hiding from me.

I don't register the clatter of footfalls behind me. I don't sense them charging up the hall or throwing themselves through the open door. They stop short right at my back. I only quiet when Nathan grabs me and pulls me away from the bed, twirling me like a ballerina trap-trap-trapped inside a music box and then wrapping me in his arms.

I quit howling like his chest is an Off button, no, a muzzle, a vegan leather gag like the one they keep in Sabrina's nightstand, but I'm choking, still, struggling to breathe as my hot breath dampens his T-shirt.

But the screaming doesn't stop, it's not me anymore it's Sabrina, and I feel Nathan look over at his wife and this is the problem, three people means no one to comfort Sabrina and he loosens his vise grip around me and I wither. He props me against the wall, where I drop to the ground, and then reaches for Sabrina's elbow. She's wrapped her arms around Elizabeth's shoulders and is crying into her neck so the whole bed shakes.

And I watch, my whole body one big set of eyes, as he disentangles Sabrina's arms and drags her over to where I sit and she droops to the floor too. She curls her hands around the crook of my arm, tight as a blood pressure cuff, and I must be dreaming, hallucinating, because I suspected that Nathan and Sabrina had hurt Elizabeth, and Renee thought so as well, and Diane and Elizabeth's extended family and maybe the detectives, too, but *no one had*, that's the twist: She was fine all along.

But look at her now.

Movement at the door—it's Virgo, seated in the doorway like it really is a threshold. Virgo and Sabrina and I watch as Nathan, eyes grim, presses two fingers to Elizabeth's throat. After a few frozen seconds he makes a horsey, snorty sound and backs away.

"Fuck," he says. His back hits the wall and he, three, plops to the floor.

We sit that way for a minute, Sabrina squeezing my arm like a boa constrictor. Finally Virgo gathers her courage and leaps, all gymnast-graceful, onto the foot of the bed. Nathan and I spring into action, shooing her off and out the door.

We linger there and Nathan goes back for his wife, he offers her his hand and she stands and we shuffle into the hallway. I pull the door closed behind us. Like we can pretend it never happened, out of sight, out of mind. *Whoops, sorry,* like when you open up the wrong dressing room.

"I'll get my phone," I finally say. It's like I'm moving underwater, every step slow and weighted.

"Wait."

I turn back, and Nathan wets his lips and says it again. "Wait. Let's just think."

You know the feeling when you've been staring at a brainteaser for too long, turning it over in your mind, and all of a sudden—*aha!*—the answer is there, wholesale, and you can't believe you didn't see it all along?

That's how it hits me. *Eureka!* Someone killed Elizabeth. Someone in this house.

I could be locked in a mansion with a murderer.

"'Think'?" I repeat. My heart grows more and more staccato. "We need to call the cops."

Sabrina stands behind him, shoulders hunched. Her eyes are wide and vacant. The horror inside me is charged and ferocious and too big, pressing against my head and chest and throat. If I don't let it out, I'll explode like a spoiled can of tomato paste.

Nathan picks his way over to me and grabs my hands. I recoil, my fingers clammy-cold in his grip. He looks deep into my eyes. "Let's talk about this."

I open my mouth but only a dry, quavering sound comes out.

"Kelly, breathe." He interlaces his fingers with mine. "Look at me. It's okay."

"But she's—they're looking for her." My throat bobs and I begin to slide my fingers out from his. "We're in way over our heads. We need to call nine-one-one." Just like I threatened to last night. Only now, for real.

"No." He tightens his fists.

Fresh fear bolts through me, a fluorescent streak. "Let me go."

"We're not calling the cops."

"Of course we are. Let go." The floor squeaks as I rock back. He switches his grip and, in a flash, he's holding my wrists.

"The cops will arrest us and put us in jail." His voice is steady, lower than usual. "They will charge us with murder. That can't happen."

"Stop it. You're scaring me." My abdomen hollows. I jerk my arms, try to wrestle away, but he's unflappable, unstoppable. Cold-eyed and calculating—a sociopath straight out of central casting.

"Think about it, Kelly." Sabrina steps forward. She's shaking all over, her teeth chattering. *Oh my God, she agrees with him.* "Nobody knows she's here; she's been missing for months. But *someone* did this. Someone's going down for it." She comes closer. "Think about all the physical evidence. How this will look."

The horror inside me is changing shape, zapping, a cloud of vapors set on fire. I turn toward the door and picture what's behind it: the bundle formerly known as Elizabeth Kessler. Our DNA clinging to her like glitter. Fingerprints like spots on a dalmatian. I touched her shoulder; she's stretched on my duvet. Sabrina gathered her in a sobby hug.

"Not to mention, everyone in the precinct is a fan of Renee." Nathan shakes his head. "There's no scenario where calling the police ends well for us."

You did this. Coldness fans through my torso. It's the only thing that makes sense—the only reason he'd want to keep the cops away. A clang of insight that nearly knocks me off my feet: *If they could kill their lover in cold blood . . .*

There's a gun in the house, a loaded gun in Nathan's nightstand. Do I need to get to it first? How can I call for help?

"We're not calling the cops." Nathan dips his chin. "If we call nine-one-one, you're going down too. Jail time, a trial. The end of life as we know it." Our eyes bore into each other's, mine pleading, his set. What if I say no? If I spit in his face and rush to the bedroom in a mad dash for my phone?

"Is that a threat?"

Nathan raises his eyebrows. "No. Just a fact."

Sabrina leans against the wall, her eyes unfocused. *He's right.* My arms go slack and Nathan releases them.

"Look . . . we're already on lockdown." He stuffs his hands in the pockets of his sweatpants. "No one's coming in or out. We get to decide how to handle this."

My heart hasn't slowed. Will it burst in my chest?

"I don't understand." I pull away and turn my head. "Nathan. I don't understand what happened."

A look zips between them. I remember my raggedy sleep, my vague impression that people were moving. Did one of them follow her into the spare room? How did she die?

I gaze down at my own hands, gripped in front of my heart. Clean, unblemished. The gash from when I tore apart Mike's office is mostly healed now, a dark splotch near my thumb, irrefutable evidence of the first time I snapped.

I take in their hands, too, all normal, none red.

I hear again the wicked thoughts my brain hissed right before I fell asleep: *I hate this woman. I need her gone.*

No. I would never, ever hurt anyone. Yes, I've had bad thoughts take over my body and turn into actions, but I could never in a million years hurt someone, let alone kill them.

I glance back and forth between their faces. It's like we're telepathically connected, a triangle of consciousness: *One of us did this. One of us is guilty.*

My jaw is so tight, it would crack if I opened it. My eyes ache to dart toward the front door, *get away,* but I force them to connect with Nathan's instead.

"Okay," I say, my voice shaking. "You're right."

"Good," he grunts. His shoulders drop and he leans against the catwalk's banister. "Let's just think."

And I take off.

I pound down the front stairs two at a time, *thump-thump-thump* as fast as a woodpecker, and throw open the front door. I know someone's behind me as I sail down the stone steps and rocket onto the driveway, pavement scalding my bare feet, pajamas flopping around me, I need to be quicker, I have to reach the gate, it's getting larger now, looming, almost there, if I can—

I reach the iron and bring my finger to the keypad, heart exploding in my rib cage, fingers shaking as I push them against the bubbled buttons, *ten-forty-three.*

Two flashes of red, a beep. *No.* I jiggle the iron, desperate.

I type it in a second time, more deliberate, 1-0-4-3.

"Kelly!"

I jump and twist around. Sabrina's alone, closing the distance between us. I throw my back against the gate, terrified.

"Kelly, stop." She jogs the last few yards between us. She shakes her head. "No one's going to hurt you. But Nathan changed the code."

My chest heaves. "He needs to let me out."

"We can't. No one can go in or out." She's crying, too, her face raw and young.

I grip the gate's bars and scream onto the street. The sound echoes and comes back to me, unnoticed. I drown into sobs and tip my forehead against the cool iron. Goddamn Tanglewood snobs tucked away in their fortresses.

"Kelly, let's go back inside." She twists her hair over one shoulder. "I know you're scared. I am too. But we need to work together. Okay?"

I turn around. "I'm not going back in there," I snarl.

Her chest caves. "Kelly. We love you. But do you see how this looks?"

I gaze up at the house, its windows like unblinking eyes. Heaviness fills my insides. And suddenly it's obvious. "You're saying this makes me look guilty." Trying to flee the scene of the crime. I'm the one with the clearest motivation, right? I even articulated it to myself yesterday: *I need her gone*. And they don't know about the clash I had with Elizabeth before bed.

I frown. When did *they* come upstairs last night?

Sabrina touches my arm. "Let's figure this out together. Okay? It's going to be okay."

I lean against the gate, vertigo diving through my skull. It's clear and terrible: I don't really have a choice.

And then I feel it, a dropping sensation as the veneer falls away.

The stone walls I thought were meant to keep neighbors from peering inside.

The gate at the mouth of the driveway, here to protect us, keep us together.

The fence at the edge of the subdivision, blocking out the world.

I thought they were there to keep us safe.

But now they're trapping me inside.

CHAPTER FORTY-EIGHT

Nathan's waiting for us in the foyer. "Nobody leaves." His voice is tense, warning. "And no one goes anywhere near their phone or laptop."

"How do we know what *you* were doing while we were outside?" I snap. Nathan's studying my face with quivering intensity. Is he trying to figure out if I did it? Or does he know I'm innocent because he scrubbed the blood from his own hands?

"I didn't do anything, I swear." He shakes his head. "I ran to my office and changed the code, then I came straight down here." His chin trembles. "I can't—after everything—I can't believe I couldn't . . ." He starts to cry and Sabrina touches his arm. Acid creeps up my throat. *What is going on?*

"What are we *doing*?" My voice cracks. "What's the plan?"

"I don't know! I don't know." Nathan rubs his temples.

Finally Sabrina pops the question we've all been waiting for: "Who did this?" She shakes her head. "It wasn't me."

"It wasn't me either," Nathan says, his voice almost a groan.

"I didn't. I swear I didn't."

"Well, somebody did this." Sabrina looks frantic. Her eyes dart back and forth between us. "And no one's come in or out. So what happened?"

Nathan frowns. "Kelly went to bed first," he points out. "We don't know what she was doing upstairs."

My eyes bug. "What are you talking about? You had *way* more opportunity to do it. While I was *asleep in your room*."

"We were together," Sabrina murmurs. "We cleaned up the kitchen and had another glass of wine and talked and . . ."

"We were down there for a long time." Nathan's voice is accusatory. "With the dishwasher running. You two were upstairs. Alone."

"This is absurd." My knees buckle and I drop a few inches, like a kid mid-tantrum. "You could've done it together, for all I know." They're the real unit, after all.

"But we *didn't*." Sabrina grabs my shoulders and tips her forehead onto mine. "We need to trust each other."

I step back, my heartbeat loud in my throat. "You're sure it's just us here? That no one else could have come in?"

Nathan nods. "This place is Fort Knox."

"Elizabeth got in somehow." I'm like a lawyer arguing my case. If I can win this argument, everything will make sense again. "This is exactly what she was worried about. She thought Renee was going to kill her."

Nathan sags. "Renee had no way of getting in here."

"But Elizabeth—"

"Elizabeth lived here." Nathan's words are a blade, slicing into mine. "She knows—she knew the door code."

I whimper. "I didn't do anything. I don't even know her."

"Exactly." Nathan's jaw is set, his mouth a straight line. "She meant nothing to you."

"Let's all take a breath." Sabrina shifts her weight. "Let's think for a second."

I turn to her, clocking her pursed mouth, her huge eyes narrowed with calculations. Why would either of them hurt her? They seemed so relieved, even overjoyed by her presence.

How well do I really know the Lamonts? What's beneath the tip of the iceberg?

Sabrina glances up the staircase behind Nathan. "Let's close the curtains so nobody can see into Elizabeth's . . . into the guest room."

We all look at each other queasily, and together climb upstairs. "I'll do it," Nathan says, and then he huffs into the room. The curtains make a hissing noise and the room blackens.

"Now what?" I ask when he steps grimly back into the hallway. Sabrina closes the door, and now there's a body in *my* bed, blood coagulating on *my* comforter. What the hell went on in there?

"Should we search the house?" I suggest. Even in the morning light, it's like a haunted mansion now, danger lurking in every corner. "We could look for any sign of someone getting in." I *need* this to be an outside job. I need to trust the Lamonts again. Our family is crumbling by the second and I'm grabbing at the pieces.

"And I guess we should lock up our electronics. Since we're not going to call the cops." Sabrina's eyes dart between ours. "This is a group decision, yeah? Everyone's in agreement?"

It's like there's a band around my lungs, squeezing tighter and tighter. We stare at each other and the only sound is a distant trilling bird, amplified by the crystalline silence inside. Virgo swishes by my feet and I jerk at the feel of her.

"No phones," Nathan says. "Rina's right."

They both turn to me and finally I give a curt nod. I don't know what else to do. I don't want them calling the cops and blaming me. Is this idiotic, going along with their cover-up, their joint vow of silence? We're yoked together now, accomplices; every minute that passes without us calling the police tightens the ropes around us.

Like a noose. No, a garrote. Am I signing on to be strangled?

"My laptop and phone are up here," Sabrina announces. Her eyes and nose are impossibly red. "I guess we should all go together." She shuffles down the hallway and into her bedroom. She's not remotely nervous about the possibility of someone else being here—of, say, Renee still crouching in a corner, ready to strike.

Is it because she knows something I don't?

Nathan and I follow. Sabrina snatches her phone and laptop from the chair near her side of the bed. She starts to read a notification on her screen, and even to unlock it, knee-jerk, but Nathan pulls both devices from her. "I'll do the same," he promises, holding down a button to turn her phone off. She blinks at him, miserable, then walks to his side of the bed and powers both of our phones down as well.

"We should search the room, right?" I prompt again. This is all wrong. They're not nearly afraid enough; they know something.

We fan out to peek behind curtains and furniture. It feels like the most terrifying game of hide-and-seek: *Ready or not, here I come!* I fling open the door to the walk-in closet, heart thrashing, half expecting to find another human huddled inside.

Invaders everywhere. A week ago, *I* was the one hiding here, watching Nathan through the two-way mirror after I realized someone had moved the—

"Security camera," I call, gazing at the naked tripod.

"Huh?" Nathan pops out of the en-suite bathroom.

"The one at the gate," I say. "Why didn't we think of that right away?" I narrow my eyes at him. He was just at his office computer, clicking a button to change the gate code. Did he already watch the video? Did he have time to alter it?

Nathan nods. "You're right. Come on, let's check it. My laptop and iPad are in there too."

My pulse speeds when he pushes past me and into his office. He stops at the desk and we crowd around him as he wakes his monitor. A shiver rustles down my back.

Am I shoulder-to-shoulder with a murderer?

CHAPTER FORTY-NINE

Nathan brings up a grainy, grayscale view of the end of the driveway. My brain reads it as a photograph, and then a leaf blows by.

He rewinds past my confrontation with Sabrina. He zooms back ten hours, eleven. He pauses on his SUV returning from the Ritz.

So no one came in. It was just the four of us last night.

And then there were three.

"Renee had to find another way in." My voice is desperate. "Maybe she was watching from the cemetery. Maybe she knows Elizabeth was here."

"I doubt it." Sabrina whisks away her tears. "She'd be speed-dialing her cop friends or busting down the door."

"I can't overstate how much she hated us even before Beth went missing," Nathan adds.

"It's true." Sabrina fights to keep her voice steady. "We helped Elizabeth file reports that got her suspended."

"She used all the leverage she could to cast suspicion on us after Beth disappeared." Nathan's still eerily calm, matter-of-fact. "She wasn't officially on the case, obviously, but she has clout." He hangs his head. "I'm sorry, Kelly. I thought we were safe here."

I stiffen. "Well, yeah. I wish you would've told me your partner disappeared from here and her evil cop ex had it out for you. That would've been useful intel." There's a beat as the words land, *Oh shit, was that out loud?*

They don't correct me or grow defensive or leave. Sabrina murmurs, "You're right."

"Neither of you had *any* idea why she was here?" I try to stare at both their faces at once, searching for any microexpression, a sign of guilt.

Sabrina shoots me a wild, pitiful look. "No idea. I swear to you."

"She didn't say anything about money? Or needing your help? Or moving back in, or . . . ?"

"Nothing!" They're both shaking their heads, brows high.

I scoff. "No hunches? There must've been a reason."

Sabrina pinches the bridge of her nose. "She didn't tell us, I swear. And I was so grateful to see her—that she was okay—I didn't ask. I thought those questions would come later. I thought . . ." And then she's weeping, barely able to breathe. How indescribably awful: to lose the one you love, and then find them, only to immediately lose them again.

Nathan rubs her back, his face tight and drawn. My insides curl with suspicion. He still seems more uncomfortable than sad.

"And you, Nathan?"

He shakes his head. "No idea. I . . . we really had no idea where she was. All this time, we were praying she wouldn't turn up dead." It hangs there, like a song that ends on a wrong note.

I want to believe them. God, do I ever. But if they didn't do this . . . who did?

Cold dread wrings my spine. *I hate this woman,* I told myself. *I need her gone.*

Nathan begins yanking cords out of the computer like someone pulling the plug on life support. I step back and look around the office. My eyes fall on the pyramid on the far wall, etched with the Atwood family crest. What if there's more in here—what if Nathan's got another firearm tucked away? I'm entirely on their turf; I'm unmoored, and the sunny spare room, the one I falsely thought of as mine, is sealed off from the world now.

Nathan plops his computer on top of Sabrina's and they both turn to me.

"My laptop is in my bedroom, I think."

We glance that way.

"I didn't see it when I closed the curtains," Nathan says. "You're sure?"

"No. But I don't know where else it could be."

"Let's check the rest of the house first," Sabrina says. "Maybe you left it somewhere else."

We continue our sweep, making sure we're alone, checking for chinks in the security, looking for evidence that this was an outside job. I feel like we're Dickens characters wearing nightshirts and holding oil lamps and scurrying around a spooky mansion. We find nothing; the house is sealed up tight.

In Sabrina's office, I pause in front of the messy desk. I know what's in the locked drawer, pinned flat by years of cards and ticket stubs: that Polaroid of Elizabeth's bruises, undated and context-free. Yesterday they all shared the Tale of Renee's Reign of Terror with me, taking turns like it was a goddamn oral history.

A cold shock slips through me. What if some of it was just that: a tale? What if all three were colluding on an agreed-upon version of events, the story that would exonerate one of them—perhaps the true source of the documented battery—of any past wrongdoing . . . ?

I feel a whoosh through my ears and squeeze my eyes shut.

That night in the hot tub, water rushing up my nose. The musical crash of breaking china when they argued in the kitchen all those weeks ago. That bluebird-day walk with Sabrina, the one when she told me about getting doxxed: *Nathan lost it. He walked out there and punched the guy in the face. The guy's bleeding from the nose and he calls the cops on Nathan.*

A knot forms in my belly. What if Nathan occasionally turned his anger onto Elizabeth when they were still in a relationship? What if *that's* why Sabrina took the photo—analog, indiscriminately damning—and kept it locked in a drawer?

What if, last night, Elizabeth did something to piss him off? That secret invitation Sabrina told me about in the bubble bath—*leave Na-*

than, run away with me. What if Elizabeth asked her again yesterday, and Nathan found out? What if he believed he'd just lost me and he was about to lose the other two women who mattered to him too?

"Ready to go?" Nathan is right behind me and I jump, heart racing. I turn back to him—those eyes I always found so warm, those smirky lips now stretched into a line—and manage a weak nod.

I can't *ask* them. ("Why, yes, Kelly, I'm a hot-tempered monster! Solid detective work.") And if he doesn't know that Elizabeth once tried to cut him out, the last thing I want to do is invoke his wrath now.

He'd never hurt Elizabeth, I tell myself. *He loved her. See how glad he was to have her back yesterday?*

But what I'm really trying to convince myself of is simpler.

He'd never hurt you.

I cry on and off as we finish canvassing the house. In the mudroom closet I spot the picnic blanket we lounged on while we watched the fireworks on the Fourth of July. I close my eyes and time-travel back—explosions in the sky and in my chest, my heart kapowing with the Lamonts' gentle touches. It feels like it's been months, years—but it wasn't that long, just a blip on an otherwise empty calendar full of days that never ended but weeks that flew by.

On the screen porch, we peer at the pool from which I saw someone lurking in the trees. The hot tub where I nearly drowned, where Nathan inflicted violence on me, intentional or not. I find myself leaning away from him, trying to keep Sabrina between us when we stand. It becomes a cadence I can't ignore: *Plan, plan, I need some kind of plan.*

Hope dwindles like a candle's flame as we eliminate every possibility: There's no entrance into the attic, no way someone could've climbed to a second-floor window. No tears mar the screens, and every window is intact. If anyone came in, they moved like a ghost, diaphanous and silent.

The only room left is mine. Elizabeth's. An anonymous, faceless guest.

We linger in the hallway. The tension is like mustard gas, seeping into my lungs, burning the air sacs.

"Let's get this over with," Nathan says, and he pushes open the door.

When I see her, I let out another small cry. It's so tempting to drop a sheet over her, but no one wants to disturb the body. Nathan checks the window—sealed tight, latched from the inside.

Obviously. Just a regular second-floor bedroom serving as a mausoleum.

Nathan heads into the closet and I tiptoe past the bed. I spot it again: Elizabeth's backpack, red as a cardinal. I kneel on the floor and lift it. My pulse ratchets up my chest, tick-tick-ticking. I hold my breath and unzip the top: a toothbrush and paste, face and body wipes. The banal needs of a functional body.

All useless now to the corpse lying faceup beside me.

I double over, close to vomiting. I'm about to drop the bag when I feel a rectangle of stiffness along the back.

I frown and peer inside, nosing my hand into the bag's crevices. There's a hidden compartment flat against the bag's back panel.

My fingers recognize it instantly: a photo, smooth and matte. Another Polaroid? More evidence of their love—or of abuse?

But then I slide it out and stare in confusion.

It's not a photo at all. It's mostly black with swirls of white marbling it like layers of sediment. The white is vaguely triangular (*like our relationship,* my brain spits out, *a triangle with a corner missing is just a dot looking over at a line*), and slowly, hands shaking, I turn it right-side-up.

That's a head. A nose. Floating in an amoeba-shaped pool like the one out back.

I squint to read the tiny font on the bottom, and a gasp escapes my throat.

Elizabeth Kessler was thirteen weeks pregnant.

CHAPTER FIFTY

Sounds soften and my vision blurs, like I've plunged underwater.

"Hey." Sabrina looms behind me and my senses sharpen. "What's that?"

As I hold out the ultrasound image, the thoughts latch together all at once: What if Sabrina already knew? She and Elizabeth could've found a moment alone yesterday. Elizabeth could've whispered her secret into Sabrina's silky hair, trusting that Sabrina would know what to do, how to help her.

I flash back to Sabrina on one of my first nights here, uplit by pastel pool lights: *That's why I don't want children . . . I have no model for good parenting.* Nathan confirmed it, in the same breath divulging her two miscarriages: *I wanted to keep trying, but Rina was done.*

The kid she never wanted—little fingers and a big head, as smooth and round as a shoehorn. Here it is, inside Elizabeth's womb. The woman who—according to Sabrina—loved her a tiny bit more than she loved Nathan; the woman dead on the bed behind me. Pregnant with her husband's baby.

What if Sabrina saw that Elizabeth could give Nathan what she couldn't—the family he desperately wanted? What if she recognized how much the discovery would mess up her marriage, and, in an angry fit—

Sabrina snatches the sonogram from my hand and stares at it, her eyes inscrutable.

"What did you find?" Nathan calls as he bursts out of the closet. I twist around to look at him—he's got my laptop pinned under his arm—and when I turn back, the sonogram is gone. Sabrina is calmly sifting through the drawers of my nightstand. Damn, that was smooth.

I stare at him blankly, heartburn plucking at my chest, then lift the backpack again. "I went through her things."

"Just her toiletries and stuff," Sabrina adds. I squint at her. Why hide it from him? Is she worried he'll become suspicious of her if he learns of the pregnancy, like I did?

But then another theory locks into place, the most convincing one yet: What if *Nathan* was the one who already knew? What if he and "Beth" had a whispered conversation in the dark? If he's the dad, it makes sense she'd tell him first.

But what if he wasn't overjoyed like she hoped? Maybe he was horrified about what it could mean for his reputation. What if he demanded she get an abortion, destroy the evidence of his extramarital relations? What if they fought?

I look up at him as I stand. He'd do anything to protect himself. His career, his image. He made me delete photos on the spot; he snarled at me about not posting anything to my feed hinting at our "unconventional" arrangement. Fathering a child with a young woman he knew through work . . . it wouldn't look good.

Nathan likes for people to please him, buoy his ego; on more than one occasion he'd joked about "marrying up" and called Sabrina an out-of-his-league "trophy wife."

Maybe the opposite is true too. If a woman—an accessory, a set piece—threatened to destroy his image, he might lose it. Maybe it'd drive him to . . .

"Let's get out of here." Sabrina's by the door, eager to leave.

I steal a glance at Elizabeth's flat midsection. *Elizabeth was pregnant.*

Was she here to terminate the pregnancy? To demand child support? Hell, how do you even get an ultrasound when you're off the grid?

Then I look up at the brown-red blood stiffening alongside her head. There it is: a hole above her left ear, a quarter-sized window exposing her insides to the world. The wound is vaguely rectangular. An image rises: my right hand closing around something hard and cold and sharp, and a wild swing. That's what it would take—some blunt object arcing out a path like a machete in the jungle, *swish-swish*.

I jerk and step back, pulse clobbering. I hurry into the hall and close the door behind us.

Downstairs, we gather in the breakfast nook. Sabrina fetches us glasses of water, but I feel too stuffed with fear to drink. We were Nathan's shadows as he carried our electronics into the first-floor bathroom, pushed the button on the inside knob, and locked them inside. I can feel them right beside us, pulsing with potential, each a coiled spring.

My breath is shallow, high up in my lungs. I'm lightheaded and marathon-tired. If no one broke in, there are only so many possible perpetrators, and they loop through my mind: *Nathan, Sabrina, both of them together.* Dizziness zooms through my skull. Am I hyperventilating?

"We need to think," Sabrina finally says. Her eyes and nose are a painful-looking red. "What could have happened?"

My fingers are freezing cold. I narrow my eyes and scream in my head. *Why did you hide the sonogram from Nathan? What else are you hiding from him . . . and me?*

"It had to be Renee," Nathan says quietly. "She was in the neighborhood. Beth thought Renee would try to kill her. It's obvious."

I swing my head to look at him. This sporadically violent man who wouldn't let me leave, and who thought he might lose it all. Why the change of tune?

"But how would she get in and out?" Sabrina says again.

"Well, if not her, who?" he snaps. There's that anger again. Bubbling out like pus from a blister.

Be trusting, Kelly. Give them the benefit of the doubt. I mash my knuckles against my eye sockets. Everything is at stake: My freedom, my found family. My life. If I can solve this puzzle—if I can find the compelling alternative theory that proves their innocence—I'll win the lottery again, restoring my trust in the Lamonts and my safety in this house.

I turn to Sabrina. "You said you have some stalkery fans. Has anyone been harassing you lately? Did someone, I don't know, come looking for you and get confused when there were two other women in the house?"

Sabrina pushes a napkin against her tears. "Nothing lately. Nothing weird." A rough, gaspy breath. "There are always some miserable trolls in my DMs, but nothing threatening."

Nathan rubs his beard. "Plus, people aren't exactly traveling to Deerbrook to meet their favorite author these days."

Another beat. *Nathan. Sabrina. Both of them together.* I grab my glass, arm shaking, and water sloshes from the top.

"Elizabeth's family?" I suggest. "Her aunt or cousin or those boys?"

"But the security camera . . ." Sabrina says.

I let out a frustrated noise. "Diane?"

She opens her palms. "They all wanted to *find* Elizabeth, not kill her."

"But you said Elizabeth had issues with them. And that they're friendly with Renee," I point out. "The Atwoods and Diane—all of them."

"They like Renee because she's good at convincing people she's an angel who just wants what's best for Beth. *Goddammit.*" Nathan pounds his fist on the table, and Sabrina and I wince.

I fold my frigid hands together. God, it's cold. Nathan cranked the air conditioning to keep the body from smelling. To delay *putrefaction*, a gross word for a vile process.

"Well, she didn't hit *herself* in the head," Sabrina groans, cueing a fresh spurt of tears. I watch her carefully. Is she faking it? With her big eyes and eloquent words, Sabrina always seemed to wear her heart on her sleeve. But that could've been an act, too, the work of a highly skilled thespian. Because I watched her calmly hide the ultrasound. I know she kept it from Nathan when Elizabeth asked her to cut and run. And when I was new here, falling hard and fast, she hid details about their missing ex from me.

Cold rinses through my belly as I think back. Her calls and texts and DMs were nothing but cheerful in the weeks after Elizabeth disappeared—an act so convincing I swallowed it whole. I was stupid to take her words at face value these last few months. Why should I believe her now?

My teeth start properly chattering again, a quake that travels down my spine. Nathan makes a grumbly sound and I peek at him. He's staring into space, his eyes like red-hot coals.

Angry, unpredictable Nathan. Perhaps he did it, and now he's starting to wonder if—my God—he might get away with it.

Nobody confesses. Hours pass. We barely speak. We relocate to the basement, the farthest spot from the body. We move in small roves, keeping an eye on each other when one of us tromps to the bathroom or refills a water glass.

The rectangle of sky outside the basement window darkens. Sabrina cries on and off. Nathan looks increasingly grim, and when I stare hard in the bathroom mirror, I barely recognize myself—eyes wild, skin mottled, jaw juddering like I'm out in the tundra.

"Kelly!" I jolt at the sound of Sabrina's voice. I dry my hands and return.

"Rina was saying we need a plan." Nathan looks decades older. Sabrina too. The horrible thought unfurls again: Did they kill her together? Is one of them covering for their spouse? Are they plotting to frame me, make me take the fall?

"A plan?" I repeat.

Sabrina nods. "In the morning, it'll start to smell. We'll have to make a decision."

"A decision?" I'm a damn Furby, parroting back their words.

Nathan clears his throat. "Call the cops, or—or do something to get rid of it."

It takes a second to sink in and then I let out a strangled cry. I'm in a Lifetime movie and I want out, this is torture, how is this my life? Burying a corpse or, or chopping it up and driving it to the nearest body of water . . . or dissolving it, somehow stocking up on acid and, and—

"We live next door to a cemetery," Sabrina says.

I picture that cratered area in Brinsmere, the concentric circles of tombstones. I picture us digging in the night, tilling freshly disturbed soil to evade notice. Watching for witnesses.

"It's not a bad idea," Nathan admits. "As far as anyone knows, she's still missing."

She sniffles and stares at her lap. "We should do it tonight," she says. "Once it gets dark enough. And then we'll clean the hell out of the bedroom, and in the morning it'll be over."

They're looking at me. I will my heart to stir, to refill that all-consuming love I felt for them both as recently as . . . wow, was it just yesterday? I want to believe that they're doing this out of love, that this really is the end, that there will be no more Polaroids beneath the dresser and stowaways in the cellar and secrets and betrayals and lies—no more Elizabeth, if we can get through tonight.

That we can go back to what we were.

But I'm not sure it's true. Not after today.

I look into their faces: Sabrina's Bambi stare, Nathan's bristled beard. I didn't think either was capable of this, but . . . now that I know about the pregnancy, I have to admit they both have motive. And for all my waffling, I know only one of them to be violent. Sabrina is calm, controlled—she never acts without thinking. Nathan's more emotional, unpredictable. I feel it, my gut choosing a side. I've known Sabrina for twenty years. Nathan, on the other hand . . .

I flash back to that moment in the kitchen, cracking jokes as we made lunch for our hike. I was so giddy over their cheap flattery—*the prettiest hair, super hot, a very beautiful woman*—that I missed the compliment Nathan cited as his favorite: *I make those I love feel safe.*

I never thought to ask: What happens if that love turns off like a light?

And now I know. Nathan locked me inside the property and stripped me of my phone and laptop. The self-described "gun-toting good ol' boy," the one who built his identity around his ability to eliminate threats, stopped counting me as part of his tribe.

Elizabeth got cut out even sooner. And look what happened to her.

But I'm out of options. I'm under his thumb and trapped in his house and maybe he's telling the truth, maybe if I go along with their plan, I can still make it out of here alive.

So I open my mouth and muster the energy to reply: "Okay."

And with that, I feel a swooping sensation so intense, the world goes black.

CHAPTER FIFTY-ONE

I drop onto the sofa, head swimming, then blink until the snow in my eyes starts to clear. There's the fizzy, record-scratch moment—*what just happened?*—and then I register that I almost passed out.

I lean back against the cushion, but my head clangs with pain. The bruise on the back is a tender peach.

"I need to lie down," I say.

"Actually, we should try to get a little sleep before tonight," Nathan says. "It's going to be a marathon, and I'm running on fumes. The adrenaline will only get us so far."

"I want to sleep in my bed," Sabrina announces.

Nathan sits up straighter. "You two should nap. I'll get everything ready in the meantime."

"No. You can't—we can't leave you with the laptops." Sabrina blinks at him. "That was your idea. Anyone could pick that bathroom lock."

I watch them carefully. Is this choreographed? What do they know? Personally, I was hoping to get a minute alone with Sabrina—I'm dying to ask why she hid the sonogram. She knows I've seen it, and for some reason, she must believe Nathan hasn't.

"Good point," he replies. "We should all be in the same room."

Great. Now we'll be trapped in an even smaller space.

Upstairs, Nathan draws the curtains and pulls something from his nightstand. The gun. The loaded gun he's always said he needed to protect his family.

And now he wants us to believe he did nothing while his last love was murdered?

He settles into an armchair in the corner. "I'll keep an eye on things," he says. "Just in case."

I don't like it, don't like anything about it, but their bed is so soft and Sabrina is already asleep next to me and I'm jealous, so jealous, I ease onto a pillow next to her, carefully avoiding the lump on my skull. This is so messed-up: taking a disco nap a few rooms away from a corpse so that we'll have the energy to inter it tonight. I should be working on a plan. I should think of a way out of this . . . I could . . .

I wake to the sound of a crying baby, and when I open my scratchy eyes, it takes a few seconds to sort it out. That's Virgo, letting her most plaintive yowl rip. I sit up, head and hip and shoulder aching in protest, and look around the room. It's dark; it could be any time, ten P.M. or four in the morning. Time is meaningless now, except that we have shit to do. A body to bury. A skeleton in our closet.

The yowling intensifies and I slip off the side of the bed. Nathan's asleep in the armchair, his head lolled to one side, and next to me Sabrina stirs but doesn't wake. I tiptoe to the closed door and crack it open, and Virgo slips inside and swirls around my ankles, eel-like.

I look out into the hallway. Nerves flick along my spine. This is my chance. I can't run—without the gate code, I can't escape the property—but if I can break into the downstairs bathroom and grab my phone, I can call for help.

But . . . I'm still not sure I can do it. I'll look every bit as guilty as them, right? And it'll be a she-said-they-said situation, their two stories refuting mine. Plus . . . what if Nathan's telling the truth? What if it really will be over once we ditch the body in a few hours? Can we truly bury the hatchet along with their ex?

I'm stuck. Nathan stirs in the armchair behind me and my pulse explodes. I take a step back.

I can't do it. I'm not bold enough. I'll close the door and crawl back into bed and go along with their plan.

But then—I feel the familiar mic-feedback whine, high-pitched and irresistible. I peer into the hallway and realize it's telling me to return to Nathan's office. I take a step and it intensifies, like there's an invisible rope pulling me forward.

You're missing something. There's something they're not telling you. Do it do it do it.

I slip into the hallway, quiet as a lynx. I push the office door open and peer inside; starlight frosts the heavy desk, spotlighting a wood surface that looks off-balance. It takes me a second to process: There's a blank square where his laptop should be, a gap as apparent as a missing tooth.

I close the door behind me and turn on the light.

Something's amiss.

I can feel it, this offness, ringing like an earache. I do a slow pan, taking in Nathan's prim loveseat, the glossy leather desk chair, the monitor with a screen like a black hole. I turn to the floating shelves, and my eyes narrow at the stone pyramid. It's in its proper spot, polished and shiny, reflecting the lamplight like a tiny lighthouse. Has anything in here changed since we crowded around Nathan's computer to check the security footage earlier today? Or . . . or since yesterday, when the four of us watched Renee deliver cupcakes meant for me?

The symbol on the paperweight has captured my gaze so many times in Brinsmere, and now I feel it thrumming, calling to me, asking me to lift it. When I do, shock lashes through my arms and legs.

The shine, that's what's bothering me. It's been wiped clean. The streaks my fingertips left in the dust have disappeared. But the symbol carved inside—

No. No no no no no no.

The word becomes a cadence, a horrible, unbroken stream. Because the engraved symbol—it's filled now. The etching made perfect canals to capture Elizabeth's blood.

I've found the murder weapon.

And it belongs to Nathan.

I look down at the floor and gasp. It's obvious now—there's a faint outline on the hardwood, the remnants of blood soaked and then scrubbed. Someone killed her here. Killed her and then carried the body into my bedroom, planted her square on the bed. Someone strong and sure-armed. Relief and fear fuse together all at once: *It wasn't me.*

"Drop it."

I jerk and look up, and then it's like the wind's knocked out of me, lungs collapsed, all my life shrunk down to what I see in front of me.

There's Nathan, arms shaking. But what draws my attention most is what's clutched in his hands.

The gun pointed right at my heart.

CHAPTER FIFTY-TWO

The pyramid tumbles from my hands and hits the floor, *thunk*.

"Nathan, wait." I'm weirdly calm. It's like the fear has reached a frequency so high it can only be heard by dogs. "Think about what you're doing."

"Kelly, no." Sweat drips down his cheek; his eyes are wild. "No, no, no."

I watch fury roll through him. He thought he'd get away with it; he liked me contained and controlled and grateful, always making him feel like a hero. He liked me on my knees. I raise my hands. I bide my time, like Virgo. If I were a cat, my tail would be flicking, vicious but controlled.

"That's the murder weapon," he says, nodding his chin toward it.

I frown. "I know."

"Jesus Christ, Kelly." His voice is craggy, desperate; is he about to burst into tears? He never thought he'd be caught. "Fuck."

He shakes his head again and, oh, I can see everything, my vision is sharper than a bald eagle's. I spot the hole in his T-shirt a few inches above the hem. I see the sweat on his brow braid into a salty bead and roll into the corner of his eye, *blink*. I watch Nathan angle the gun down while his other wrist whisks across his forehead.

Now. My bare soles ram against the floor and sail through the air before pushing off again. His eyes and mouth widen in unison, three O's, but he doesn't have time to react as I torpedo toward him.

He throws his arms out in surprise and my nerves pop, *shit*, I need to get away but now he's *blocking the door*.

And so I improvise—I barrel into his outstretched arm, throwing him off balance. He cries out and I whirl around, shoving my back to his front and pinning his forearm against my side, pushing him against the wall, locking him in place, the way Sabrina held me still as Nathan choked me in the sizzling hot tub.

The gun's still dangling from his palm and I reach for it, scrabbling. An angry groan erupts out of him and he claws at my wrist with his free hand, cursing. When that doesn't work, his hand flies to my body, clutching wildly at my waist, my breast, and finally, my throat.

Checkmate. The back of my head snaps tight against his chest and white-hot pain makes my stomach contort with nausea. I hold still, dizzy and sick, and he slides his arm around my neck so my head's locked inside his elbow.

The seconds fan out, wide and clear and deafeningly quiet. He tightens his headlock and starts to draw the gun back in. I feel the crush of his tendons on my throat. It's the Jacuzzi all over again, alarm bells ringing, my windpipe compressing like a trash compactor, *I need air.*

Instinctively, I scratch at his forearm. But his grip is too strong and the struggle keeps pressing his pec against my head wound, which buzzes so loud and bright it's like a hive of hornets all sting-sting-stinging the same spot.

I see flashes of light, bright as fireworks. My shoulders start to slump in defeat.

And then, from the corner of my eye, I notice two things:

One, the gun in his right hand isn't pointing at me.

And two, it's within reach.

I thrust my hands out to wrench it away, but his wrist jerks up and I grab for the grip again and—

Bang!

It's so loud the world goes silent, the only sound the fizzy hiss of rushing water, of roaring rapids and whorling hot tubs, *shhhhhhhh*. And then I'm thrown forward off my feet, I'm airborne, weightless, who knew I had wings I can *fly*, but there's weight behind me, Nathan, and then I smash into the hardwood face-first, a heavy mass stretched along my back, and I bounce once and feel my nose crack under the pressure.

I'm still.

Screaming—the wailing is so large it's a tide, it's a tsunami and I'm trapped underneath while this deep scream jangles all the molecules above me. I lie there for a moment, confused. Then adrenaline surges and I roll myself out from under the bulk on top of me, which is, I realize, Nathan.

No. The floor bucks beneath me and I stagger back. My butt hits the desk and I lean against it. I stare and stare and stare at Nathan, now rolled onto his side.

He's not moving.

Sabrina's in the doorway, her mouth twisted in a Munchian scream. I taste copper as blood pours down the back of my throat. My ears haven't stopped making that shrill, hissing ring. It's too much, this cacophony and blood.

And then my eyes stitch together what's next to her. The white wall alongside the door. The scarlet splashed across it like spray-paint.

Moving like a sleepwalker, I take a few steps toward her. I look down again and my angle is different now, a new POV. It's like something in a movie, something that can't possibly be real.

That's fake blood, it's got to be.

A fake bullet hole in his chin. Makeup.

There's no way the back of Nathan's head is splattered across the wall.

CHAPTER FIFTY-THREE

Time freezes over, three seconds, five, my brain frantically trying to reinterpret the input from my cones and rods, *run it again, that can't be right*. It's like there's a tornado inside me, twisting and twirling, and I drop to my knees a few feet away from Sabrina.

She stops screaming and switches to a wobbly sobbing sound.

"Sabrina," I finally say. I can feel my vocal cords trembling. Talking hurts; my trachea is on fire.

As if my voice unfroze her, she rushes to Nathan and kneels, hugging him to her and repeating his name like she can undo this, wake the dead.

Finally she gasps, a huge, rickety inbreath, and faces me. "*What did you do?*"

My heart thrums; my ears roar. A single thought muscles its way to the surface: *We need to get out of this room.* I fill my lungs with air and stagger toward the door, clutching her arm and dragging her into the hallway, where she melts to the floor. I crouch over her, listening to the steady wheeze deep in my ears. For a while, I can't form a coherent thought—just a loop of *oh my God oh my God oh my God.*

I swallow, digging down deep. "Sabrina, listen to me."

Whimpering, she glances up.

"I know this is hard to hear, but—he killed Elizabeth." Saying it aloud, I feel the floor tilt again like a storm-sieged ship. "Listen to me. The stone pyramid, that's the murder weapon—he killed her in there. And when I found it, he—he attacked me, he tried to shoot me, he . . ." I disintegrate into sobs. I press my eyes closed but the image strobes again: fire-engine red forming a big firecracker on the wall, the kind that drips and weeps. *This isn't happening*.

Her eyes are feral, glassy. I peer into his office and see his bare feet lolling on the floor, and my stomach pitches.

"I don't know what to do," she whispers, her whole body shaking. "I don't know what to do."

Her quivers grow more intense and I shuffle her into her office. I set her on the purple couch and slide the blanket from the back around her.

"Oh, Sabrina." I smooth her hair behind her ear, the way she's done to me so many times. Back in the hallway, I close the door of Nathan's office and stumble into my bathroom to fetch water for her. When I catch myself in the mirror, I flinch: Blood is smeared above my lips like garish lipstick, with a fresh trickle still seeping from my nostril.

I can't look. I'm not allowed to look.

Water slops over the cup and coats my fingers. *Focus, Kelly*. I carry it back to Sabrina and, kneeling, help her hold it to her lips. She drops the glass all over her lap, and the wetness seems to wake her.

"Sabrina, listen." I snatch up her cold hands and hold them in mine. "We can't just sit here. I'm so sorry, but—we need to act. Can you look at me?"

Her huge eyes make the long, slow climb from her lap to mine. She shakes her head. "What did you do?"

"Sabrina. Listen to me. Nathan killed Elizabeth. In his office. And he tried to kill me too. We need to get help, okay? Can you do that?"

She lets out another strangled sob, an approximation of *oh God*. "He didn't do it," she whispers.

I squeeze her fingers. "He did. I'm sorry. He attacked me. He—"

"No. I know him. He couldn't."

I think for a second, wiping blood and snot and tears from my face. "Did he tell you he didn't?"

She nods. But the hatred in his eyes, the guilty flash of surprise—I know what I saw.

"Listen, I noticed someone got up from our bed last night. And there's no way *I* could've carried her into the guest room without making a mess—dragged her, maybe, but then there'd be a, a trail of blood." Bile bubbles through my voice.

"No." Sabrina keeps shaking her head, harder and harder. "No. I didn't do it, and he said he didn't do it either and I believe him, and he refused to believe that you killed her. I *told* him it couldn't be somebody from the outside, but he said there was no way you'd . . ."

An ember of doubt smolders in my chest—why was he defending me, what was he playing at? But then I smother it. Just more manipulation, more lies. "Sabrina." I wait until she meets my eyes. "He . . . he looked at the paperweight and admitted it was the murder weapon. There's dried blood on it, Sabrina. It's hard for me, too, but . . . but how else do we explain . . . ?"

She hooks her feet on the sofa and curls her forehead onto her knees, the way you'd cry alone in a shower.

"And—and we know he can be violent, right? From when he punched the doxxer." I point to my neck. "He started choking me, Sabrina. I know you don't want to hear this, but . . ."

"Nathan." She whispers it into her knees, then lifts her head, her face bleak. "I've known him since college. He's good. He would never, ever hurt Elizabeth. He wouldn't hurt anyone."

"He hurt me," I point out. Too quickly.

She thunks her forehead back onto her thighs. Grief is welling up inside me like a basement mid-flood. *Oh God, Nathan. How could you?*

"But why?" she chokes out. "He loved her. We were both so relieved."

Nathan's possible motives are spinning around me like horseflies. "You said she tried to get you to leave Nathan. Were they fighting before she disappeared? Or—or did he somehow find that out?"

She groans. "No. No way. The relationship was *fine*, she just . . . she'd only dated women before, and she loved Nathan but it was complicated, dating both of us, and she wanted to know if I . . . if we . . ." She turns away, tears gushing. "But she only asked me once. And we agreed to never talk about it. There's no *way* Nathan knew."

How can anyone really know what's in someone else's head, the patterns and hunches gathering in corners like dust? She believes he had no idea. And I suspect she's wrong.

"Are you sure she never asked *him* to run off with her?" I say. "Maybe they were in contact . . . maybe something was going on between them."

"No," she replies weakly. Her eyes are closed; I can't tell if this has occurred to her. "They weren't in touch. She—she didn't even have a phone."

I stroke her hair. True, I hadn't spotted one among Elizabeth's belongings. But I need Sabrina to see what I see.

So I pounce: "The pregnancy."

She groans again. "He didn't know. It seemed like she was working up the courage to tell us something, but we never found out what." Laboriously, her eyes reach mine. "We didn't have that long together before *you* showed up."

Her words are a tossed ax, but I tense and let them hit me handle-first. *Focus, Kelly.* "But she could've told him, right? Maybe late last night. Were you ever apart?"

Her chin wobbles. "I . . . I don't know, I don't think so, we went to bed after you, and . . ."

They strobe again, the wretched explanations I don't want to look at head-on. If Nathan and Sabrina were side by side all night . . . whether the killer was Nathan or Sabrina or the two working as a team, it's possible they colluded on the half-assed cover-up. Nathan could have lifted the slight body and carried it down the hall while Sabrina scrubbed the floor and the pyramid. And if that's true, then she's still acting, feigning ignorance to cover her own ass.

But I look at her, at the grief and betrayal coursing through her. Love bulges in my chest and I believe her. I *know* her.

Nathan's the angry one, not Sabrina.

She mashes her hand across her face. "You think Nathan's the father?"

"The timing matches up, right?"

"It does." Her knuckles fly to her mouth to hold in a burp. Heart-burn, like her whole system's ablaze.

"Why did you hide the sonogram?"

"To protect him." A braying sound, like an injured animal. "I thought if he saw it, if he knew his first child was dead too . . ."

So Sabrina believed he had no idea Elizabeth was pregnant. She was trying to be a good wife and shield him from that pain.

I set my hand on her foot. "You know him best. What would he have done if he found out? Would he have been excited, or . . . ?"

Her sobs reach a new apex, so violent and loud they're like a storm raging through her. "He'd do anything to keep the news from getting out." She leans forward and buries her face in my neck.

"I didn't kill Elizabeth," I whisper. "Did you?"

Against my chest, she shakes her head no.

"Okay. Then it's over." I lift my head and wait for her to meet my eyes. "I love you."

Even as I say it, my brain cues up a movie montage—so many mem-ories with Nathan. How he joked and cajoled and chuckled and his eyes glittered with glee when he cracked you up. How he was grabby in bed, appreciative and intense.

I need to be right.

I nod and she nods and she mouths the word *okay* and I rest my head on hers. "We're going to be all right," I whisper. "Shhhh."

She pulls me tighter and we sit there, swaying slightly, both gushing tears.

CHAPTER FIFTY-FOUR

We move quickly—we don't have long before the blood dries, before our slowness requires explanation, though Sabrina points out that it'll take a while for anyone to be dispatched out here. The part of me that floats above my body marvels at my focus, my calm—I'm in charge now, calling the shots. So different from the old me, who went along with everything.

We identify the points where we ourselves broke the law, first by honoring Elizabeth's wishes and not reporting her appearance to the authorities, then by not calling 911 when we found her body in my bed. So we go through our story, down to the minute. It's not hard because the only thing we're tweaking is our motivation, taking away some of our agency, making ourselves more obedient, less unlikable.

Elizabeth left her hideout in Santa Fe and surprised the Lamonts. She begged them not to call the police because she'd seen Renee on the property—verifiable, true. I came home from a staycation at the Ritz and was shocked by her appearance (also true), but we all agreed she'd contact her family in the morning (a tiny fabrication). Late last night, Nathan and Elizabeth must've slipped into his office to discuss her pregnancy (see: the sonogram, Exhibit A) and, whether it was a crime of passion or premeditated, he bludgeoned her with a stone object, panicked, dropped her in the spare room, wiped down the weapon and floor, and returned to bed. Check, check, check.

And here's the gap, the period when we should've called the cops but didn't. So we cast Nathan as the villain he turned out to be: He changed the gate code when I tried to flee (hence the video of me making a run for it and Sabrina grimly guiding me back inside); he commandeered our technology, stashing it somewhere secret so we couldn't call for help. If you squint, it's all true, so why mention the part where we went along with his plan? When I finally slipped away, we'll say, he confronted me with the gun and shot himself in the ensuing struggle.

Shaken and scared, we'll say, Sabrina and I raced around the house searching for our phones. That's when we discovered the ultrasound and put two and two together.

And here we stumble, a spiky clash inside the stupor of trying to deal with everything.

"So we're going to admit that the three of you were in a relationship?" I ask.

"No . . . no, let's just say they had an affair. Or, no, that we don't know who the father is—that's better."

"But if they weren't sleeping together . . . why would Nathan kill her for being pregnant with someone else's baby?"

She shrugs. "We don't know what happened in the office. We weren't there."

I think for a second. "If it sounds like they were having an affair, it won't look good for *you*. Scorned wife and everything."

And she rubs her eyes. Cross and too flippant. "Then it's a good thing I didn't kill him."

I crawl over it in my mind. I nod and we move on with our story-weaving. But a thought rises up, a shadow: *I thought* Nathan *was the one who cared about keeping the three-way relationship a secret.*

Theirs. And ours.

Finally, *cut*—our story's set like papier-mâché and we freeze it in place, going over it again and again to make sure it's solid. We tell it back to each other as we pace around the upstairs, and Virgo sprints back and forth along the catwalk, riled by our anxiety. Nathan killed Elizabeth and held us hostage, and when I tried to escape, the gun went off in the ensuing struggle. It's like the lyrics to a song we're trying to memorize. We test each other. We find holes and sew them up. We're grateful we live in the suburbs, where screams go unnoticed, where gunshots echo off the rocks and trees.

We finger the physical evidence. Sabrina finds the camcorder—no Wi-Fi connection, thank *God*—on a closet shelf and shoves it into the microwave, *snap, crackle, pop*. I slouch into the kitchen and pull paper towels out from under the sink, and a dull observation makes me freeze: *Did I leave the bleach spray in here?*

But . . . no. No time for that now. Nathan was rushing, eager to wipe down the office floor, and he tossed it here instead of in the mudroom. I snatch up the bottle and head back upstairs.

In Nathan's office, I hold my breath and creep past his form on the floor, swallowing the sick inching up my bruised throat. I wipe the fingerprints—his and mine—from the pyramid and place it back on the shelf; he'd do that himself if he were trying to get away with it. I clutch the knob of his locked closet door and the shelves of his desk, miming searching for our electronics, though I know they're in the bathroom. I stamp my hands around the office window so we can say I was trying to jimmy it open and escape when the confrontation oc-curred. We survey our work, shaky and wild-eyed. This'll do. *This has to work.*

Finally we use a credit card to pop the bathroom lock. I feel a surge of emotion at the sight of my phone, its screen stippled with alerts of cheery, banal things. I can't touch it. It's from the Before Times. A dif-ferent Kelly used that phone to post Instagrams and reply to silly WhatsApp threads and pretend her life was more together than ever. Was it just two days ago that I shared that selfie from the pool?

Sabrina places the 911 call, her voice hysterical, holding my gaze as she screams and sobs and speaks with the dispatcher. In the predawn, we sit on the front steps to wait for the ambulance, like we're the survi-vors at the end of a horror movie. I listen so hard my ears feel pricked, swiveled forward like satellite dishes. Finally we hear the shrill whoop in the distance and, a few minutes later, spot their glittering lights.

The sirens grow louder and louder, so loud I press my palms to my ears, and then Sabrina swears and climbs off the steps, sprinting to the end of the driveway.

She's running. She's trying to get away. My brain spits out accusations like a janky drinking fountain.

Then the gates that stanch the driveway start moving, just in time, and Sabrina walks back toward me, a hissing night breeze rippling her hair, her eyes and jaw set. She's so beautiful—terrifying and unknowable.

She could have done it, the gremlin whispers.

But she didn't, I silently murmur back.

I stand too. I cross to her and reach for her hand.

She grabs it, squeezes once, a hard, quick pump.

"Here they come," she says.

There's time for one final thought, a flicker before the cops zoom up the driveway and commandeer my attention: *She knows the new gate code.*

And then they're here.

CHAPTER FIFTY-FIVE

The police precinct is surprisingly nice, not like I was led to believe from detective shows—all those municipal dollars mean eggshell walls and hardwood floors, and the scent of our taxpayer bracket gets us kind treatment, an empathetic tech who apologizes as he swabs some cells from the wet warmth of our mouths.

Now I'm alone with the detective in an interview room, one with worn metal chairs and a scratched wooden table and a window overlooking the parking lot. No two-way mirror to speak of. Not like in the Lamonts' bedroom.

I go cold all over. We were so focused on the events of the last few days, Sabrina and I didn't discuss head-on what we'd tell them about *our* relationship. I assume we're pleading platonicness, too . . . but yikes, lying about my love life in a police interview feels far more high-stakes than misleading, say, Amy. Look how badly I bungled it with Megan.

Er, Renee.

Detective Schaefer starts the tape recorder, rattles off the date and time. She's got black hair pulled into a tight bun and long, curly eyelashes. My chest tightens. Is she a friend of Renee's?

"Do I have your permission to record this?" she asks.

"Of course."

Deep breath in and *shoom,* we're off, moving fast like the sphere in a pinball machine. We walk through the whole day in detail, starting with the minute I drove home from the Ritz and encountered a surprising new houseguest. My confidence grows every time we move ahead in my recounting, like this is a board game and I'm inching closer, closer to the end.

Yes, I'd met up with Renee voluntarily, but she led me to believe she was someone else. No, I had no idea she knew Elizabeth or even the Lamonts. My insides twist as we navigate this point—*stick to the facts, Kelly, share what you know is true*—but the detective remains impassive and moves on to the next point, another bead in the necklace I'm stringing.

I repeat details whenever she asks for them. I'm cooperative—an ideal witness, a model victim, recounting my story with weary yet brave tenacity. I'm hyperfocused on every word, my brain clinging desperately to details, to logistics, anything to keep it from replaying that moment in Nathan's office, the shot heard 'round my world. I pick at my nails and touch my swollen nose and fight off the image that appears when I close my eyes: blood spattered on the white wall. The black hole in Nathan's chin.

When we get to that point in the story, I break down crying.

"I was so scared," I say. "I wasn't even trying to get ahold of the gun—I just wanted to get it away from me."

She wants details, the choreography of how he pinned me in place, squashed my throat in the crook of his arm. It's all tangled in my head, but I do my best to recount the battle blow-by-blow. She leans over the table, squinting, as I tip my head back to show her the bruises. She says she'll need to photograph them, and I let tears soak into my mask. "I'll do whatever you want," I tell her. "I want this nightmare to be over."

She circles back to things I've said. I cry and stammer but I don't falter, I clear my throat and say, "Pardon?" when I can't hear the question or need another second, and God, it's easy to spin my shaking hands and hummingbird pulse as symptoms of trauma, not reasons I'd fail a lie-detector test.

I *am* traumatized. I'm squeezing myself together, balancing precariously like a cairn on a beach. I need to get through this questioning and the follow-ups and then, only then, can I exhale, tumbling into a jumble like a stone stack piled too high.

"What was the nature of your relationship with the Lamonts?" she asks, several hours into the interview.

Here it is. They'll ask Sabrina, too, and if only one of us tells the truth, the other will be caught in a lie. "Like I said, I didn't meet Nathan until I got there. I went to high school with Sabrina. She offered me a place to stay."

"Why do you think she did that?"

I shrug. "Because she's kind. She knew I needed it."

She taps her pen against the notepad.

"When did you move in with them?"

"June sixteenth."

"When were you planning to leave?"

I shake my head. "I don't know. Whenever the pandemic ends."

She peers at me for a moment, then nods. "So it must've been going well. Living together."

"I thought so."

"Did they ever talk about Ms. Kessler?"

"They mentioned her. Like, how awful it was when they learned she'd disappeared. But she didn't come up a lot, no."

"Right." She clicks her pen. "And did anything ever happen that made you think Nathan had a violent side?"

I hesitate. Will they discover the Polaroid in Sabrina's desk? I can't tell them about that or the night in the hot tub, but there's another verifiable nugget for them to find: "Not really, but Sabrina told me he assaulted someone in D.C." I sketch in the details, running my fingers over the red scratches on my wrist. My stomach hardens with every word. When I get to the end, I hold up my arm. "I'd say last night really showed me his violent side, though. Beyond any shadow of a doubt."

Now the finish line is in sight and there's just one hurdle up ahead. My pulse clip-clops—can I really pull this off?

"So you were looking everywhere for your phones."

"Our phones and laptops, yeah."

"And you went into Ms. Kessler's room."

I almost correct her, stop. No reason to make myself sound hostile to our guest. "Right. To see if they were there."

"Did you have any reason to think they were?"

Deep breath in, deep breath out. "We didn't know where they were. We were trying to be methodical. If—I don't know, we thought maybe he put them in there because he knew we wouldn't want to go in."

She nods. "Then what?"

My vein thumps beneath my jaw. "I saw her red backpack. There was still so much we didn't understand. So I opened it and—there was the ultrasound."

"Were you surprised?"

"Shocked. I showed Sabrina right away."

"And how did she seem?"

"Also shocked. Elizabeth hadn't said anything. We still don't know what it means or who the father is." I look away, tears brimming. "I thought maybe Sabrina suspected Nathan was the father. She didn't tell me why, though. Whatever happened, it was before Sabrina and I were even in touch."

This was part of our plan: kick it all over to her. Let Sabrina—the homeowner, the wife—explain what the sonogram might mean. After all, I'm the eleventh-hour interloper; I wandered onto the scene after Elizabeth had disappeared and the dust had settled.

"So Sabrina believed her husband and Ms. Kessler were having an affair."

"I really don't know." I shake my head. "You should talk to her about it."

"Does that track with what you know about Nathan?"

On my lap, my hands clench. There's a faint scar from the gash I got in Mike's office back in Philly, and I strum my thumb over it. "I don't know. Turns out I didn't know Nathan at all."

She tilts her head, studying me. "Miss Doyle," she says. "Did you have a sexual relationship with Nathan?"

It shoots out of me like a cannon: "What? No!"

"Did he ever come on to you?"

"No!" I shake my head. "I have no idea what happened before I was there. But it never crossed my mind that Nathan would cheat on Sabrina. Or that he could hurt me." I touch my tender neck. "I barely knew him. I was just . . . a houseguest."

She watches me and I force myself to maintain eye contact, to slacken my hands, to keep from fidgeting or flinching or giving myself away. Meanwhile my insides convulse, a deep writhing that works its way up my abdomen. *A houseguest.* It isn't true. But right now, I need to sell it.

"I understand," she says, softening. "We'll get you out of here soon."

CHAPTER FIFTY-SIX

When we're well into the afternoon, the sun a lemony splotch in an overcast sky, a cop drops me off at the hospital and I finally get medical care. A radiologist settles my skull inside what looks like a giant Mentos for a CT scan, and I almost nod off despite the ear-splitting screeches and hums. A fractured nose, they tell me, but no bleeding or swelling in my skull. *Lucky,* the doctor calls me. I don't feel lucky at all.

A nurse wheels me into a hospital room and clamps a gadget on my finger, and I stare at the ceiling, breathing through my mouth and feeling a fizzy kind of awe deep in my guts: *I think that worked, I think she believed me.* An ENT pops in, his hair a feathery blackbird's nest, and tells me my nose is lined up fine; the swelling should go down on its own. Next up, a neurologist, a beautiful redhead with an expertise in traumatic head injuries, but again, such luck—no seizures, no vomiting, no confusion whatsoever.

More waiting. Someone brings Sabrina to the hospital to sit with me, and she hugs me close. I ask how she's doing and she stares miserably in response. I want to ask about the interviews, but we can't talk here. Finally the nurse reappears to clear me for discharge.

"You should be out of the woods," she says, eyes flicking over my chart.

Out of the woods. I look at her blankly, then nod.

We take a car to the hotel Sabrina booked. It's the first Uber I've taken in months, and we hold hands in the backseat like teenagers. Sabrina hasn't stopped crying, her eyes and nose as pink as raw chicken. I'm numb, still, riding out the final watts of my energy stores. They aren't letting us back into the house yet; it's a crime scene, after all.

Good. I don't want to be stepping over bloodstains in 327 Tanglewood Drive.

We check in—two queen beds, a view of a gas station, nothing fancy but nothing offensive either. Sabrina trudges to one of the beds and sprawls on the stiff maroon comforter. I find the TV remote and a home renovation show, and we let it and the ditzy commercials alike wash over us.

My belly gurgles and I look down at it, like it's a distinct entity. *How can you even think about eating at a time like this?* But we haven't fed ourselves in forever and I order pizza, then stare too long at the teenage dude who delivers it to our door: *How nice,* I think, *to be having an ordinary day.*

The greasy sight flips my hunger on like a switch, and I set the box on the desk and dig in. My nose is so swollen I can barely taste it, but I'm too ravenous to care.

Sabrina sits up. "Will I ever be hungry again?"

I look down at the slice I've nearly finished. All that's left is the crust, Nathan's favorite part: *pizza bones,* he called them, scooping them off my plate.

My stomach buckles and I stare at the crust with revulsion. I set it back in the box and turn away, bracing myself for another wave of tears.

"Kelly," Sabrina murmurs, and I turn to see her rubbing her wrists. "Can you come here?"

I collapse on the bed and wrap myself around her, our spooning position second nature. Only this time, she's racked with sobs.

"You awake?" Sabrina whispers.

It's late, the middle of the night. Skinny bands of orange light leak around the blackout curtains. I keep thinking about goofy Nathan on the drive to my birthday dinner, how he kept playing the role of a grumpy old man ("Back in *my* day . . .") because he was thirty-seven to my thirty-five. The last time things were good between us. Since my birthday, everything's been terrible.

"Yup," I reply, rolling over to face her. She's curled like a caterpillar on her side of the bed. Though she's a good six inches taller than me, she looks tiny now—frail and gaunt.

"I keep going over it in my head." Her voice bubbles with emotion: "I slept next to that man for years. And I *never* thought he was capable of hurting someone."

Except that doxxer, I think, but she doesn't need me arguing with her right now. "I know. I loved him too." God, did I ever. Now I'll never hear his belly laugh or meet those twinkly eyes again.

"And Elizabeth." A stuttering breath corkscrews through her. "I can't believe she's . . . gone. It's so unfair. First her parents abandoned her, then she got knocked around by that bitch of an ex. And when she finally escaped that, she ran to *us,* to the house she thought was safe."

I rub her arm, nodding sympathetically.

Her shoulders tighten. "I can't believe she let herself do that." I'm quiet, waiting, feeling both of our hearts beat faster. "She swore she'd be careful, we explicitly talked about it. She . . ."—and here her voice drops to a growl—"she told us she had an IUD."

The sounds of the room, the air conditioning and dull drone of traffic and roar of night insects all drop away, like when you're driving in a downpour and pass beneath a bridge. Her tone—that's not how you talk about someone you adore, someone you're freshly grieving. There's vitriol beneath her words, blame, and coldness slinks up my spine.

In the charged silence, a thought I circled earlier returns: Sabrina had at least as much motive as Nathan. The unplanned pregnancy that could've detonated her marriage, her lifestyle, her *life*—she had good reason to want it, and Elizabeth, out of the picture.

Plus . . . Sabrina insisted Elizabeth only wanted to be with her. But what if she was wrong—what if Elizabeth would have taken either Lamont? What if she told Nathan she was pregnant and begged him to run away with her, and he refused, and Sabrina got wind of her betrayal and lured her into Nathan's office late at night . . .

"Elizabeth was a mess," Sabrina whispers. "And I miss her so much." The mattress shakes with her sorrow and when I pull her to me, her limbs loosen. I push the dark thoughts away, the paranoia spilling from my pores. *Nathan did this.* He let his violent streak take over and then he freaked out when I found the weapon and that's the reality, that's why things ended the way they did. Period, end of discussion.

"I'm so sorry, Sabrina. I'm sorry." An idea blossoms. "She said she worked on a farm in New Mexico, right? Did she tell you more about that?"

After a second, she nods. "She found an alpaca farm looking for workers in the classifieds." Her lips curve into a tiny smile. "I think she loved it. Being outside, feeding and grooming them, getting to know their personalities . . ." She wipes away tears. "She didn't quite put it this way, but I think it was . . . healing. And I'm glad she had that."

I squeeze her close. "She was lucky to have you. You're one of the most amazing people I've ever met, Sabrina." I stroke her cheek.

While Sabrina sleeps, a word licks at my brain: *haunted.* At first I thought their house seemed haunted, with its peaked angles and dark corners and strange sounds late at night. Now I wonder if I'm the haunted one. Not because of some spooky, otherworldly visits—haunted by my own brain, stamped now by the events of the last forty-eight hours.

I've never been that close to a dead body before. Let alone two.

I picture investigators sweeping the house, streaming like ants up that elegant staircase, forking out into the offices and bedrooms, peeking, dusting, observing. One of the kinder cops offered to go in first with a cat carrier, and they've sent me photos of Virgo sleeping soundly on a sofa in the officer's apartment. I miss her rabbitlike fur and the warmth of her next to me in bed.

Sabrina and I talked through everything they'll find: the red backpack in my bedroom, its sonogram inside, our laptops on the floor of the bathroom. Dirty dishes in the sink, clean laundry in the dryer. Video footage of me banging against the bars of the fence; of Elizabeth creeping inside and of Renee leaving baked goods on the far side.

My chest frosts over. *Renee.* What were we thinking? We discussed Renee's role in the story we'd tell law enforcement officers, how she fit into the intricate choreography we concocted and cemented and spat back into detectives' laps. Renee, the bogeyman. Renee, the impersonator, posing as a chatty new neighbor. Renee, the specter from Elizabeth's past, violent and mercurial.

We vaguely assumed it would all get back to her. But giving a fake name isn't a crime, nor is bringing cupcakes. We didn't ask for protection or request a restraining order because the woman didn't *do* anything, not to us.

So we pushed her out of our minds. We stayed laser-focused on the plot, our plan, the story that would set us free.

My heart bangs against Sabrina's shoulder blades. We discounted Renee. We saw Elizabeth's death as severance, snipping the cord connecting Renee to the Lamonts and, by extension, me.

But now . . . she's nearby. She's likely heard about Elizabeth, about the bodies in Tanglewood and what we told the police. She might know we're here right now, tipped off by someone at the station.

And somehow, amid all the machinations, the co-conspiring, assuring each other that we were careful we thought of everything *this has to work*, we missed the most obvious part.

We failed to think about what Renee might do to us . . . *now.*

CHAPTER FIFTY-SEVEN

I slide my limbs away from Sabrina, trying not to wake her, and tiptoe across the room. I plunk the bar lock into place and feel a rush of déjà vu—was it really just three nights ago that I pressed myself against the wall of another hotel room, fumbling with the chain of another door, hands shaking, fear misplaced?

I check that the dead bolt's still secure and turn around—then jump. Sabrina's sitting straight up in bed, staring at me, coated in the sickly light of the smoke detector.

"You scared me." I press a hand to my thudding chest.

"What are you doing?"

"Checking the locks." I climb onto the bed. "Go back to sleep."

She tilts her head, studying me in the dark. "Is that it?"

I sigh. "Not entirely. I'm worried about Renee. What if she, like, comes after us now?"

"'Comes after us'?" She blinks sleepily. "For what?"

I scoff and open my mouth to answer, but come up dry. "For . . . I don't know, taking away her 'chance' to be the one who hurt Elizabeth? Or . . . I don't know, you said she's unstable and manipulative—you made her sound sadistic—you think she's just going to move on now?"

She stares at me blankly. "You're right," she finally says. "She *is* dangerous. I'm . . . it's hard to know what to think." She rubs her eyes, scowls. "I can't deal with it right now."

"Of course. Let's go back to sleep." I pull the sheets up around us. Anxieties churn, but I can't pin them down, like an eye floater that skates away when you look at it: Renee's scary, but I can't work through what to be afraid of, what she might want. What she could do.

Sabrina begins to snore softly, but I stare at the window, watching the light brighten around the edge.

The plan works. Sabrina and I are a united front, so it's not my word against hers, no she said/she said—it's our word against a skeptic's made-up interpretation, and the burden of proof is on people who'd really like to wrap this up and get home to their wives and children and steaming lasagnas, their neat suburban lives. So, as Sabrina predicted, the detectives sleepwalk through their due diligence and sign off on the version of events that's right in front of them. No one's charged with a crime. It's dizzying, the way that whole sordid forty-eight-hour period is just . . . declared . . . over.

Well, not entirely over, because the press gets wind of it—how could they not? The trashier titles splash salacious headlines on top, DOD'S D.C. SWINGER KILLS MISTRESS & SELF among them, implying he whipped out a weapon (the press was never clear on what, or how she died, or where we found her—any of the details, really) in the middle of an orgy like it was part of some deranged sex-cult blood ritual.

Sabrina pens an eloquent statement asking for privacy during this difficult time, and goddamn if her Heart of Desire series doesn't swoop back onto the bestseller list as her profile rises and readers scour the racy scenes for any whiff of autobiography. We pick up Virgo and move back into the house (where else are we going to go?) and keep the doors to my old bedroom and to Nathan's office locked. News vans, white as teeth, idle at the entrance to Tanglewood Estates, and I'm grateful again for all the wrought-iron blockades. Seclusion—we can demand it, even in the midst of two very public deaths.

We don't talk about Renee. When I don't hear from her, I relax a bit, resuming my daily walks, focusing on all the other healing I need. But Sabrina's vigilant, her energy jumpy and taut, and I spot her peering out the windows and wincing when Virgo canters on the floor behind her. It's strange, watching Sabrina morph into the one obsessed with security, double-checking the locks several times a day. She was never the paranoid one. That was always Nathan.

And, of course, me.

We're in mourning, both of us, and the grief is a wide, scented wind that loops around the house and catches us off-guard when we least expect it: while we're pulling handfuls of clean clothes from the washer or watching TV in the basement or dipping our feet in the pool, wiggling our toes and commenting on how there's a cold snap coming, and summer feels both longer and shorter than when we were kids.

Suddenly one or both of us will stiffen or our eyes will glaze over and we miss our respective lovers *so hard* we're not sure we'll ever be whole again.

One afternoon, I catch Sabrina in her bedroom, holding Nathan's sweatshirt to her nose and sucking in the scent. I offer a hug but she tells me she wants to be alone. She seems to be grieving for Nathan more intensely than Elizabeth, but I'll never know what it's like to lose a spouse.

Another day, the smoke alarm erupts and she finds me hyperventilating in the kitchen, egg blackening on a skillet—cooking it reminded me of that morning with Nathan, his front pressed against my back, our arms in sync as we tossed an egg in the air. I had no idea at the time, but our positions foreshadowed our final seconds together, grappling for his gun.

Sabrina turns off the stove and opens the windows and wraps me in her arms tight tight tight until it passes.

We're getting better. The nightmares where I'm back in Nathan's office taper and I start to believe the mantras I repeat to myself throughout the day: *I did not kill Nathan. I'm not responsible for his death.* With every sleep, it gets a little easier. I blow a few downy dandelion filaments of grief into my dreams and the night carries them off.

I'll always have a Nathan-sized hole in my heart—that's never going anywhere, how he made every light source seem brighter, every moment more Technicolor, how one time he watched Virgo saunter out of the bathroom looking aggressively nonchalant and announced, "She totally just did a drug deal," and I laughed and laughed.

We order dumplings and Thai food and rich, gluey pasta, and one time Diane stops by with a casserole—so on the nose—and Amy calls me every night and Mom and Dad send flowers and don't ask me, thank God, if anything they're reading in the papers is true. I deactivate all my social-media accounts and it's nice, in a weird, woolly way, yanking the curtains closed and being alone with our sorrow, safe in our fortress with the one other person who gets it.

In all the fuzzy silence, I realize how much processing I have yet to do—all the questions that gape like wounds when I look back over the summer. So in a desperate late-night bid to wrap my head around what happened and why, I order a handful of books about relationships. The first one I crack is on *ethical nonmonogamy,* a phrase I should've learned long before I cavalierly entered a relationship with both my hosts.

Stomach clenching, I read the book in big gulps, with the slowly dawning realization that we missed the mark. Though Nathan told me there's "no playbook," there are indeed core tenets of polyamory, ones that seem obvious when I see them on the page: honesty, communication, openness, freedom, and transparency. I'm amazed by how many of my questions the book validates—how much confusion and hurt I could've avoided by looking for the answers myself instead of depending on my partners for guidance.

Both Sabrina and Nathan laughed it off when I was hesitant to sleep with either one of them alone. We had no safe words sexually or clear parameters emotionally. Hell, when Elizabeth showed up, I had no idea whether they saw her as their ex or their long-lost partner . . . and *nobody wanted to talk about it.* Turns out you can't just deem a relationship *egalitarian*—or, more accurately, *nonhierarchical*—and expect it to magically be so.

Should I feel bitter? Arguably, Sabrina and Nathan should have known better since they'd done this before. But I was complicit, so eager to not rock the boat. And as I read, I feel energized by every page, like my consciousness is expanding. Even if I never have multiple partners again, this is relationship gold, values I'll seek out in any partnership. So what if ours was a messy, imperfect polyamory? There was beauty there, too, and learnings for the rest of our romantic lives.

I leave the book out on the counter and then bashfully ask Sabrina if she'd like to read it too. ("Maybe it'll help you with *Elite Deviance*," I stammer, and she laughs kindly.) Over the next few days, I notice her bookmark sinking through its pages. The sight warms me. She's changed me, and in some small way, maybe I'm changing her too.

We eat in the dining room now—a change of scenery, without Nathan's empty chair staring back at us across the breakfast nook. One night, heart racing, I ask Sabrina over dinner if I should look into getting a new apartment. She blinks, confused.

"For both of us?"

A smile plays on my lips, the kind you try to hide, like when you're listening to a funny podcast on a bus in the Before Times.

"I meant for me."

She shakes her head, mystified. "Why would you do that?"

I refresh my wine. "I wasn't sure you still wanted me here."

"Kelly." She waits for me to meet her eyes. "Be honest. Where do you *want* to live?"

I think back to those long May days when I was still in Philadelphia. Before I came down here, before we'd even seen each other in person, seen or kissed or touched. Even then, I could tell Sabrina anything, our smartphones like the window in a Catholic confessional. She was non-judgmental, a superb listener . . . but also faraway and faceless. Can I do it again? Summon the bravery to be real with her?

"I want to stay here," I say. "With you. Or, if you want to sell the house and go back to the District or, hell, wait until we can take airplanes and move to, I don't know, Madrid—I don't care where we go. I just want to be with you."

"Phew." She leans back, swirling her wineglass. "Because I thought you were gonna say you're done with me. And all I want is to be with you."

We exchange a beam—personal, special, our world for two. I was ready to bury a body in the dead of the night for her. That's how much I love her—how much she means to me. And after all that, she wants me too.

I clear my throat. "Um, I know you looked at that book I suggested. About ethical nonmonogamy." My pulse picks up its tempo but I can do this, I can state my needs and ask for clarity. "I know we were kinda making it up as we went along, but it talks a lot about . . . communication. Expectations, parameters, all that stuff. So . . . I guess what I'm asking is . . ."

"Oh, Kelly, I'm so sorry." Sabrina's eyes are wide and regretful. "We went about it all wrong. So let me put it all out on the table: Right now, I only want to be with you. And I want you to only be with me. I understand if that's not what you're looking for, but—"

"*Sabrina.*" I set my hand on hers. "We're good. That's exactly what I want too."

"Oh, thank God." She pretends to slip out of her chair in relief.

I grin and swig the last of my merlot. "Hey, we're not glomming on to each other out of some weird, codependent trauma bond, right?"

She considers. "I guess we can't change the fact that we're bonded by trauma," she admits. "But I choose you because I want you. Not because I need you."

A few months ago, rejection would've unfurled in my gut at my beloved saying she didn't need me, because what else was I there for? From childhood on, my self-worth—no, my *identity* was swaddled in what I could do for others, how I could anticipate their needs and make myself indispensable. But look at Sabrina, independent as a cat. Free to choose whomever she'd like, and here she is, choosing me.

"So let's move," I say.

"Really?"

I squeeze her fingers. "What's keeping us?"

"Wow. You're right." She looks around the dining room. "This place is haunted. And I'll always be looking over my shoulder for Renee. We could have a fresh start."

Away from the bloodstains and Diane, the grieving Atwoods finally justified in their suspicions. Another smile I have to keep from overtaking my face. "Where should we go?"

She clangs a nail against her wineglass. "What about New York?"

I do miss city life: taking public transportation into the labyrinth of skyscrapers; the shimmering curve of a downtown river; cars whizzing around, headlights steady, and feeling that same energy winding through my blood vessels.

But . . . we're still in a pandemic. "Do we want to be in a city? With everything going on?"

She rests her chin on her fist. "From what I've heard, New York's back. Outdoor dining everywhere, everyone wears a mask, and my God, you should see the rent prices right now."

My smile spreads down my chest and up to the top of my head. "What if we start with something short-term?" I say. "Then we can try it out and look at neighborhoods." Virgo head-bumps my ankle and I rub her ears. "What do you think? Would you like to be a city cat again?"

She meows and Sabrina and I laugh.

"I'll take that as a yes!" Sabrina stands to clear our plates. "I'll start looking at places tonight."

CHAPTER FIFTY-EIGHT

We have sex that night, fingers trailing on each other's skin for the first time since . . . since the incident, since all that.

"I missed this," I tell her as we cuddle afterward. "I missed you."

"I missed you too."

I smile into her skin. "It's so wild that I didn't even know I liked women. Or that I could be with more than one person at once. You opened up this entire other world to me, you know? Got me out of my comfort zone."

"Lucky me." She skims her nails up my arm. "That's a tough thing for people to realize: Just because something feels *different* doesn't mean it's bad or wrong."

"Exactly." I weave our fingers together. "You know what's funny? Nothing about it seemed weird to me. It actually felt really natural." My thumb strokes hers. "What felt dangerous was letting go of Mike, our whole traditional future together. But, like, the safe zone isn't where any growth happens."

"Yes!" She sits up a bit. "And yet that's the messaging we always get:

'Don't rock the boat! Don't make any noise! Otherwise, some people might, gasp' "—she turns to me—" '*not like you.*' "

She's so pretty when she's worked up. Lightning in her eyes, her shoulders squared. I smooth my hand over her hip. "Well, I like you. Both in spite of and because of how you stir the coals." I lean over and kiss her shoulder.

The place she finds is perfect: an airy, furnished three-bedroom in Boerum Hill, with trees peeking into every window. It's all earthy corners—a dining table sliced out of a tree, an overstuffed suede couch with faux-fur blankets sliding off its back. She contacts a realtor about selling the mansion. I feel newly nostalgic for the Tanglewood house, touching its banisters and doorframes like it's an old, rheumy dog.

In my darkest hours, I try to picture it: Nathan's confrontation with Elizabeth, the moment he doomed himself. I feel desperate for answers, furious there's nothing I can do to make it make sense, no rabid gum-shoeing that can soothe the gremlin, *do it do it do it*. But I'm getting better at pushing the feeling away, at staring the thoughts down head-on and watching them shrink until I can breathe again.

Nathan did it. We'll never be sure of why or how, and I'll have to live with that ambiguity, left alone with the messy facts. I choose my ending and build my life around it because what other choice do I have?

None. No alternate because this is it, my everything—Sabrina and me with our fingers entwined, a solid couple in a churning world.

For so long I thought my happy ending would be me posing in a yard with two gorgeous children and my tall, handsome husband, a big house behind us and a nice car out front, two-dimensional perfection for all the world to see.

But did I ever really want that? Or did I accept the only future that was available to me as a kid growing up in Libertyville, the ultimate M.A.S.H.-game prophecy hanging low like a ticket at a deli counter?

This is better. Wilder and truer. I'm hers and she's mine and our beautiful, shared life inside these walls is for us alone to see.

So, in our final weeks at Tanglewood Estates, I relax. I get on the waiting list of an excellent psychiatrist in Manhattan. I lift weights in the cool basement. I research job opportunities in New York and say goodbye to the mansion, admiring its perfect pool and original front doors and scattered, golden light. It's not the home's fault it was the site of certain horrors—lies and murder, the spilling of blood. It was the site of beauty, too, moments that crowd out the ugliness like tender orange flowers poking up from the compost.

This is where I fell in love. This is where I discovered freedom. This is where I said goodbye to my imagined life with Mike and wiped clean the program that was running in my brain, an autopilot future that I marched toward like a zombie. Mike is wonderful and I don't regret our years together . . . but that wasn't enough, and that's okay.

It feels right when we make dinner together, Sabrina carefully chopping potatoes with the knife skills I taught her. It feels right when she bounds outside and cannonballs into the deep end while I'm swimming laps, enjoying one of the last warm days. It feels right when we sit outside and watch the sun set, purples and pinks and some shy peachy coral, and remark on how dusk comes sooner now, the final days of summer shrinking before our eyes. I wrap my arm around her and she rests her head on my shoulder and we sit like that until night blots out the entire backyard.

I'm in the downstairs bathroom clipping Virgo's claws, her an impatient bowling ball in my lap, when my phone buzzes. Virgo rolls off my thighs and hops onto the toilet lid, and when I check the screen, I feel like I've dived into an ice-cold lake.

I'm very sorry for your loss. And I owe you an explanation.

It's from Renee, who's still in my phone as Megan, and my stomach clenches. I think back to those early emails from Mike, the ones that threw me into another kind of tailspin, but this is different. Worse. More unbelievable.

Another text appears, impossibly long, and my heart thud-thud-thuds as I read it:

> You are going to hear one account of things from Sabrina, and I want to share the other side: the truth. Elizabeth is a cheat and a liar. I never hurt her. I'm not some scary stalker ex. Months after I broke up with her, she stole from me and then disappeared, and when I learned the last place she was seen was near the Lamonts', I became obsessed with figuring out what happened to her. Since she got me suspended, I had nothing but time to think about her. I thought the answers might be inside Sabrina and Nathan's house . . . and when you showed up, I thought you were my ticket to getting inside. I lied to you about my name, but nothing else. (I didn't even say I was straight . . . you started calling my ex "him," so I went with it.) I'm sorry I lied to you. I actually liked hanging out with you and felt bad I was doing it under false pretenses. And when even birthday cupcakes didn't get you to stop shutting me out, I figured Sabrina and Nathan had gotten to you and told you to stay away from me.

"Sabrina?" I call, struggling to stand. She's still typing. I could block her right now but I don't, and the typing dots dance and then *bing*, more lines, words I hoover up:

> I probably should cut ties but I thought you deserved to know the truth: I NEVER LAID A FINGER ON ELIZABETH. Why would her family take me in if I was abusing her?! You really think I could get them to like me and hate the Lamonts FOR NO REASON? No one on the planet is that persuasive. Here's the thing: I got to see the report after Elizabeth accused me of assault and battery.

My pulse batters in my neck and makes my hands shake so violently, I almost drop the phone. But there's more.

> I know *I* didn't give her those bruises. But someone did. And I'm worried you're next.

CHAPTER FIFTY-NINE

I rush to finish the text, which concludes as I knew it would:

> Given how close Elizabeth was with Nathan and Sabrina and
> how much time she spent with them . . . all I'm saying is, I'm
> not surprised by the awful news about Nathan. And I still don't
> trust Sabrina.

My stomach pitches and I lean against the counter, breathing hard.
I knew "Megan" always gave me a good vibe. I had misgivings about the
story Elizabeth and the Lamonts cooked up about Renee—*stories,* more
accurately, always shifting, slippery as an eel.

Bzzzt—one more text blisters through.

> I couldn't sleep at night if you didn't know everything so that
> you could make an informed decision. I'm truly sorry and I
> won't contact you again.

I hear footfalls above me, Sabrina on the move. Is Renee really warning me that my partner could hurt me? All the suspicions come flooding

back: how Sabrina knew the gate code but wouldn't let me out; how her voice dropped to a growl when she told me Elizabeth was supposed to have an IUD. Or even how she refused to talk about Elizabeth before any of this started—Nathan could discuss the past, but not Sabrina. She kept saying it was out of hurt, but what if it was out of something even hotter, more motivating: hate?

"Did you yell for me?"

She's right outside the cracked-open door and I jump. Virgo trots over to her, and as Sabrina pushes the door open Virgo flops onto her back, purring.

I hesitate—Sabrina's eyes are so wide, wild with concern. She's been dishonest with me before . . . and now I truly know what a good liar she is. Look how skillfully she clipped Elizabeth out of their story when we first rekindled our friendship. Look how smoothly she hid the ultrasound from Nathan. Behold the jarring mismatch between her hysterical voice and dull gaze when she placed the 911 call, and how masterfully she lied to detectives the morning after her husband died—look at what she pulled off.

But then my thoughts zag another way: No, what *we* pulled off. *I* lied to the police that day, too, something I never thought I could do. Mike's voice echoes, flummoxed and agitated: *I don't know who you are.* And I feel the same. Over the last few months, I've discovered so many new facets of myself. I fell in love with a woman. I can love and be with more than one partner at a time. I'm on the fence about motherhood. And I'm more Machiavellian than I ever would have thought: Witness how level-headed I was after the tussle with Nathan, how I convinced Sabrina we needed a master plan, how I looked that detective in the eye and lied through my teeth . . .

Total honesty is toxic to a relationship, Amy told me. *What matters is trust.*

"I wasn't yelling for you." I slip my phone into my pocket. Of course Renee is still trying to manipulate me—convince me she's a perfect angel. If she had *any* dirt on the Lamonts, she'd use it. And even if— God forbid—Elizabeth *did* get those bruises at 327 Tanglewood Drive, they had to be from Nathan, the violent one. There's nothing there.

Sabrina stoops to pet Virgo's cheek. They're all I have now, and with a linking sensation, I realize I'm all Sabrina has too. Of course I can trust her. They can't *both* be telling the truth, and Renee is a certified con artist. Nathan was a carefully camouflaged monster, but Sabrina, she's the good one, the woman I love. It's too late to rewrite our ending now—the story makes sense, the narrative we put together from the broken pieces in front of us, the blood on the office floor.

I thumb the scar on my right palm. I believe her.

I wrap her in my arms. "I can't wait to move with you," I say.

It's the last time we'll sleep in the house. Sabrina conks out next to me, but I can't turn my brain off. It's the anxiety I typically get right before a trip, but turned up to eleven—because of the pandemic, because of the guilt I feel leaving Nathan's memory behind, because embarking on a new life together is equal parts exhilarating and terrifying.

Something is bothering me about tomorrow's drive, and finally I roll over and snatch my phone from the side table. The nightstand's drawer is cocked open and for a second, I think I spot a metallic gleam inside. I scramble for the reading lamp—but the drawer's empty, of course. Nathan's gun is miles away in an evidence locker.

We're safe.

I open Google Maps and tap on the address of our rental in Brooklyn. It shows me the route, a blue line along I-95, almost as the crow flies. Washington, D.C., on the lower left, New York in the opposite corner. And only one other city—one other location is big enough to merit its name on the map.

"What is it?" Sabrina rubs her eyes.

I stare at the screen a moment longer, suddenly sure. "Philadelphia," I say.

"Huh?"

My plan straightens up inside me. "I want to see Mike. In person. For closure." I swallow hard. "I want to stop there on the way to New York."

She props herself up on her elbow. "Are you sure?"

I nod. "I'm finally ready. To try to be friends, you know? He's a good guy, Sabrina. He's given me space and, and respected my boundaries and I'm ready for things to not be tense again."

She drags herself up to sit. "Okay. I understand."

"It'll be quick. A pit stop. And . . . and I can get more of my things while we're there."

She sends a sad smile up toward the ceiling. "We could send a courier. It's okay if you want to stop, but don't pretend it's for practical reasons."

"You're right." I nuzzle my head on her shoulder. "To be honest, I miss him. Not romantically—not at all. But he was an important part of my life for a long time." My stomach squeezes; it still feels wrong to discuss my ex with my partner. But if I've learned anything this year, it's that I need to be vulnerable. After all we've been through—after I entered the intricate double Dutch of her romantic past, the marriage that opened into a triad, Elizabeth's disappearance and swift blink in and out—I have to be free to discuss my own baggage. "And . . . I know this sounds weird, but the fact that I *can* talk to him makes me feel like I *should*. I'm lucky he's still around when the last few weeks have shown us that . . . that the people you love can go away like *that*."

She nods, blinking back tears. "That's true."

"I love you," I say. "I can't wait to move to Brooklyn with you. But I need this. Okay?"

"Okay." She gazes at me for a second. "I love how kind you are." And she kisses me soft and sweet.

CHAPTER SIXTY

I twist to look behind me as we pull away from the gate. Our things hulk in the back of the car, clothes and kitchen appliances and books and electronics piled so high I'm not sure Sabrina can see out the rear windshield. Through the wing mirror, I watch the black gates seal us out. But most of the reflection is just me, eyes eclipsed by sunglasses, lips drawn.

"Goodbye, house," Sabrina says softly.

Curves in the road push our shoulders to the right and left. The trees blush harder the farther north we get. Eventually we turn off a long two-lane road onto the highway. My gut writhes. I can't picture Mike clearly, even after all those times I kissed his face. I'm worried I won't recognize him.

I'm afraid he'll be a stranger.

Hours later, Philadelphia appears in the distance, blue-green skyscrapers sliced into rectangles or tapering into triangles where they meet the sky. Sabrina turns on the blinker to exit the highway. It clack-clack-clacks like a ticking time bomb.

"You're sure you want to do this?" She eases to a stop at a red light. "You can still bail. You don't have to prove anything to anyone."

I flail for a second, then remember: I want a hug, mutual acknowledgment of all we shared. I'll wish him the best and then lift off like a goose, beating my wings, heading for a new climate at the end of a long season.

"I need this." I reach out and squeeze her hand. "Thanks for coming with me."

Ominous clouds curdle the sky. My pulse gathers speed. Wow, I really got used to being surrounded by trees and hills and birds, by the halcyon hush of the far-out suburbs. We wriggle into the city and the noise and crowds and billowing trash seem to beat against the SUV.

We roll past important historic monuments, glittery bursts of mosaics, and the glossy, orange-tinged green of Rittenhouse Square. The GPS's impassive voice sends us worming around a few final turns, and then—

"There," I say. Our building. A rowhouse nearly identical to the ones abutting it, with neat brick and black shutters and a half-circle window over the front door. It looks impossibly narrow now, the bars over our first-story windows tarnished and grotesque.

It's perfect! I'd called when we first entered this apartment at the start of the year. Mike looped his fingers through mine, kissed my cheek. I gasped and grinned. *I think this is it.*

"Is this it?" Sabrina asks, snapping me back. Her voice is thick with kindness, like I'm about to put my dog down.

"Sure is," I finally say. He knows we're coming; he was nice about it when I texted early this morning. I couldn't call. Couldn't hear his voice. Man, this is going to be hard.

She gazes out the windshield. "Do you want me to come in?"

"No. That'd be weird." I haven't decided yet if I'm going to tell him about Sabrina and me. The tabloids never got ahold of that detail, instead garbling the backstory and dubbing me "a childhood friend marooned in the gated community after fleeing Chicago like so many city-dwellers." As if 327 Tanglewood Drive were a desert island, as if I were shipwrecked and stranded and sunburned.

"I'll find somewhere to park," she says, "and then I'll hang out in Rittenhouse Square. Call me when you're done, okay?"

"Thanks." I turn to Virgo on the seat behind me. "Ready?"

My heart thrashes as I ring the doorbell. I glance over my shoulder, but Sabrina's already gone. I feel unmoored. Like I really did wash up here, sputtering and half-drowned.

There's the deranged buzzer and I enter the vestibule. My feet creak on uneven planks, and then I see him standing in our door.

His door. The door. A door to a place I once lived.

He looks exactly the same, yet entirely different. His hair is a Q-tip—he must have shaved his head at some point—and he's buzzed away the beard he grew in the spring. But those blue eyes, those thin, playful lips, it's all him, details I know so well. Something oozes open in my ribs, and I cross to him and set my purse and Virgo's carrier on the floor.

"Mike. How are you?"

After a moment's hesitation, he opens his arms and I step into them, pressing my head against his chest, and he smells like him and though the romance is gone, though our capital-L Love leaked away before the pandemic even started, I do care about him. I missed him.

After a minute he gives that final, closing squeeze and we break apart. The tears in his eyes match my own and we laugh self-consciously.

"Come inside!" he says, with try-hard cheer.

I step into the living room, marveling. He did it—he hung framed pictures on the walls and unpacked those last annoying boxes.

"It looks great." It's more cramped than I remembered, but that's on account of my living in a mansion for months. He's done well.

"There's some stuff in the office I wasn't sure if you wanted." He sticks his hands in his pockets. "You might want to go through it. I'm . . . I'm really glad you contacted me."

"I am too. It's good to see you." I've never befriended an ex before, and it feels good. Mature. Like I'm doing something I can feel proud of later.

Virgo meows and Mike looks at the carrier with trepidation. He pulls at the zipper, then brightens as she trots out. She leans into his pets, her eyes blissfully closed, and Mike grins.

"You seem surprised!" I chuckle.

"I . . . I wasn't sure if she'd remember me." He smiles crookedly, scratching her chest. Abruptly she stands and then skims into the office. We follow and Mike ruffles her silky fur, and we laugh as she flops onto her side, purring.

"So, New York, huh?" he says. It's easier this way, with us both keeping our eyes on Virgo.

"Yeah. I'm excited. And . . . and you can come visit Virgo whenever you want." I wasn't planning to say this, but it suddenly feels obvious.

"Thanks. My buddy Carl, from Madison? He lives there now. So I'll have a few reasons to make the trip."

He switches from crouching to sitting on the hardwood, and I do the same. I clear my throat. "So, hey. I wanted to . . . to thank you. For being honest about how our relationship wasn't working."

He doesn't respond, just methodically runs his palm over Virgo's belly. She crunches and stretches her front paws in the air. The motion makes me think of a sea urchin opening and closing.

"I didn't see it at first," I continue, "and obviously it took a while for me to come around, but you were one hundred percent right."

Virgo, overstimulated, flicks her head up and bites the fleshy pad of Mike's thumb. He pulls his hands onto his lap as she darts under the desk.

"Y'know, it wasn't fair of me, saying I wouldn't reschedule the wedding but not actually breaking things off. I wanted to have my cake and eat it too." He's trying to keep from crying. If we were still together, I'd clutch his hands and help him slow his breath.

"I know. We were both at our wits' end." My voice wobbles. "It sucked, but it's good we figured out we shouldn't marry each other. And I've been wanting to say thank you, too, for being solid. With all the things I had to worry about over the last couple of months, and with all the shitty stuff I went through . . . you made it easy for me."

A little sob shakes through him. "You're just so . . . *fine*," he says. "I wasn't expecting that."

"Oh, jeez. Do I seem that way?" My laugh sounds slightly deranged. "It's only sometimes. It's been *a lot*. I don't know how much you read about it, but . . . it was like living through a scary movie."

"Sounds like it." He looks stiff, overwhelmed. I wonder if he suspects us—Sabrina and me, the three-way relationship, any of it. "I don't know how you stayed in that huge house after all that."

I stare at the scratched hardwood floor. I'm glad he hasn't asked me what happened; I don't want to walk anyone through it. "It's hard to explain. It still felt like home. I . . . I was happy there. After here. Sorry, I don't mean to be cruel. But . . . I did a lot of growing there." I look up at him. "But how are you? I'll feel better knowing you're okay too."

"I thought you'd come back after that." He shakes his head, dismayed. "When I heard? I was worried about you."

"I was fine! I *am* fine."

"You were living in a house of horrors." His voice loudens and I see it clear as day: how eager I once was to be his emotional shepherd, to help him process whenever he was upset. *It's not your job anymore,* I remind myself. However he works through strong feelings (or doesn't) is no longer my concern.

"Mike."

"I just wanted to protect you, I . . ."

An icy silverfish runs up my neck—he sounds so much like Nathan. "*Mike.* I know you care about me." I can't help it—I cuff my hands around his arm, and he droops a little. "It's okay that you weren't there. But I'm asking a second time: Are you okay?"

He looks at me, lips quivering, then lowers his head. His hands sit limply in his lap. They're dry and cracked like he's been scrubbing them nonstop.

"I'm okay," he whispers. He looks up. "Ready to go through your stuff?"

We chat while I sift and sort, and he relaxes, like the worst part is over. I pick out some books, Virgo's favorite scratching post, a jewelry box full of baubles I'd all but forgotten. He's on the list to adopt a dog; he got nothing but praise in his first work review. His dad's doing well in Iowa. In some ways, Mike really does remind me of Nathan, now that I see him—the loyalty, the big laugh, how he'd do anything for his tribe. The thought fills me with a bubble of sorrow and I turn away, blinking.

Virgo swishes around the apartment, at ease. Mike and I can still joke around and make each other laugh. It's good; this is good.

We finish going through the boxes and stand. He opens his arms again and we hug, swaying a little, like we're dancing.

"Well, good luck in New York," he says into my hair.

"Thanks." I let out a rickety laugh. "I'll try not to be involved in any front-page news up there."

"Okay, phew." He laughs, too, his chest bouncing. "Good plan. No more scandals involving the Department of Defense."

"No more missing persons in the house," I add.

"No more dead bodies in your bed."

I stiffen and he steps back, cheeks red. "Sorry, too soon?"

A sick feeling swirls in my stomach, and I swallow. "Guess so, yeah. I . . . I should find Virgo." I stagger into the hallway, calling her name, and hear a rustle in the bedroom. A charged, heavy feeling gathers in me as I kneel by the bed, then slowly lower my face to the floor.

Wake up, Kelly. It's back, the deep, desperate wanting, alarm bells looping through my head. *Put it together. It's right in front of you. Do it do it do it.*

I blink into the silty dark as lumps come into focus. A box of light-bulbs. A forgotten shoe. Dust carpets the debris—clearly Mike hasn't cleaned under here since I left.

Wait—that sparks something, a dim light in my consciousness. But what? I finally spot Virgo in the center and our eyes lock. I flatten my body and slide farther under the bed; dust coats my shirt, my hair. I grab at the thought again, still just out of reach: *He hasn't cleaned under here.* With the cleaning supplies.

The ones we keep under the kitchen sink. Unlike . . .

The alarm bells are louder now, a siren, and it's coming into focus, the moment that made dread pool in my belly. I'm halfway under the bed, waist-deep, and the box spring claws at my shoulder.

"C'mere, Virgo. Time to go."

I stretch my arm out as far as I can and she watches calmly, an inch past my fingertips. Heart banging against the hardwood floor, I rewind the last few minutes, to the conversation that ended on such a dissonant chord.

No more scandals involving the Department of Defense.

No more missing persons in the house.

No more dead bodies in your . . .

My blood turns icy, slushy in my veins, everything cold, dis-traught, *no.*

No more dead bodies in your bed. None of the news reports, the tab-loids or TV segments or column inches of crispy-soft newsprint ever included this detail.

Horror bangs through me and I jerk and bedsprings scrape my skull. Virgo tenses at the sound, then shoots out from under the bed. I scram-ble to slide backward, palms skidding in the dust. My head hits the bedframe as I get my feet under me and stand, then whirl around—

And come face-to-face with Mike.

He steps back, pushing the door closed behind him. I rush to reor-der my expression, but it's too late.

He's seen it. After five years, he can read me like a book.

"I—I need your help getting Virgo." My voice buzzes through my whole body.

But his face is reddening by the second, mouth twisting, Adam's apple jerking. He knows he slipped. "It—it was on the news, the dead girl—"

The sound of a waterfall pounds in my ears. "I won't tell anyone."

He starts to cry and this makes him furious, like his tear ducts have betrayed him. Alarmed, Virgo gallops back under the bed.

"Mike, please," I say, choking on my breath. "*Please.*"

He takes a step toward me and stops, his toes a millimeter from mine. My legs press against the bed as he tips his chin lower, lower, until his face is an inch from mine.

"I . . . I didn't mean to." He swallows thickly, his lips trembling. "I thought it was you."

CHAPTER SIXTY-ONE

"What are you talking about?"

"You humiliated me." His voice is shrill, hysterical. "I never wanted any of this."

I feel like my skull's expanding, out out out like a balloon, about to explode.

"You left me. You dropped me like I was a piece of toilet paper stuck to your shoe." He presses his shaking fingers against his mouth. "I was so depressed and you just left me here, alone, in this piece-of-shit apartment. You didn't even look back." Tears gush down his cheeks. "You were having the time of your life down there, seeing someone new, not a care in the world. Never once thinking about *me*." He thumps his chest.

Something he said the last time we spoke echoes back to me: *All this time to think, it's not healthy*. I left him alone in this prison-bar apartment, his whole life compressed within its four thin walls. While I was lounging around a mansion, loving and beloved, Mike was in solitary confinement.

And he lost it. He. Did. Not. Do. Well.

"You know how I know I didn't matter to you?"

I stare back, teeth chattering.

"Because you told me. I was a goddamn *butt dial* to you. And then! You didn't even *acknowledge* my message."

My eyes widen, bewildered, and his face darkens. "You don't remember it."

My brain is careening over the last few months, quick as an eagle, and finally I spot it: "My birthday." His voice memo—I figured I'd reply later, and then . . . then the newspaper, then the Ritz, then Elizabeth.

He nods and wets his lip. "And not only did you not acknowledge it, you replied with a fucking selfie. On Instagram."

I rear back. Mike doesn't even *use* social media; I had no idea he was keeping an eye on me.

"*I'm so* fucking *grateful to year 34 for pushing me to take a leap of* faith *and make choices that are* authentic *to me*," he recites from memory, his voice high and taunting. "*The life I never expected is better than I dared to hope. I'm so* goddamn grateful *to those I get to love . . .*" He steps closer and replaces the falsetto with a growl: "*and I'm happier than ever.*" A single, grunting laugh, the meanest noise I've ever heard him make. Tears drip down my neck.

My pulse is thunderous, swelling like applause. I wasn't even *thinking* about him when I wrote that caption. "I'm sorry," I say, my voice tiny. "I didn't think you'd see it."

Wrong answer—he puffs up like the Hulk, tendons tightening on his throat. "Of course you didn't," he roars. "You don't give a shit about me anymore."

He breathes hard as a fresh wave of rage rocks through him. I flash back to him in our bedroom, days after his mother died, when he punched the wall and then sobbed as I bandaged his hand.

This time, it's not going to be a wall.

"That's not true, Mike. I've always cared about you. I *love* you." Help—I need to call for help. My mind races around the apartment, searching for the nearest connected device. My bag's by the front door, right?

"I gave you the benefit of the doubt," he goes on. "I thought maybe the couple you were staying with was messing with your head. Keeping you away from me. I mean, you always go along with things."

My stomach sinks. It's almost exactly what Sabrina said to me all those months ago at the brewery. Is it true? Am I merely a reactor, bandied about like an acorn in a storm drain?

No. I won't just go along with this. Mike flexes his jaw, and I feel a fresh jolt of alarm.

"I needed to see you." His eyes are wild, glazed. "I had to go down and see it for myself. Find out what was actually going on. I thought—if I could just see what my Kelly was really up to . . ."

My Kell-Bell. I'd always found it endearing. Now I see it for what it really is: a claim to his possession.

"I took the next Amtrak. I called a cab. And then I discover there's two fences keeping me away from you? Fuck that."

My heart's beating hard in my hands and feet. His face is so close, I can see the pores on his nose, the sweat on his forehead.

"I hadn't come all that way for nothing. So I paid the damn taxi. I hit the little buttons to call the house. I even waved at the stupid camera so you'd know it was me. And you just . . . ignored me. Like you'd ignored my message. Didn't even bother to tell me why."

"What are you talking about?" We couldn't access the main gate's CCTV, only Nathan's camera at the end of the driveway. When did Mike try to get in? I scramble to do the math: If he saw the birthday selfie around noon and took the next Amtrak and traveled another hour to Deerbrook . . .

He puffs up his shoulders. "Don't lie to me. Don't do that."

"I'm not, I didn't know you—"

"I told you not to lie."

He waits for me to nod, then continues. "I started walking around the gate. Followed it into the cemetery next door. And I discovered I could get close to the house from there." He narrows his eyes. "In fact, I could see inside. Right into an office. And do you know, Kelly"—his head comes even closer, kissing distance—"do you know what I saw?"

It hits me: the chime of the entry system; *we'll get your presents later.* Oh Jesus, the three of us in Nathan's office, curtains spread like legs . . .

He sees the revelation on my face, snorts. "How. Fucking. Dare you."

I whimper, shrinking beneath him.

"This is how you decide to fuck with me? By *rubbing it in my face?*"

I cry and cry, my guts wringing like the tears are coming from deep inside. "I'm sorry you saw that, Mike." *Tell him what he wants to hear. Hide how it was so much more than sex.* "I made a mistake. But I swear, I had no idea you tried to come by. I never would've . . ."

"You were furious when I asked you for a threesome. A one-time thing." His words shoot out through clenched teeth. "You were horri- fied. Like I was a terrible person for even asking. And then the second you got away from me . . ."

"You're right, Mike. It was a stupid rebound thing and I was just going along with it." My voice climbs higher and higher. "But please believe me, I had no idea you were there. I would never try to hurt you like that—*never.*"

He gazes at me, then looks away. "So I got out of there. Found a hotel within walking distance. Stopped at a liquor store on the way. I was *done* with you."

You weren't, though.

"And then . . . I woke up hungover and angry and miserable the next morning and I just, I couldn't leave. I couldn't come back here with my tail between my legs." A loud, pitiful sniff. "I hadn't slept in probably three days and I couldn't think straight. I was acting like such a pussy— hiding like a scared little boy. And . . . something switched. I knew what I had to do." He peers at me, his eyes lobster red. "I'd go into the house. And I'd make you fucks pay."

His chest heaves. Fresh fear squirts through me, like paint splatter- ing onto a canvas. I'm rapt, watching with a rubbernecker's dark fasci- nation.

"So I waited until it got dark. Finished a handle of Jack. And I walked right up to the house."

My heart thumps, every nerve on high alert. I shake my head, still wanting this to be false, the wild ravings of a lunatic. "Past the gate?"

He gives a broody shrug. "I climbed a pine tree near the back fence. It wasn't hard to get over."

Whoa. The only camera is at the foot of the driveway. All of Nathan's security measures—felled by a damn fir.

He closes his eyes like he's reliving it, locked in his own mental re-enactment. "The side door was open."

"What?" They drilled it into me the day I moved in: *Lock the doors, lock the doors.*

"I could see it from the driveway, there was light coming from inside. So I went up to it and it was open an inch. It felt like a sign or something, like God had left the door cracked for me."

Confusion twirls, and then it hits me: I knocked instead of entering the code when I got back from the hotel. I set Virgo's carrier on the ground and Nathan was distracted and distant as I shuffled inside and, Lord, did we really not seal the door behind me? The *one night* we slacked on security . . . it's like everything that came after was predestined, a twist of fate.

Mike mashes his fists against his teary eyes, digging them in hard enough to bruise.

"As soon as I stepped inside, I saw Virgo—but when I reached for her, she took off. It pissed me off, like everyone had abandoned me . . . her too. Like, did I hallucinate our entire relationship?"

"Mike." No wonder he was on-edge around her.

"I walked around the whole house." His voice is as compressed and impenetrable as a diamond. "I felt like I was dreaming. I'd spent months picturing you in your fucking Barbie Dreamhouse. It didn't seem real."

I press my hands over my open mouth. My brain's doing something desperate, begging this story to end differently. *Get out of the house, Mike. Go back to Philadelphia. Leave us alone.*

"I walked around the basement. I walked around the kitchen. I went upstairs and pushed a door open just enough to see that bearded asshole asleep in his bed."

My heart is a drumroll; my hands and feet hum. This was the day Elizabeth showed up at the house—a whole drama Mike somehow missed. Did he not notice my sleeping body in the Lamonts' bed?

"The next room was the office." It's a whisper, so tiny yet barbed enough to fill the entire room: "The room where I saw you fucking. On the desk. On the couch. Everything in that room, it's like—it's like it was mocking me." His pulse throbs in his corded neck. "I noticed this thing on the wall. This little pyramid. Exactly what I was looking for—heavy and sharp. And I picked it up and went back into the hallway and . . . and the next room, it was yours."

I'm frozen, vibrating with terror. The rest of the world has disappeared and it's just us, spotlit in a tiny corner of the universe, one listening as the other confesses to murder.

He shouldn't be telling me this. Because once he's told me . . .

"I went in. I saw your lotion on the nightstand and Virgo's toys on the floor. For a second I was relieved you were in there and not sleeping with the couple."

Elizabeth; he mistook Elizabeth for me.

He shakes his head. "You were sound asleep. I left the light off and you didn't even stir as I went over to the bed. You were turned away, curled up the way you like to sleep, so all I could see was your hair. I was feeling like . . . like a *cuck*, this pathetic guy who couldn't even keep his girlfriend—who couldn't keep anything in his life together. A complete failure." He pauses to groan, a crude, guttural sound. "I . . . I raised the pyramid"—he lifts a hand—"and I held it there, and oh, God, I was ready to do it, to bring it down and make you pay for how you treated me." Tears gush down his face; a line of snot forms under his nose, shiny as a snail's trail. My own hot tears pour over my chin and down my throat.

Nathan. Nathan was innocent.

Thanks to me, Nathan and Elizabeth are dead.

Mike tries to compose himself. "But I couldn't do it. You have to believe me. It was like waking up from a dream, like, *What the hell am I doing?* Because I'm not a murderer. Please tell me you believe me."

"I believe you," I whisper, but it's rote, a lie to keep him calm. Who is this man?

He grunts, his throat jerking. "So I went back into the office and I was going to put it away. The stone thing? And . . . and then . . ." He collapses into more sobs, sobs that shake his whole body, turning the inch between us charged and muggy. My body's ablaze with fear, knowing this story is a ticking bomb counting down its final moments.

"She surprised me, Kelly. She must have heard me in the office, she came out of nowhere and I still had the pyramid in my hand and I spun around, I was trying to *defend* myself, but it didn't—it didn't swing through the air like I thought, it made this wet, spongy sound and when I looked, I couldn't see the tip, it was . . ." He bawls, his shoulders juddering like a chainsaw. "That's when I realized it was *her* I'd seen in the bed. My head was spinning, like—is this even the right house? And I— I didn't know what to do. I wasn't thinking. I carried her back to the bedroom. I found cleaning supplies downstairs and wiped down the floor and pyramid and then I went to the kitchen and scrubbed my hands until they were raw." He shakes his head, hysterical. "Where *were* you? What the fuck was going on?"

An idea like a tongue of light at the top of a cave. "No one's looking for you, Mike." I gulp. "You saw the headlines. You got away with it. Nathan took the fall for everything."

His eyes are pressed closed; a sob shakes out of him.

"You know it's true—it's the reason you agreed to meet me, yeah? You're in the clear. As far as anyone knows, you were never there." I wait for him to meet my gaze. "Mike, it's *me*. We can move past this. It's over—you're free."

"I'm not free!" he roars, and I wince. His hand works in and out of a fist. "I can't sleep, I can't eat, I can barely think. And when I do fall asleep, I wake up screaming from the nightmares." A hunk of spit flies off his lips. "I keep seeing her face, Kelly. I see all that blond hair and the pyramid and my hand and, oh God, the moment when I realized what'd happened, and she looked right at me, like she could see into my soul."

He grabs my chin and I let out a scream. His eyes narrow. "None of this—*none of this*—would've happened if it weren't for you."

CHAPTER SIXTY-TWO

Everything goes very, very still. A scrim drops over the rest of the room and the only sound is Mike's bellowing sobs, strangled like they're being wrung out of him, mixed with my own cries.

Clink. Clink, clink. We both turn, squinting into the light. Someone from the street outside is banging on the rusty window guard.

"You okay?" It's a young guy, college-aged. He grabs a bar where it curves like a rib and peers inside. "I heard shouting. Do you need me to call someone?"

Mike takes a half step back, and cool air rushes into the space between us. He makes a loud snuffling noise. He isn't going to answer, I realize. It's up to me.

Clarity like a beam of light: I could end this. Brace myself and tell that stranger *Yes, please call the cops, do it now before Mike gets away*.

We have so much intel for law enforcement. New developments. A break in that open-and-shut case about who killed Elizabeth Kessler and Nathan Lamont.

My neck swivels and I lock back on Mike's eyes. They brim with shame. He mouths: *I'm sorry.* And then his knees give out and he drops to the floor, quick as a coin in a well. He cups his hands over his face and accepts his fate.

I flash to how we must look to the fellow in the window: a domestic dispute, probably, a man and a woman, blue-eyed and well-matched, both awash in emotion. Mike looks guilty as sin—the wife-beater begging for unearned grace.

It was kind of the passerby to stop. To care. I'm not trapped. I'm not in Tanglewood, inside two concentric circles of wrought-iron gates. I'm not cut off from the world and stuck in our own horrible, untouchable dome, social isolation at its most stifling.

Mike tips onto his side and curls into the fetal position. He chokes on his sobs and his arms clutch at his body as if to hold it together. It's over. He knows it.

Maybe he knew it from the second I walked in the door, the truth straining against the walls of his heart, then leaking out like air from a sagging balloon. To my surprise, a peculiar sensation surfaces: recognition, empathy. And then it clicks—I know firsthand how jealousy can push you to the breaking point when you're isolated and alone and the world is spinning out.

I stare at him. I think of the punched wall, the dented sofa, the ATV rental guy whose eyes bugged as Mike nearly lost control. For years, I repeated it to myself like a chant: *Mike's terrible at emotional regulation, but* . . . And then I let the end dangle. *But he'd never hurt me*—that's how I wanted it to conclude. That made him safe; that made it okay.

And now I know the true end of the sentence: *But then again, so am I.*

A sob catches in Mike's throat and turns into a snort, then a cough. My insides tug. All those loyalties—to Nathan, to Sabrina. To the man I would've married.

And then, deep in my mental battle, another candidate enters the ring.

Me. My freedom, my life. All the dominoes that'll topple over, *plink,* if I turn him in.

I think back to that tense twenty-four hours locked in the house with Elizabeth's body. I feel the bulk of Nathan's arm necklaced against my throat as we tussled in his office in the middle of the night. I feel the weight of the gun in his hand, the clock-arm twist as the barrel swung. The overly air-conditioned police precinct, where the detective asked me, glass-eyed: *Tell me again why you couldn't call for help?*

I see it with piercing lucidity: If Nathan's innocent . . . they'll know we're guilty. Crimes of omission, of cover-up, of perjury and obstruction of justice.

I shoot the man at the window a shy, apologetic smile. "Thanks so much for checking. But we're fine." I kneel and Mike looks up in shock. He sits and watches as I take his hand. "We're working through some stuff."

The kid shrugs. "All right. Have a good day." He lopes away, out of the window frame, his peephole view on our life. We'll never see him again. He'll never know he was a key player, the one who held so much power in his hands—the power to ring the alarm and summon the authorities, to recast two already salacious deaths.

Mike touches my hand to his cheek. He squeezes his reddened eyes closed and I allow it, a tender moment, the cottony rush of his gratitude.

He's locked in his own kind of prison now. And I see all the times I should have known—when his own father derided him for crying at a funeral; how he learned that pride is power and anger's the only acceptable way to handle hurt. He hid the truth when he lost his job and when we didn't reschedule the wedding; he didn't even want to alert our guests when we officially called it off. All the time I struggled with love versus distrust, two ends of a tug-of-war, I failed to notice the third point forming a triangle: pride, the hard shell that keeps you from being real.

"Now what?" he asks.

Virgo slinks up behind him. She fixes me with a flinty stare, like she's waiting for the answer too.

I pull my hand away. "Now I get my stuff," I say. "And I leave."

I'm unsteady when I burst out of the townhouse, blinking into the pearly day, overcast but still too bright. I stagger down the sidewalk, a bulging bag pinned under one arm, Virgo's carrier gripped in the other. I couldn't get out of there fast enough. Mike's words are still ringing in my ears, the chorus he repeated as I rushed out of the apartment: *Forgive me, forgive me, forgive me.*

I said he was forgiven. My final lie to him. I'll try, someday, when he's a distant memory, when I can think of him without my heart pretzeling into a panicky knot. But he's not first in line.

Nathan. The accusations I've been carrying around in my chest for months, horrible things I ascribed to him . . . he was innocent all along. Through this new lens, everything he did—all the actions that seemed so sinister, changing the gate code and locking away our electronics and insisting we bury the body together—point to the same conclusion, antithetical to the one I drew: He *hadn't* done it and couldn't bring himself to believe that Sabrina or I had either.

He loved us. And all he wanted was to keep us safe.

Walkers clog the sidewalk and I pick my way around them. I pause at an intersection and the scene begins to play in my head, the moment I've worked so hard to suppress:

Drop it. I turned around and faced him and his arms shook like an old diesel engine.

We stared at each other. Sweat dripped down his cheek; his eyes were wild. *Kelly, no. No, no, no.*

Something rolled through him then—what I took to be fury. But alarm, shock, horror . . . from the outside, they all look alike. And they're all understandable responses to realizing something unthinkable about someone you love.

I should know.

That's the murder weapon. He nodded at it. Not confessing—observing. Making the same conjecture I had seconds earlier.

I know, I said, frowning.

And he was defeated, dismayed. He believed his partner, his love, had killed Elizabeth. Then he uttered his last words, ones I read entirely wrong: *Jesus Christ, Kelly.*

My vision fogs and my head fills with static, and I lean against a lamppost, swaying. I set Virgo down and she meows at my ankles and though I yank down my mask, I can't get enough air, my breath is short and quick and too high. I clutch at my breastbone as my body floods with panic, screaming for oxygen, I'm like a scuba diver without a tank, a surfer yanked under a riptide, *air I need air oh my God I need—*

"Are you okay?"

A woman has stopped, her eyes crinkling over her mask. I gesture at my mouth, trying to form words but nothing comes out. Darkness pulls at the margins of my vision; tingles swamp my hands and feet.

She digs in her purse and whips out a small cloth rectangle, which she unfurls into a blue shopping bag.

"Hold this over your mouth," she orders. "Make a seal."

I do as I'm told, pushing my hot breath into the nylon, feeling the bag puff and shrink like an external lung as I suck my exhalations back inside. After a few seconds, the tingling subsides and my head seems to float back down to my shoulders.

"Thank you so much." I hold out the bag.

"Keep it." She continues on her way. I watch her shrink into the distance.

She helped me. *Saved* me. Not because she loved me or knew me or considered me part of her tribe.

For seven months, it's been drilled into my head: *Stay away from strangers; avoid other people at all costs.*

Anyone could kill you.

A dangerously seductive mantra for someone whose brain tends toward everyday paranoia. Pull up the drawbridge; fill the moats. Cinch the drawstrings of our lives until one mansion on a hill is all we know.

But it's clear now: We need each other. Three people aren't enough to make a world.

I know what I have to do. Tears sting my eyes as I turn in the direction of Rittenhouse Square.

CHAPTER SIXTY-THREE

A few blocks later, I spot the glossy crown of Sabrina's head. My pulse ticks back up as questions form like clots in my brain. The things I need to ask her and truths I need to share. There's a break in the clouds and she's sitting in the stippled sunshine, enjoying the warm October day. My heart slumps under the knowledge that things will never be the same again.

"How'd it go?" Sabrina chirps. It's cinematic—the mom in the movie cluelessly asking her kid how their day at school was.

I lower Virgo's carrier and settle onto the bench. Strangers stroll past, each the protagonist of their own melodrama: a pregnant woman in a raspberry dress, a couple arguing about weekend plans, two teenage girls with their masks looped defiantly over their forearms. Sabrina's iced coffee jingles as she shakes it.

"That's all your stuff? It's less than I thought." She gestures at the IKEA bag under my arm, puffed like a piece of popcorn. "I could've gotten the car."

"I was hoping we could talk."

Her eyebrows lift. "Of course."

"There's something I need to tell you." My heart thumps. Can I do this?

She leans closer. "Okay . . ."

I stare down at my hands. "A while ago—like, right after I discovered the camcorder—I . . . I went through some of your things. In your desk."

She rears back, her forehead crinkling with hurt. "Wow."

"I know. I'm sorry. I knew it was wrong. I was . . . I was desperate for more information, and you'd told me not to ask about Elizabeth. And I found something. A Polaroid of her with a black eye and bruises."

She shakes her head. "I can't believe you did that."

"I'm sorry." I'm crying again, feeling that pressure beneath my eyes and nose. "I didn't know what else to do. But once I found that—and it was right after the incident in the hot tub, and . . ."

"You think *Nathan* gave her those bruises?" Now she's crying, too, fury gathering in her eyes. "They were from Renee. When she accosted her in her apartment in D.C." She shakes her head. "We convinced her to report it. She gave a bunch of photos to the police. But we kept one, because we were worried they would . . . conveniently misplace them." She looks away. "But they didn't. That's what finally made them open an investigation and put her on leave."

"Got it." I sink a little at the confirmation. *Nathan.* An innocent man, guilty only of trying so hard to protect us.

That cold, calculating side—the one I misread as conniving, even Machiavellian—was Nathan's way of coping, his own form of grief. He'd just lost one woman he loved; he wasn't about to lose the other two.

I take a deep breath. "I'm really sorry I went through your things. It's something I'm working on. Trusting people. Believing that they're not hiding things from me." I picture the chain linking the childhood me—tense, worried—to the girl spurned by her college boyfriend, then the twenty- and thirtysomething who repeated the pattern. I wasn't *wrong* to see threats everywhere, not exactly. Whatever you watch for, you'll find.

"There's something else," I say. "It's about . . . that night."

Sabrina peeks up at me. "Go ahead."

"Why . . . Why did you let him trap me? When you had the new gate code?" My voice cracks as I get it out, something that's been bothering me below the surface for months now. My heart speeds, remembering. Jabbing my fingertips against the keypad, *ten-forty-three*. Realizing there was no way out.

Her frown distorts her entire face. "We had no idea what was going on. For all we knew, you could've . . ." She doesn't finish, but I fill it in silently, a terrible Mad Libs: *You could've told others about our secret relationship. You could've ruined our lives.*

You could've been guilty, a murderer on the run.

They never trusted me either. They proved it that first sex-mussed morning: *Don't tell anyone anything.* It was always about appearances, how it would look to the outside world. It was always about controlling the narrative.

And in that sense, we're no different from Mike. *You humiliated me,* he screamed. Prioritizing pride over facing our own messy feelings.

Sabrina takes my hand. "What happened with Mike? What's going on?"

At her touch, I feel that closed circuit, warmth from the way she's connected to me. God, I chose them so fully. I fell right into their arms and lapped up everything they told me about how wonderful I was, so that I wouldn't notice the red flags: power plays, omissions, gaslighting, lies. Betrayals that skidded us down a path toward two deaths—the demise of two complex humans who weren't innocent, not entirely, but who never deserved what befell them.

Sabrina squeezes my fingers and a sob escapes my lips. As long as we're together, I won't ever be free from Nathan and Elizabeth.

I could tell her. Open my mouth, wet as a wound, and tell her the truth about Mike.

But now I'm choosing my own secrets. Controlling the narrative. Deciding whom to trust with what, and if Sabrina and I couldn't ever fully trust each other, well.

It's time to become my own vault.

"It's . . . man, this is hard." Tears wet my cheeks and she touches my shoulder, alarmed.

"What is it?"

I sniffle, then force it out: "I need to be on my own for a while."

Her face crumples. "What are you talking about?"

I stare down at my lap. "Seeing Mike, I realized I . . . I went right back into my old pattern. Wrapping my whole identity up in a relationship and losing myself in the process."

Her eyes fill like a glass of water.

"I went straight from seeing him to seeing you," I continue. "It's not fair to anyone, but especially to me." I peek at her. "And it's the same thing for you. You guys hadn't even broken up with Elizabeth. There's no way you were over her. And now . . ."

She runs her hand down her hair. "Now we all need to heal," she finishes.

I nod. "It's not only that. I get that you're not ready for us to come out as a couple. I'm not sure I could deal with that right now either." I swallow. "But I need a relationship I can shout from the rooftops, you know? No matter how many people it's with. I want all that love and joy to be out in the sunshine." I tip my head back, allowing the UV rays to warm my bare skin. Let them burn me, age me, destroy my cells with their ferocious power—for the moment, just a moment, they're worth it.

I grab her hand. "I love you, Sabrina. I'm here for you, and after all we've been through together . . ." I shake my head. "I'll always be here for you. But . . . as a friend."

She's quiet. People stroll past, some masked, some faces bare. I know there's more, something I can't quite put into words. I'm finally growing comfortable with the idea that there's a whole world out there, big and stretchy and irrevocably changed. And *I've* changed, so I'll attract different people too. I'm not even sure whom or how many I'll choose to let in, to love. But I've got time to figure it out.

Finally Sabrina nods. "I kinda knew it. We've been through so much awful stuff together. I don't think anyone expects me to be fine—let alone in a new relationship—after my husband . . ."

She trails off. My stomach drops like a rock in a gorge, freefall.

If she knew I'd brought this on them . . .

I look into her face, at her wide green eyes and curvy lips, the face I fell for on Instagram all those months ago. I could still tell her. *Here's what you need to know about Nathan. Here's the truth that will set you free . . .*

But she yanks me into a hug and I let her. The timbre of her touch has changed; it's a friend hug now, qualitatively different. Still, I kiss her wet cheek.

"Are you still coming to New York?" she asks, wiping under her eyes.

"Hell yeah."

In the carrier next to my feet, Virgo meows, agreeing.

CHAPTER SIXTY-FOUR

Brooklyn—I love it, the bustle, the fat, fire-hued boughs forming tunnels over streets of sepia brownstones, the playgrounds bubbling with children and parks fizzing with groups of friends. It's strange, living with my ex, but not as horrible as I'd have thought (and far superior to cohabiting in purgatory back in Philadelphia). Sabrina and I transition into friendship so seamlessly, I wonder if she was thinking about breaking things off too. Well, good. I'm not the fragile woman who pulled up to her house in June. This isn't my beautiful house; that's not my beautiful wife.

Amy and I FaceTime regularly; Mom and Dad volunteer to drive out and visit, but with strict quarantine protocols it'd still be weeks before we could hug. I don't want them catching anything along the way, so I ask them to stay home.

I love them and they love me. But I don't *need* them right now.

I redouble my job-search efforts and find remote work at a boutique PR firm based in Illinois. On weekends, I take long walks to other neighborhoods and wander their main drags. In Williamsburg I pause outside a chichi sex shop to gaze at the gleaming goods in the window: vegan ball gags and high-end nipple clamps and so many vibrators and dildos, smooth and curved, like miniatures of the rockets billionaires launch into space. I recognize one from Nathan's stash, and then I'm just a weirdo crying in front of a sex shop.

You make me feel good: That's the compliment I identified as my favorite. And I do want to be kind, I do. But what's left if I'm not defined by my mirror image, something I can't control—the reflection in others' eyes?

I tried the perfect-on-Instagram filter, my identity scattered into shards and cast back on my two thousand followers' screens, a holographic human. With Mike, I donned the doting-future-wifey costume. And then I swung like a pendulum from the top of a white picket fence—I tried to be one corner of a triangle, giving and good.

But I'm not defined by the gaps I fill. I'm just Kelly—weird and wide-eyed and messy and dynamic, unapologetically whole.

I jump—a salesperson is behind the display casing, watching me. I jump and step back, then give an apologetic wave.

They reach for the door and pull it open with a jingle. "Want to come inside?" They've got friendly eyes and a half-shaved head, with blue fingernails gripping the handle.

"No, thank you!" I start to apologize and swallow it instead. "Maybe another time."

I have lunch alone at a French-style sidewalk café, slicing quiche with a fork and watching a trickle of passersby: parents with sticky toddlers, gaggles of teenagers, twentysomethings hauling loaded grocery bags. After paying the bill I head up the main street for a final window-shop, marveling at all the things you can buy, all the goods that promise to make life better. It's a trap, isn't it? None of it will last; none of it will save you. No one else can save you either.

I can save my fucking self.

It's such a simple thought, but tears lurch into my eyes. I am worth saving entirely on my own. Not because someone claimed me. Not because I earned it. Not because others approve of me. Because I deserve to live.

I walk by a crystal shop, then stop in my tracks. I turn slowly and squint at the display in the window. Among the sparkly rocks and smudge sticks, large prints of tarot cards rest on stands, and my heart rate zooms as I home in on one.

TEMPERANCE., it says along the bottom, as if it were a complete sentence. An angel with outstretched red wings fills the frame. But what makes my pulse hammer is the symbol on the chest of her white robe.

A triangle. Inside a square. Not a perfect match for the one on the headstone in Brinsmere, but not far off either.

With a tinkle the glass door flies open, and I leap back.

"Come on inside!" The shopkeeper's got a deep, friendly voice and a mass of salt-and-pepper curls.

I hesitate, then point to the print. "Can you tell me about this card?"

"Of course! Come on in."

The shop smells like palo santo, smoke and mint. She plucks the image off its stand.

"Temperance is sort of the good fairy of the pack." She gazes at it, and below the mask, her neck wrinkles into a ladder of chins. "It's a Major Arcana card, which means it's extra powerful. It comes right after the Death card—that's number thirteen, this is fourteen." She sees my widened eyes. "Oh, don't worry. The Death card isn't about anyone dying. It indicates the death of an old way of thinking, or some phase or situation that isn't serving you. The end of an era." She taps the print in her hands. "So Temperance—well, think of Death as a wildfire that flattens the entire landscape. Temperance comes next—an angel flying over the blackened earth. Deciding what'll be built next."

Goosebumps prickle up my neck.

"People also forget that temperance can mean *tempering*, like tempering steel," she continues. "Making it stronger—more elastic—by heating and cooling it."

"What does the symbol mean?" I point. "On her robe."

"Ah, the chest plate." She turns the print over. "The square represents masculinity and matter, and the triangle represents femininity and spirituality." She flips it back around. "It's about finding harmony between the two extremes. Letting them work together."

"Within a relationship?" I ask.

She smiles. "Within yourself."

I nod. It doesn't look that much like the Atwood crest, really. A couple geometric shapes coincidentally arranged in a similar manner.

"If a card calls out to you," she says, "it probably has something to teach you."

I thank her and start to turn away. Then, surprising myself, I reach for my wallet and tell her I'd love the print.

I'm not sure where my new walls will be, the stick-figure square and peaked roof that'll become my house. But I'll frame this, I decide. It's my first purchase for my next home.

"Ready, monkey?" Virgo is curled like a seashell inside her carrier. She blinks at me through its mesh side, then flings a paw over her nose.

I straighten up and gaze at the monitor again. A throng of people stand in a scattered horseshoe, six feet apart, waiting for the track number to appear. I already checked a bag of my meager belongings. It was strange to hand it over to the man in a red cap—weird to know I didn't feel attached to anything inside, wouldn't care if it wasn't waiting for me in Chicago later this week. Now I've got a backpack loaded with books and snacks and little Virgo by my side. I'm looking forward to the nineteen-hour train ride. The chance to be somewhere new.

Apartment walk-throughs stud my schedule; there's a one-bedroom in Lincoln Square I'm particularly excited about. I already have dates with friends and old coworkers on the calendar, time carved out for people eager to bundle up and sit outside with me. Amy can't wait for me to experience their fancy grill and backyard firepit. My parents are beside themselves with excitement too. Mom keeps sending me links to outdoor, socially distanced activities.

I won't tell any of them about Nathan and Sabrina and me. It's too painful—too personal, a wound that's only just begun healing. But when I'm ready, I'll reactivate my dating apps. It feels obvious now: I want a relationship that celebrates who I am and engages me with the world, instead of cutting me off. I'll change my "looking for" settings and see what interesting folks—monogamous or otherwise—are out there, regardless of gender. And the "want children?" field? I'll check "open to kids."

A track number blinks onto the sign in tandem with a muffled announcement, and the group shuffles toward the exit. Chicago! I can't believe I'll be there again, almost exactly a year after I left. For a while, it felt like the whole city had disappeared, that our patch of Virginia was all that existed.

When I reach the platform, a February wind chills the air. I'm heading for the back, peering through the windows for an empty row, when my phone jolts in my pocket. A spurt of panic—*of course you're not getting out of here this easy*. It could be the Deerbrook cops—six whole months after I fed them a story that was more wrong than I even knew, they're on to me; they've noticed an inconsistency. Or perhaps Renee was lying about leaving me alone, lulling me into complacency. Maybe it's Mike. I told him not to contact me, but I didn't block him either. We haven't spoken since that October day, but if that terrifying anger uncoils again, I want to know.

Maybe it's Sabrina, suspecting the truth.

This is all your fault, Kelly.

It is Sabrina, but she's breezy, texting me from the roomy condo she bought in Windsor Terrace: "Safe travels today!"

I time-travel back to the first time we connected last year—my fangirl messages on her Instagram, her sweet and frequent replies. Time folds and that moment is once again now, and though a novel virus is sweeping the country, though the world's bucking and crumpling around me, though Mike is about to call off our wedding and I hate Philly and I have no friends no love no nothing, there's Sabrina's message, quivering with care. Maybe I loved her then; maybe we were destined to come back together all those years after high school.

She couldn't contact me on those apps if she wanted now. Last week I wrote social-media posts announcing I was done curating a fake, polished exhibition of my life. Then I deleted all my accounts.

"Thank you!" I write back. I'll send her a photo of Virgo on the train. I smile and slip my phone away.

Sabrina's started dating again, and I'm happy for her. At first, she mostly courted couples, but now she's seeing a poly fashion designer who has several other partners—and when Sabrina introduced us last week, I instantly liked her. Me, I'm not interested in mate-seeking just yet. I'm content to be a dot, a point in space, dense and strong and undeniably here.

Another announcement squawks onto the track: "Attention all passengers, this is the last call, last call for the Lake Shore Limited Train to Chicago with intermediate stops in Buffalo, Cleveland, and South Bend."

I clomp up the train stairs and push a button to enter a car. I don't look back as the door swings shut behind me.

EPILOGUE

SIX MONTHS EARLIER

This one will stick.

Elizabeth is sure of it, her confidence growing with every hour she spends in their home. Clearly Nathan and Sabrina are still in love with her, even if they did invite that nosy doppelgänger into their home—a stand-in, a Band-Aid while they mourned Elizabeth's departure. She checks her red backpack and slides it under the bed. This time, everything's coming together.

She's learned from each time she's taken off. She's getting smarter, scrappier. The first departure wasn't a choice: Her parents, their eyes wide with fear, shoved fifteen-year-old "Lizzie" on a plane to live with her well-to-do uncle, a fey man near a strict all-girls school that accepted her post-expulsion. The sting of abandonment turned to opportunity when she got a spot in a university whose price tag made her eyes water. Her uncle didn't know how to pay for her room and board, so she quietly moved from the dorm to a cheap rental and convinced her uncle that students must pay their bills directly, since they are, after all, over eighteen. Her uncle liked throwing money at problems, and Elizabeth was one. Wealth, she quickly realized, meant security, and by the time she graduated, she had $40K saved—more than enough to move to D.C. and leave behind the family that never wanted her.

Inside the cozy confines of her first romantic relationship, with a big-eyed, take-no-shit police lieutenant, she thought she'd found the sense of belonging others ascribed to their own families . . . but when Renee broke up with her, she learned that love wouldn't provide the safety she'd hoped. Money, then. She set up a secret online bank account (conveniently, apps aren't great at verifying a client's identity). One night, she begged Renee to come over and, while her ex was in the bathroom, used Renee's Venmo password to clear out her savings account. It was bafflingly, laughingly simple, and there's no way to report funds stolen when, as far as anyone can tell, you yourself initiated the transfer.

When Renee wouldn't stop calling and then stopping by, demanding she return the money, Elizabeth whispered into ears—her network's, then Renee's, then finally Renee's workplace—about Renee's abusive ways. Never mind that the bruises Sabrina documented were from swinging a hammer into her own face, neck, and side. That's the funny thing about calling someone a liar—there's no way for them to refute it, and the accusation wriggles into reality like shards of fiberglass into skin.

By then, the Lamonts were her everything. *This is it,* she thought, *just what I've been looking for.* A manly dude, a self-assured woman, the huge house, constant promises to keep her safe. But dating them both was hard, harder than she anticipated. All the emotional labor and stinging jealousy and always being a liiittle off-balance, like their mansion was the hull of a ship, gently rocking.

She'd been certain Sabrina would say yes when she offered an escape route. Surely she'd recognize that oafish Nathan was dead weight. He was always so pleased with himself for wanting to protect women, but did he ever pause to question why they *needed* protection? Fighting *that,* instead of imaginary bad guys, bogeymen that made him feel like a hero, their knight in shining armor? No, he didn't. The worst kind of so-called feminist, by Elizabeth's estimation—rolling up his sleeves to protect the patriarchy.

But dammit if Sabrina wasn't more loyal than Elizabeth expected. Her proposal only made things awkward, and after a couple months of lockdown, Elizabeth realized she couldn't put the genie back in the bottle.

So . . . she left. It wasn't her most elegant exit, but she liked the idea of starting fresh, and of a vague halo of suspicion hazing over those who'd hurt her: her parents and uncle and even Sabrina, whose rejection was like a clump of cancer cells, growing under the skin. But most especially Renee, whose emotional abuse she'd recast as physical. Elizabeth considered taking something with her when she ran, something strategic: videos from Nathan's camcorder, things they wouldn't want leaked. She did set aside a few salacious Polaroids to carry in her bag— insurance—but they got lost in the shuffle.

And anyway, blackmail's so *sadistic*. By then she knew the smartest tack was keeping the door open to the Lamonts, to their love. She learned from that mistake with Renee: Let the mask slip and they'll hate you from that day forth, and people who hate you generally don't want to help you. You catch more flies with honey than vinegar, etc.

The first few weeks in Santa Fe were like something out of a dream— *forget the Lamonts, I don't ever want to go back*. The people were friendly and the alpacas plush and the sunlight rich and golden, making her skin hum with pleasure. But boredom settled in, as it always does. And then, as she was beginning to wonder where to go next, another off-ramp appeared like a gift from the universe. On the third day of vomiting in a shared bathroom, she smiled into the toilet. A miracle. A permanent tie between herself and the Lamonts and their ostentatious fortune.

But first, she'd have to make a miraculous reappearance. Renee— that's it, she'd blame Renee's violence for her sudden departure and claim Renee was the reason they had to keep her hidden now. She'd share her news with Nathan first, let him decide whether to rope in Sabrina too. Then she'd slip out again, her only connection to her old life a secret bank account Nathan would top off for the rest of her life. Hush money or child support—it didn't much matter how he viewed it. She's not yet sure if she'll keep the child. At first she figured she'd order pills to end the pregnancy, but now she's growing attached to the little bean.

She crosses to the corner of the room she once thought of as hers. Elizabeth will find a way. She always does. There's a reason her family is scared of her, especially her parents, who knew from middle school onward that she was different. Darker, smarter. They didn't tell anyone, not even her extended family, but she knows her rich uncle and silly aunt Lydia and cousin Michelle have complicated feelings about her too. Sabrina said Michelle's boys dropped dead animals at their door. Perhaps they inherited whatever genes blinked on in Elizabeth, the streak that makes her unique.

In the closet, she runs a hand over Kelly's clothes. Kelly, her very own Single White Female. She was a surprise, but earlier tonight, when Sabrina returned Elizabeth's kiss right in front of her, she knew this anxious blond woman was nothing to worry about. She knows Kelly's type: a nervous hamster eager for someone else to tell them what to do. So she did—Elizabeth cleared things up when they were alone. Kelly won't call Renee or 911. She'll follow directions and stay out of Elizabeth's way.

She thought of everything. She was careful. She flicks off the light and falls asleep.

Hours later, Elizabeth jostles awake, sweaty in her sheets. Her door is open a few inches and a bar of moonlight impales the room. Was someone here, watching her sleep?

She rolls down the covers and creeps to the door. A gentle racket leaks from Nathan's office. Her pulse ticks up. This is it, her chance to talk to him alone. To tell him about the pregnancy. To explain that the baby is the most important thing.

She tiptoes down the hallway, pausing in front of the office door. She smiles to herself.

This time, she thinks, *everything will go perfectly.*

ACKNOWLEDGMENTS

People who've picked up my previous books know exactly whom I'll thank first: YOU, hi, you're amazing and I love you. My readers are the damn best—sensitive, observant, and intelligent—and it's a privilege to continue writing for them. I'm honored that you let me (and shades of my own shame and vulnerability and messy, "unlikable" thoughts) into your life for a few hours. Thank you so very much, truly, for spending your precious time, attention, and money on this twisted tale. I hope that it not only entertained you but also made you think and question and feel.

Thank you to everyone bravely standing up for the rights of queer people. I was finishing edits on this book when a shooter opened fire at Club Q in Colorado Springs, and in the aftermath, several prominent Republicans said truly horrific things about the LGBTQ+ community. The silence from the rest of the party—and from those I know who vote for the GOP—was deafening. I'm begging my readers to loudly reject fearmongering, hatred, dehumanization, and the condoning of violence, both at the ballot box and in conversations with their networks. My life literally depends on it.

Thank you to my partner, Julia Dills, who's shown me so much love, grace, and acceptance on this journey. I'm beyond grateful that, after thirty-four years of identifying as straight, I finally found the courage to live authentically—and there you were. You're my favorite adventure buddy, climbing partner, pet co-parent, and, well, *person*, and I'm so lucky to get to love you.

I can't fully express my gratitude for my blood and soul sister, Julia Bartz—my OG brainstorming partner and collaborator (remember "The Ghost Gang"?) and my biggest cheerleader. I'm thrilled for you and your 2023 debut, *The Writing Retreat*—the book is terrific, and you deserve every bit of your success.

The Spare Room would still be a hot mess if it weren't for the brilliance, patience, and guidance of my crit partner Leah Konen. I'm grateful for all the long walks, pep talks, and plot doctoring sessions, not to mention fifteen years of ride-or-die friendship. Huge thanks as well to Danielle Rollins for the careful early reads and genius suggestions that helped snap the plot into focus. Thank you to Megan Collins, whose beta read and excellent feedback upleveled the manuscript, and whose friendship, support, and humor make this whole "authoring" thing much more manageable. I owe a similar debt of gratitude to Jennifer Keishin Armstrong, Caroline Kepnes, Julia Phillips, and Melissa Rivero—I can't imagine my writing life without any of you.

More broadly, I don't know what I did to deserve so many kind, caring, wonderful people in my orbit, but I'm grateful to the friends who make my life brim with love, including Lianna Bishop, Blaire Briody, Megan Brown, Cristina Couloucoundis, Kate Dietrick, Lindsay Ferris, Alanna Greco, Ross Guberman, Michael Howard, Leigh Kunkel, Abbi Libers, Booters Liebmann-Smith, Kate Lord, Emily Mahaney, Anna Maltby, Erin Pastrana, Teresa Pattitucci, Katherine Pettit, Marie Rutkoski, Katie Scott, Nicole Stahl, Andrea Stanley, Jennifer Weber, and many others.

Special thanks to Peter Rugg for the jokey early-lockdown text convo that sparked this idea *months* before I myself moved in with a benevolent childhood friend and her family outside DC. Spooky! (To clarify: My stint in a spare room was decidedly throuple-, missing-person-, and dead-body-free.)

I'm perpetually dazzled by my agents at CAA. Alexandra Machinist: How do I *begin* to thank you for making all my writing dreams come true? Beyond your unparalleled agenting prowess, you're a warmhearted, hilarious soul and I feel honored to be your client. I'm also grateful to Josie Freedman for the encouragement and friendship in addition to all the skillful, tireless work selling my books for the screen.

I can't believe I get to work with the best of the best at Penguin Random House—how are you all so fantastic? Hilary Rubin Teeman: It's been six years (!) since you took a chance on a booze-soaked hipster mystery no one else wanted to publish, and I'm still pinching myself that I get to work with you. Your instincts and ability to pinpoint what I'm trying to say—and blow it up into a book, something people will actually enjoy reading—are extraordinary. Caroline Weishuhn: I'm in awe of you—your thorough, thoughtful edits; your spot-on suggestions; and the grace and aplomb you bring to every step of what can feel like an overwhelming process.

Sarah Breivogel and Katie Horn: Sweet Lord, are you good at your jobs! Working with you is always a highlight—boy, did I luck out in the publicity department. To my marketing team, including Debbie Aroff, Corina Diez, and Kathleen Quinlan, thank you so much for all your hard work (and sorcery!) making sure people actually *know* about the 100,000 words I spent years writing. Thank you to my sensitivity reader, whose feedback not only took the manuscript to the next level—it also challenged and elevated my thinking. And to everyone else who had a hand in turning this Word doc into a bona fide book—copy editors, proofreaders, designers, typesetters, and more—I see you and appreciate you.

Cheers to the booksellers, librarians, and book influencers (especially on Instagram and TikTok, where creators blow me away with their creativity and generosity). You work so hard to help readers find books that will resonate with them, and it means the world to us authors. Thank you.

I'm very grateful to my family for their continued love and support, especially Mom and Dad, Tom and Cathy, and my *nagymama,* herself a spectacular storyteller.

Finally, in case anyone needs to hear this today: You're beautiful and whole exactly as you are. To those who fear repercussions from embracing their authentic selves—I'm sending love, solidarity, and strength. You deserve acceptance and joy, and the world is so much better with you in it.

ABOUT THE TYPE

This book was set in Ehrhardt, a typeface based on the original design of Nicholas Kis, a seventeenth-century Hungarian type designer. Ehrhardt was first released in 1937 by the Monotype Corporation of London.